MIRACLES & MISCHIEF:
NOH and KYŌGEN THEATER IN JAPAN

MIRACLES & MISCHIEF:
NOH and KYŌGEN THEATER IN JAPAN

SHARON SADAKO TAKEDA

IN COLLABORATION WITH

MONICA BETHE

WITH CONTRIBUTIONS BY

HOLLIS GOODALL

TOM HARE

KAWAKAMI SHIGEKI

KIRIHATA KEN

CAROLYN A. MORLEY

NAGASAKI IWAO

TANABE SABURŌSUKE

LOS ANGELES COUNTY MUSEUM OF ART
AGENCY FOR CULTURAL AFFAIRS,
GOVERNMENT OF JAPAN

Published by Los Angeles County Museum of Art,
5905 Wilshire Boulevard, Los Angeles, CA 90036

Published on the occasion of the exhibition
MIRACLES AND MISCHIEF: NOH AND KYŌGEN THEATER IN JAPAN,
Los Angeles County Museum of Art,
November 10, 2002–February 2, 2003.

This exhibition was organized by the Los Angeles County Museum
of Art and the Agency for Cultural Affairs, Government of Japan.
It was supported in part by awards from the museum's Costume
Council, the National Endowment for the Arts, and The Blakemore
Foundation.

Transportation assistance provided by All Nippon Airways.

In-kind support is provided by K-MOZART 105.1, the official
classical radio station of the Los Angeles County Museum of Art,
and the Radisson Wilshire Plaza Hotel.

Director of publications: **STEPHANIE EMERSON**

Editor: **THOMAS FRICK**

Editorial assistance: **SARA CODY**

Designers: **LORRAINE WILD WITH JESSICA FLEISCHMANN
AND ROBERT RUEHLMAN,** composition based on the Tataminet
grid concept by Jessica Helfand and William Drenttel

Rights and reproductions coordinator: **CHERYLE T. ROBERTSON**

Supervising photographer: **PETER BRENNER**

Printer: **TOPPAN PRINTING CO., INC.,** Tokyo, Japan

ISBN: 0-87587-188-7
Library of Congress Cataloging-in-Publication
Control Number: 2002110591

Front cover: **SHŌJŌ MASK,** catalogue 184; *back cover:*
SHIOFUKI (SALT BLOWER) MASK, catalogue 99; *endsheet*s:
YORE MIZUGOROMO (detail), catalogue 16; *frontispiece:*
**KARAORI WITH SNOW-LADEN CAMELLIAS AND GENJI
CLOUDS** (detail), catalogue 70; *copyright page:* **KAN NŌ ZU,**
catalogue 113; *page 6:* **KATAGINU WITH RADISH AND MALLET,**
catalogue 33; *page 8:* **JŌ (OLD MAN) MASK,** catalogue 84.

Most photographs are reproduced courtesy of the creators
and lenders of the material depicted. For certain artwork and
documentary photographs we have been unable to trace copy
holders. We would appreciate notification of additional credits for
acknowledgment in future editions. All performance photographs
featured in this catalogue are credited to USHIMADO Masakatsu.

Pages 2, 42, 51–53, 61, 63, 66, 75, 79, 86, 109, 164–65, 191, 197, 214,
238, 241, 250: National Noh Theatre; pp. 11, 59, 186: © Metropolitan
Museum of Art; pp.12, 111, 118, 205: Tokugawa Art Museum,
Nagoya; pp. 27, 30, 47, 49, 51, 58, 66, 70, 78, 81, 96, 124, 129, 160,
173, 185, 193, 197, 201, 212–13, 217–18, 223, 229, 231, 233, 236, 238, 243,
258, 260, 262: Agency for Cultural Affairs, Tokyo; pp. 32, 91,
155, 262: © Museum Associates/LACMA; pp. 47, 57: Nara National
Museum/Shrine; p. 56: Chūōkōron-shinsha, Tokyo; pp. 60, 168, 170,
183, 216, 233: Toyohashi City Art Museum; pp. 80, 82, 89, 109–10,
169, 173, 192–93, 235, 245, 250: Hayashibara Museum of Art,
Okayama Prefecture; pp. 103, 105, 110, 115: KAWAKAMI Shigeki;
pp. 111, 118, 204: Tokugawa Art Museum, Nagoya; p. 137: KANDA
Yoshiaki; p. 205 left: Fujita Museum of Art, Osaka; p. 205 middle:
Kongō Noh Theatre; p. 257: © Indianapolis Museum of Art.

NATIONAL
ENDOWMENT
FOR THE ARTS

FOREWORD

International exchange between museums and cultural institutions results from the efforts of individuals whose dedication and vision provide a forum for the dissemination of knowledge. This is the spirit in which *Miracles and Mischief: Noh and Kyōgen Theater in Japan* has been realized. We are extremely pleased to have a continuing relationship with the Agency for Cultural Affairs, Government of Japan (Bunkachō), and to be partners in bringing the cultural heritage of Japan's oldest form of theater to the United States. *Miracles and Mischief* unites in a comprehensive way the exquisite costumes, masks, musical instruments, libretti, and paintings of the noh and kyōgen traditions, and we are very honored to be the only venue for this exhibition.

Miracles and Mischief is the product of over five years of research and planning by Sharon Sadako Takeda, senior curator and department head of Costume and Textiles at the Los Angeles County Museum of Art. She has worked tirelessly with colleagues and scholars in both the United States and Japan to produce this catalogue, which not only documents the exhibition but also embodies a deep understanding of noh and kyōgen theater. It is our hope that this publication will be a primary resource for years to come.

We are grateful for the generosity of the many sponsors who have made this exhibition and publication a reality. Among them, the Costume Council of the Los Angeles County Museum of Art has provided generous support to the department of Costume and Textiles and to this exhibition in particular. We additionally thank the National Endowment for the Arts for recognizing the importance of this project, and the Blakemore Foundation for its insight.

We would also like to express our gratitude to the many institutions and individuals who generously lent their works of art to *Miracles and Mischief*, and particularly to Kawai Hayao, commissioner of the Bunkachō, and his staff for negotiating the Japanese loans for the exhibition. Many of these loans have been given the designation Important Cultural Property by the Japanese government, and we consider ourselves extremely privileged to be able to bring them to Los Angeles. We hope visitors to the exhibition will obtain lasting pleasure from seeing these marvelous treasures.

ANDREA L. RICH
President and Director
Los Angeles County Museum of Art

PREFACE

Every year the Agency for Cultural Affairs, the Bunkachō, oversees exhibitions that highlight the outstanding cultural properties of Japan, in order to deepen an understanding of our culture and history. I take enormous pleasure at the opening of this new exhibition at the Los Angeles County Museum of Art, which has co-organized other presentations with us in the past.

Miracles and Mischief: Noh and Kyōgen Theater in Japan concerns *nohgaku*, which represents the traditional performing arts of Japan. Since its establishment around the fourteenth century, nohgaku has evolved by combining the masquerade musical of noh and the comedy play of kyōgen. This amalgamation of the subtle expression of human delicacy in noh and the representation of cheerful passion in kyōgen has had an immense influence on other theatrical arts, including *kabuki* and *ningyō jōruri bunraku*.

Though it focuses on costumes, *Miracles and Mischief* also includes other crucial objects, including masks, paintings, songbooks, and musical instruments. The costumes on display are of numerous types, each worn in accordance with the age, gender, and social status of the character it helps portray, and all revealing magnificent textile techniques as well as rich and unique designs.

In May 2001 the multifarious art of nohgaku was selected by UNESCO as one of the first Masterpieces of the Oral and Intangible Heritage of Humanity, and *Miracles and Mischief* is the first comprehensive exhibition on this subject outside of Japan. I am certain that visitors will appreciate the brilliant array of objects related to these performing arts, and I hope this exhibition serves as a doorway to a more profound understanding of Japan.

Finally, it is my hope that this exhibition will contribute to further friendship and mutual understanding between the people of Japan and the United States. I would like to express my gratitude to the owners of the art works in the exhibition, who kindly consented to lend them, and to all individuals in both countries who made *Miracles and Mischief: Noh and Kyōgen Theater in Japan* possible, including Dr. Andrea Rich, president and director of the Los Angeles County Museum of Art.

KAWAI HAYAO
Commissioner
Agency for Cultural Affairs,
Government of Japan

KAN NŌ ZU (WATCHING NOH)
Edo period, c. 1607
Kobe City Museum
catalogue 113

RITUALS, DREAMS, AND TALES OF ADVENTURE: A MATERIAL HISTORY OF NOH DRAMA

TOM HARE

Noh drama is a six-hundred-year-old performance art devoted in large part to the inner lives of ghosts. The very idea that ghosts might have lives is disconcerting; admittedly, those lives are really afterlives, with a retrospective view of a life before death, so in a certain sense we introduce some distortion by insisting on "the lives of ghosts." All the same, in many noh plays a ghost or spirit is the central figure, or *shite* (pronounced "sh'tay"), and however distant in time the events that formed that ghost's prior life, they remain at the forefront of the shite's mind and motivate his or her appearance in the dramatic present of the play.

The most important character after the shite is an interlocutor (a representative in his way of the audience), known as the *waki*. The waki's appearance is usually the first thing that happens, and the interaction of the shite and waki provides the kernel of paradox that sets a typical noh play in motion.

A given play may call for other characters as well. The shite and waki may each appear with companions (*tsure* and *wakizure*, respectively). Often another character, the *ai-kyōgen* (or simply *ai*), appears about three-quarters of the way through a play (usually while the shite has retired backstage for a costume change) to give an account in simpler language of events already discussed or enacted. In some plays a child (the *kokata*) may appear. There is always a chorus, usually of eight voices, which chants descriptive texts or takes over the shite's or waki's lines at certain important points (in particular, when the shite is dancing).

An instrumental ensemble consisting of a flute and either two or three drums completes the cast, providing accompaniment to the chanting of the shite, waki, and chorus (and more rarely the ai) or performing strictly instrumental music (especially when the shite is dancing). Finally, there are several staging assistants, who sit on stage and manage props, occasionally helping to straighten costumes and such.

Although noh and kyōgen come from the same roots, they are distinguished in performance today and have different stage conventions. The main character in a kyōgen play is, as in noh, termed the shite; however, the secondary character is not called the waki, but rather the *ado*. Though it is unusual for secondary characters on the noh stage to take the roles of antagonists, the ado may well take an adversarial role vis-à-vis the shite of a kyōgen play. There may be tsure and kokata in kyōgen, as in noh, and occasionally a musical ensemble, but only rarely is there a chorus. Kyōgen are far more concerned with living characters than noh, and ghosts are much rarer.

The aesthetics of noh and kyōgen have been maintained from the late 1300s by performance guilds, or schools. The conventions of performance, costuming, choreography, the choice of masks, and many other performance details that shape the character of noh are dependent upon the judgments made over the centuries by influential members of these schools.

TSUKINAMI FŪZOKU ZU
(EVENTS OF THE TWELFTH MONTHS) (detail: twelfth month)
Muromachi period, sixteenth century
Eight-panel screen; ink and colors on paper
Each panel: 24 1/16 ~ 24 3/8 x 15 11/16 ~ 16 5/8 in.
(61.1 ~ 61.8 x 39.9 ~ 42.2 cm)
Tokyo National Museum
Important Cultural Property
figure 1

TOYOKUNI SAIREI ZU (CEREMONY
AT THE TOYOKUNI SHRINE FESTIVAL) (detail)
Edo period, seventeenth century
Pair of six-panel screens; ink and colors on paper
Each screen: 65 7/8 x 138 7/8 in. (167.2 x 352.6 cm)
Tokugawa Art Museum, Nagoya
figure 2

THE ARCHAEOLOGY OF NOH

Miracles and mysteries surround the origins of noh and kyōgen. The early literature of noh tells of performances commissioned by the sick that led to their recovery, and oracular dreams where gods command that gifts be awarded to particular actors. There are uncanny tales about masks, assertions of the supernatural powers of distant ancestors, romantic claims of aristocratic lineage, martial tragedy, and hints of espionage.[1]

The archetype of all noh performance is the manifestation of a god under a famous pine near Nara, a tree memorialized in the painted pine on the back of every noh stage (fig. 3), reflecting the origins of noh and kyōgen in religious rituals. Even today, at the annual Onmatsuri (Grand celebrations) at the Kasuga Shrine in Nara, a series of performances maintains the tradition of the medieval festivals in which noh and kyōgen had their beginnings (fig. 1). The scene depicted in *Ceremony at the Toyokuni Shrine Festival* (fig. 2) gives one version of this early history, showing the leaders of the four oldest schools of noh (Kanze, Konparu, Hōshō, and Kongō) in competitive performance before the sacred pine.

Screen paintings of noh became popular by the sixteenth or seventeenth century, too late to give a firsthand picture of noh in its earliest days (cat. 113, p. 10). Instead, early artifacts such as masks are the most eloquent witnesses of noh and kyōgen at their birth.

The earliest masks usually show the cheerful, wrinkled visage of an old man, carved of wood, gessoed, painted, and finished with a long beard and eyebrows like pom-poms. The features are consistent enough from one example to the next to define a type: the wrinkles are symmetrical, almost always in concentric groups of three. The eyes are shaped like inverted smiles. The nose is broad and the lower jaw is carved of a separate piece of wood, which is tied to the upper part of the mask. The two sections of the mask are attached in such a way that they seem to articulate a broad smile, completing the expression of the wrinkles and eyes. A long wispy beard is affixed to the chin (or, if it is missing, the holes by which it was once attached are evident).

Many of these masks are painted white, though there are some, usually smaller ones, that are black. The black masks sometimes have mustache hair as well as a beard. Taken together, masks of this type are important material evidence of noh and kyōgen in their earliest days.

NOH STAGE
Ōe nōgakudō, Kyoto
figure 3

OKINA MASK
Nanbokuchō period, fourteenth century
Nyū Shrine, Nara Prefecture
catalogue 137

SANBASŌ MASK
Muromachi period, fifteenth century
Nyū Shrine, Nara Prefecture
catalogue 143

When white, this archetypal mask is called Okina (cat. 137, p. 14, is a celebrated mask of the type, though the pom-pom eyebrows have been lost) and when black, Sanbasō (cat. 143, p. 15). Today they belong exclusively to the play known as *Shikisanban*.[2] In the play as currently performed, three characters have important roles. The first performs without a mask, the second wears the white Okina mask, and the third the black Sanbasō mask. All three sing and dance in an ancient ritual to the accompaniment of eight choristers and an ensemble of flute and drums. The play is commonly performed at the New Year and on other special occasions, and holds a unique place in the noh and kyōgen repertory as a representative of both genres, with an ancient but rather nebulous sanctity. The text recited is in large part incomprehensible (which seems to have been the case even in the late 1300s), and there is hardly any plot. The ritual event of the performance itself is the source of the play's riveting interest.[3]

Old Okina masks are thought to partake of divinity and are afforded reverential treatment. This is evident in the way the mask is brought onstage in performance, in an exquisite lacquered box (cat. 138, p. 181), and in the way it is attached to the actor's head in full view of the audience. *Shikisanban* is the only noh play in which a mask is donned in this manner, and it is unique in other ways as well.

NOH, YET NOT NOH

Shikisanban is the oldest play in the noh tradition, and is exemplary in its music, costumes, movements, vocal delivery, and other features. Categorizing it as noh acknowledges the ancient pedigree of the art and places *Shikisanban* with the two hundred and fifty or sixty plays in the modern repertory. But calling it "not noh" suggests that it can be considered as much a kyōgen play as a noh play and thus belongs to an ancient comic tradition, just as old as but far less self-conscious and text-based than noh.

"Noh, yet not noh" also indicates that *Shikisanban* can be seen as a religious event, whereas noh in the more generic sense is an entertainment. That distinction has been at issue since at least the 1380s, and even today *Shikisanban* evokes a kind of religious awe. Yet despite its claims on Buddhist theology and its demonstrable links to Japanese medieval religion, *Shikisanban* is also powerfully entertaining.[4]

**TSUKINAMI FŪZOKU ZU
(EVENTS OF THE TWELVE MONTHS)**
(detail: fifth month, *taue*)
Muromachi period, sixteenth century
Eight-panel screen; ink and colors on paper
Each panel: 24 1/16 ~ 24 3/8 x 15 11/16 ~ 16 5/8 in.
(61.1 ~ 61.8 x 39.9 ~ 42.2 cm)
Tokyo National Museum
figure 4

"Noh, yet not noh" points to technical specifications as well. The fact that the white Okina and black Sanbasō masks mentioned previously have detached jaws distinguishes them from all other noh masks. In this *Shikisanban* shows a continuity with earlier forms of masked dance and drama such as the *bugaku* of the ancient court.

Naturally noh has changed over the centuries, but the performance tradition reaches from the modern stage deep into the heart of medieval Japan. This lineage can be traced, through the names of historically identifiable individuals, as far back as the middle of the fourteenth century. Earlier than that, though the tradition is no less established, it is almost entirely anonymous.

In those early days noh was called *sarugaku*, and it enjoyed popularity at shrines and temples near Kyoto and Nara, the centers of secular and religious power in Japan's high Middle Ages. The word is written with Chinese graphs for "monkey" and "music," but it probably meant, in effect, "to behave in a comic manner." Sarugaku was only one of a number of performing arts competing for patrons in the relatively peaceful days of the late fourteenth and early fifteenth centuries. *Dengaku* (field music), the semiprofessionalized music played for rice-planting rituals (*taue*), was closely akin to sarugaku, an important rival influence (fig. 4). There were also several generically distinct kinds of itinerant songstresses, singers of devotional tales and narratives of tragedy and war, charismatic preachers, proselytizers and hucksters, and professional magicians and acrobats.[5]

Sarugaku troupes fulfilled certain religious responsibilities, entailing performance at shrines and temples, notably in Nara and around Lake Biwa. These performances were the contributions of a rural agricultural class to celebrations that also included Buddhist liturgical pageants and elite classical arts, such as the bugaku mentioned above. By the late fourteenth century sarugaku seems to have gained a degree of popularity and dynamism that separated it from the more formal elements of these performances. It never lost a sense of celebration, however. Noh performers and theorists over the centuries have insisted that celebration is a fundamental and inseparable element of the art. The Japanese word they use to express this is *shūgen*, (literally "auspicious words") and in the performance of *Shikisanban* this tenor of celebration is apparent everywhere. Though much of the text is only marginally comprehensible, it clearly refers to peace, prosperity, and benevolent rule, evoking images of the pine and the crane, which are thought to flourish for a thousand years. The tortoise, believed to live for ten thousand years, is also prominent. In costumes and related items all these motifs appear frequently (see, for example, cats. 142, p. 183; 145, p. 185).

DEUS EX MACHINA

The aspect of noh that offers evidence of its ancient religious heritage also begins, in the fourteenth century, to show some departure from it. Although Okina masks seem clearly to represent the oldest stratum of noh, they are joined not much later by masks of daemons, and then, before long, by masks of old men unlike those represented by the Okina mask.

The daemon masks represent fearsome lower-ranking gods and divine spirits. They intimidate because of their power, but they are not necessarily hostile to human interests (which is why they might be termed "daemons" rather than "demons"). The play *Kamo* provides an example of the role these creatures fill in noh, and there is evidence of them in later plays as well.[6] See, for example, the illustration of a play called *Kuzu* from a handscroll of noh and kyōgen performance belonging to the Tokyo National Museum (cat. 118).[7]

The performance depicted must be a particularly celebratory one, given the larger than usual chorus and the extra attendants for the ensemble musicians. Especially striking are the characters at the front of the stage, where a daemon in a maroon *kariginu* robe and red *hangire* pants dances vigorously before a character dressed as a goddess (with a crown, a green *maiginu* jacket, and white *ōkuchi* trousers).[8] The smaller figure at the front, stage left, is a child actor (kokata) portraying the emperor.

The tale that forms the basis of this play is about the escape of the young emperor from the clutches of dangerous enemies. In the scene depicted we find him successful in having eluded them due to the efforts of the divinities dancing in his honor.

The god appearing at the end of this play wears one of the two major types of daemon masks, the Ōtobide (compare cat. 151, p. 191), which has bulging eyes and a mouth opened wide to reveal a tongue behind gilded teeth. Examples can be found from the late fourteenth century (and perhaps earlier); they attest to the miraculous character of an important early strain of noh performance.

The first act of the same play also shows evidence of some important early character types: the emperor's two enemies threaten an old couple with a drawn bow and a menacing halberd. The old man and woman are themselves gods, but they are disguised as aged peasants. Their masks show a greater individuality and naturalism than Okina masks.

These new types of masks foreshadow a great change in sarugaku from the late fourteenth to the early fifteenth century, one that in a sense turns sarugaku into noh. Soon the Okina masks, daemon masks, and masks of old men will be supplemented by those of young men and

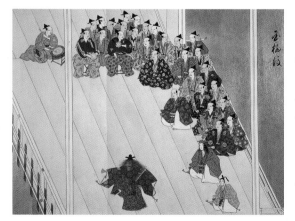

NŌ KYŌGEN EMAKI
(NOH AND KYŌGEN PICTURE SCROLLS)
(details: *Kuzu*, acts 1 and 2)
Edo period, eighteenth century
Tokyo National Museum
catalogue 118

women, as well as a greater variety in the old men. These masks are used in explicitly human roles, and the developments they portend are closely associated with two men, Kannami Kiyotsugu (1333–1384) and his son, Zeami Motokiyo (c. 1363–c. 1443).

KANNAMI AND ZEAMI

By all evidence Kannami was a uniquely successful and beloved performer, a large man who could nonetheless carry off the roles of beautiful women and young boys convincingly. He particularly valued the roles of madwomen and daemons. Zeami, his son, was also a renowned performer and the author as well of a majority of the most celebrated plays in the repertory. Zeami had important ideas about training, performance, aesthetics, philosophy and, in the end, about being itself.

Most of what we know about Kannami comes through Zeami, who seems to have been eager to advertise the genius of his father (whether out of gratitude or as a promotional strategy for his own troupe). It is difficult, therefore, to disentangle father from son, but it is clear that the two shared a pragmatic interest in the audience. For Kannami this meant appealing to the interests of important patrons, but also keeping in touch with the tastes of the common people of rural communities around Nara, his home base.

One of the plays most plausibly attributable to Kannami, and most likely to reflect his strategies of performance, is *Jinen Koji* (Lay-priest Jinen).[9] The play concerns the heroic rescue of a young girl from slave traders. Jinen tries to win her release by returning to the slave traders the goods with which they bought her, but in the end he has to perform a sequence of dances and entertainments before they are persuaded to let her go (cat. 118).

This play reveals Kannami's interest in *monomane*, or dramatic imitation. He was celebrated for being able to perform the role of the young lay priest convincingly even when he was a middle-aged man. Even more tellingly, the sequence of dances with which Jinen placates the slave traders demonstrates Kannami's recognition of the importance of dance and song for the new art of noh. One of the keys to his success with patrons in the capital was his adoption of dance genres that had been entirely separate performing arts. In *Jinen Koji* several independent dances are performed in the last half of the play.

Although there was a musical element in Kannami's performance that cannot be fully resurrected, we know that he brought music of a new rhythmic sophistication to his performances. He provided them with an entertaining diversity of music and dance as well as a proficiency in various types of dramatic imitation.

Zeami acknowledged the importance of traditional audiences for sarugaku, but he was also keenly aware of the rich opportunity offered by the patronage of the military class and court

**NŌ KYŌGEN EMAKI
(NOH AND KYŌGEN PICTURE SCROLLS)**
(detail: *Jinen Koji*)
Edo period, eighteenth century
Tokyo National Museum
catalogue 118

aristocrats in Kyoto. He tailored his plays, his instructions to his troupe, and presumably his acting to those new audiences. This meant bringing well-known classical poetry and incidents from celebrated romances to the stage. It also meant an increasing concentration on the inner lives of the characters, particularly the shite.

Zeami's efforts provoked a great change in noh at the beginning of the fifteenth century. Kannami's knowledge of the elite culture of traditional Japan is difficult to gauge, but it is clear that Zeami was familiar with philosophical aspects of Buddhism as well as with classical poetry and literary narratives from the preceding centuries.

He left behind a repertory of around fifty plays and diverse observations about training, aesthetics, and composition methods. His son Motoyoshi set down his memoirs, which contain additional information on these matters and a broad range of comments on the culture of his times, which actors were good at what, who made fine masks, and so on. These texts provide a unique view of the development of medieval Japanese theater.

Zeami's writings on the composition of noh plays demonstrate that his deepest interest was in human subjects. He wrote plays about gods, bodhisattvas, and other supernatural beings, but his most celebrated works and the comments he made about acting in the critical commentaries he left behind point to a fascination with the emotional lives of people, from warriors to ladies of the old court to mothers in the marketplace. He harbored serious reservations about the unrefined daemonic roles that had been so important to his father. When he wrote about daemons, he gave them a human sensibility.

This concentration on the human introduced a dynamic tension between the ideological requirements of celebration (*in-shūgen*) and the broader emotional spectrum of a drama that now treated not only gods and miracles but also the deep ambivalences inherent in human life: love, loneliness, resentment, anger, longing, and fear. We cannot ignore, in this context, the great difference between Kannami and his son Zeami in terms of education and access to a cultural legacy.

What we know of Zeami from his writing is mirrored to some extent in noh artifacts, primarily masks. During Zeami's time a typology of characters emerged, and masks began to show the diversity necessary to exploit the potential of the texts he was writing. Zeami identifies, for instance, a Warai-Jō (Laughing Jō) mask, carved by one Yasha, to be used in the play *Koi no omoni* (The heavy burden of love), and another called Kouji-Jō as appropriate for the last act of *Oimatsu* (The aged pine).[10]

THE CANON OF NOH PERFORMANCE

The awareness that a particular mask should be used for a particular play shows a developing noh performance canon: the understanding that particular plays are to be performed in specific ways with prescribed masks, costumes, props, music, and choreography. In Zeami's time this canon was in a formative stage, but it lent to noh from an early date a sense of classical standards that grew stronger with every century of performance.

Hand in hand with the new mask types came innovations in the structure of noh. Zeami deployed extended temporal perspectives to broaden and deepen his subjects' lives, with the result that many of his central characters are ghosts.

The play *Tadanori*, named for a famous twelfth-century warrior and poet, is one excellent example.[11] Another is *Matsukaze*, which had been popular on the sarugaku stage even before Zeami brought it to its contemporary form.[12] It is the story of two sisters, Matsukaze (Pining Wind) and Murasame (Sudden Shower), peasants who make a precarious living by extracting salt from seawater. They had become the lovers of an aristocrat, Ariwara Yukihira, when he was exiled to the Suma seacoast, where they live.

In the dramatic present of the play, the sisters reappear as ghosts on the Suma coast to relive their longing for Yukihira, who had long since returned to the capital (fig. 5). The climax occurs when Matsukaze, the elder sister, imagines that Yukihira has come back in the form of a pine tree on the beach. This scene, a favorite throughout the history of noh, embodies the genre's legacy of mad-women and is, indeed, one of the finest mad pieces. Matsukaze's "madness," however, is in some interpretations a more accurate assessment of reality than the conventional perspective of her sister Murasame. It culminates in a pervasive meditation on the complexity of perception and emotion.

In the scene from *Nō kyōgen emaki* illustrated (cat. 118), the two sisters are dipping brine from the sea into a cart. The props are delicate and colorful, but the text tells us that the labor is exhausting. Despite the drudgery of the work, the sisters' thoughts move from their weariness, to recollections of poems their lover once recited, to images of moonlight on the waves. Although they are peasants, they embody the refinement of a centuries-old courtly aesthetic; though ghosts, their

PERFORMANCE OF MATSUKAZE
figure 5

NŌ KYŌGEN EMAKI
(NOH AND KYŌGEN PICTURE SCROLLS)
(detail: *Matsukaze*)
Edo period, eighteenth century
Tokyo National Museum
catalogue 118

emotional worlds could hardly be more vital and human.

By having ghosts as his central characters Zeami established a religious or philosophical viewpoint from which to look back to a life that could be enacted or otherwise evoked onstage at signal moments. In this process the main characters come to a clearer awareness of their identity, their significance, their loves and hates. Plays of this type often end with the implicit assumption that the subject has moved on spiritually to a new and clearer life, or even to enlightenment.

Many noh plays about ghosts make it explicit that those ghosts are appearing in dreams. This has given birth to the major genre called *mugen* (dream vision) noh. These plays, very likely the invention of Zeami, represent the majority of the repertory.

As *Matsukaze* comes to an end, Matsukaze and Murasame disappear in a sudden shower, which moves on, leaving only the wind soughing through the pines. The entire play finally seems merely a dream in the mind of the waki, but no less significant for that.

DRAMA OF THE LIVING

By contrast, plays about characters who are alive during the dramatic present of the play are termed *genzai* (contemporary) noh. Zeami wrote both types, but his genzai plays often take the form of mugen noh by framing the last act as the ecstatic trance or derangement of the shite. Mugen noh became the dominant genre; even some plays that are technically classified as genzai have a structure and content closely akin to mugen. One such play is *Kantan*, based on a Chinese legend about a magical pillow that enables one to attain enlightenment.[13]

Kantan opens uncharacteristically with a speech by the ai, who explains that she has come into possession of the magical pillow. The scene then switches to the shite, a young man named Rosei. He feels he has passed his youth in a daze and must make his way to Mount Yōhi to learn about the matters most central to his life. As night falls, he reaches the village of Kantan and finds lodging.

The innkeeper promises to cook him some millet porridge, but suggests that in the meantime he take a nap on her magic pillow. Rosei quickly begins to dream. Now (in a formally unique innovation), the waki comes onstage, taps the platform where Rosei is asleep (cat. 120), announces

**CHŌKEN WITH WISTERIA,
FOLDED PAPERS (NOSHI) AND PRIMROSES**
Edo period, eighteenth century
Fujita Museum of Art, Osaka
catalogue 17

himself as an imperial messenger, and tells Rosei he has been entrusted with the throne.

Rosei is hurried off to the capital in a palanquin. A magnificent palace is described, and the messenger informs Rosei that fifty years have passed since he attained the throne. He is given a magic elixir and watches the auspicious dance of a child, then takes center stage himself to perform another celebratory dance. Thereafter he returns to the platform and goes to sleep once again. The innkeeper returns to inform him that his porridge is ready. Rosei realizes he has had a remarkable dream and that he no longer feels the need to seek the meaning of life on Mount Yōhi.

It is not known who wrote *Kantan*, but the play is popular and frequently performed. It presents a charmed vision of China, even with its implicit message of "bloom where you're planted." It shows the impact of Zeami's mugen format on the broader repertory and at the same time provides evidence of the increasing formalization of dramatic roles in noh.

Many of the greatest noh plays are centered on female subjects like Matsukaze and Murasame. Zeami was clearly enraptured by women of diverse classes and experiences. The tradition since Zeami has validated his interest and affords the greatest reverence to plays about women.

This focus may fairly represent Zeami's taste, or his response to the tastes of his patrons, but it also appropriates the aesthetic of such rivals as Dōami (?–1413) and Zōami (fl. c. 1400–1410). The latter is credited with the invention of a mask type, Zō-onna (Zōami's woman), one of the most beautiful and elegant of women's masks (cat. 148, p. 191). When human masks first appeared in noh they were only identified broadly as Wakai Onna (young woman, cat. 94, p. 64) or Wakai Otoko (young man, cat. 82, p. 61), but if Zō-onna really was invented by Zōami – and this is to some degree an open question – then it represents a ramification and specialization in the masks used for human roles similar to the one noted earlier for gods' masks.

STAGE CLOTHING

We don't have a precise idea of the stage attire in Zeami's and Zōami's day. It would probably not be correct to refer to "costumes" in that early period, because stage clothing seems not to have been clearly distinguishable from clothes worn in a variety of offstage circumstances. Many items worn onstage had been bestowed on the actors at previous successful performances. Court diaries from the fourteenth and fifteenth centuries refer to occasions when grandees and members of their entourage threw garments onstage out of appreciation. One entry from 1423 remarks on Zōami receiving various robes. Another mentions a total of eighty-three articles of clothing given for a certain performance. In an entry in the military chronicle *Taiheiki* (Chronicle of great peace), the garments received on the occasion of one performance are said to have formed a veritable mountain, representing a huge expenditure.[14]

In Zeami's writings there is a clear awareness that, above all, the attire of high-ranking characters must be carefully researched and fitted according to the actual practices of aristocrats, so that a sartorial gaffe doesn't taint an otherwise fine performance. As for the particular garments worn in his time, there are only vague indications. By the fifteenth century, however, Japan had a very sophisticated system of clothing design and a minutely inflected code of dress in the emperor's court, among high-ranking samurai, and among the clergy. (This sophistication is already evident in the literature of the tenth and eleventh centuries, especially in the celebrated *Tale of Genji*.)

In the noh of Zeami's day clothing became an adjunct to identity. In two of the most celebrated plays of the time, *Matsukaze* and *Izutsu* (At wellside), the central characters (beautiful women living at the seaside and in the country) use court robes, left as keepsakes by long-gone lovers, as a means of achieving an ecstatic unity with them. In modern performances of these plays, robes known as *chōken* (cat. 17, p. 23) are employed: when the women put on their lovers' chōken and court hats, they are possessed by them; in a sense, they become them (fig. 6). It's not clear if the chōken proper existed in Zeami's time, but the plays in question make clear that a garment of some sort was used for the same purpose.

In *Aoi no ue* (Lady Aoi), another important play, we find that a major character is represented by a robe alone (in this case a *kosode*). This play is a variation on a famous incident in the *Tale of Genji* where the hero's principal wife, the Lady Aoi of the title, becomes possessed by a number of malevolent spirits while in labor. One spirit is particularly tenacious. It turns out to be – quite literally – the embodied jealousy of another of the hero's lovers, a woman called Lady Rokujō. Lady Rokujō is the

PERFORMANCE OF IZUTSU
figure 6

25

**NŌ KYŌGEN EMAKI
(NOH AND KYŌGEN PICTURE SCROLLS)**
(detail: *Aoi no ue*, act 2)
Edo period, eighteenth century
Tokyo National Museum
catalogue 118

central character in the play; the title character appears only as the kosode (cat. 118).[15] The kosode, front and center on the stage, is easy to identify. *Aoi no ue* most likely dates from the late fourteenth century, and along with plays such as *Matsukaze* and *Izutsu* it emphasizes the importance of attire in noh, even if the precise nature of the costumes used at the time is not known.

In the early fifteenth century images and motifs emerged that subsequently became fundamental elements of noh costuming. The crane, for example, has traditionally symbolized good fortune, long life, and celebration and thus is entirely predictable on the costume of the Sanbasō character in *Shikisanban* (cat. 144, p. 184). Similarly, the fans used in celebratory plays (cat. 142, p. 183; cat. 146, p. 185) became a common and very generalized indication of the auspicious.

The image of a plantain covered with snow has a more specific meaning, underscoring the relationship between noh as it developed in the early fifteenth century and the Buddhism of the great Zen institutions of the time.

NOH AND ZEN

In Zen poetry of the Muromachi period (1392–1568) there is a fascination with paradox, often expressed in vivid images. One monk speaks of quince blossoms under the blazing summer sky, something that does not exist in nature, since the quince blooms in the early spring. In another case a monk speaks of the plantain burdened by the weight of snow, again a paradox, since the cold of winter would force the plantain to die back to its roots. The occurrence of these images in poetry and painting exemplifies the creative power of imagination, an indispensable tool not only for aesthetic pleasure but also for religious awakening.

Although the garment on which it is depicted is from about a century and a half later than the heyday of Muromachi-period Zen, the image of the plantain under snow (cat. 48, p. 27) exemplifies in its small way the legacy of Zen in noh, which dates back to the late fourteenth century. Zeami used Zen vocabulary in his writing on noh and was eventually interred in a Zen temple. Still more explicitly engaged in Zen was his son-in-law and ultimate artistic heir, Konparu Zenchiku (who even included the "Zen" graph in his name).

Zenchiku (1405–c. 1470) lived in politically more fractious and dangerous times than Zeami but nonetheless seems to have had a more extensive classical education. He followed his father-in-law in creating a body of critical writing on noh, its aesthetic values, and its relation to East Asian philosophical thought.[16] Zenchiku is also thought to have composed a play, *Bashō* (The plantain), in which the paradox of the plantain under snow occupies a prominent place. In this way he acknowledged a debt to Muromachi Zen and revealed himself as an exemplar of the mysterious Higashiyama culture.[17]

NUIHAKU WITH SNOW-LADEN PLANTAIN
Momoyama period, sixteenth–seventeenth century
Hayashibara Museum of Art, Okayama Prefecture
catalogue 48

Ashikaga Yoshimasa (1436–1490), the central shogun of the Higashiyama culture, was a strong patron not only of noh but also of painting, tea, garden design, and a host of related arts that came to characterize medieval Japanese culture. Zenchiku seems to have composed several of his plays during Yoshimasa's lifetime, and the aesthetic he valued most highly, of dark, monochromatic mystery and philosophical reflection, seems to symbolize the Higashiyama age itself. It was a time of deep spiritual inquiry and great seriousness in the arts. Zenchiku, driven out of Kyoto by war, devoted much of his life to learning about Zen and other forms of Buddhism, as well as Confucianism and native Japanese religious thought. This is reflected in his 1466 treatise *Rokurin ichiro hichū* (Secret notes on the six circles and the one dewdrop, cat. 121, p. 30), which concerns the way the natural world is expressed in noh by what Zenchiku calls "the circle of forms."[18] The wonderfully delicate accompanying illustration in gold gives visual expression to the schematic understanding of noh aesthetics that Zenchiku developed. The text proper provides clear evidence of the intellectual debt Zenchiku owed Zeami, in that he refers to several of the aesthetic standards the latter had set earlier in the century.

BROADENING THE AESTHETIC

In the most general sense, the canon of noh was established by Kannami and Zeami. The basic principles of dramatic imitation, certain aesthetic ideals and formal matters (such as the structure of the mugen play), and the importance of chant were clearly delineated by them. The development of the performance canon progressed gradually in the hands of Zenchiku and his competitors. The political fragmentation of war-torn late fifteenth- and early sixteenth-century Japan may have contributed to the decline of some of the rivals of Zeami's and Zenchiku's descendants. Kyoto was largely destroyed in the course of battles between daimyo and contestants for the position of shogun. The elimination of the palaces, shrines, and other performance venues forced actors and artists out of Kyoto, provoking a rapid development of interest in noh and related arts in provincial settings.

Patrons and conditions of patronage changed somewhat, and the great refinements of Zeami's and Zenchiku's noh, while appreciated by sixteenth-century audiences, did not provide most of the inspiration for new plays. That inspiration came from simpler intellectual and aesthetic structures, which favored the visual over the aural and allowed an interest in plot, which had been present in early noh, to resurface again. Zenchiku's grandson, Konparu Zenpō (1454–c. 1532), and Zeami's grandnephew, Kanze Nobumitsu (1435–1516), not only added several enduring plays to the repertory, some with riveting plots, but also provided more detailed instructions on the use of masks, costumes, and music than had been seen before.

Zenpō wrote a major treatise on the art of noh, *Zenpō zōdan* (Conversations with Zenpō, 1513), which differed from those of his grandfather and great-grandfather in that it contained little abstract speculation about aesthetics and spirituality. It was, rather, a book of anecdotes and comments about performance practice. As such it set the tone for a proliferation of noh-related writing in the sixteenth and seventeenth centuries and provided a detailed view of the development of noh performance. By the time of Zenpō, for example, we find explicit textual reference to a more carefully ramified canon of performance than in the time of Zeami and Zenchiku. He mentions details about masks, costumes, and dances that cannot be found in earlier writing.

There is also clear evidence at this time of the penetration of the aesthetics of noh into life outside the theater, something that would become ever more apparent in the seventeenth century and thereafter. In *Zenpō's Songbook* (cat. 124, p. 31) for example, is a text for the play *Sumidagawa* (Sumida River) in the hand of Zenpō. It also incorporates musical notation (note the small dots arrayed along the right side of the words of the text). Its practical purpose, however, is supplemented by a beauty of design and embellishment that associates noh with a decided elegance and wealth. In this case the text has been written in a beautiful, fluent hand, carefully balanced on the page with neither corrections nor cross-outs. In other manuscripts from the same group one even finds graceful illustrations added to the text. One cannot help but notice the striking contrast between this lovely article and the extant playscripts in Zeami's hand (fig. 7, p. 31). In the latter there are no illustrations, no fine bindings or embellishments. Even the writing itself is a modest practical expression of the spoken text, in the barest Japanese script form, *katakana*.

Writers outside the guilds of Zeami, Zenchiku, and their contemporaries in the Hōshō and Kongō schools also show a fully professional and sophisticated understanding of noh performance. Among the best examples is the work of Shimotsuma Shōshin (1551–1616), an actor and dramaturge associated with the great Honganji temples of southern Kyoto.

Playwriting in the late fifteenth and early sixteenth centuries demonstrates a broadening of the aesthetics of earlier noh, with strong new plays following in the tradition of Zeami as well as remarkable works that take an entirely different approach to dramatic interest. One of the most important plays in the repertory, *Dōjōji* (Dōjōji Temple) dates from this time, and in its earliest version is likely the work of Kanze Nobumitsu.[19]

Dōjōji provides the opportunity to consider the evolution of noh music from its earliest days into its maturity in the seventeenth century. Chanting was of great importance to noh from the days of Kannami and Zeami. The latter specifies five types of music and makes claims suggesting that he believed music was closely intertwined with the well-being of the state. Dance was also important to Zeami; he saw song and dance as the two basic elements of noh performance and as the first elements in the training of young actors.

**ROKURIN ICHIRO HICHŪ
(SECRET NOTES ON THE SIX CIRCLES
AND THE ONE DEWDROP)** (detail)
Konparu Zenchiku (1405–c. 1470)
Muromachi period, 1466
Hōzanji, Nara Prefecture
catalogue 121

**ZENPŌ UTAIBON SUMIDAGAWA
(ZENPŌ'S SONGBOOK, "SUMIDA RIVER")**
Konparu Zenpō (1454–c. 1532)
Muromachi period, fifteenth century
Nogami Memorial Institute for Noh Studies
at Hōsei University, Tokyo
catalogue 124

MANUSCRIPT OF EGUCHI (detail)
Zeami Motokiyo (c. 1363–c. 1443)
Muromachi period, 1424
Handscroll; ink on paper
10 3/16 x 72 11/16 in. (25.8 x 184.6 cm)
Hōzanji, Nara Prefecture
Important Cultural Property
figure 7

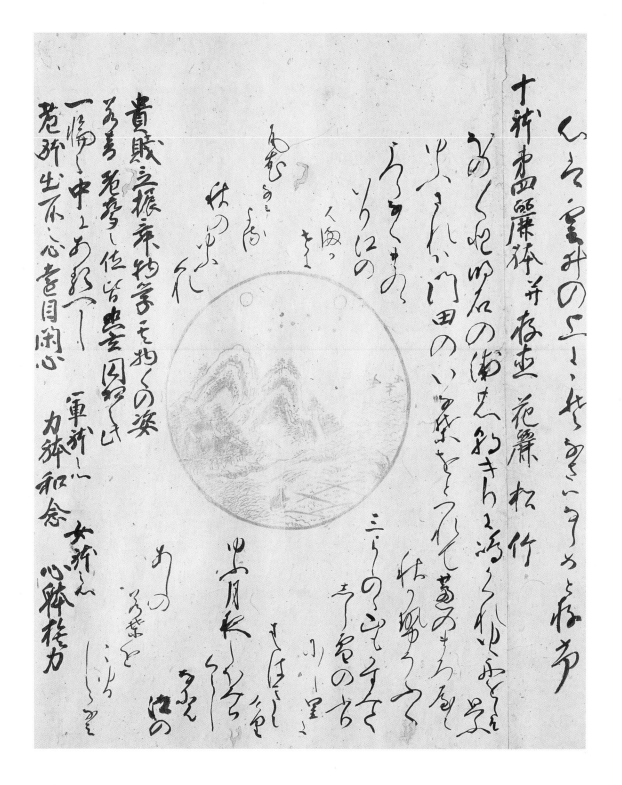

Flute and drums were used in early performances, but it is not known whether the noh flute had yet been given its unique physical structure or whether Zeami recognized a distinction between the two types of hourglass drum, the ōtsuzumi (cat. 131) and kotsuzumi (cat. 130), although this distinction is fundamental to noh music today.[20]

By the time of *Dōjōji* there is reason to believe that noh music had become much more systematized and was probably structured in roughly the same way as it is today. Ironically, *Dōjōji* reflects this as much because of its many musically unique features as because of its commonalities with noh music in general (cat. 119).

Mai, a common word for "dance" in Japanese, usually connotes a relatively stately and often slow dance, in which the dancer's posture remains for the most part upright and the choreography is based on a sequence of circular movements around the nearly square noh stage.[21]

There are a few mai with unique melodies and musical structures, but the majority share a single flute melody of four lines and a characteristically segmented structure. The common melody, called *ji*, occurs in repeated segments separated by a short structural marker called *dan*, followed by melodic sections called *oroshi*, which are unique to a specific mai and usually to a specific position within a given mai. Variations in mai occur not only because of these specific melodies but also because of the widely diverse tempos at which different mai are performed. There is, moreover, a "demeanor" (*kurai*) associated with each mai, related to, but not entirely dependent upon, its particular tempo.

In *Dōjōji* we find that the *kyū no mai* (fast dance), in departing dramatically from the typical mai, throws into relief what a mai more commonly does. The *Dōjōji* kyū no mai is, as its name

ŌTSUZUMI (LARGE HOURGLASS DRUM BODY)
WITH WIND AND THUNDER GODS
Edo period, seventeenth century
Museum of Noh Artifacts, Sasayama, Hyōgo Prefecture
catalogue 131

KOTSUZUMI (SMALL HOURGLASS DRUM BODY)
WITH AQUATIC MOTIFS
Momoyama–Edo period, seventeenth century
Los Angeles County Museum of Art, Gift of Julia and Leo Krashen
M.84.103.1
catalogue 130

KO NŌ KYŌGEN NO ZU (OLD NOH AND KYŌGEN ILLUSTRATIONS) (detail: musicians)
Edo period, seventeenth century
National Noh Theater, Tokyo
catalogue 119

suggests, the fastest of all the mai in noh. Uncharacteristically it does not contain the oroshi sections that give most mai their unique identity. The speed at which this mai takes place is accentuated by the fact that it comes after a slow, intensely focused passage called the *ranbyōshi*, in which the shite dances a highly eccentric dance to the solo accompaniment of the kotsuzumi drum and the drummer's shrieks.[22] Shortly after the ranbyōshi and kyū no mai, the shite leaps into a bell prop, just as it comes crashing down on stage. This mai, then, marks the juncture at which the enticing dancer of the first part of the play is transformed into a terrifying serpent.

The kyū no mai in *Dōjōji* punctuates the dramatic climax of the play, which is true of many types of mai in numerous noh plays, but also illustrates, in its stark contrast with the mai in plays by Zeami and Zenchiku, the different kind of appeal characteristic of several noh plays of this era.

The plays of Zeami and Zenchiku maintained their popularity, but Nobumitsu, Zenpō, and other playwrights quite naturally looked for something different from their predecessors. Nobumitsu, compared with Zeami, had little concern for the delineation of a character's inner life and wrote plays about the conflict between good and evil with clear heroes and villains. Zenpō exhibited a somewhat more diverse range of interests but, like Nobumitsu, he valued pageantry and gave prominent roles to child actors.

TALES OF ADVENTURE

One of Nobumitsu's greatest successes was a play called *Ataka*, named after the place where a barrier was erected to stop the hero Yoshitsune from evading the charges brought slanderously against him in the court of his half-brother, the shogun Yoritomo.[23]

Yoshitsune is played by a child actor. The shite is his senior retainer, the brawny warrior Benkei. Nine additional actors join their retinue in tsure roles, and there are others onstage with the waki (cat. 118). Such numbers lend an entirely different air to this play than a more typical Zeami or Zenchiku production. The text makes it clear that this is a battle of good versus evil, a great adventure in the saga of an ill-starred hero who will eventually – as the audience knows – meet a tragic end. In *Ataka*, Yoshitsune's party is victorious through guile, and they escape. In the course of events, though, Yoshitsune, the lord and master of all, must pretend to be a common laborer, and Benkei is forced to beat him before the barrier guards to give credence to the pretense. The play gives only a limited perspective on the interior lives of its characters, a relatively stereotyped vision of feudal loyalty and solidarity. It is nonetheless an exciting drama exhibiting a sophisticated understanding of how the space of the noh stage can be used to great dramatic effect.

Like other plays of its time, *Ataka* seems psychologically simpler than earlier, shite-centered dramas, and points ahead to the kabuki and the puppet theater of the Edo period (1615–1868). It should come as no surprise that when recreated as a kabuki play centuries later *Ataka* found a wildly appreciative audience under the title *Kanjinchō* (The subscription list).

In its development from the late fourteenth century to the seventeenth century and beyond, noh changed from an innovative and adventurous form of avant-garde drama to a highly refined and self-conscious classical drama. There are significant discontinuities in this process, but noh's classicism, and the interest in establishing a performance canon, were present from as early as the days of Zeami. In subsequent centuries his predispositions were refined and transformed into the orthodoxy of noh, even as supplementary traditions of performance found ways to coexist, sometimes in a kind of dynamic tension, with that orthodoxy.

By the beginning of the seventeenth century, the political situation in Japan had undergone a major change. Three important military leaders, Oda Nobunaga, Toyotomi Hideyoshi, and Tokugawa Ieyasu, had brought the country out of the chaos of the Warring States period (1467–1568), and within three decades created one of the most stable political structures of the early modern world, the Tokugawa state.

Nobunaga, Hideyoshi, and Ieyasu were all enthusiastic connoisseurs of noh. Hideyoshi in particular was an ambitious amateur who performed in plays written for, and about, himself. Once the Tokugawa shoguns had secured their hold over Japan in the mid-seventeenth century, noh performers

安宅

NŌ KYŌGEN EMAKI
(NOH AND KYŌGEN PICTURE SCROLLS) (detail: *Ataka*)
Edo period, eighteenth century
Tokyo National Museum
catalogue 118

came under the direct supervision of the shogunate. In exchange for salaries, recognition of status, and professional certification (which allowed recognized schools a monopoly on performance), the actors had to demonstrate their lineage, abide by a strict system of administration, and prepare repertory lists from which any play could be commanded for performance within three days. The relationship between noh and its patrons had been of great importance to the development of the art since the days of Kannami and Zeami, but under the Tokugawa regime this relationship had more influence on performance than ever before.

Apart from the Kita school, which was certified around 1619 as an offshoot of the Kongō school, only the original four schools of Yamato (now Nara) acting were recognized. This meant that rival performance styles, which had been relatively widespread during the previous centuries, were eliminated. The division between the actors who played shite roles and those who played waki roles was institutionalized, and schools developed licensing procedures, highly formalized regimes of artistic transmission, a centralized administrative structure called the *iemoto* system, and other controls.[24]

The artistic consequences of these structural and political changes were wide-ranging. On the one hand, the requirement that schools produce lists of their active repertory led to the elimination of many plays from performance and the radical curtailment of new texts. (Of all the plays in the modern repertories of the five schools, only *Fuji* [Wisteria] was composed during the Tokugawa [Edo] period.) Amateurs and professionals were strictly separated, and restrictions were imposed on noh performance before commoners, even as noh was exalted as the official performing art of the samurai class. Improvisation, which was apparently an important element in medieval performance, was dramatically reduced and survived only vestigially in the modern era.

On the other hand, economic security and conservatism regarding the repertory led to the polishing of acting technique and extraordinary refinement in the performance canon. These restrictions made room for the development of kabuki and the puppet theater in the seventeenth and eighteenth centuries. Ironically, even though full-fledged noh performance became less accessible to commoners, other aspects of noh reached ever more broadly into Japanese life. Amateur noh chanting became a popular activity. Noh plays were printed in increasing numbers and were even used as text-books in commoners' schools during the Tokugawa period. Some of these were mass-produced from wooden blocks and were readily available at affordable prices. Others were executed with extraordinary care by artists of the first rank using precious materials. In printed books reputed to have been created by one of the foremost artists of the time, Hon'ami Kōetsu (1558–1637), a touch of luxury is provided by the powdered mica used in the paint for the cover designs (cat. 126, p. 38–40). In some cases the pages were printed even more extravagantly, including printed images in gold and silver under the texts themselves.

With the Meiji Restoration of 1868 and its aftermath, the institutions of noh suffered a dangerous crisis. The patronage of the samurai class had sustained noh and enabled its refinement from the seventeenth through the early nineteenth centuries, and the elimination of that class, particularly the demise of the shogunate at its head, provoked radical changes in the way noh was supported. When the shogun was deposed and left Edo for his family's traditional domains, the noh actors he patronized left with him. This was also true for a majority of the other actors in the employ of high-ranking daimyo in the shogunal administration, though a few stayed behind in Edo (soon to become Tokyo). Noh was not performed for several years, and many thought it had come to an end. Because, however, of the efforts of several important men in the first generation of Meiji Japan, noh weathered the storm of the late 1800s and came into the twentieth century as a cherished part of Japan's medieval cultural heritage.

Noh maintains a generous and well-to-do audience base at the beginning of the twenty-first century. In recent decades new works, along with revivals of plays that had not been performed for centuries, have been brought to the stage by intrepid performers. Noh has influenced theater in the West to some degree, notably in plays by W. B. Yeats and Bertolt Brecht. It has had a significant influence on the development of avant-garde drama in Japan, specifically in the work of Suzuki Tadashi. If, however, no dramatic forms have displaced noh in its more than six-hundred-year history, it is because noh has had something unique to offer its audiences. This exhibition catalogue offers a palpable sense of why that remains as true today as it has been at any time in the history of noh.

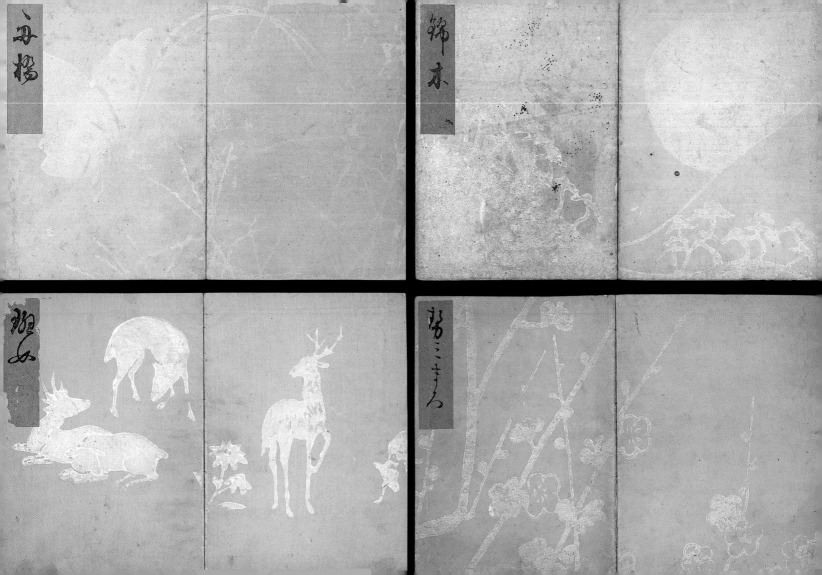

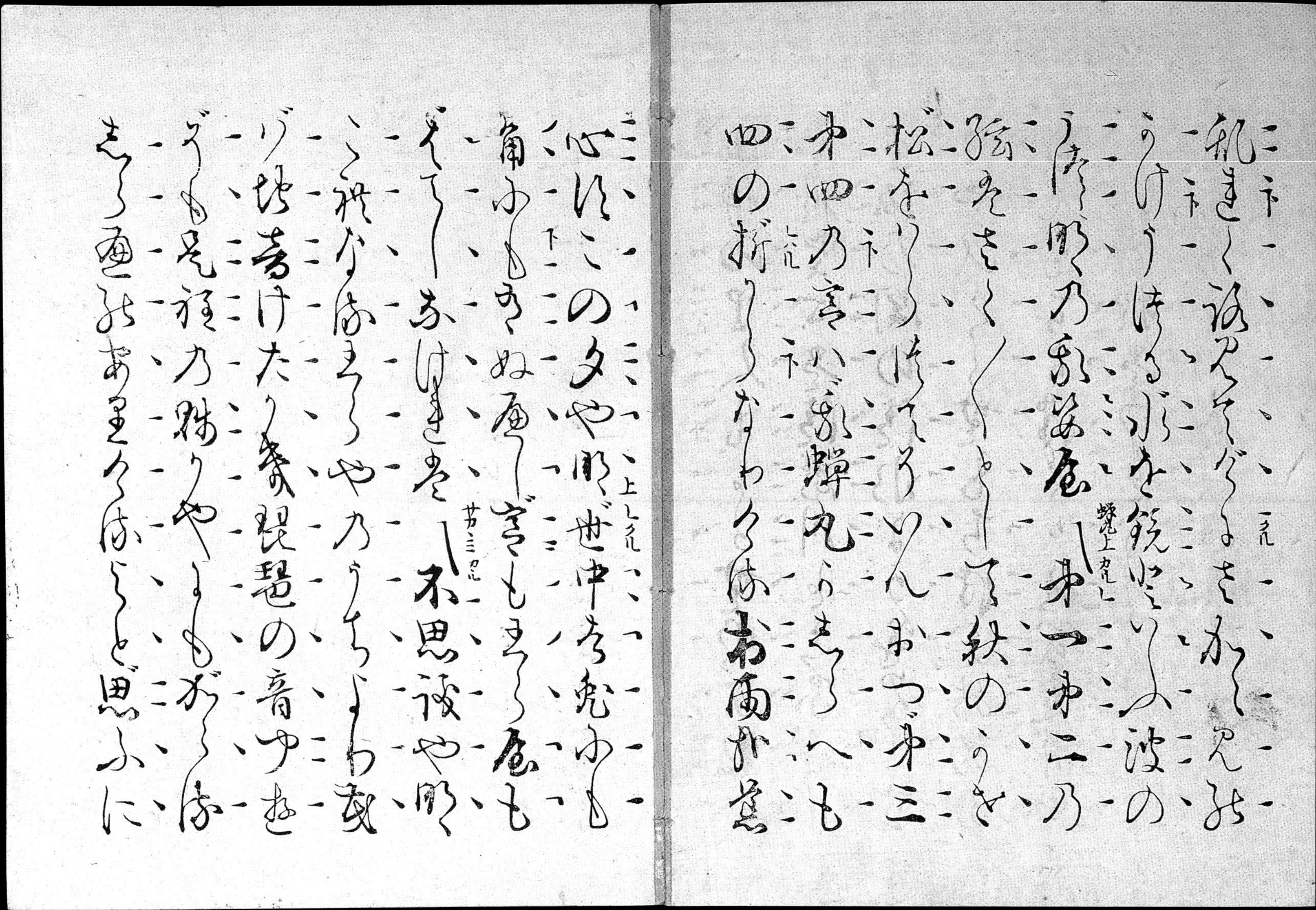

NŌ UTAIBON
(NOH SONGBOOKS)
Hon'ami Kōetsu (1558–1637);
published by Suminokura Soan (1571–1632)
Edo period, seventeenth century
Agency for Cultural Affairs, Tokyo
catalogue 126

1. Some of the clearest accounts of these events are to be found in the memoirs of the great actor Zeami, entitled *Sarugaku dangi*. The most authoritative Japanese edition is to be found in Katō Shūichi and Omote Akira, eds., *Zeami, Zenchiku*, Nihon shisō taikei, vol. 24 (Tokyo: Iwanami Shoten, 1974).

There are two translations currently available in English, one in J. Thomas Rimer and Masakazu Yamazaki, tr., *On the Art of the Nō Drama: The Major Treatises of Zeami* (Princeton: Princeton University Press, 1984), 172–256; the other in Erika de Poorter, *Zeami's Talks on Sarugaku: An Annotated Translation of the Sarugaku Dangi, with an Introduction on Zeami Motokiyo* (Amsterdam: J. C. Gieben, 1986). I have discussed some of these in *Zeami's Style* (Stanford: Stanford University Press, 1986), 27–28.

2. There are some technicalities regarding the title of this play that I am avoiding here for the sake of clarity. Some only use *Shikisanban* to refer to historical and festival performances of the play. They might call the play *Okina*, but that invites confusion with the mask of the same name. The play can also be called *Okinamai* (The Okina dance) but that might result in mistaking the whole play for the dance done by the old man of the first half.

3. Noel Pinnington has written about *Shikisanban* recently in "Invented Origins: Muromachi Interpretations of Okina Sarugaku," *Bulletin of the School of Oriental and African Studies*, 61, no. 3 (1998).

4. Bernard Faure discusses *Okina* and its religious and anthropological significance in a forthcoming book from Princeton University Press.

5. For a Japanese introduction to noh, including its artistic antecedents and relatives, *Bessatsu taiyō: Nō*, edited by Omote Akira (Tokyo: Heibonsha, 1978) is excellent and readily available.

6. The best modern printed texts of representative noh plays are to be found in *Yōkyokushū*, 2 vols., edited by Yokomichi Mario and Omote Akira in the series Nihon koten bungaku taikei, 41, 42 (Tokyo: Iwanami Shoten, 1960 and 1963). A translation of *Kamo* by Monica Bethe can be found in Karen Brazell, ed., *Traditional Japanese Theater: An Anthology of Plays* (New York: Columbia University Press, 1998), 193–206.

7. A translation of *Kuzu* can be found in Kenneth Yasuda's *Masterworks of the Nō Theatre* (Bloomington and Indianapolis: Indiana University Press, 1990), 391–410.

8. For the specialized vocabulary of costume, see checklist of the exhibition in this volume.

9. A translation can be found in Royall Tyler, *Pining Wind: A Cycle of Nō Plays* (Ithaca: Cornell University East Asia Papers, no. 17, 1978), 138–54.

10. There is as yet no English translation of *Koi no omoni*, as far as I can tell. *Oimatsu*, however, is translated in Shimazaki Chifumi, *The Noh*, vol. 1 (Tokyo: Hinoki Shoten, 1976), 141–67, as well as in Makoto Ueda's *The Old Pine Tree and Other Noh Plays* (Lincoln: University of Nebraska Press, 1962), 1–11.

11. *Tadanori* is readily available in English translation in Royall Tyler, *Japanese Nō Dramas* (London: Penguin, 1992), 264–76. There is also a translation in Shimazaki, vol. 2, 89–125. A full translation with extensive commentary can be found in Hare, 188–211.

12. *Matsukaze*, indeed, was also popularly performed as dengaku, and the dengaku performer Kiami may have had a hand in the musical composition of the play or one of its antecedents. *Matsukaze* has been translated many times. One of Tyler's versions is readily available in *Japanese Nō Dramas*, 183–204. A detailed guide to the play including a full transliteration and Tyler's translation is to be found in Monica Bethe and Richard Emmert *Noh Performance Guide: Matsukaze* (Tokyo: National Noh Theatre, 1992).

13. *Kantan* is available in translation in Arthur Waley's *The Nō Plays of Japan* (London: George Allen & Unwin, 1921) and subsequent reprints, e.g. (Rutland, Vt.: Charles E. Tuttle, 1976), 193–204.

14. The quasi-historical chronicle of medieval Japan, *Taiheiki*, records the prodigious payments to dengaku actors in clothing as well as precious metals. See Helen McCullough's translation, *The Taiheiki: A Chronicle of Medieval Japan* (New York: Columbia University Press, 1959), 131.

15. *Aoi no ue* is translated in Waley, 179–89 (he calls the play *Aoi no Uye*), and there is a detailed guide to the play in Monica Bethe and Richard Emmert *Noh Performance Guide: Aoinoue* (Tokyo: National Noh Theatre, 1997). It is also one of the plays that caught Ezra Pound's attention. His version, entitled *Awoi no Uye*, is most accessible in Ezra Pound, *Translations* (London: Faber, 1953), 323–31. The play and its classical antecedents have been discussed in Janet Goff's *Noh Drama and the Tale of Genji* (Princeton: Princeton University Press, 1991), 125–39, and there is an article in which I compare the play with another important play about Lady Rokujō in *The Distant Isle, Studies and Translations of Japanese Literature in Honor of Robert H. Brower* (Ann Arbor: Center for Japanese Studies, University of Michigan, 1996), 183–205.

16. See Arthur Thornhill's study of Zenchiku's thought, *Six Circles, One Dewdrop: The Religio-Aesthetic World of Komparu Zenchiku* (Princeton: Princeton University Press, 1993).

17. The Higashiyama culture takes its name from the "Eastern Hills" (i.e., *higashi yama*) of Kyoto, where the Ginkakuji, or "Temple of the Silver Pavilion," is located. This temple was, from 1483 to 1490, the residence of the shogun Ashikaga Yoshimasa. Yoshimasa was a miserable ruler, and political centralization during his administration broke down in a ten-year-long war which set the stage for a full century of disorder, violence, and maladministration known to the Japanese as the Warring States period. The dates of the Higashiyama period are not clearly defined, and extend before and after the period of Yoshimasa's residence in the Eastern Hills at the Ginkakuji.

18. I.e., Zōrin; see Thornhill, *Six Circles, One Dewdrop*, 58–59.

19. A translation of *Dōjōji* by Donald Keene can be found in Brazell, 193–206.

20. For a more detailed discussion of the instruments of noh see checklist of the exhibition in this volume, p. 261–3.

21. An important distinction exists between mai, in this case, and odori, another kind of dance known in kabuki, which in general takes a more left-right orientation in performance, and in which the dancer often departs from an upright posture to bend at the hips, neck, or knees.

22. A more detailed description of this remarkable dance is found in Monica Bethe's essay, in this volume, p. 206–10.

23. A translation of *Ataka* can be found in Yasuda, 91–132.

24. The five schools are exemplary of the institutional situation in the Tokugawa period, but technically speaking they are only the five schools of shite acting. There are also schools of waki acting and schools (several each) for kyōgen, and for each of the instrumentalists in the ensemble.

KASSHIKI (ACOLYTE) MASK
Muromachi period, sixteenth century
Seki Kasuga Shrine, Gifu Prefecture
catalogue 81

THE BIRTH AND EVOLUTION OF NOH MASKS

TANABE SABURŌSUKE

Masks have been studied from a variety of perspectives, including those of cultural anthropology, art history, and folk studies, but few scholars have considered them historically. In most societies masks have appeared for defined periods of time and in set types; this may be why their evolution has rarely been a primary consideration. Japanese masks are perhaps one of the great exceptions to this rule.

Japanese masks date back to the Jōmon period (11,000–300 BC). Examples range from shell masks to variously shaped clay masks (fig. 8) to pieces of cloth with attached clay ears, noses, and mouths that were presumably worn over the face. These artifacts may have been placed on the dead as talismans to ward off evil, or used as "vessels" for the convulsed faces of possessed shamans, or employed in a type of dance, or clay facial parts may have been intentionally broken off an existing mask to serve as votive objects during medical treatment. All these scenarios imply magical purposes.

The Yayoi (300 BC–AD 300) and Kofun (300–552) periods, from which there are very few objects related directly to masks, appear to have been a fallow era for the creation of such artifacts. However, recent excavations have unearthed a fragment of a wooden mask from a seventh-century site in Hyōgo Prefecture. This mask could well have served some magical purpose, as the quality of the wood differs markedly from the wood used to make the *gigaku* masks described below. Since it is difficult to imagine the complete absence of this basic human art form during these periods, it seems possible that mask-related artifacts were made instead from perishable materials such as wood, cloth, or leather.

The Asuka period (552–645) saw the introduction of gigaku (mimed skits using masks) at essentially the same time as Buddhism was brought to Japan, with gigaku masks (fig. 9, p. 44) imported along with the performances. Gigaku, like Buddhism, arrived via the Korean peninsula, but there seems to have been a recognition that its origins lay in performances from the state of Wu in South China. Remaining artifacts suggest, however, that the real origins of gigaku should be traced to lands west of China proper, and that the art was later perfected in China with the creation of dances including strong dramatic elements. In the seventh century the form of the masks was already essentially fully realized.

By the Nara period (645–794), the influence of cosmopolitan Tang China (618–906) had grown strong, and dances were being imported from most Asian countries. These were ordered and amalgamated in the early years of the Heian period (794–1185) into a form suitable for the society

CLAY MASK
Late Jōmon period, 11,000–300 BC
Clay
6 1/8 x 5 1/2 in. (15.5 x 14.0 cm)
Tokyo National Museum
figure 8

and culture of the time. In this way *gagaku* (ceremonial music) was born. Among the gagaku pieces, those that included dance are known as *bugaku*, and among these, some used masks (fig. 10). It should be noted that bugaku was essentially pure dance, and lacked the dramatic elements of gigaku. This difference had quite a large impact on the construction of the masks: the stronger the dramatic element, the more realistic the mask's expression, while the stronger the pure dance element, the more abstract and stylized the expression. From the Heian period through the Kamakura period (1185–1333) bugaku was the major form of performance in Japan. It spread from the central capital area to the provinces, leading to a dispersion of the mask designs as well. Generally speaking, the bugaku masks from the early years of the Heian period still retained a naturalistic character, but by the late Heian they had become completely stylized.

At about the same time as the bugaku masks were being perfected, masks began to be created for various types of religious ceremonies, such as Shishi and Haeharai (fig. 11) (young-boy masks with broad foreheads, small features, and bright expressions) and Kuchitori (masks with clenched mouths), used in rituals memorializing the completion of a Buddhist statue or the construction of a pagoda. There were also masks representing deities and saints, such as various Bodhisattva (*bosatsu*), the Eight Guardians (*hachibushū*), and the Twelve Devas (*jūniten*). Other masks were made to represent various demons chased out of the precincts during purification ceremonies (*tsuina*), at the Imperial Palace, the "demon-chasing rites" (*oni oi*) among the commoners, and the Buddhist ritual known as "chasing off the white demons" (*byakki hashiri*). The pursuers of these demons, known as *hōsōshi*, *ryūten* (dragon god), or *bishamonten* (Vaiśravana) wore equally frightening masks easily mistaken for demons. In the shrines as well, when the deity was taken out in a palanquin (*mikoshi*) and paraded around, his way was first purified by parade leaders performing either lion dances (*shishimai*) while wearing lion masks (*shishigashira*) or king's dances (*ōmai*) while wearing long-nosed masks (*hanataka*). The extant examples mostly date from after the Heian period, though many show influences from bugaku masks in their construction and technique.

As these highly refined dance and ceremonial masks evolved during the long Heian and Kamakura periods, masks of demons and deities were created with magical intent to fulfill folk beliefs and were dedicated as offerings to shrines or temples. Presumably the performance arts of *sarugaku* and *dengaku*, early forms of what would become noh, arose from a similar folk base, namely the agricultural society of the commoners. Among these performance types, *Okinamai* (*Shikisanban*) came to be treated as a separate tradition of its own, and masks for *Okinamai* appeared all over the country. These early examples are often considered to be noh masks, but in fact masks made during the Nanbokuchō (1333–1392) and early Muromachi (1392–1568) periods, while noh itself was developing, were still in an evolutionary stage.

In the older noh masks an unfinished simplicity and strength are combined in a way that projects a primitive folk energy. Their construction techniques reveal the influence of masks used in pre-noh performances and ceremonies. The mature form of noh masks developed out of this older form, transcending aristocratic refinement and incorporating both dramatic and dance aspects, embodying a delicate harmony of the realistic and the abstract. They combine elements drawn from the foreign-inspired masks that formed the mainstream of Japanese mask history until the Middle Ages with aspects of magical folk masks that were born in primitive times and never quite died out. Thus emerged a characteristically Japanese type of mask.

CHICHINOJŌ MASK
Nanbokuchō–Muromachi period, fourteenth century
Pigment on wood
Height: 6¹³⁄₁₆ in. (17.2 cm)
Nyū Shrine, Nara Prefecture
figure 12

BUGAKU MASK: SAISŌRŌ
Heian period, twelfth century
Colors and lacquer on wood
Height 7⅝ in. (19.5 cm)
Tamukeyama Hachiman Shrine, Tōdaiji, Nara
Important Cultural Property
figure 13

OKINA AND DEMON MASKS

A well-known commentary on masks and mask carvers appears in the *Sarugaku dangi* (Account of Zeami's reflections on the art of sarugaku), a collection of Zeami's thoughts on his art compiled by his son and containing information up to 1430.[1] Zeami begins with Okina masks and *oni* (demon) masks, following the order in which these mask types were incorporated into sarugaku and thus recounting the original character of sarugaku. The *Sarugaku dangi* also mentions names of carvers such as Nikkō and Miroku (both late tenth century) in connection with Okina masks, but these names (like the so-called "god carvers" of the early-modern writings about mask-carver families) have strong overtones of Buddhism and suggest only a tangential relation to any likely actual carvers.[2] Nevertheless, they do indicate that the creation of Okina masks long predates Zeami's time.

Four types of masks were used in the medieval version of *Okinamai*: Okina (cat. 137, p. 14), Sanbasō (cat. 143, p. 15), Chichinojō (fig. 12, p. 45), and Enmeikaja. Of these, all except Enmeikaja have a detached chin (*kiri-ago*, or "cut chin"): the lower jaw is carved separately and then attached with a cord, so that the chin shakes with the movement of the dance. It is often thought that this construction is related to that of the bugaku mask Saisōrō (fig. 13, p. 45), but there may be a different source. In the Saisōrō mask, as in some other bugaku masks, the separately carved chin is tied to separately carved eyes, so that movement of the chin activates rotation of the eyes. For prototypes of the Okina masks it is possible to point to the Korean old-man's mask, Hae, as well as the Tudi and San Wang masks used in demon-chasing purification rites (*nuo xi*) in Daozhen Xian, in the Guei Zhou province of China. Similar detached-chin examples are also found among Indonesian masks. Although it is unclear when these masks were first created, their existence may point to a common source, most probably emerging somewhere in China and then migrating to the south and east.

Putting aside such speculation, the formative period for *Okinamai* masks from the Kamakura period that are comparable with bugaku masks in technique is rather early, and is exemplified by the Okina and Sanbasō masks in Nyū Shrine, Nara Prefecture, which are most likely from before the beginning of the Muromachi period. The copying of such Okina and Sanbasō masks began earlier than the replication of other types. Fewer examples remain of Chichinojō and Enmeikaja masks, which ceased to be used frequently at some point in the development of *Okinamai*.

While the form of *Okinamai* masks changed little over the years, the demon masks attained great variety, developing along with the early development of noh. A pair of red and black demon masks, one with the mouth open (fig. 14), the other with the mouth closed (an "ah-un" pair),[3] are owned by the Kanze school, which attributes them to Prince Shōtoku (574–622), and designates them as original model masks (*honmen*).[4] Painted with red and black lacquer and with eyes and teeth covered by gilt bronze plates, the masks are inappropriate for use in noh; presumably they are from early performance

ONI (DEMON) MASK
Kamakura–Nanbokuchō period, fourteenth century
Red lacquer and metal on wood
Height: 7 3/8 in. (18.3 cm)
Kanze Bunko
figure 14

KOTOBIDE MASK
Muromachi period, 1475
Nagataki Hakusan Shrine, Gifu Prefecture
Important Cultural Property
catalogue 89

BESHIMI MASK (front and back)
Chigusa Saemon Dayū
Muromachi period, 1413
Naratsuhiko Shrine, Nara Prefecture
catalogue 88

The carved inscription on the back gives the date and the name
of the carver as Chigusa, whom Zeami mentions as skilled.

forms that existed alongside sarugaku and dengaku. These masks, carefully preserved from generation to generation, derive from pre-noh "ah-un" masks such as Hanataka (long nose), used in such dances as Ōmai and Hōken; Ryūten (dragon god) and Bishamon (a deity), used in demon-chasing rites; and the demon masks (*oni men*) used as shrine offertories. When incorporated into sarugaku these were reinterpreted as bulging-eye, open-mouthed ("ah") Tobide masks (cat. 89, p. 47; cat. 151, p. 191) and clenched-mouth ("un") Beshimi masks (cat. 88, p. 47; cat. 178, p. 214). The process of increasing differentiation can be seen in the *Sarugaku dangi*, which mentions at least two "ah" and two "un" masks.[5]

The Beshimi mask (cat. 88) at Naratsuhiko Shrine in Nara Prefecture is an example of the "un" style from the earliest period, bearing a 1413 date and an inscription by Chigusa, a carver known to Zeami.[6] The Kotobide mask (cat. 89) from Nagataki Hakusan Shrine in Gifu Prefecture, dated to 1475, already adheres to the standard form. The Akujō mask (cat. 87, p. 49) belonging to Oyama Shrine in Ishikawa Prefecture bears an inscription by Yamato Higaki Motoshichirō, and it is likely that the work comes from the period he was active (c. 1492–1500). It is not clear how the demon masks such as Akujō, *shishiguchi* lion masks, and Ikazuchi (god of lightning) developed, but many examples of similarly exaggerated expressions are depicted in the handscrolls (*emaki*) of the late Middle Ages. The Akujō mask from Oyama Shrine is a ferocious demon-style mask that also has a dignity worthy of the main actor in the play.

By the seventeenth century, those demon masks that were easy to use as noh masks became set and copied. The Ōtobide (cat. 151, p. 191) and Chōrei Beshimi (cat. 178, p. 214) at Toyohashi Uomachi Noh Association in Aichi Prefecture are typical examples of copies (*utsushi*) made from a model mask.

THE REPRESENTATION OF DEAD SPIRITS AND MALICIOUS DEITIES

In his treatises Zeami distinguishes among eight general types of noh masks such as "aged man" and "young man." A closer look at his writings, however, reveals further differentiation within these general types, with variant masks representing different men and women, although at that time the names of individual masks, their correlation with role types, and the modern mask categories had not yet been established. Around the end of the Muromachi period and in the Momoyama period (second half of the sixteenth century), the mask types became more fixed. The secret noh writings of that time, such as the *Hachijō kadensho* (Eight volumes of flowery treatise on noh) and Shimotsuma Shōshin's *Dōbushō* (Excerpts on children's dance, 1596) demonstrate that essentially all the standard noh masks used today were established by that point.[7]

Noteworthy are the Hannya and Ja (snake) masks belonging to the demonic masks previously described, and the male and female ghost masks, many of which contain "ryō" in their

AKUJŌ (EVIL OLD MAN) MASK
Muromachi period, sixteenth century
Oyama Shrine, Ishikawa Prefecture
catalogue 87

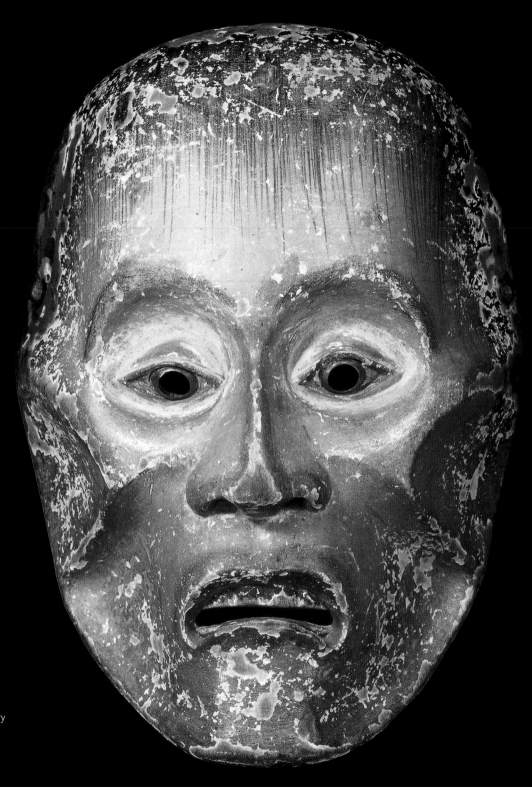

YASE-OTOKO MASK
Muromachi period, sixteenth century
Pigment and metal on wood
Height: 8 ½ in. (21.6 cm)
Mitsui Bunko Museum, Tokyo
figure 15

YASE-OTOKO MASK
Deme Zekan (d. 1616)
Momoyama–Edo period, seventeenth century
Toyohashi Uomachi Noh Association, Aichi Prefecture
catalogue 86

YASE-ONNA MASK
Edo period, seventeenth century
Oyama Shrine, Ishikawa Prefecture
catalogue 90

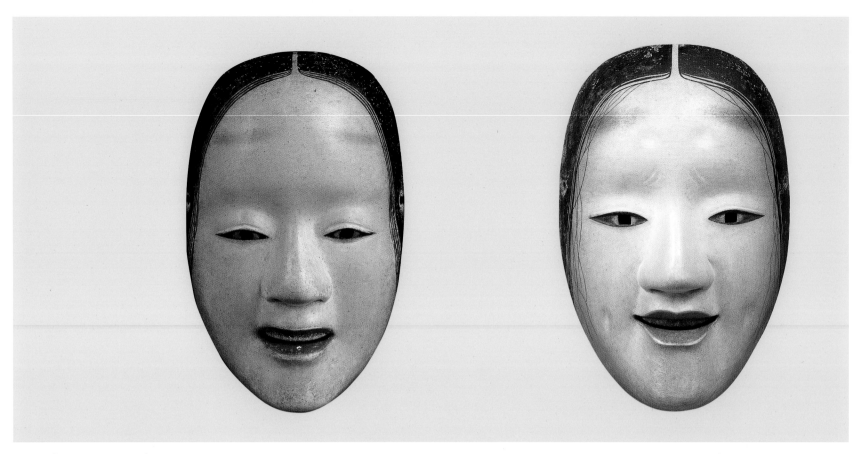

DEIGAN (GOLD-PAINTED EYES) MASK
Edo period, seventeenth century
Toyohashi Uomachi Noh Association, Aichi Prefecture
catalogue 93

MASUGAMI MASK
Edo period, seventeenth–eighteenth century
Pigment on wood
Height: 8 ⅜ in. (21.3 cm)
Hikone Castle Museum, Shiga Prefecture
figure 16

names, such as Ryō haya-otoko, or Onna-ryō. Ghosts appear in a large portion of the plays written by Zeami, and the many ghost masks that were made attest to their continued prominence in noh plays written after Zeami. An early example of this type is the superbly expressive Yase-otoko mask from the Mitsui Bunko Museum in Tokyo (fig. 15, p. 50). The Yase-onna (cat. 90, p. 51) from Oyama Shrine, Ishikawa Prefecture, a somewhat later example, is an exemplary piece among women's masks. The Deigan ("gold-painted eyes") mask (cat. 93) from Toyohashi Uomachi Noh Association, Aichi Prefecture, dates from the Edo period (1615–1868). As its name implies, the whites of the eyeballs have been painted with gold. A few loose hairs fall along the sides of the face. Straggling strands of hair become more prominent on the Masugami (fig. 16) mask. In these masks the eyes and hair signal the extent of the character's excitement or psychic confusion. The Yase-otoko mask, for example, has metal inserts in the eyeballs to heighten its emotional intensity.

The face expresses personality; the eyes express the heart. Accordingly, the amount of gold used in the eyes serves as a measure of the agitation or intensity of the grudge born by a character,

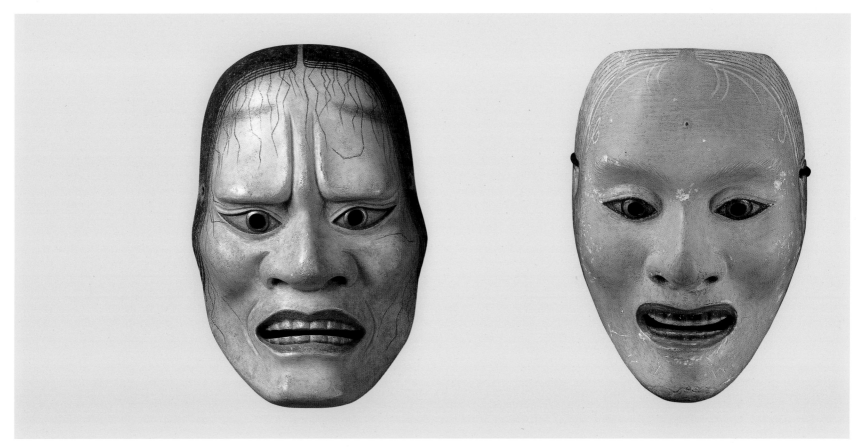

HASHIHIME MASK
Edo period, seventeenth century
Oyama Shrine, Ishikawa Prefecture
catalogue 95

YAMANBA MASK
Momoyama–Edo period, seventeenth century
Toyohashi Uomachi Noh Association, Aichi Prefecture
catalogue 97

which can range from the vengeful spirit (*onryō*) masks to the malicious deity (*kijin*) masks. Medieval demons are not all inhuman, like those who labor in hell, but include also the spirits of the dead and fierce gods. Noh masks represent a spectrum of beings, from ordinary people to vengeful ghosts to fierce demons and fantastic gods. The expression in the eyes of the Tobide and Beshimi masks discussed previously corresponds to the degree of their ferocity. Of course the hair, beard, and fleshiness can temper the impact.

The Hashihime mask (cat. 95) from Oyama Shrine and the Yamanba mask (cat. 97) from Toyohashi Uomachi Noh Association are women's demon masks that have metal eye rings. The first, used in the old play *Hashihime* (Bridge princess), expresses the terrifying vengeful attachment of a woman that drives her to become a demon. The mask is used today in the play *Kanawa* (Iron ring), where a woman wishes to curse and kill a man. The second mask is particular to the play *Yamanba*, and represents a woman who has lived for many years in the mountains as a kind of female hermit or demoness.

HANNYA MASK
Iseki Jirōzaemon Chikamasa
Momoyama period, 1558
Museum of Noh Artifacts, Sasayama, Hyōgo Prefecture
catalogue 96

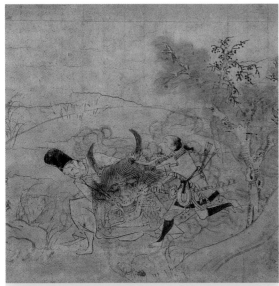

**HIDAKAGAWA SŌSHI EMAKI
(ILLUSTRATED LEGEND OF HIDAKA RIVER)** (detail)
Muromachi period, fifteenth century
Handscroll; ink and colors on paper
6¼ x 548⅓ in. (15.8 x 1394.2 cm)
Private collection
Important Art Object
figure 17

**TSUCHIGUMO SŌSHI EMAKI (ILLUSTRATED
LEGEND OF MONSTROUS SPIDER)** (detail)
Kamakura period, fourteenth century
Handscroll; ink and colors on paper
11½ x 385¼ in. (29.3 x 976.0 cm)
Tokyo National Museum
figure 18

The strongest expression of female vengeance is found in the Hannya masks, (cat. 96; cat. 174, p. 213). The most prominent characteristic is their horns. Although examples of pre-noh masks with one, two, or three horns represent a demon, the noh masks with two horns belong to the snake family, and these are restricted to female vengeful spirits. In the twenty-third book of the *Taiheiki* (Chronicle of great peace), the section entitled "Seven Things about Ōmori Hikoshichi" describes a woman who becomes a monster with horns:

> Suddenly she became a demoness eight feet tall, with mirror eyes [possibly metal inserts], and seemed to be drenched in red. Her upper and lower jaws were dislocated, and the corners of her wide-open mouth reached back to the base of her ears. Her eyebrows were painted over and over with lacquer until they spanned the forehead, and from her parted hair grew up calf horns of about 5 *sun* [15 cm] tall and covered with scales.

Many similarly transformed creatures appear in the painted handscrolls of the late Middle Ages, such as the *Ōeyama ekotoba* (Illustrated legend of Ōe mountain) at the Itsuō Art Museum, Ikeda City, Osaka Prefecture and the *Tsuchigumo sōshi emaki* (Illustrated legend of monstrous spider, fig. 18) at the Tokyo National Museum. Some of these are depicted with bull-like horns sprouting from their foreheads on either side of parted hair, with eyebrows converging over fierce eyes, gaping mouths exposing tusks, and animal-like ears. These are probably not representations of women, but rather modeled after street gangsters, called "big boys" (*ōwarawa*) because they sport a child's hairstyle. Nevertheless, these depictions are worth considering in relation to the creation of the demon masks.

Dragon figures feature prominently in the noh play *Dōjōji* (Dōjōji Temple). The basis for this drama is a tale appearing in the eleventh-century collection *Honchō hokke genki* (Miracles of the lotus). This type of legend normally develops over time, and by the end of the Muromachi period it had split into a number of versions. As a noh, the story first appears in the play *Kanemaki* (Bell coiling), attributed to Kanze Kojirō Nobumitsu (1435–1516). Additionally, quite a number of pictorial versions of the Dōjōji legend exist, among which the *Hidakagawa sōshi emaki* (Illustrated legend of Hidaka River), by an unknown artist, is interesting for its relationship to noh masks. The main setting is the Hidaka River, where a woman jumps into the water while chasing a priest. In the river she transforms from an upper-class woman into a dreadful figure with angry eyes and wide-open mouth (fig. 17, p. 55). Next she grows horns and flashes her firelike tongue. Her body takes on the form of a dragon (snakelike but with four legs), and she winds around the bell in which the monk has hidden. Finally, when she breaks the bell and clings to the priest her head has transformed entirely into that of a dragon.

The characteristics are so similar that it is tempting to think that this representation of a demon with horns may have been copied from the Hannya noh mask. The handscroll is thought to be from the mid-Muromachi period and might be considered proof that Hannya-style masks had been invented by that time. A forerunner of the Hidakagawa scroll can be found in the third scroll of the "Gishō-e" section of *Kegonshū soshi eden* (Illustrated biography of the patriarch of Kegon-sect Buddhism), in Kōzanji temple, Kyoto. Here the girl Zenmyō (Chinese: Shan-miao) turns into a dragon while chasing after the priest Gishō, who has set out to sea (fig. 20, p. 57). The woman featured in the Dōjōji legend is painted in the *Dōjōji engi* (Illustrated legend of Dōjōji Temple) owned by Dōjōji Temple of Wakayama

Prefecture with a head like a dragon, but her body has no legs: that is, she has the body of a snake (fig. 19).

From the ancient period up to the early Middle Ages, dragons and snakes were represented quite differently. By the time these paintings were made, however, a blending of the two seems to have occurred. In ancient folk ideas the water god was frequently represented in a female form and was often connected with snakes or dragons. In other words, this blurring between female figures, snakes, and dragons has deep roots. Various snake-related noh masks include Shinja (true snake), Deija (gold snake), and Kitsuneja (fox snake), as well as Hiragata Hannya and Ukigi no hannya. Older extant examples display significant variation – even given some regional differences, it appears that the snake masks were created earlier than the Hannya masks and have a longer tradition.

Comparing these early snake masks with Hannya masks, it is evident that the animalistic, evil expression of the former has been discarded and a human factor added, giving rise to what might be regarded as a dignified demon style. This may reflect the shedding of the sarugaku, dengaku, and folk mask styles in favor of masks more suited to noh. Prized examples of early Hannya masks include the Eisei Bunko Museum Hannya (cat. 174, p. 213) once owned by Tsutsui Junkei, and the Hannya owned by the Museum of Noh Artifacts, Sasayama, with an inscription from 1558 by Iseki Jirōzaemon Chikamasa (cat. 96, p. 54). Concurrent with the invention of the Hannya type, other snake masks were in all likelihood also undergoing changes. The period of this conversion presumably corresponded to the time of maturation and great flourishing of noh itself.

In 1394, as recorded in the *Kasugasha rinjisai shidai* (Accounts of special festivals at Kasuga Shrine), the Renshōbu biwa legend was performed as *Ōmi* sarugaku by low-ranking priests.

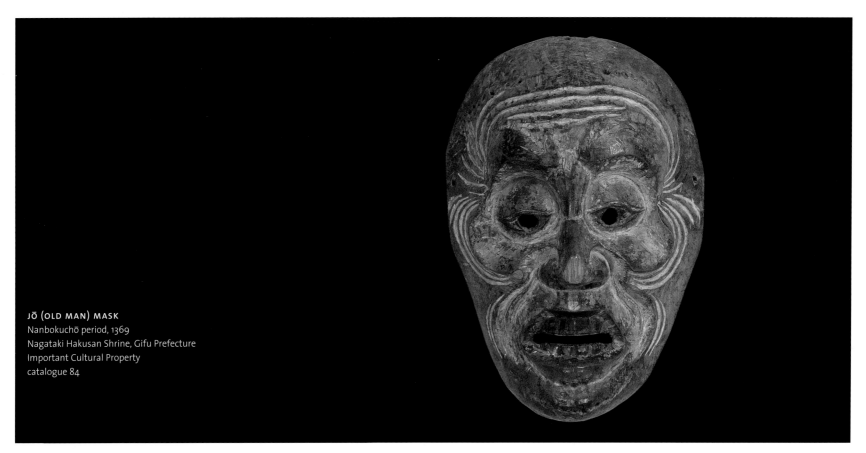

What masks were used for the dragon king and the dragon god? The mask traditionally considered a dragon mask at Kinomoto Shrine in Murou (and now kept in Shōfukuji Temple in Nara Prefecture) is a Tobide mask, and the one presently used in noh to represent dragon gods is the Tobide-variant Kurohige: both are demon-style masks without horns. It may be possible that the actors wore separate dragon crowns atop their heads.[8] This would imply that there was no confusion between dragons and snakes up through the Nanbokuchō period. However, distinguishing between dragon and snake demons (whether male or female, with or without horns) continues to be problematic.

MASKS OF OLD AND YOUNG MEN AND WOMEN

The variety of human masks expresses the core of noh, and these include masks of men and women of all ages. While each type has a name, some special masks bear names that specify their use for a single role within a single play. The human masks are categorized according to subtle criteria of modeling and painting. Naturally these evolved along with the art of performance and were fully developed only at the beginning of the modern period (the late sixteenth century).

KOJŌ MASK
Edo period, nineteenth century
The Metropolitan Museum of Art, Rogers Fund, 1925
catalogue 85

Of these human masks, the first and most important to appear were those of old men (Jō). In the Middle Ages the elders of the family or village were respected as being closest to the gods. In noh as well, after *Okina*, the old men who transform into various gods in *waki* noh are viewed as divine in nature. Consequently, these masks were created early in the development of noh; one that bears an inscription dates from 1369 and belongs to Nagataki Hakusan Shrine in Gifu Prefecture (cat. 84). Its primitive execution nonetheless contains a fervent life energy born of the fields and paddies. Of note are the elements of its construction that connect it to later old-men's masks – namely, the holes for implanting hair in the forehead and chin, as well as the shape of the mouth. Of a somewhat later date, the Jō mask that Kanze Jūrō Motomasa (Zeami's son) donated in 1430 to the Tenkawa Benzaiten Shrine in Nara is fully equipped with the characteristic elements and has become very much like a standard noh mask. Over time a rich variety of old-men's masks were created to correspond to the many levels of deification. The Kojō mask (cat. 85) in the Metropolitan Museum of Art is typical of the Jō masks that emerged from this process.

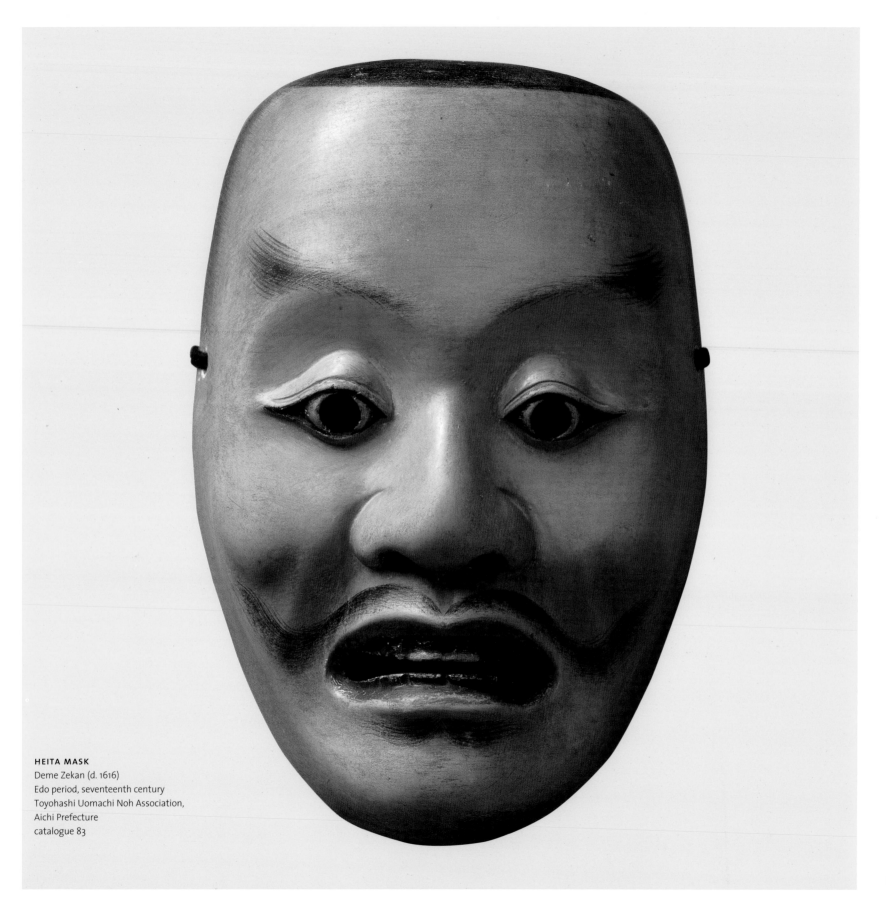

HEITA MASK
Deme Zekan (d. 1616)
Edo period, seventeenth century
Toyohashi Uomachi Noh Association,
Aichi Prefecture
catalogue 83

WAKAI OTOKO (YOUNG MAN) MASK
Muromachi period, sixteenth century
Seki Kasuga Shrine, Gifu Prefecture
catalogue 82

Many noh plays are based on episodes in classic tales, such as those featuring members of the nobility as found in *Tales of Ise* or the *Tale of Genji*, or those featuring warriors, such as *Tales of the Heike* and the *Genpei Seisuiki* (Rise and fall of Genji and Heike). Men's masks corresponded to each of these role types, the most representative being the Chūjō and Heita masks. Examples of the completely matured form of these masks dating from the early seventeenth century are owned by the Toyohashi Uomachi Noh Association (cat. 156; p. 197: cat. 83, p. 60). For comparison with earlier versions from the late Middle Ages, it is worth referring to the young man's mask in Seki Kasuga Shrine, Gifu Prefecture (cat. 82, p. 61) and the Kasshiki mask (cat. 81, p. 42) from the same shrine, which depicts a youth in his teens. The Kasshiki mask is worn for roles of acolytes who tend to the daily lives of priests, and perhaps because of the fashion for same-sex love, there are quite a number of charming, attractive examples from the Middle Ages through early modern times. Also in the same genre are the masks of Dōji and Jidō, used for roles of youths who resemble sprites; the Shōjō mask (cat. 184, p. 223), in the same style but painted red, represents a wine sprite featured in a Chinese legend.

Many of these men's masks do not represent living people, but rather dead spirits. The main roles of the warrior plays (*shura* noh) are of this type: typical examples include the Chūjō mask used in *Tadanori* (cat. 156, p. 197) and the Heita mask used in *Tamura*. Still, for certain roles of deceased warriors some actors might substitute a mask such as Mikazuki (fig. 21). Mikazuki is suitable for super-human male roles or for gods with human aspects; indeed, such beings that stand between the human and the demon-gods carry considerable importance in noh. An actor will choose his mask depending on how he feels about the main role of the play. Although regular male roles were apparently performed without a mask in Zeami's time, as male masks began to be created, each emphasized human qualities, endowing them with an otherworldliness at the heart of noh.

Women's masks followed a similar course as men's (though with fewer variations), but as women's roles are by definition difficult for men to perform unmasked, they are thought to have developed earlier than men's masks. The mask that corresponds to the male Jō masks is Uba (grandmother). In addition, there are some special elderly woman's masks used only in the "secret" noh about old women (*rōjomono*) that depict the withered form of the aged poetess Ono no Komachi.[9] Some of

MIKAZUKI MASK
Deme Genri (Yoshimitsu, d. 1705)
Edo period, seventeenth–eighteenth century
Pigment and metal on wood
Height: 6 in. (15.2 cm)
Toyohashi Uomachi Noh Association, Aichi Prefecture
figure 21

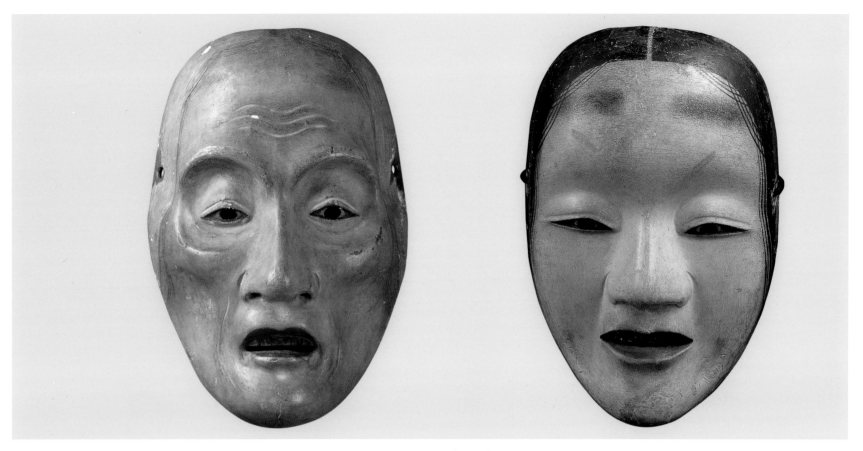

RŌJO (OLD WOMAN) MASK
Momoyama period, sixteenth century
Hikone Castle Museum, Shiga Prefecture
catalogue 91

SHAKUMI MASK
Deme Chōun Yasuyoshi (d. 1774)
Edo period, 1774
Toyohashi Uomachi Noh Association, Aichi Prefecture
catalogue 92

these, such as the Rōjo mask (cat. 91) in the Ii family collection stored at the Hikone Castle Museum, Shiga Prefecture, are very similar to the female ghost mask Yase-onna (cat. 90, p. 51). Masks for middle-aged women are represented by either the Fukai or the Shakumi (cat. 92) mask, such as that from the Toyohashi Uomachi Noh Association.

Masks of young women (often considered the most typical genre of noh masks) exist in many types. The Ōmi-onna mask (cat. 170, p. 212) from the Tokyo National Museum is used not only for the *shite* (main actor) in the first act of *Dōjōji*, but is also suitable for somewhat rustic roles. Zō-onna (cat. 148, p. 191) has a dignity appropriate for angels, such as the moon maiden in *Hagoromo*, who wear filigree crowns (*tengan*).[10] Ko-omote (cat. 162, p. 202) represents the archetypal young woman, and among young women's masks is the one with the most youthful charm. Ko-omote masks were always in great demand; in the premodern era they were sought after by all schools of noh actors and also by the various daimyo collectors. The Waka-onna (cat. 94, p. 64) mask stored in Rinnōji, Tochigi Prefecture, dates from a period just before this, when the form of women's masks was not yet standardized.

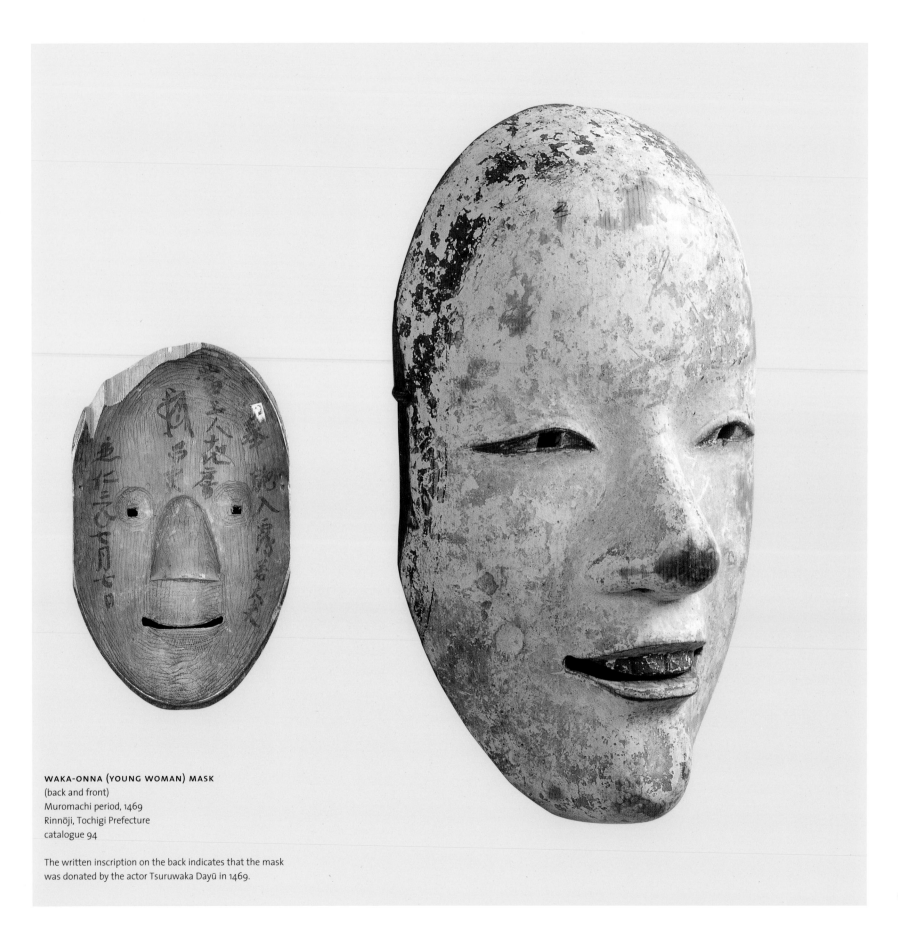

WAKA-ONNA (YOUNG WOMAN) MASK
(back and front)
Muromachi period, 1469
Rinnōji, Tochigi Prefecture
catalogue 94

The written inscription on the back indicates that the mask
was donated by the actor Tsuruwaka Dayū in 1469.

STATUE OF CHILD SHINTO GOD
Nanbokuchō period, fourteenth century
Wood
Height: 40 in. (101.5 cm)
Takada Hachiman Shrine, Ehime Prefecture
figure 22

WOMAN'S MASK
Kamakura–Nanbokuchō period, fourteenth century
Pigment on wood
Height: 6⅞ in. (17.5 cm)
Nagataki Hakusan Shrine, Gifu Prefecture
Important Cultural Property
figure 23

In fact, the development in young women's masks can be traced by studying the ones stored at this shrine, with examples dating from 1469, 1583, 1598, 1605, and 1635.

What provided the sculptural model for these masks, particularly the young figures? One explanation finds parallels for some masks with medieval Shinto sculpture. For instance, the crease lines between the eyebrows on statues of male Shinto gods and the dimples on the cheeks of young male and female Shinto statues appear to have been incorporated into noh masks (fig. 22). In this case Shinto sculpture seems a more persuasive model for noh masks than the single female bugaku mask, Ayakiri, or the various bugaku men's masks. On the other hand, it is important to recognize the expressive similarities between bugaku masks and the stylized, decorative early women's masks, such as that in Nagataki Hakusan Shrine, Gifu Prefecture (fig. 23), and Enmeikaja of the *Okinamai* masks. Among the old masks considered to be Enmeikaja, some do indeed share structural and technical characteristics with bugaku masks.

SHIOFUKI (SALT BLOWER) MASK
Edo period, eighteenth century
Eisei Bunko Museum, Tokyo
catalogue 99

OTO MASK
Muromachi period, fifteenth century
Seki Kasuga Shrine, Gifu Prefecture
catalogue 98

KYŌGEN MASKS

Kyōgen are short plays that began by satirizing the confessional and mimetic elements of the original sarugaku and dengaku, and that continue today to provide a comic contrast to the solemn, refined noh dramas. Since the world of kyōgen is that of the present – that is, kyōgen enacts the immediate reality around us – the actors do not wear masks for the majority of the plays, just as actors representing men in present-day noh (*genzaimono*) do not wear masks. In addition, kyōgen has none of the mystification that flavors noh; in this sense kyōgen still retains the old form of sarugaku and dengaku. Indeed, among many of the kyōgen masks considered old, quite a few exhibit this essential aspect of the early style.

Naturally, there are fewer kinds of kyōgen masks, yet they can be categorized similarly to the noh masks. They can be divided into five categories: (1) masks for *Okinamai*, Sanbasō (cat. 143, p. 15), and Enmeikaja (it is unclear from what period these were performed by kyōgen players); (2) masks for demons and Shinto god figures: Bishamon ("ah"), Buaku ("un"), and Fukunokami (god of good fortune), believed to have developed from the Enmeikaja mask; (3) masks used for low-ranking gods or the spirits of smaller beings such as mosquitoes or crabs (Usobuki, Kentoku, and Noborihige); (4) women's masks, such as Oto and Fukure; (5) masks of animals such as Saru (monkey) and Kitsune (fox).

Although it might appear that many kyōgen masks have little in common with noh masks, in reality they may well have emerged from the same background. The supreme examples are the monkey and fox masks. Both figures have been revered since medieval times – the monkey as the mountain-king servant of the Hiyoshi Shrine, and the fox as the servant of the Inari Shrine of good harvest. The monkey mask (cat. 101, p. 150) known as Sannō Daigongen (great manifestation of the mountain king) from Mibudera Temple in Kyoto, and the fox mask (cat. 100) from Naratsuhiko Shrine, Nara Prefecture, are most probably the oldest examples of this type and date back to the Muromachi period, if not earlier.

The Shiofuki (salt blower) mask (cat. 99) from Eisei Bunko Museum in Tokyo is an Edo-period variation of the Usobuki (lie puffer) mask, while the Oto mask (cat. 98) from Seki Kasuga Shrine in Gifu Prefecture is an old work filled with the energy of rural agricultural life. The archetype for Usobuki and Oto may well be in Indonesian masks (as mentioned earlier regarding Okina); the possibility of their sharing a common ancestor is intriguing. After noh spread throughout Japan and became the province of the upper classes, commoners turned to various types of Shinto performance (*kagura*), and the masks for these remarkable Shinto plays contain vestiges of kyōgen masks and of some noh masks.

KITSUNE (FOX) MASK
Muromachi period, fifteenth century
Naratsuhiko Shrine, Nara Prefecture
catalogue 100

EXAMPLES OF MASKS BY MASK CARVERS

Many aspects of the history and identity of noh mask carvers are as yet unclear. For example, those mentioned in Zeami's *Sarugaku dangi* – including Okina mask carvers Nikkō and Miroku (late tenth century); demon mask specialist Shakuzuru (late thirteenth–early fourteenth century); Echi Yoshifune from Ōmi, Shiga Prefecture (active 1375–1379); Ishiōbyōe from Echizen, present-day Fukui Prefecture (late thirteenth–fourteenth century); famed women's mask carver Tatsuemon from Kyoto (early fifteenth century); elderly-man's mask carver Kouji (Yamato [now Nara], fifteenth century); Yasha, Bunzō, and Tokuwaka (all fifteenth century) – have many masks attributed to them, but unfortunately, no extant examples can be irrefutably proven to have been made by any of them. Chigusa is the only name mentioned by Zeami that can definitively be matched with a carved inscription (cat. 88, p. 47). By the late Muromachi period, however, a number of carver's names can be matched with specific masks, particularly in the provinces of Ōmi and Echizen, Shiga and Fukui Prefectures, respectively. Masks made by the founders of the three main lines of mask carvers – Jirō Saemon Mitsuteru of the Echizen Deme line, Kazusanosuke Chikanobu of the Ōmi Iseki line, and Daikōbō Kōken of the Ōno Deme line – have recently come to light, and scholars can begin to establish the styles of the various artists.

It is well known that the powerful unifier of Japan, Toyotomi Hideyoshi (1536–1598), had a great love for noh, but the fact that he also composed his own noh and encouraged the creation of noh masks deserves special mention. This patronage continued through succeeding generations in the Tokugawa household and was taken up by the various daimyo; accordingly, the number of noh mask carvers proliferated. About the time of the fifth Tokugawa shogun, Tsunayoshi (1646–1709), the Kodama family and the Deshi Deme family split away from the Echizen Deme family, creating the three competitive lines. Until this time, each of the carver families included one or more outstanding craftsmen, some of whom had received official recognition by being granted the title of *tenka ićhi* (best under heaven). After the late seventeenth century, however, this appellation grew so common that it becomes difficult to grasp the individual styles of the carvers.

The study of the carvers requires that one have a clear picture of the works and other sources, but for reasons such as those outlined above, the circumstances at present make this very difficult. The proliferation of carvers copying masks using similar techniques and styles is a major reason why accurate identification of many carvers remains difficult. Copying sometimes went so far as to replicate the older masks' insignia. Inscriptions were often added later and include attributions such as "I guarantee this mask was made by Shakuzuru." In addition, of course, there were attempts to raise the market value of masks. The process of thoroughly investigating the masks owned by members of the five schools of noh actors and collected by the various daimyo has just begun.

Translated by Monica Bethe

1. Translations into English can be found in J. Thomas Rimer and Masaku Yamazaki, *On the Art of the Nō Drama: The Major Treatises of Zeami* (Princeton: Princeton University Press, 1984) and Erika de Poorter, *Zeami's Talks on Sarugaku* (Amsterdam: J.C. Gieben, 1986). Twelve mask carvers are mentioned by name – two, Nikkō and Miroku, are associated with Okina masks; the others, known today as the Jissaku (Ten carvers), were presumably contemporaries of Zeami, and each was associated with a genre of mask (demon, old man, young woman, etc.) See the concluding section of this essay.

2. Edo-period treatises and commentaries on mask carvers tried to systematize the material. In the process they traced the beginnings of noh masks back to the Nara-period legendary beginnings of sarugaku, claiming that Okina mask makers included such famous figures as Prince Shōtoku (the statesman responsible for the official adoption of Buddhism), literary educator Ōmi no Mifune, Kōbō Daishi (the founder of esoteric Buddhism), and a man called Kasuga.

3. "Ah-un" refers to paired statues of fierce human or animal figures, such as temple lion dogs (*shishi*), set up to guard shrines and temples. One opens his mouth wide to say something ("ah"), but before he can fully utter it the other has acknowledged and agreed with him, uttering "un."

4. Masks considered particularly appropriate for given roles were designated as "main" masks (*honmen*) and used as models to be copied when multiple samples were deemed necessary. By the Edo period almost all the masks made were copies (*utsushi*) of model masks.

5. This sentence refers to section 173 of the *Sarugaku dangi*, which reads (de Poorter translation):

The *tobide* of the Deai troupe, the *tenjin* mask, *ōbeshimi* and *kobeshimi* of our troupe are all [made by] Shakuzuru. The *ōbeshimi* is called *Yamato-beshimi* in [Sarugaku of] other provinces. It is this [kind of] mask. The *ōbeshimi* and the *tenjin* mask have been handed down since Kan'a [Kannami]. The *tobide* [mask] represents Kan Shōjō [Sugawara no Michizane], who is disgorging a pomegranate. The *tenjin* mask has had this name since it was worn in the play *Tenjin*. [One day] a man borrowed it, but he had a strange divine revelation in a dream and gave the mask back. It was kept in our house [without being used], but again he had a dream, and now it is worn [again]. The *kobeshimi* [mask] was worn for the first time by Zeshi [Zeami]. Nowadays there is nobody else who can wear it. With that mask he started to perform *Ukai*. With other masks he performed *Ukai* [more] gently. [An actor] also has to wear masks according to his level.

6. The *Sarugaku dangi* contains one reference to Chigusa (tr. de Poorter): "As for man masks, those made by Chigusa are reputed to be very good masks."

7. *Hachijō kadensho* is an eight-volume compendium of secret writings on noh, compiled at the end of the Muromachi period. It provides important information regarding the song, instrumentation, staging, and teaching of the time. Although it claims to be based on Zeami's *Fūshikaden*, only a small portion is taken from Zeami. Other segments reproduce other writings, such as the notes of a *tsuzumi* (drum) player, Miyamasu, of the early sixteenth century. Since it was reproduced in print quite early, it provided technical information for both professionals and amateurs, including the daimyo studying and patronizing noh. Shimotsuma Shōshin (1551–1616) was a Honganji monk and noh actor. He inherited a connection with the Kanze school, but was primarily affiliated with the Konparu school and received many of their secrets, recorded in his numerous writings on noh. The *Dōbushō* records three volumes about staging the Konparu noh.

8. Today the costume for dragon-god roles includes a large dragon crown and the Kurohige mask. Both pictorial and written records suggest that this was already common practice in the Edo period and may, as the author suggests, reach back to the fourteenth century.

9. The term "secret" refers to the difficulty of these pieces, for which there are special teachings, and which are performed only by mature actors of considerable age. Ono no Komachi was a skilled poetess who lived in the early Heian period and was renowned for both her beauty and her pride. She is featured in five noh plays, where her portrayals range from a young courtesan to an elderly beggar to a ghost tormented by an unrequited suitor.

10. The various noh schools have different traditions concerning which mask is used for which role, particularly for young women's masks. In the Kanze and Hōshō schools, Zō-onna is the standard mask for the moon maiden in *Hagoromo*, and it is also used for the shite in the first act of *Kamo*, indicating her hidden godliness. The Konparu and Kita schools use Ko-omote in *Hagoromo*, which is the tradition followed here in the selection of a costume for that piece.

KARIGINU WITH HERONS AND REEDS
Momoyama period, sixteenth century
Neo Kasuga Shrine, Gifu Prefecture
Important Cultural Property
catalogue 1

FASHIONABLE DRESS OR THEATRICAL COSTUME: TEXTILES AND THE EVOLUTION OF NOH ROBES

SHARON SADAKO TAKEDA

The colorful stiff brocades, subdued airy gauze fabrics, or soft, shiny silks decorated with multicolored embroidery and metallic foil utilized to construct noh costumes are some of the most sophisticated woven and embellished textiles of Japan. Magnificent noh costumes, worn in combination with carefully chosen masks, envelop the actor and transform his body into an often voluminous, abstracted sculptural form concealing all individual physical features except for the hands and part of the face and neck. The costume's fabric, cut, drape, color, and design motifs function as visual indicators that assist an initiated audience in identifying such matters as the character's sex, age, social status, and emotional state. Animated by the actor's subtle, stylized, and highly controlled movements, masks and costumes help transport the audience to an illusionary world that transcends time and space.

Noh costumes came to be made from luxurious and expensive textiles as a result of the long tradition in Japan of presenting cloth and clothing as tribute (fig. 24). An unusual custom that had audience members spontaneously tossing garments onto the stage to actors out of admiration or as a reward for an excellent performance was practiced as far back as the Heian period (794–1185). At that time popular entertainment forms enjoyed by all classes included *bugaku* (court dance) and *sangaku* (acrobatics, mimes, and short plays performed at shrine and temple festivals), also known as *sarugaku*.[1] Entertainers performing in public did not charge admission fees, but it was expected that spectators would throw garments (*kazukemono*) onto the stage instead.[2] Members of the audience were from various levels of society, and while separate viewing areas were defined, it appears that everyone participated in the tossing of garments. A late-Heian-period chronicle reports, "No fixed amount was demanded, and the unique reward was given spontaneously and according to the enthusiasm and financial status of the spectator."[3] In this way a variety of clothing styles, from simple hemp garments worn by commoners to elegant silk robes of the nobility, fell into the hands of performers.

During the early twelfth century the ruling class allowed actors to wear the sumptuous attire they bestowed (which was normally deemed inappropriate for people of lower social standing) not only for stage performances but also in the streets during public festival parades and mass dances.[4] These increasingly popular events provided circumstances where the upper and lower classes commingled. Enjoyment of the entertainment of commoners such as *dengaku* (field music) led aristocrats to patronize

KASUGA GONGEN REIGEN-KI (detail)
Takashina Takane (fourteenth century)
1309
Set of twenty scrolls; ink and colors on silk
Height: 16¼ in. (41.2 cm)
Imperial Household Collection
figure 24

their own individual performance troupes.[5] Such support included generous endowments of textiles and clothing that reflected the taste of wealthy benefactors.[6]

ARISTOCRATIC AND SAMURAI STYLE

The wardrobes of Heian aristocratic women and men included various styles of robes with large open sleeves (ōsode) and generously cut and pleated bifurcated skirts or trousers (hakama) (fig. 25). Female courtiers draped multiple layers of monochromatic lined robes (uchigi) arranged in sensitively chosen color combinations to form part of an ensemble known as kasane shōzoku.[7] Attire for noblemen included the formal ensemble known as sokutai with hō, its outermost covering. Kariginu and nōshi, two kinds of round-neck, wraparound outer mantlelike robes, shared the form of the hō, but did not consistently follow the strict color-code etiquette of the court, since the garments were for daily wear.[8] The kariginu (literally, "hunting robe") was initially informal apparel worn in public. Constructed of fine-quality bast-fiber (asa) cloth, kariginu lacked side-seams and had braided cords laced along the outer edges of the sleeves. The cords could be pulled to gather and tighten the large wrist openings so that the massive sleeves would not hinder the wearer during activities such as hunting.[9] Nōshi were everyday apparel accepted as formal wear when combined with the proper court headgear (kanmuri).[10] A distinguishing feature of the nōshi is the two bands at the hemlines that connect the front and back panels of the garment's body. Both the kariginu and the nōshi were worn with sashinuki, long hakama with ties along the hem so that each pant leg could be secured at the ankles, creating a full silhouette. As outer clothing, kariginu and nōshi could easily be removed and thrown to actors on a public stage. Both garment forms would later be slightly adapted and adopted as noh costumes, as seen with the sixteenth-century Kariginu with Herons and Reeds (cat. 1, p. 70) and the nineteenth-century Nōshi with Phoenixes and Clouds (cat. 5, p. 74). This occurred in part because numerous plays were based on classical literature and the lives of Heian aristocrats.

The Kamakura period (1185–1333) saw the rise of a military government (bakufu) organized by Minamoto Yoritomo (1147–1199). Yoritomo controlled most of eastern Japan and based his government in the provincial town of Kamakura. He secured political power over the entire country from the imperial court when he was granted the title of seii tai shōgun (supreme commander) in 1192. The

THE ILLUSTRATED DIARY
OF MURASAKI SHIKIBU (detail)
Kamakura period, mid-thirteenth century
Ink and colors on paper
Width: 8 ¼ in. (21.0 cm)
Gotoh Museum, Tokyo
National Treasure
figure 25

Kamakura shogunate allowed the emperor and his household to maintain their refined and aesthetic way of life in the old imperial capital of Heian-kyō (now Kyoto). With the diminishing power and wealth of the imperial family, the aristocratic style of dressing gradually became simpler. The military elite, envious of the inherited cultured lifestyle of the imperial family, attempted to emulate the ways of court life, resulting in a unique warrior style that was a synthesis of aristocratic tradition and samurai innovation. The aristocrat's informal kariginu, for example, was appropriated and transformed into formal wear by utilizing exotic silk fabric from China's Southern Song dynasty (1127–1279). Clothing styles were also borrowed from commoners and lower-ranking warriors. These outfits of ōsode jackets and hakama, called *hitatare* and *suō*, were made of high-quality bast-fiber cloth and became part of the conventional wardrobe for samurai.

DEVELOPMENT OF NOH AND NOH COSTUMES

During the succeeding Muromachi period (1392–1568) military rule continued under the leadership of the Ashikaga clan. Ashikaga Takauji (1305–1358) was appointed shogun in 1338 and moved his government back to Kyoto in order to keep a watchful eye on political rivals. This placed the powerful military elite physically closer to the aesthetic courtly pursuits, and this proximity would prove to have great influence on art and culture for years to come.

Takauji's grandson Ashikaga Yoshimitsu (1358–1408), a talented military leader and cultural aesthete, witnessed a performance by Kannami Kiyotsugu (1333–1384) and his eleven-year-old son Zeami Motokiyo (c. 1363–c. 1443) at a *kanjin* (subscription) sarugaku noh performance at Kyoto's Imakumano Shrine in 1374. Just sixteen years old himself, Yoshimitsu was captivated by Zeami's beauty and talent. He took both father and son along with their sarugaku noh troupe under his patronage. With shogunal sponsorship came access to some of the best artists, musicians, poets, and Zen philosophers of the day. The impact of this contact contributed to the gradual transformation of sarugaku noh into a stately and sophisticated theatrical art by Kannami, Zeami, and their Kanze troupe.

Drawing upon resources at hand, entertainers utilized their own ordinary dress as well as proffered attire. The military aristocracy presented actors with rare luxurious imports from Ming dynasty China (1368–c. 1644) that included sophisticated silk brocades with supplementary wefts of gold-leaf paper "threads" or *kinshi* (*kinran*), plain gauze-weave silk (*sha*), gauze-weave silk with gold-leaf paper supplementary weft patterning (*kinsha* and *rokin*), and gauze-weave silk impressed with gold leaf (*inkin*). A 1399 entry in *Kōfukuji kuyōki* (Record of the memorial service at Kōfukuji) notes that kariginu made of kinran, which had become an established mode of samurai dress for special occasions, was worn by Yoshimitsu.[11] According to a 1427 entry in *Mansai jugō nikki* (Diary of the Reverend Mansai) Zeami received a kinran kariginu from the shogun along with two thousand bolts of silk.[12] After this occurrence, kinran

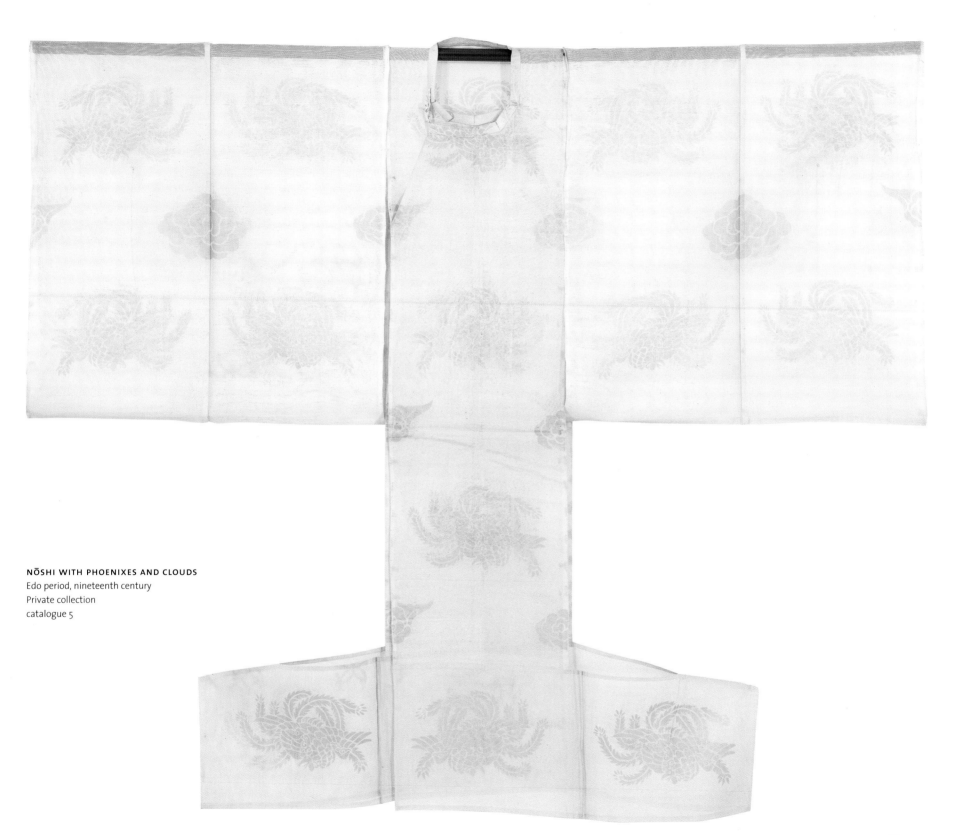

NŌSHI WITH PHOENIXES AND CLOUDS
Edo period, nineteenth century
Private collection
catalogue 5

KARIGINU WITH LIONS AND FLOWERS
Momoyama period, sixteenth century
Seki Kasuga Shrine, Gifu Prefecture
Important Cultural Property
catalogue 2

textiles and clothing were frequently given to actors as payment and rewards for kanjin productions held at shrines and temples. Increasingly, special cloth and clothing offerings were made backstage prior to an appearance rather than at the conclusion of a performance.[13] In a gesture of gratitude, the head actor of the school (*tayū* or *dayū*) would don a newly acquired garment or hold the robe or textile gift in his arms while performing a dance called *kureha no kiri o mau*.[14] Special performances given in appreciation for costume donations (*shōzoku tabari no nō*) were staged in front of a distinguished audience before the official beginning of special events such as the Kasuga Wakamiya Festival in Nara, as noted several times in *Sarugaku dangi* (An account of Zeami's reflection on art, 1430).[15] Since this established mid-Muromachi-period etiquette dictated that actors immediately employ gifts of clothing onstage, it is reasonable to assume that the offerings may have included not only fashionable attire as spontaneously presented in earlier times, but also expensive clothing consciously made with the notion that it would be worn on stage, to the delight and satisfaction of the patron.

During this formative period of noh, costume guidelines were not yet clearly defined but mimicked what was worn on the streets by the various social classes. Treatises written by Zeami on the art of noh include his observations of performances and a few comments on what actors wore (including type of garment, fabric, color, style of draping, and motif). Zeami repeatedly stressed the importance of an actor dressing appropriately for his role. In *Fūshikaden* (Secret writings on the style and flower of acting, 1400–1418), he describes the research that the male actor should undertake before playing various types of women's roles: "If the actor's style of dress is unseemly, there will be nothing worth watching in the performance…The fact that an actor takes great care with his costume means that he is truly anxious to perform his role as well as possible."[16] In *Sarugaku dangi*, Zeami felt that the costume for Okina in the ritual play of the same name should be appropriate for an old man who symbolized happiness and longevity. Using a costume made of silk and gold kinran would be unsuitable. Instead, Okina should wear a robe of basic colors (*seishoku*). Zeami favored attire that would befit a character rather than glittery impressive costume for dramatic effect. His nephew On'ami (1398–1467), on the other hand, unreservedly used eye-catching kinran to create splendid theatrical costumes that captivated the audience.[17] This elaborate style was nurtured by the patronage of shogun Ashikaga Yoshinori (1394–1441). On'ami succeeded Zeami as leader of the Kanze troupe in 1428, and so began the elevation of noh costumes from normal street fashion to a set of rarefied costumes designed to transfix the audience emotionally.

While a number of literary sources from this classic period of noh document textiles and dress presented to actors by the upper classes and even by Buddhist monks, there are few surviving textiles and virtually no extant documented noh costumes from Zeami's day. This may be due to the fact that the civil conflict known as the Ōnin Wars (1467–1477) ravaged the country and especially Kyoto, the center of silk textile production. Everything, including noh costumes, was terribly damaged or destroyed by fires during this cataclysmic period, according to *Daijō-in zōjiki* (Miscellaneous records of Daijō-in, 1470).[18]

Resident weavers in Kyoto, who had kept up with the demands for silk textiles required by the aristocracy and military elite for rituals, ceremonies, and daily life, fled to the provinces for safety. Many settled in the seaport city of Sakai (in present-day Osaka Prefecture), joining a community of immigrant Chinese weavers. Sakai had prospered as a trading base during the wars when access to the shogunate's main port of Hyōgo (now Kobe) was thwarted. Imports from China continued to enter Japan through Sakai. Japanese textile artisans were stimulated by their exposure to the talents of Chinese weavers residing in the area and by the diverse textile imports, which included kinran, sha, kinsha, *donsu* (silk damask), and *ōdon* (a satin-weave textile consisting of silk warps and cotton wefts with additional silk and gold-leaf paper patterning wefts). The Muromachi-period *Kariginu with Lions and Flowers* (cat. 2, p. 75) is constructed of ōdon. Most of these sophisticated textiles would not be produced domestically until the Momoyama (1568–1615) and early Edo (1615–1868) periods (cat. 112).

Merely a decade after the conclusion of the Ōnin Wars sumptuous noh costumes began to appear and receive notice. According to an entry in *Inryō-ken nichi roku* (Daily record of Inryō-ken, 1435–66 and 1484–93) dated the twenty-first day of the first month of 1489, Kongō Dayū (the head of the Kongō school), Kongō Matashichi, and Kongō Shinsaburō appeared on stage with costumes that were outstanding in quality.[19] Further documentation notes that both the nobility and the shogun presented Ming kinran and donsu to actors.[20] Even amateur actors were seen performing in costumes made from imported kinran and donsu. It can be concluded, therefore, that professional actors were already wearing equally sumptuous if not superior costumes at this time. In *Zenpō zōdan* (Conversations with Zenpō; 1513) the actor Konparu Zenpō (1454–c. 1532) remarked that imported fabric from China (*karaorimono*) was used to construct noh costumes. Zenpō also wrote words in Chinese graphs (*kanji*) that can be read in Japanese as "maiginu" and "chōken," evidence that distinctive costumes for noh had materialized by the early sixteenth century. While the term chōken in Zenpō's day probably applied to a different type of garment than today's chōken, by the Edo period, jackets such as *Maiginu with Young Pines on Abstract Snowflake Pattern* (cat. 26, p. 78) and *Chōken with Weeping Willow and Swallows* (cat. 18, p. 79) were unique to noh.

Around 1570 Toyotomi Hideyoshi (c. 1537–1598), the warlord credited with unifying the country under a new feudal hierarchy after the fall of the Ashikaga shogunate, encouraged displaced weavers in Sakai to return to Kyoto and resettle in an area that had functioned as the Western Camp during the Ōnin Wars.[21] A new wave of immigrant craftsmen escaping from Ming China brought their refined technical expertise of fabricating gold-leaf paper "thread" (*kinshi*) and weaving kinran.[22] As a result, by the end of the sixteenth and beginning of the seventeenth century, domestic weavers had

SHOKUNIN TSUKUSHI-E
(VIEWS OF ARTISANS AT WORK) (detail: weavers)
Edo period, seventeenth century
National Museum of Japanese History,
Sakura, Chiba Prefecture
catalogue 112

**MAIGINU WITH YOUNG PINES ON
ABSTRACT SNOWFLAKE PATTERN (YUKIWA)**
Edo period, eighteenth century
Noda Shrine, Yamaguchi Prefecture
catalogue 26

**CHŌKEN WITH WEEPING WILLOW
AND SWALLOWS**
Edo period, eighteenth century
Toyohashi Uomachi Noh Association,
Aichi Prefecture
catalogue 18

gained the technical knowledge to reproduce a wide range of Ming-style textiles.[23] More than five thousand looms in the Kyoto weaving district of Nishijin (Western Camp) produced silk textiles for the imperial court, military elite, temples, monasteries, and noh actors.[24]

THE FLOWERING OF THE TEXTILE ARTS AND NOH COSTUMES

Early observations and documentation of how specific types of textiles and costumes were used expressly for noh were recorded by a Momoyama-period amateur actor, Shimotsuma Shōshin (1551–1616). In *Shōshin nōdensho* (Book of Shōshin's instructions on noh) and *Dōbushō* (Excerpts on children's dance, 1596) Shōshin lists two types of kosode-style robes that were standard costumes for female roles: the woven *karaori* and the embroidered and gold-leafed *nuihaku*. These garments, named after the textile techniques used to produce them, were stylish both on- and offstage. In the Keichō era (1596–1615), toward the end of the Momoyama period, Kyoto artisans began to weave Ming-style brocade known as karaorimono. These domestically produced karaori were designed to appeal to Japanese aesthetics. Flowers of the four seasons, embodying the refined sensibilities often found in classical Heian-period poetry, were the most popular motifs. The noh robe *Karaori with Chrysanthemum, Paulownia, and Weeping Cherry Tree Blossoms* (cat. 61, p. 112) combines blossoms associated with spring (paulownia and cherry) and autumn (chrysanthemum). All three motifs have been popular since the Heian period. The colorful supplementary pictorial wefts (*e-ito*) delineating the motifs span the surface of the twill-weave ground in long, soft floats, giving the impression of being embroidered rather than woven.

Japanese embroidery, like weaving, was influenced by imports from the continent. Before it was used to adorn clothing, it primarily enriched Buddhist devotional textiles. Sixteenth-century Japanese embroidery methods included the use of soft, untwisted silk floss (*hira-ito*) that embellished the surface of the base fabric, leaving only tiny dots of visible stitches on the reverse side of the cloth, which was reinforced with a paper backing. This technique, which was influenced by Ming embroidered textiles, is known in Japan as *ura nuki* (literally, "nothing on the reverse") or *watashi nui* (bridging stitch). It flourished in the Momoyama period, when stylish kosode were covered almost entirely with embroidery.

SHOKUNIN TSUKUSHI-E
(VIEWS OF ARTISANS AT WORK) (detail: embroiderers)
Edo period, seventeenth century
Suntory Museum of Art, Tokyo
catalogue 111

NUIHAKU WITH SNOW-LADEN REEDS AND BIRDS
(detail: watashi nui embroidery and silver leaf)
Momoyama period, sixteenth–seventeenth century
Hayashibara Museum of Art, Okayama Prefecture
Important Cultural Property
catalogue 47

KARIGINU WITH HERONS AND REEDS
(detail)
Momoyama period, sixteenth century
Neo Kasuga Shrine, Gifu Prefecture
Important Cultural Property
catalogue 1

These fashionable embroidered robes weighed less and were more pliable than brocaded robes. Momoyama-period embroiderers secured the long watashi nui stitches, which were susceptible to snagging, with thin silk threads stitched in a manner that created patterned details, such as veins on the leaves of plant motifs (cat. 47). Comparable artistic patterning of binding warps (*toji*) used to secure long supplementary weft floats on woven fabric, however, was not achieved with the drawloom until the Edo period (fig. 39, p. 111). Another hallmark of Momoyama-period embroidery is the occasional abrupt color change (*irogawari*) within a single component of a motif. The leaves on the embroidered *Kariginu with Herons and Reeds* (cat. 1) are executed in this manner and convey an unrealistic portrayal of plant life compared to the more realistic portrayal of birds.

The combination of embroidery (*nui*) with metallic leaf (*haku*) is referred to as *nuihaku*. During the Momoyama period kosode worn by upper-class women as well as costumes used by noh actors were decorated with nuihaku, as evident in a number of extant examples. A lightweight plain-weave cloth called *nerinuki* made with an unglossed silk (*kiito*) warp and wefts of glossed silk (*neriito*) was typically used for sixteenth-century nuihaku noh robes. The smooth surface of nerinuki was well suited for the ultra-thin gold or silver leaf adhered within the interstices of the plump watashi nui embroidered motifs on Momoyama-period noh robes such as *Nuihaku with Snow-Laden Reeds and Birds* (cat. 47, p. 80 and 82). Reflective metallic-leaf decoration was recognized as an effective embellishment for stage costumes in the late-Heian period, when aristocrats were known to give costumes decorated with gold to dengaku and sarugaku actors.[25] Gold (in the form of gold leaf affixed to paper with lacquer, and then cut into very narrow strips and used as supplementary wefts) was not introduced into woven textiles until the Edo period, when kosode made of heavy woven fabrics were no longer fashionable but were utilized almost exclusively as noh costumes.

Contrasting blocks of color (*dangawari*; literally "levels different") found on sixteenth-century nuihaku such as *Nuihaku with Grasses, Poem Papers, Serpentine Line Pattern, Plank Bridges, and Snow-Laden Willow Branches* (cat. 50, p. 83) are created by binding off sections of the nerinuki prior to immersing the fabric into a dye vat. The embroidered motifs fill each color block but remain within the borders of each design block. Likewise, woven motifs of sixteenth-century karaori do not cross the borders of color blocks created by tie-dyeing the warps (cat. 61, p. 112). Dangawari and other organizational concepts for design spaces such as *katamigawari* (literally, "split body") with different fabrics and patterns divided on the right or left side of the garment, as seen in *Nuihaku with Scrolling Clematis Vines, Eulalias and Scattered Fans* (cat. 52, p. 85), and *katasuso* (literally, "shoulder and hem") with patterns concentrated in the areas of the shoulder and hem as seen on *Nuihaku with Snow-Laden Willow Branches and Abstract Pine-Bark Lozenges* (cat. 46, p. 86), are visually striking and seem expressly made for the stage. Yet these whole-garment patterning layouts appeared on street clothing as early as the thirteenth

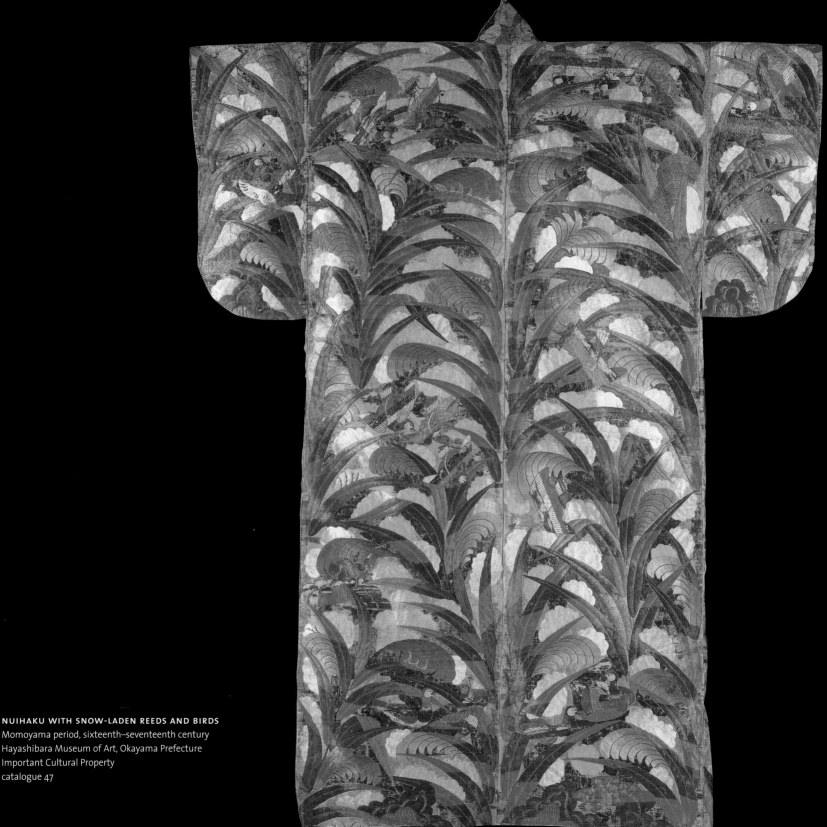

NUIHAKU WITH SNOW-LADEN REEDS AND BIRDS
Momoyama period, sixteenth–seventeenth century
Hayashibara Museum of Art, Okayama Prefecture
Important Cultural Property
catalogue 47

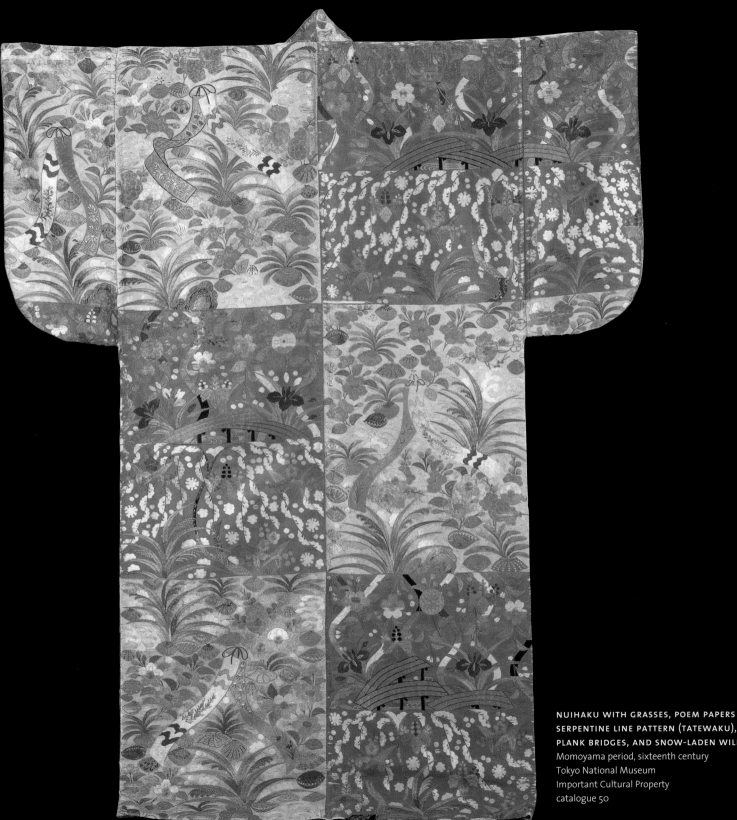

**NUIHAKU WITH GRASSES, POEM PAPERS,
SERPENTINE LINE PATTERN (TATEWAKU),
PLANK BRIDGES, AND SNOW-LADEN WIL**
Momoyama period, sixteenth century
Tokyo National Museum
Important Cultural Property
catalogue 50

century and are depicted on the early-fourteenth-century scroll of the *Kasuga Gongen reigen-ki* (Miracles of the deities of Kasuga Shrine; figs. 26, p. 84 and 28, p. 87). Dangawari and katamigawari patterning may have had their origins in the frugality of commoners, who pieced together fragments of several tattered garments in order to make one complete garment, but it became very stylish in subsequent centuries. The seventeenth-century noh robe *Atsuita with Poems* (cat. 71, p. 82), for example, was conceived as a katamigawari-style garment prior to the weaving of the fabric. Careful planning and calculation were necessary before the silk and gold-leaf paper supplementary wefts were skillfully woven into yardage with the words of six poems from an eleventh-century imperial anthology. The writing not only appears in the correct orientation, but the words seem to be brushed onto the fabric by a calligraphy master.

Katasuso-style nuihaku noh robes can have simple straight-line borders or curved borders resembling the irregular shoreline of a sandy beach (*suhama*). A kosode with a suhama design is depicted on a young woman in the early-fourteenth-century *Kasuga Gongen reigen-ki* (Miracles of the deities of Kasuga Shrine, fig. 28, p. 87). The design format is also seen on *Nuihaku with Scattered Fans and Snow-Laden Willow Branches* (cat. 45, p. 87), a sixteenth-century robe once belonging to the Konparu school and now in the collection of the Tokyo National Museum, as well as on a young-woman's kosode that was donated to Ura Shrine in Kyoto (fig. 27, p. 87). It is unclear if the Tokyo National Museum nuihaku started out as fashionable attire and was later presented to a Konparu actor, or if it was originally created as a noh costume. The shoulder and hem areas of both robes are covered with multicolored silk embroidery and gold leaf that contrast starkly with the smooth negative space of the white lustrous nerinuki ground fabric.

Breaking away from the confines of pattern blocks, the artisan began to move toward a more unified pictorial patterning with *Nuihaku with Lilies and Oxcarts* (cat. 49, p. 88). The outer limits of the garment itself restrict the exuberant motifs and the design reads more like a painting. Magnification of pictorial elements such as the lilies is a device used in Momoyama-period painting. This enlargement, along with the asymmetrical placement of the lilies rising up from the hemline on a relatively blank monochromatic background, anticipates the direction that the popular Kanbun-style kosode took in the early Edo period. Instead of gold leaf covering the small voided areas between densely embroidered motifs, large-scale vertical serpentine lines known as *tatewaku* are composed of a stenciled gold-leaf pattern of tiny geometric elements (now barely visible). Tatewaku are part of a design vocabulary of traditional patterns favored by aristocrats (*yūsoku mon'yō*) during the Heian period. The oxcarts also allude to Heian courtiers.

Elegant kosode worn by upper-class samurai women during the Keichō (1596–1615) through Kan'ei (1624–1644) eras (fig. 29, p. 89) share the same color palette and decorative techniques seen on the noh robe *Nuihaku with Scattered Crests of Wild Cherries and Scrolls* belonging to the

KASUGA GONGEN REIGEN-KI
(MIRACLES OF THE DEITIES OF KASUGA SHRINE)
(detail: dangawari patterning)
Takashina Takane (fourteenth century)
1309
Set of twenty scrolls; ink and colors on silk
Height: 16 ¼ in. (41.2 cm)
Imperial Household Collection
figure 26

NUIHAKU WITH SNOW-LADEN
WILLOW BRANCHES AND ABSTRACT
PINE-BARK LOZENGES
(MATSUKAWABISHI)
Momoyama period, sixteenth–seventeenth century
Seki Kasuga Shrine, Gifu Prefecture
Important Cultural Property
catalogue 46

**NUIHAKU WITH SCATTERED FANS
AND SNOW-LADEN WILLOW BRANCHES**
Momoyama period, sixteenth century
Tokyo National Museum
Important Cultural Property
catalogue 45

**KOSODE WITH PAULOWNIA
AND SPRING PLANTS**
Momoyama period, sixteenth century
Silk plain weave (*nerinuki*)
with silk embroidery and gold leaf (*nuihaku*)
46 ³/₁₆ x 39 in. (119.0 x 99.0 cm)
Ura Shrine, Kyoto
Important Cultural Property
figure 27

**KASUGA GONGEN REIGEN-KI
(MIRACLES OF THE DEITIES OF KASUGA SHRINE)**
(detail: kosode with suhama pattern)
Takashina Takane (fourteenth century)
1309
Set of twenty scrolls; ink and colors on silk
Imperial Household Collection
figure 28

NUIHAKU WITH LILIES AND OXCARTS
Momoyama period, sixteenth century
Tokyo National Museum
Important Cultural Property
catalogue 49

**NUIHAKU WITH SCATTERED CRESTS
OF WILD CHERRIES AND SCROLLS**
Momoyama period, sixteenth–seventeenth century
Hayashibara Museum of Art, Okayama Prefecture
Important Cultural Property
catalogue 51

**KOSODE ON SCREEN (KOSODE FRAGMENTS WITH LEAVES,
FANS, AND PLANTS)**
Momoyama–Edo period, seventeenth century
Silk figured satin (*rinzu*) parti-colored (*somewake*) with silk
and gold thread embroidery, and stenciled gold leaf
68 7/8 x 68 7/8 in. (174.9 x 174.9 cm)
National Museum of Japanese History, Nomura Collection
Sakura, Chiba Prefecture
figure 29

SURIHAKU WITH PICTURE CARDS (SHIKISHI)
AND GRAPEVINES
Momoyama period, sixteenth century
Tokyo National Museum
Important Cultural Property
catalogue 39

Hayashibara Museum of Art (cat. 51, p. 89). Constructed of figured twill on plain weave (*saya*), a type of textile first introduced from China at the end of the sixteenth century and produced in Nishijin by the close of the Keichō era, the Hayashibara nuihaku is decorated with *nuishime* (stitch and bind) and *bōshi* (capped) *shibori (*tie-dyed) motifs on a crimson ground. The robe is further embellished with silk embroidery and gold-leaf stenciled patterns. Keichō-Kan'ei era embroidery is typically sparse, with stitches that are shorter and tighter than those seen on earlier robes. Instead of spanning only the surface of the fabric, stitches also cross the reverse side, which lacks a paper backing. The gold-leaf stenciled patterns on the dark brown tie-dyed elements are small and delicate. These stylistic and technical modifications may have occurred because the figured twill on plain weave was thicker than nerinuki and its uneven surface was not suitable for large solid areas of gold leaf. A decline in the quality and quantity of imported silk due to the downfall of the Ming dynasty may have also been a factor in the embroidery becoming sparser and the stitches shorter. A larger and more nebulous influence was simply the changing of artistic taste. Designated an Important Cultural Property by the Japanese government, *Nuihaku with Scattered Crests of Wild Cherries and Scrolls* embodies one of the last moments when fashionable kosode shared aesthetics with noh theater costumes.

In the Kanbun (1661–1673) through Genroku (1688–1704) eras, the use of gold leaf on fashionable kosode lessens and is supplanted by gold embroidery thread (*yorikinshi*; gold-leaf paper strips wrapped around a core of cotton or silk floss). Gold- and silver-leaf embellishment (*surihaku*), however, remains primary on a certain type of noh costume that takes its name from the technique. Worn as undergarments by actors playing female roles, surihaku noh robe motifs range from elegant pictorial designs, as seen in *Surihaku with Picture Cards and Grapevines* (cat. 39), to strong geometric motifs like the triangular scale pattern (*uroko*) worn by demonic female characters (fig. 30), to small repetitive patterns, as on *Surihaku with Autumn Grasses* (cat. 41).

Dress among the samurai and wealthy merchant (*chōnin*) classes in the late Momoyama and early Edo periods began to shift away from kosode made of stiff, heavy brocaded textiles and moved toward lightweight dyed kosode accented with embroidery, and traces of gold leaf. The innovative free-hand paste-resist dyeing technique known as *yūzenzome* revolutionized decorative design on kosode in

ACTOR WEARING SURIHAKU WITH TRIANGULAR SCALE PATTERN IN PERFORMANCE OF AOI NO UE
figure 30

SURIHAKU WITH AUTUMN GRASSES (detail)
Edo–Meji period, nineteenth century
Los Angeles County Museum of Art, Costume Council Fund
catalogue 41

**ATSUITA WITH FLOWERS IN LINKED HEXAGONS
(KIKKŌ) AND WISTERIA ROUNDELS**
Edo period, seventeenth century
Tokyo National Museum
catalogue 74

**ATSUITA WITH PAULOWNIA CRESTS
AND TEMPLE GONGS (UNPAN)
ON LINKED HEXAGONS (KIKKŌ)**
Edo period, eighteenth century
National Noh Theater
catalogue 77

ATSUITA WITH CHINESE LION-DOGS (SHISHI)
Edo period, eighteenth century
Tokyo National Museum
catalogue 78

the late seventeenth and eighteenth centuries. Kosode made with brocaded textiles gradually became obsolete in fashionable circles but remained critical to the world of noh. Costumes made of stiff woven fabrics could be draped in sculptural forms and utilized to great advantage on stage (fig. 32, p. 98).

Atsuita are kosode-style noh robes made of heavy brocade similar in weave structure to karaori but worn by male characters. The term atsuita, meaning "thick board," refers to thick (*atsu[i]*) textiles that were wrapped around thin wooden planks (*ita*) for transport. Instead of the feminine floral motifs that identify karaori, atsuita can range from simple stripes or checks to patterns typically characterized by strong geometric or Chinese-inspired designs like legendary animals (dragons and phoenixes) and Buddhist implements that are considered masculine.

Silk supplementary weft-pattern motifs on both atsuita and karaori robes in the early seventeenth century appear to have almost equal importance to the ground weave as seen in *Atsuita with Wisteria Roundels and Flower-filled Linked Hexagons* (cat. 74, p. 92), whereas a distinction between foreground and background emerges later as in *Atsuita with Paulownia Crests and Temple Gongs on Flower-Filled Linked Hexagons* (cat. 77, p. 93). Eighteenth-century weavers were able to outline motifs and create minute details, as demonstrated on the eighteenth-century *Atsuita with Chinese Lion-Dogs* (cat. 78). By skillfully arranging limited colors of supplementary wefts (usually between ten and fourteen), taking care not to repeat the same color combinations, weavers created an illusion of a wider color pallette. And by simply changing the background color and shifting the alignment of the brocaded cloth, two similar but different looking robes can be created. Compare two karaori with the same supplementary weft patterning of autumn grasses and butterflies: one with a green and white background in the collection of the Ōtsuki Seiinkai (cat. 69, p. 96) and a red and white version belonging to the Tokyo National Museum (fig. 31, p. 97). Such ingenuity combined with technical expertise characterizes mid-Edo period weavers.

Over the centuries, changes in the sociopolitical framework of Japan have affected the development of both noh and the textile arts. Competition between the military elite extended to their patronage of noh and their participation as amateur actors. Daimyo ordered expensive noh costumes to be given to their favorite actors as well as for themselves. As a result of this important patronage

ATSUITA WITH CHINESE LION-DOGS (detail)
Edo period, eighteenth century
Tokyo National Museum
catalogue 78

**KARAORI WITH AUTUMN GRASSES
AND BUTTERFLIES**
Edo period, eighteenth century
Ōtsuki Seiinkai, Osaka
catalogue 69

**KARAORI WITH AUTUMN GRASSES
AND BUTTERFLIES**
Edo period, eighteenth century
Silk twill weave with silk and gold-leaf
supplementary weft patterning
54 ¹¹⁄₁₆ x 55 ¹⁵⁄₁₆ in. (139.0 x 142.0 cm)
Tokyo National Museum
figure 31

of noh, textiles produced domestically reached a high level of sophistication. Woven and decorative techniques that had been fashionable during the Momoyama period – weft patterning, embroidery and surihaku – remained in use for noh costumes and continued to evolve, finally reaching a creative and technical peak in the eighteenth century.

After attaining the title of shogun in 1603, Tokugawa Ieyasu celebrated by presenting a three-day noh performance at Nijō Castle in Kyoto. Noh then became an official part of Edo-period ceremonial rites in addition to its connection to religious institutions. During the long peaceful reign of the Tokugawa shogunate, many government edicts were issued, including legislation on noh acting methods and costuming.[26] These laws adversely affected innovation and by the Genroku era a standard set of noh costumes was codified. Today, while strict rules dictate a costume's use, the noh actor selects color combinations and motifs from his wardrobe that will best express his interpretation of the character he is to portray. Infused with symbolic meanings that help convey the dramatic emotions of the role, noh costumes also represent centuries of textile and costume history.

KARAORI DRAPED IN NUGISAGE STYLE,
TSUBO-ORI STYLE, AND KINAGASHI STYLE
IN PERFORMANCE OF EGUCHI
figure 32

NOTES

1. P.G. O'Neill, *Early Nō Drama: Its Background, Character and Development 1300–1450*. (London: Lund Humphries, 1958), 4. Sangaku (Chinese: *sanyue* or *san-yueh*) was first imported from China to Japan in the eighth century. During the tenth century the terms sangaku and sarugaku were interchangeable.

2. One of the earliest records of the custom of audience members impulsively taking off their clothes and throwing them at actors on a public stage can be found in the *Shin sarugaku ki* (A chronicle of new sarugaku), also known as *Shin sarugō ki*, written during the late Heian period by Fujiwara no Akihira (c. 989–1066). See Jacob Raz, *Audience and Actors: A Study of Their Interaction in the Japanese Theatre*. (Leiden: E.J.Brill, 1983), 48.

3. Ibid.

4. People from diverse walks of life such as warriors, priests, and dengaku players intermingled in public wearing lavish garments for the Gion Festival of 1127. See Raz 1983, 59.

5. When imperial regent (*kanpaku*) Fujiwara no Tadazane (1078–1162) retired and moved away from the capital of Heian-kyō, he brought along dengaku troupes for his amusement when he resettled in nearby provincial Uji.

6. Raz, 80.

7. The basic kasane shōzoku ensemble included an unlined undergarment (*hitoe*), worn closest to the body, and a hakama. Additional articles of clothing, such as the apronlike *mo* that attached at the waistline and trailed behind the wearer, would be added to the kasane shōzoku for formal occasions. Since the sixteenth century, the popular term for kasane shōzoku has been *jūnihitoe* (literally, "twelve unlined robes").

8. The color code system used for distinguishing hierarchy within the imperial court originated in China.

9. Kariginu are mentioned numerous times in the *Eiga monogatari* (A tale of flowering fortunes), a chronicle of aristocratic life during the tenth and eleventh centuries. See William H. and Helen Craig McCullough, tr., *A Tale of Flowering Fortunes: Annals of Japanese Aristocratic Life in the Heian Period, vols. I & II* (Stanford: Stanford University Press, 1980).

10. *Kanmuri* (literally, "crown") is a tall ceremonial or court hat. Lower-ranking courtiers wore *eboshi*, which is rounder and flatter.

11. Kitamura Tetsurō, "Kinsei no kosode to nō shōzoku" (Early modern kosode and noh costumes) in Kitamura, ed. *Taiyō some to ori shirizu: kosode nō shōzoku* (Tokyo: Heibonsha, summer 1977), 61–70. The military elite competed among themselves in presenting imported textiles and clothing fashioned from rare materials to actors under their patronage.

12. Kitamura Tetsurō, *Nō shōzoku* (Noh costumes) in *Nihon no bijutsu*, no. 46. (Tokyo: Shibundō, 1970), 21.

13. Kitamura 1977, 66. Cloth, a traditional form of taxation and tribute, was another popular form of payment and reward for performances during the Muromachi period. A Kanze performance at the Kiyotaki Shrine in 1425 yielded a total of three thousand rolls of silk. In 1428, On'ami, Zeami's nephew and future successor as leader of the Kanze troupe, received fifty thousand rolls at the shogun's Muromachi Palace and Zeami's son Motomasa (c. 1394–1432) obtained five thousand rolls of silk for a performance at Daigoji Temple. See Michele Marra, *Representations of Power: The Literary Politics of Medieval Japan*, (Honolulu: University of Hawaii Press, 1993), 108.

14. Kitamura 1977, 69. *Kureha* is also the name of a noh play. For translation, see Royall Tyler, *Japanese Nō Dramas*, (London: Penguin, 1992), 170–82.

15. See Erika de Poorter, tr., *Zeami's Talks on Sarugaku: An Annotated Translation of the Sarugaku Dangi with an Introduction on Zeami Motokiyo* (Amsterdam: J.C. Gieben, 1986), 82, 165. The term *shōzoku* currently refers to high-quality clothing, whereas the word *ishō* indicates more common clothing. Noh costumes are referred to as nō shōzoku while kabuki costumes are called kabuki ishō.

16. J. Thomas Rimer and Yamazaki Masakazu, tr., *On the Art of the Nō Drama: The Major Treatises of Zeami* (Princeton: Princeton University Press, 1984), 11.

17. Man'sai, the principal of Daigoji Temple, presented On'ami with indigo blue silk and gold brocade at the kanjin performance of 1430.

18. A diary of the head priest Jinson. Kitamura 1970, 23.

19. Kitamura 1977, 67, and Kitamura 1970, 23.

20. As recorded in *Ōdate Jōkō-ki* (Diary of Ōdate Jōkō; 1538–1542) and *Tamon-in nikki* (Record of Tamon-in; 1478–1617). Kitamura 1970, 23.

21. Kitamura 1970, 24. Toyotomi reportedly presented imported kinran to actors of the four main noh schools. Today the area is still known as Nishijin and remains a center for textile production in Kyoto.

22. Wendell Cole, *Kyoto in the Momoyama Period*. (Norman: University of Oklahoma Press, 1965), 72.

23. In the beginning of the Edo period during the Gen'na era (1615–1623) kinsha and a variation of kinsha that combined plain gauze weave (sha) with plain weave (hiraori) and gold-leaf paper supplementary wefts was first produced in Takeyachō, Kyoto, by merchants who were trained by a Chinese weaver in Sakai. These fabrics were known as Takeyachō-gire. See Nishimura Hyōbu, ed. *Orimono* (Weaving) in *Nihon no bijutsu* no. 12, (Tokyo: Shibundō, 1967), 71.

24. Cole, 72.

25. As recorded in *Gyokuyō* (The gem note), written by Kujō Kanezane in 1179. See Kitamura, 1970, 20.

26. Authoritative regulations on the manners of noh actors were issued by the government in 1647.

KARAORI WITH AUTUMN GRASSES
Edo period, eighteenth century
Tokyo National Museum
catalogue 66

THE DEVELOPMENT OF THE KARAORI AS A NOH COSTUME

KAWAKAMI SHIGEKI

Kōjien, the preeminent dictionary of the Japanese language, gives the following three definitions for the word "karaori":

1) A woven textile imported from China. Also, a general term for something resembling such textiles. Karaorimono.

2) A silk textile with a 2/1 twill foundation weave and colored supplementary weft patterning creating colorful and beautiful patterns.

3) A type of noh costume. The most lavish and elegant type of outer robe, which is fashioned from karaori cloth. Used primarily for female roles.

As the first definition suggests, the word "karaori" – literally *kara* (Chinese) and *ori* (weave/textile) – originally referred to textiles imported from China. Over time, however, the word gradually came to refer to a particular weave, and then to a style of garment for which this weave was used. Though the *Kōjien* touches on it only briefly, there was a long period preceding the adaptation of the karaori as a noh costume during which Chinese textiles were incorporated into the Japanese context. The following essay reviews this history, explores the processes and circumstances through which karaori textiles came to be used as noh costumes, and examines the changes undergone by these costumes themselves over time.

THE KARAORIMONO USED BY THE ARISTOCRACY

Japan's textile history was heavily influenced by ancient China. Although the Japanese practice of sending official envoys to its continental neighbor ended abruptly in 894, commercial interaction with China actually accelerated after this time, with numerous Tang (618–906) trading ships arriving in Japan. This trend became even more marked during the Song dynasty (960–1279).

As suggested in *Makura no sōshi* (The pillow book) by Sei Shōnagon (flourished late tenth century) – which lists *karanishiki* as one of the "splendid things"[1] – luxurious silk textiles imported from China were highly prized by the Japanese aristocracy during the Heian period (794–1185). The names of these fabrics, including *nishiki* (compound or multicolored weaves), *aya* (twill damasks), and *ra* (complex gauzes), would be prefixed by "kara" to exhibit their Chinese origins, leading to terms such as karanishiki and *karaaya*. Whether or not the imported textiles of the day included the kind of 2/1 twills with supplementary floating wefts known today as karaori is unclear – no actual examples have survived, and there are no references to such weaves in textual sources.

One existing Heian-period textile that would seem to be a predecessor to our modern definition of *karaori* is found on the borders of several sutra wrappers from the temple of Jingoji, in northeastern Kyoto. The wrappers are part of an original set of five hundred made to cover manuscripts of the entire Buddhist canon (Japanese; *issaikyō*), which were donated to the temple in 1185 by the retired emperor Goshirakawa (1127–1192). The nishiki[2] textile used around the border of this wrapper, known as

**JINGOJI TEMPLE KYŌCHITSU (BUDDHIST SUTRA WRAPPER)
WITH CHINESE BOYS AND FLORAL SCROLLS** (detail)
Silk twill weave with silk supplementary patterning wefts (*nishiki*)
Heian period, twelfth century
12 x 19 ⅞ in. (31.5 x 50.6 cm)
Kyoto National Museum
figure 33

Chinese Boys and Floral Scrolls (fig. 33), is highly unusual in that its design is executed not with multicolored compound wefts, but through the use of weft floats. It has a foundation weave of 2/1 twill, with supplementary pattern wefts extending continuously from selvedge to selvedge. These pattern wefts are inserted between every foundation weft and have a 5/1 twill binding structure (fig. 34). The karaori textiles used for contemporary noh costumes have a 2/1 twill foundation weave with floating supplementary pattern wefts, each separated by two shots of foundation weft (fig. 35). In addition, the supplementary wefts of today's karaori textiles are discontinuous, extending only the width of each individual pattern, as opposed to the continuous supplementary wefts of the Jingoji sutra border. Though there are clear structural differences between present-day karaori and the Heian-period *Chinese Boys and Floral Scrolls*, it is important to note their analogous characteristics: ground weaves of warp-faced three-harness twill and patterns formed of longer supplementary weft floats.

During the Nara (645–794) and Heian periods, the most common types of nishiki textiles were weft-faced compound twills, also called samite (*nuki nishiki* or *ikin*), with multiple polychrome wefts forming both the background and the pattern colors. Such samites typically have two different warps, a binding warp that creates the foundation weave structure (either plain weave or 2/1 twill) and a hidden warp that separates the colored wefts running across the front of the textile from the unneeded weft colors on the back (fig. 36). This compound structure allows for either pattern colors or background colors to be brought to the surface as necessary.

The weave structure of *Chinese Boys and Floral Scrolls* is based on a different principle. The foundation structure resembles less the samites described above than a damask weave, in that it

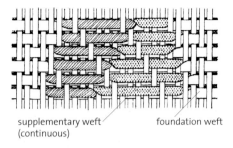

supplementary weft
(continuous)

foundation weft

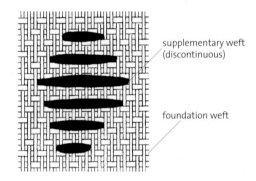

supplementary weft
(discontinuous)

foundation weft

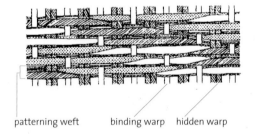

patterning weft   binding warp   hidden warp

**WEAVE STRUCTURE OF CHINESE BOYS
AND FLORAL SCROLLS**
figure 34

WEAVE STRUCTURE OF KARAORI
figure 35

**WEAVE STRUCTURE OF SAMITE (NUKI NISHIKI
OR IKIN) WITH A 2/1 TWILL BINDING**
figure 36

has only a single set of warps. The addition of supplementary patterning warps into this structure is an entirely new technique more akin to textiles with discontinuous supplementary weft patterns. Such new techniques were imported from Song dynasty China into Heian Japan, where they were copied and adapted for use in the clothing of the nobility. The term "karaorimono" would seem to refer to one of these new textile genres.

Evidence that karaorimono were used for aristocratic garments can be found in sources dating to the Kamakura period (1185–1333). *Bun'ei gonen inmai goran ki* (Record of the retired emperor's viewing of dances in Bun'ei 5), which relates the retired emperor Gofukakusa's viewing of *bugaku* performances in 1268, gives descriptions of the types of robes worn by aristocrats for particular dances. For example, four male courtiers performing a dance entitled *Rindai* all wore *kariginu*[3] robes of karaorimono. One of these four wore a layered outfit (*kasane*) in the color combination known as "cherry blossom" (*sakura*), comprising a white robe layered over a red robe. It further describes that the outer layer had a woven pattern of cherry blossoms. The other three dancers wore kariginu of karaorimono with woven designs of cherry blossoms or cherry blossoms with bellflowers or willows.

Aristocratic women also wore garments made from karaorimono textiles. In the aristocratic diary *Myōkaiki* (Record of the marvels of the three great ministers), the entry for the twenty-fourth day of the fourth month of 1260 describes how, on a viewing of the Kamigamo Shrine Festival, the former empress Ōmiyain (wife of the retired emperor Gosaga, r. 1242–1246) wore layered robes of gauze-like raw silk (*suzushi*) karaorimono with a woven pattern of bamboo in the color combination known as "iris" (*shōbu*): that is, a blue robe over an underrobe of dark pink. Other sources describe how noblewomen wore garments of karaorimono when making donations at temples and shrines. In *Shōkunmon'in onsan gu ki* (Humble record of Empress Shōkunmon'in's giving birth), the entry for the twenty-third day of the first month of 1303 tells of Shōkunmon'in (wife of Emperor Kameyama, r. 1259–1274), who donated a robe of karaorimono with a design of wisteria and mandarin oranges when visiting Iwashimizu Hachiman Shrine, south of Kyoto. It also tells that Empress Eifukumon'in, wife of Emperor Fushimi (r. 1308–1313), donated a robe of karaorimono with a wisteria pattern to Kyoto's Kamigamo Shrine.

The karaorimono mentioned in these examples seem to have had both the colors needed for specific aristocratic layering combinations and the Japanized patterns favored by Heian period nobility. *Meigetsuki* (Record of the clear moon), a courtly diary by Fujiwara Teika (1162–1241), mentions in its entry for the twenty-ninth day of the twelfth month of 1229 that a weaver in Kyoto had just woven karaaya, showing that, despite their name, these "Chinese damasks" were indeed being produced in Japan.

THE KARAORIMONO INCLUDED AMONG SHRINE TREASURES

Though the word "karaorimono" appears frequently in early documents and literature, unfortunately there are no extant examples of what the aristocrats of the Kamakura period (1185–1333) actually wore. We do have, however, a number of sacred garments donated to Shinto shrines during the medieval period, which appear to have been made in accordance with contemporaneous stipulations for courtier dress. The textiles used in such garments all have foundation weaves of 2/1 twill and include such variations as *futaeorimono*,[4] *karaorimono*, *ukiorimono*,[5] *kataorimono*,[6] and *katajiaya*.[7] The karaorimono examples all have floating pattern wefts over warp-faced three-harness twill ground weaves – the same structure as karaori textiles today.

The oldest surviving example of karaorimono is *Uchiki of Karaorimono with Triple Roundels of Facing Cranes*,[8] a court lady's robe that is part of the material legacy of Tsuruoka Hachiman Shrine in Kamakura. The shrine treasures are thought to have been donated by the retired emperors Goshirakawa (1127–1192) and Kameyama (1249–1305). Though they do not have inscriptions or other certifiable ways to pinpoint their years of manufacture, the objects appear to be from the Kamakura period, when compared with the Nanbokuchō-period (1333–1392) treasures of Kumano Hayatama Shrine in Wakayama Prefecture. This uchiki robe has floating supplementary weft patterns over a ground of 2/1 twill. These supplementary wefts are of various colors and are brocaded only in the individual pattern areas – i.e., they do not extend from selvedge to selvedge. This textile structure is identical to the one described in the second *Kōjien* definition of karaori.

The treasures of Kumano Hayatama Shrine, in the city of Shingū, Wakayama Prefecture, were donated in 1390 by the emperor, retired emperor, shogun, and various provincial lords. They are accompanied by a contemporary inventory that corresponds with the extant treasures, from which we can deduce exactly what was meant by the term karaorimono in the late fourteenth century. The inventory (today existing only as an Edo-period [1615–1868] copy) tells us that a sacred garment fashioned in the style of a court lady's robes was offered to the sun goddess Amaterasu Ōmikami at the Wakanomiya sanctuary. The entry reads as follows: "One *usuginu*.[9] Light green with a raised pattern of multicolored karaorimono roundels on a damask ground that has a floating design of small hollyhocks. Lined with light green damask of tabby on a plain weave foundation with a design of widely spaced lozenges." One of the extant robes in the Kumano Hayatama Shrine fits this description perfectly (fig. 37). This uchiki is fashioned from a textile that is today classified as futaeorimono, literally "two-layered weave": a self-patterning ground weave embellished with a second pattern formed by supplementary wefts. Typically futaeorimono have ground weaves of 2/1 twill with diapers of floating foundation wefts; the "raised" designs are created with weft floats that are brocaded only across the width of each individual pattern section. The name "two-layered weave" comes from this juxtaposition of a patterned ground and this supplementary pattern, using the same brocading technique as in karaorimono. Indeed, we can see from the shrine inventory that the word "karaorimono" might also refer to this supplementary raised pattern itself at the time.

Through these examples we can see that the costumes offered as shrine treasures during the medieval period correspond to *Kōjien*'s second definition of karaori. From the documentary sources mentioned previously we know that the karaorimono was being woven with highly Japanized motifs by the Kamakura period, if not earlier. The "kara" in karaorimono had already been divorced from its original meaning of "Chinese" and had become associated with the traditional, luxury textiles favored by the courtier class since the Heian period.

UCHIKI WITH BUTTERFLY ROUNDELS ON HOLLYHOCK DIAPER (overall and detail)
Silk twill weave with weft floats (*futaeorimono*)
Nanbokuchō period, fourteenth century
71 x 66 ¼ in. (180.3 x 168.4 cm)
Kumano Hayatama Shrine, Wakayama Prefecture
National Treasure
figure 37

THE KARAORIMONO USED BY THE SAMURAI CLASS

The warrior, or samurai, class came into power in Japan at the beginning of the Kamakura period and created a distinct fashion culture to distinguish themselves from the nobility. Because their lives were based on stoicism and frugality, samurai families sought functionality in dress, which lead to a simplification of their costumes. Men began to wear outer robes such as *hitatare* or *suō* that tucked into *hakama* (wide trousers). This simplification increased in the late medieval period, when a sleeveless outfit called a kataginu hakama was adopted, allowing the *kosode*,[10] which had previously been used as an inner layer, to emerge. Women's costumes followed this trend, with the kosode – the female aristocratic undergarment – used increasingly as outerwear, even rising to the status of ceremonial dress for samurai women during the Muromachi period (1392–1568).

While the samurai class praised frugality, they also had a great love for garments made with woven textiles, which they regarded as superior to surface-dyed fabrics. The result was that the clothing of upper-class samurai families became increasingly luxurious, with karaorimono revered as one of the most precious weaves, even being fashioned into kosode. One example is found in the entry for the twenty-seventh day of the eighth month of 1434 in *Mansai jugō nikki* (*Diary of the Reverend Mansai*), which tells that a karaorimono kosode was received as a gift by the wife of shogun Ashikaga Yoshinori (r. 1429–1441). Another diary, *Kanmon gyoki* (Record of things seen and heard), tells in the entry for the twenty-fifth day of the fourth month of 1438 that Yoshinori's favorite consort was gifted with kosode of karaorimono. Similar records also include descriptions of *kinran*[11] and *donsu*,[12] both woven textiles of Chinese origin, but it is important to note that the karaorimono mentioned here refer not to *Kōjien*'s first, broad definition as textiles imported from China, but – like kinran or donsu – to the second definition as a particular weave structure.

During the Muromachi period the wearing of karaorimono became an exclusive privilege of the samurai. Documentary sources detailing the stipulations of etiquette for the warrior class, such as the 1482 *Otomo kojitsu* (Protocol manual for samurai retainers) and the 1528 *Sōgo ōsō shi* (*Sōgo*'s great protocol manual), indicate that the wearing of karaorimono was permitted only among the shogun and the very upper echelons of samurai society, or by those upon whom such garments were bestowed. In other words, karaorimono garments had become a status symbol of the warrior class.

THE EVOLUTION OF THE KARAORI AS A NOH COSTUME

The noh theater by Zeami Motokiyo (c. 1363–c. 1443) during the Muromachi period moved away from the imitative theater of the day to establish a more symbolic and universal idiom. This new theater evoked the ethereal world of *yūgen*, in which dream and reality become intertwined. However, it would be some time before costumes evolved into more symbolic robes that rejected realism in favor of a style unique to the noh stage.

In Zeami's time imitative noh was still the norm. In his *Fūshikaden* (The transmission of the flower of acting style), he writes that in imitative noh it is acceptable for ordinary women to appear only in outer robes and kosode. However, it is essential for imperial concubines, ladies-in-waiting, and other high-ranking women to wear hakama as well. They should also, he cautions, be very careful that the way they wear these outfits be appropriate to their status. These caveats reveal that the costumes used for noh performances at that time were departing from the ranks of everyday fashion. Everyday garments were indeed making their way into the performance repertoire through a practice called kosode *nugi* (taking off the kosode) or suō nugi (taking off the suō), in which a member of the audience would give an article of his own clothing to an actor as a sign of respect and appreciation. Such donated robes would then be transformed into costumes for the noh stage. *Tadasugawara kanjin sarugaku nikki* (Diary of subscription sarugaku performances along the Tadasu riverbank), dated 1464, describes a set of performances that continued over a period of three days, during which time 237 garments were given to actors as a result of kosode nugi. As the bestowal of costumes on actors gradually became an established custom, it also became standard for members of shogun families to give karaorimono and other kinds of luxury kosode to noh actors as ritual gifts at New Year's celebrations and on other important occasions. The use of such lavish, top-quality kosode exclusively for performance costumes likely evolved from this practice.

Textual evidence for karaorimono used in noh costumes can be found in *Zenpō zōdan* (Various sayings of Zenpō), which relates the teachings of actor Konparu Zenpō (1454–c. 1532). It describes Zenpō's father, Sōin (1432–1480), wearing karaorimono for his *shite* role as Utsusemi, in the play *Go* – a *kazura* (woman's) noh based on the *Tale of Genji* and now lost – at Tanzan Shrine in Tanomine, Nara. It also tells of a noh performance that took place at the Kyoto mansion of Ōuchi Yoshioki, in which karaorimono robes that did not contain red were worn for the plays *Ugetsu* and *Mutsura*. In a text called *Hogoura no sho* (Scribbles on the back of scrap paper), written by Zenpō later in life, he stipulates that woven textiles and karaori are inappropriate for lower-class roles. By Konparu Zenpō's day karaorimono was conscientiously being chosen for use in noh theater costumes.

One other point of interest in Zenpō's writings is that he uses the term "karaorimono" in *Zenpō zōdan*, but uses the word "karaori" by the time he wrote *Hogoura no sho*. It is difficult to imagine that the karaorimono worn for the role of Utsusemi and the karaori deemed inappropriate for lower-class female roles were entirely different. In fact it is much more likely that these two terms refer to exactly the same type of costume. *Zenpō zōdan*, which was recorded by a man named Tōemon, details Zenpō's art and teachings in and around the year 1513. Though the specific date of *Hogoura no sho* is unclear, it is thought to have been written during the Eishō era (1504–1521). From this we can surmise that the textile previously called "karaorimono" gradually became known as "karaori" in the first half of the sixteenth century.

Shimotsuma Shōshin (1551–1616), an amateur actor who mastered the plays of the Konparu school, wrote a work on the noh theater called *Dōbushō* (Excerpts on children's dance) in 1596 in which the use of karaori is mentioned in six of the seventy plays discussed. His later book, *Shōshin nōdensho* (Book of transmission of the noh of Shōshin), records karaori use in thirteen of fifty-three plays. For example, the play *Nonomiya* (The wildwood shrine) calls for "a white kosode with a sash alone or with a karaori or *nuihaku* (kosode with embroidery and gold leaf) robe on top; any of these are acceptable." For *Yuya*, it directs actors to wear "a kosode of either karaori or nuihaku." This tells us that, at the time, karaori and nuihaku were used interchangeably.

However, the role of the karaori was changing. In contrast to Zeami's earlier promotion of the hakama as the essential garment for upper-class women's roles, the Keichō-era (1596–1615) *Hachijō kadensho* (Eight volumes of flowery treatise on noh) prescribes that "the fundamental outer robe should be the karaori." Indeed, it was during the Momoyama period (1568–1615) that the karaori became established as a type of noh robe. Used most frequently for women's roles and young noblemen, this was the costume most appropriate for manifesting the elegant and evocative beauty of *yūgen*.

THE KARAORI OF THE MOMOYAMA PERIOD

Toyotomi Hideyoshi (1537–1598), the warlord who unified Japan in the Momoyama period, was well known as a noh connoisseur, even performing the dances himself. Hideyoshi is recorded as having worn karaori for some of these performances, including one at Fushimi Castle, in Kyoto, on the twenty-forth day of the fifth month of 1595, in which he wore a karaori kosode for the lead role of the noh play *Kantan*. The aforementioned text *Dōbushō* stipulates that for the *Kantan* dream dance "a kosode is tucked up over *ōkuchi*,"[13] suggesting that karaori kosode were standard for this dance. However, the karaori and nuihaku kosode used for stage costumes were not yet being fashioned in a style distinctive to the noh theater.

Evidence for the similarities between everyday kosode and noh costumes can be found in a text called *Sōdenshō* (Book of collected teachings), by Shimotsuma Shōshin. A chapter called "Measurements of Implements Used in Noh" gives the tailoring dimensions for noh costumes such as kariginu, *chōken, maiginu, mizugoromo, happi, sobatsugi, hangire, sunbōshi, kazuraobi, koshiobi*, and *hachimaki* but does not mention the measurements for kosode. The "Women's Noh" chapter of the same book, however, advocates actors to "wear kosode with long sleeves and show only the ends of your fingertips," which would seem to suggest that the kosode of the day may have had wider sleeves than ordinary robes. In actuality, however, the extant Momoyama kosode that were used as noh costumes exhibit no difference in sleeve length from other kosode of the era, and many of them retain distinctive design elements – such as "split body" (*katamigawari*) or alternating color blocks (*dangawari*) –

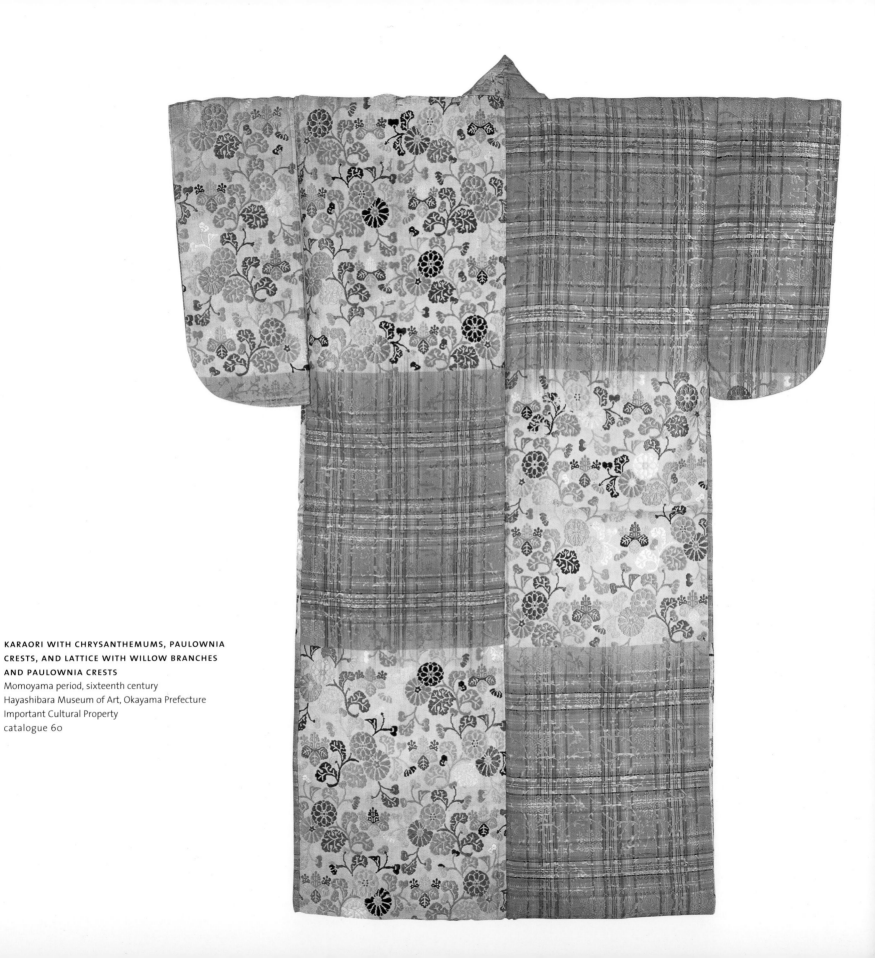

**KARAORI WITH CHRYSANTHEMUMS, PAULOWNIA
CRESTS, AND LATTICE WITH WILLOW BRANCHES
AND PAULOWNIA CRESTS**
Momoyama period, sixteenth century
Hayashibara Museum of Art, Okayama Prefecture
Important Cultural Property
catalogue 60

carried down from medieval kosode. One example of this is *Karaori with Chrysanthemums, Paulownia Crests, and Lattice with Willow Branches and Paulownia Crests* in the collection of Hayashibara Museum of Art (cat. 60, p. 109) with its distinct design of alternating bands, its relatively wide body, and its narrow sleeves – all typical characteristics of Momoyama kosode. There are many parallels between the karaori kosode worn daily by upper-class women and the karaori used on the noh stage during the Momoyama period.

There are a number of extant examples of karaori noh costumes from the Momoyama period, but unfortunately none has a clear date of manufacture. Nor have many of the actual karaori kosode worn by upper-class women survived. Perhaps our best evidence for defining karaori of the Momoyama period is an altar cloth (*uchishiki*) pieced together from the disassembled parts of a karaori kosode, which was discovered – along with six others – at the Kyoto temple of Kōdaiji during a 1990 inventory by curators of the Kyoto National Museum.

The temple of Kōdaiji was built in 1606 as a personal memorial temple by Kōdai-in, wife of Hideyoshi, after her husband's death. One of the seven altar cloths discovered there (fig. 38) has an ink inscription telling us that it was given as an offering to Kōdaiji in the year 1607. At the time it was common practice for wealthy patrons to refashion their favorite kosode into altar cloths and offer them to temples with prayers for their own future security or as a memorial for someone deceased.

The 1607 altar cloth appears to have been made and donated by Kōdai-in herself; consequently the kosode from which it is made must have been worn by Kōdai-in before this time. The fact that the designs contain a large amount of red suggests that it was used before her husband's death in 1598. Its clear provenance and creation date makes this karaori uchishiki extremely valuable. Using it as a standard in comparison with contemporaneous karaori altar cloths and noh costumes, we can identify the following characteristics of karaori from the Momoyama period.

Momoyama-period karaori have a ground weave of 2/1 twill with Z-twist binding, with floating supplementary wefts inserted between every two shots of ground weft. This is in accordance with the second *Kōjien* definition. As discussed in the first three sections, this structure was inherited from the karaorimono used for aristocratic dress.

The patterns are composed of block-shaped pattern units repeated twice across the fabric width. These are also repeated up and down the length of the textile, and may be inverted either vertically or horizontally in some cases (cat. 60). These repeats are also typical of woven patterns. Momoyama-period karaori textiles are generally around forty-two centimeters in width, of which the patterns take up approximately forty centimeters. Most have two pattern repeats across the width of the cloth. Smaller patterns that are repeated three times

UCHISHIKI (BUDDHIST ALTAR CLOTH)
WITH PAULOWNIA AND VERTICAL SERPENTINE
LINES (TATEWAKU) (detail)
Momoyama period, 1607
Silk twill weave with silk supplementary weft patterning (*karaori*)
Kōdaiji, Kyoto
figure 38

KARAORI WITH CHRYSANTHEMUMS, PAULOWNIA
CRESTS, AND LATTICE WITH WILLOW BRANCHES
AND PAULOWNIA CRESTS (detail)
Momoyama period, sixteenth century
Hayashibara Museum of Art, Okayama Prefecture
Important Cultural Property
catalogue 60

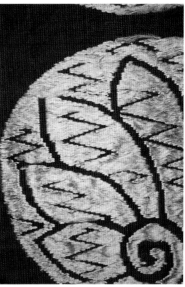

YUTAN COVER WITH TRIPLE HOLLYHOCK
ROUNDELS AND LINKED HEXAGON PATTERN
(KIKKŌ) (details)
Edo period, seventeenth century
Silk twill weave with silk supplementary patterning
wefts (*karaori*)
26 x 59 ⅝ x 25 ⅝ in. (66.0 151.5 x 65.0 cm)
Tokugawa Art Museum, Nagoya
figure 39

across the width are less common. In the vertical direction there are examples of exact repeats of the same pattern, and of the pattern being alternated with horizontal and/or vertical inversions. Textiles with a vertical repeat in which the pattern is alternated with its horizontal inversion are most prevalent. The length of the pattern varies but few are longer than fifty centimeters, making them shorter on the average than the patterns used in Edo-period karaori.

> The supplementary weft brocade is executed in untwisted silk with long floats.
> Because they have no intermediate binding points, the floating wefts are long
> and soft giving the textiles a rich voluminous sensibility.

The key point here is the lack of binding points on the pattern wefts. Binding points are warps that cross intermediately over long weft floats in order to shorten the length of the floats. These binding warps can unnaturally interrupt a pattern. In the karaori of the Edo period, binding was frequently used in the brocades and was even incorporated into the designs (fig. 39). During the Momoyama period, however, such binding was eschewed in favor of the softness of long, lustrous floats. This tendency is also visible in Momoyama embroideries, which are executed with untwisted floss drawn across long pattern sections, creating soft, airy designs. Momoyama-period karaori, in fact, look very much like contemporaneous embroidery, with which it has a great deal in common. One other similarity is in color:

> The background colors tend to be red, green, or white with brocaded designs in red,
> green, light blue, indigo blue, purple, white, etc., totaling approximately ten colors.
> Red was one of the most popular colors, but gold "thread" *(kinshi)* was not yet used.

Momoyama-period karaori and embroidery incorporate almost exactly the same color pallette. Red (*beni*),

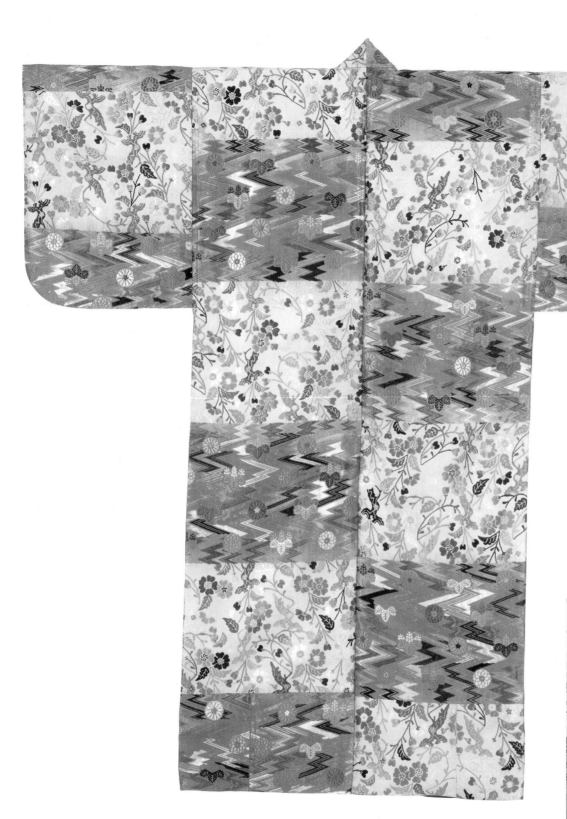

KARAORI WITH CHRYSANTHEMUM, PAULOWNIA,
AND WEEPING CHERRY TREE BLOSSOMS
(overall and detail)
Momoyama period, sixteenth century
Tokyo National Museum
catalogue 61

KARAORI WITH AUTUMN GRASSES
(overall and detail)
Edo period, eighteenth century
Kyoto National Museum
catalogue 67

dyed with safflower, was used extensively in varying shades to give costumes vibrancy. As indicated in *Zenpō zōdan*, kosode were classified by the inclusion or exclusion of red, and were called *beni-iri* (with red) or *beni-nashi* (without red). Costumes with red were used to enhance the roles of beautiful young women, while costumes without red would be chosen for middle-aged female roles. Though this distinction existed in the Momoyama period, most extant examples include red.

   The same distinction carried over into nuihaku. Nuihaku are silk noh costumes with designs executed in embroidery and metallic leaf. As in *Nuihaku with Snow-Laden Reeds and Birds* belonging to the Hayashibara Museum of Art (cat. 47, p. 82, p. 80 [detail]), nuihaku without red embroidery tend to use silver leaf, while those with red embroidery frequently use gold leaf. The inclusion of gold and silver thread did not occur in karaori until the Edo period.

   When there are alternating color blocks (dangawari) the woven patterns fall inside each band, without crossing over the borders (cat. 61, p. 112).

   This tendency is seen not only in karaori but also in nuihaku of the period. Many Momoyama textiles have designs that fit neatly into defined pattern areas, a traditional design composition that was first seen in the medieval period. This is evident in robes with shoulder and hem designs (*katasuso*), split-body coloration, or alternating pattern blocks. These carefully defined areas disappear from kosode for daily wear during the Edo period, with the patterns gradually extending across the back, as in the Kanbun kosode.[14] Traditional dangawari designs continued to be produced for noh karaori into the Edo period, but the concept of each color band as a separate pattern area gradually disappeared, with patterns extending into neighboring color bands (cat. 67, p. 113).

   Momoyama-period karaori are typified by the above five characteristics. Though we know little about Muromachi precedents, due to the lack of extant examples, it is reasonable to assume that they resembled the aristocratic garments found in medieval shrine treasures: refined textiles with brocaded patterns in three or four colors. It is when karaorimono began to be used for kosode that the textiles grew increasingly colorful and opulent. The lavish tastes of the Momoyama period also allowed for freer use of a wide variety of colors in the brocades, relieving the monotony of the repeated patterning inherent to woven textiles and making karaorimono even more luxurious.

THE KARAORI OF THE EDO PERIOD

Noh drama, which had flourished under the patronage of Toyotomi Hideyoshi in the Momoyama period, became regulated into five schools in the ensuing Edo period. These five schools were in charge of performing at official events for the shogunate and became increasingly successful.

During the Edo period, kosode used in daily life and kosode used in the noh theater gradually diverged. Textiles in which the primary patterns are woven practically disappeared from the realm of general-use kosode and were replaced by surface-dyed textiles, inspiring such trends as the Keichō era and the Kanbun era (1661–1673) kosode.

There were also changes in the karaori used for noh costumes. An important example for understanding these changes is a karaori *kesa* (Buddhist surplice) owned by the temple of Honnōji in Kyoto. This kesa, donated in 1622, has a deep brown background with woven designs of linked hexagons (*kikkō*) and hollyhocks. The small hexagons form an intricate linked repeat that almost appears to be part of the ground weave, with the hollyhocks appearing as a raised pattern (fig. 40). Raised patterns over small linked repeats are not found in Momoyama-period karaori, appearing first at the beginning of the Edo period. The same stylistic traits can also be seen in the *Karaori with Chrysanthemums and Triangles Filled with Stone Pavement Pattern* (cat. 63, p. 116) owned by Itsukushima Shrine in Hiroshima Prefecture.

The practice of scattering a raised pattern over a ground pattern recalls the futaeorimono used by aristocrats. It is not seen in noh costumes until 1620, at which time a revival of

KARAORI KESA (BUDDHIST SURPLICE)
WITH ROUNDELS OF TRIPLE HOLLYHOCKS
AND LINKED HEXAGONS (KIKKŌ) (detail)
Edo period, 1622
Silk twill weave with silk supplementary patterning wefts
21½ x 55⅞ in. (54.5 x 142.0 cm)
Honnōji, Kyoto
figure 40

courtier textiles was sparked by the marriage of Masako, daughter of Hidetada (the second Tokugawa shogun) to Emperor Gomizunoo. This wedding was a political union meant to reinforce the stability of the Tokugawa shogunate. In order to exhibit the authority of their rule, the shogunate spent an exorbitant amount on the furnishings and clothing for Masako's dowry. In the diary *Shunkyūki* (Record of moments past) the entry for the eighteenth day of the sixth month of 1620 tells that the wedding procession, extending from Nijō Castle to the Imperial Palace, contained 585 large dowry chests of clothing and furnishings. Three hundred of these were draped with karaori chest covers bearing a design of hollyhock roundels (the crest of the Tokugawa clan). Unfortunately, none of these karaori chest covers has survived, but at the Tokugawa Art Museum in Nagoya there is a similar example that originally covered one of the dowry chests of Chiyohime, oldest daughter of the third shogun, Tokugawa Iemitsu, when she married Tokugawa Mitsutomo of Owari province (now Aichi Prefecture) (fig. 41). This karaori has a pattern of large hollyhock crests over a fine hexagonal linked repeat, typical of samurai-class dowry textiles between the Genna and Kan'ei eras (1615–1644). In aristocratic textiles the ground pattern is executed with the foundation wefts; but in karaori from the beginning of the Edo period both the raised and ground patterns are woven with supplementary wefts, allowing for rich color variations in both pattern layers. The karaori of the warrior class was far more colorful than the futaeorimono of the aristocrats, a taste that is also reflected in noh costumes of the day.

One other important point about Edo-period noh costumes is the incorporation of "gold thread" (kinshi). Tokuda Rinchū, noh teacher to the Tokugawa family of Kii province, wrote in his *Rinchū hishō gaihen* (Supplementary edition to secret notes of Rinchū, 1760) that this trend was inspired by Koshōgen Shigetomo (d. 1685), the eighth head of the Hōshō school of noh. In the beginning, gold thread was used only partially within design areas, but the amount gradually increased over time, combining with the multicolored brocading to create lavish, dazzling karaori textiles.

Tokugawa Tsuneyoshi, the fifth-generation shogun, was deeply involved in noh, leading to a deep and competitive interest in noh among the provincial daimyo lords who hoped to gain his favor. The flourishing of noh around the Genroku era (1688–1704) led to the production and geographic diffusion of luxurious noh costumes. An actor named Fujita Iemon Toyotaka (1701–1758), who was employed by the Tokugawa clan in Kii Province, wrote the following in his essay collection *Toyotaka nikki* (Diary of Toyotaka):

> We have something called a karaori atsuita. It has atsuita with sixteen alternating blocks of red and lattices, over the red parts of which are two raised designs. These raised designs, which are done with floating threads resembling karaori, are of peonies, dragon roundels, and the like, woven in alternating colors. Some of the

designs are executed in damask technique.

This record tells us that the heavy brocading of karaori was also being incorporated into the atsuita costumes used for male, god, or demon roles.

Like the kosode, the shape of noh costumes changed over time. The *Rinchū hishō gaihen* tells us that the sleeves of Momoyama-period costumes were relatively short: "In the time of Lord Hideyoshi, noh costumes were narrower and shorter than garments nowadays, and the elbows were not extended out when dancing as they are today." In Rinchū's *Rinchū kenbun shū* (Collection of what Rinchū saw and heard, 1697), he tells of seeing Konparu Dayū Sokumu perform the noh play *Eguchi*. In the performance, which was held before Mitsusada, the second generation head of the Kii Province Tokugawa clan, Sokumu wore a karaori that had been given to him by Hideyoshi. Rinchū continues, "Both sleeves had been extended with a karaori of the same color. Though the patterns were the same, the difference between the old and new was obvious." This tells us that similar karaori textiles were sometimes used to extend the dimensions of Momoyama karaori, which were too small for the conventions of the Genroku era.

The essay collection *Kasshi yawa* (Night tales of the year of Kasshi) gives the words of a noh costume maker named Sekioka, then in his sixties, as follows:

The costumes for noh are tailored very differently today than when we were young.
The karaori used in women's roles and other costumes used to have wide bodies worn
to create very full figures, which looked extremely classical. Nowadays the bodies of
the garments are narrower, and the shape of the sleeves has changed greatly. In order to
give them a more contemporary shape, even if they are vintage garments, some people
have them altered by a tailor to suit modern styles.

This text gives further evidence that the narrow sleeves and voluminous bodies of Momoyama kosode (cat. 62, p. 120) were altered in the Edo period to have narrower bodies and a different shape of sleeve (cat. 64, p. 121). With the addition of other gradual modifications, noh costumes had reached a stylistic standard by the mid-Edo period that has been maintained ever since.

CONCLUSION

Though it has undergone many changes, the karaori has remained one of the most important types of noh costumes, enhancing the stage with its luminous color and brilliance. The prototype for the karaori is found in karaorimono textiles, which themselves have a long history as status symbols for the aristocracy and the samurai. When incorporated into noh costumes, karaori textiles took on their own particular style and beauty, one that was used to invoke the beauty of upper-class women. In the Penglai Palace scene of the noh play *Yōkihi*, based on the romance between the Chinese emperor Xuanzong (Japanese: Genzō) and his consort Yang Guifei (Japanese: Yōkihi), Yang Guifei traditionally receives the phoenix headdress wearing a gold karaori, evoking a symbolic beauty that transcends reality (fig. 42). The "Chinese weave" worn in this role, however, is not Chinese. The evolution of karaori is firmly rooted in Japanese textile history.

Translated by Melissa Rinne

PERFORMANCE OF YŌKIHI
figure 42

**KARAORI WITH SNOW-LADEN
MANDARIN ORANGE TREES**
Momoyama period, sixteenth century
Kyoto National Museum
Important Cultural Property
catalogue 62

KARAORI WITH BAMBOO CURTAINS
(MISU), PICTURE CARDS (SHIKISHI), POEM
PAPERS (TANZAKU), AND BUSH CLOVERS
Edo period, eighteenth century
Tokyo National Museum
catalogue 64

NOTES

1. Ivan Morris ed. and trans., *The Pillow Book of Sei Shōnagon* (New York: Columbia University Press, 1991), 109. "Splendid Things. Chinese brocade [sic]. A sword with a decorated scabbard. The grain of the wood in a Buddhist statue..."

2. "Nishiki" is a term generally used for compound weaves, either warp faced or weft faced. In some cases, however, it is also used more generally to refer to multicolored woven textiles, as here.

3. Kariginu: "Hunting robe." An aristocratic man's robe worn for informal occasions. The seam between the body and the sleeves is left partially open, allowing for freedom of movement for hunting and other physical activities.

4. Futaeorimono: The same weave structure as ukiorimono (see below), with the addition of supplementary weft brocade patterns. The name "futaeorimono" (literally "two-layered textile") comes from this luxurious use of pattern over pattern.

5. Ukiorimono: Foundation weave of 2/1 twill with the ground wefts floating to create a pattern. The floating wefts do not have a fixed binding structure, creating a soft, raised surface.

6. Kataorimono: Foundation weave of a 2/1 twill with a 5/1 pattern in the ground weft. The yarns are dyed before weaving, so warp and weft colors usually differ, allowing for contrasting ground and pattern colors (oriiro). Same structure as katajiaya.

7. Katajiaya: Same weave structure as kataorimono (above), but differs in that the textile is dyed after weaving, making the warp and weft the same color.

8. Uchiki: One of the layered robes in a court woman's outfit. Can be lined or unlined and is generally dyed a color appropriate to the season when it is to be worn.

9. Usuginu: A kind of uchiki, one of the layered robes worn by a court woman.

10. Kosode: Literally "small sleeves," referring to the narrow sleeve openings, which were antithetical to the wide sleeve openings on most aristocratic garments. Originally an undergarment in courtier dress, the kosode became increasingly used as a outer garment during the medieval period and was the predecessor to the modern kimono.

11. Kinran: Plain weave, twill, or satin weave foundation weave patterned with brocade of "gold thread" (kinshi), actually thin strips of paper coated with gold leaf. Ginran refers to similar weaves with silver-coated paper.

12. Donsu: A general term for patterned woven damask textiles in a variety of weave structures that do not contain gold or silver. Donsu textiles typically have small repeated patterns and a somewhat stiff hand, in contrast to *rinzu* (figured satin), which often has the same weave structure but tends to be softer in texture. Donsu textiles are woven with predyed yarns, while rinzu are typically dyed after weaving and are thus monotone.

13. Ōkuchi: Wide stiff hakama used in the noh theater.

14. Kanbun kosode: Named for the Kanbun era (1661–1673) during which it became popular, this genre of Edo-period kosode design typically has designs arching over one shoulder, across the back and down towards the hem.

SHOKUNIN TSUKUSHI-E
(VIEWS OF ARTISANS AT WORK)
(detail: weavers)
Edo period, seventeenth century
Suntory Museum of Art, Tokyo
catalogue 111

CHŌKEN WITH PICTURE CARDS (SHISHIKI)
AND POEM PAPERS (TANZAKU)
Edo period, eighteenth century
Eisei Bunko Museum, Tokyo
catalogue 20

Hosokawa Family

PATRONAGE: DAIMYO, ACTORS, AND NOH COSTUMES

NAGASAKI IWAO

Since the moment that noh captured the hearts of the military elite during the Muromachi period (1392–1568), it was recognized as an official art form by the Ashikaga shogunate. Local feudal lords (daimyo) as well as temples and shrines patronized noh. Impressive noh performances took place throughout the country, because daimyo felt compelled to stage high-quality productions for the Ashikaga shoguns, who traveled extensively to oversee their regional domains. This tradition continued under Oda Nobunaga (1534–1582), Toyotomi Hideyoshi (c. 1537–1598), and Tokugawa Ieyasu (1542–1616). In 1617 noh was part of the bureaucratic regulatory codes (onari) established by the Tokugawa government. Daimyo, who were required to maintain residences in both the capital of Edo (now Tokyo) and in their own feudal regions, built performance stages in both locations for public and private parties. Furthermore, daimyo were expected to learn noh performance skills such as singing and dancing as part of a warrior's education.

Noh was performed not only for official guests but also for the personal ceremonies of the daimyo – the birth of a boy, the day a boy began to wear traditional men's trousers (hakama), coming of age, marriage, and rituals of inheriting land, as well as at private get-togethers such as moon-viewing parties. The programs were designed in accordance with each event, and appropriate costumes, masks, accessories, stage props, and musical instruments were selected.

THE HOSOKAWA FAMILY

Hosokawa Fujitaka (also known as Hosokawa Yūsai, 1534–1610) had begun to learn noh under the instruction of Kanze Motohiro, head of the Kanze school (Kanze Dayū), from age seventeen, when he was a member of the shogun Ashikaga Yoshimitsu's inner circle. Continuing his support of noh, he took lessons from Kanze Mototada (1509–1583) as well as from Mototada's successor, Tadachika, and invited Furutsu Sōin, a younger brother of Kanze Kojirō Motoyori, to become the noh master of his province in Tango (now part of Kyoto Prefecture).

Hosokawa Tadaoki (also known as Hosokawa Sansai, 1563–1646) and his family members enjoyed staging noh plays. According to *Tango Hosokawa nō bangumi* (Program of the Hosokawa noh performances in Tango), performances were staged on fifty different occasions during the period from 1583 through 1599, featuring a total of 433 noh plays. Tadaoki himself proudly performed the principal role (shite) eighty-three times.[1]

Professional noh actors, including Kanze Dayū Tadachika, Furutsu Sōin, Umewaka Dayū, and Aiwaka Dayū, routinely appeared in Hosokawa family performances. Aiwaka Dayū was Tadaoki's favorite actor and followed the daimyo when he was transferred to the Chikuzen fief (now part of Fukuoka Prefecture in northern Kyushu).

The third Hosokawa daimyo, Tadatoshi, was transferred to the Higo fief at Kumamoto (now Kumamoto Prefecture in Kyushu) in 1632. Noh was a topic of correspondence between Tadatoshi and his retired father. Some of these letters contain exchanges about the noh activities of the Tokugawa shogunate, indicating that noh was an important cultural and political means for feudal lords to maintain strong relationships with the central government. The Hosokawa daimyo were very sensitive to the shogunate's favored noh actors, regularly inquiring about their performances and often inviting them to perform. Tadatoshi's son Mitsunao continued this kind of liaison with the central Tokugawa government.[2]

THE II FAMILY

From the Genroku era (1688–1704) the head families of the four main established schools of Yamato (now Nara) *sarugaku no nō* (Kanze, Konparu, Hōshō, and Kongō schools) and a newly established early-Edo noh school (Kita) lived in the capital of Edo. Each school received annual stipends from the Tokugawa shogunate of one to three million *koku* of rice (a koku was roughly enough to feed one person for one year). Families of *waki* (secondary-role actors) and *hayashi kata* (musicians) also resided in Edo.

Feudal lords throughout the country retained actors from the various noh schools. The Ii daimyo family of the Hikone fief (now part of Shiga Prefecture) was no exception. Records show that Ii Naomasa (1561–1602), the first daimyo of Hikone, had a relationship with the Kita school. In the Genroku era the Ii family began to lend support to the Kita school.[3] However, it apparently was not until the Kansei era (1789–1801) that the Ii family exclusively supported the Kita school.

Noh actors residing in the Hikone fief of the Ii family were given a social rank equal to warriors. By the end of the Edo period the numbers of retained noh acting families increased to seventeen, including shite actors, waki actors, musicians, singers, and kyōgen actors.[4] Some Ii-sponsored actors were hired for the family's residence in Edo, some for the castle in Hikone, and some were said to have been moved from Edo to Hikone. This was quite different from other government-financed noh actors, who received only the rank of townsman (*chōnin*) despite their dedication to the noh tradition.

Since noh had become the device for both entertainment and political relationships, significant development was seen in the Edo period. Noh was performed on such occasions as the shogun's public speeches, promotions, weddings, birthdays, and welcoming parties for the emperor's ambassadors paying homage in Edo. The heads of the Kanze and other schools were treated in the same manner as the Tokugawa shogunate's official noh actors, receiving their hereditary stipends. The local lords followed this custom, along with having noh theaters in their homes and castles, taking private lessons from the masters, and preparing the necessary costumes (cat. 24, p. 128).

Each daimyo competed with the others in producing large numbers of noh costumes with the finest techniques and the most beautiful designs, according to their financial abilities. The central government never stopped such activities, despite its repeated regulations limiting luxury items, particularly clothing. From the beginning of the Edo government, the local lords were forced to bear financial burdens such as *sankin kōtai* (alternate-year attendance at Edo) and the building and maintenance costs of Ieyasu's mausoleum. Encouraging their rivalry in spending their wealth on noh was part of the shogunate's deliberate strategy to reduce the economic power of potential enemies.

Noh, as a beneficiary of prosperity, began to show signs of decline when overwhelming financial distress appeared among central and local governments in the middle-to-late Edo period. As the Edo government collapsed, financial support of the schools was terminated, noh theaters were closed, and the selling of costumes for financial reasons made noh's survival itself questionable.

THE IKEDA FAMILY

The large collection of noh and kyōgen costumes in the Hayashibara Museum of Art formerly belonged to the Ikeda family of the Okayama domain. The items include kosode-type robes (*karaori, atsuita* [cat. 75, p. 129], *nuihaku, surihaku*); ōsode-type robes (*kariginu, happi, sobatsugi, mizugoromo, hitatare, suō, chōken, maiginu*); trousers (*hakama*); and accessories such as sashes (*koshiobi*), headbands (*kazuraobi*), and headgear.

Some objects from the Momoyama period (1568–1615) and the first half of the Edo period are said to have been the property of the Fukushima family of the Hiroshima domain and the Mizutani family of the Matsuyama domain. Both clans were dismantled during the Edo period.[5] Most of the early Edo costumes, however, were collected by Ikeda Mitsumasa (1609–1682). His son Tsunamasa (1638–1714) and grandson Tsugumasa (1702–1776) were perhaps responsible for the mid-Edo period costumes in the collection, which are superb in both technique and design.[6] The largest portion of the Ikeda collection dates from the late Edo period. Credit for the overall quality of the Ikeda costume collection must be given to these two notable collectors.

Ikeda Shigemasa (1839–1899) lived during both the Edo and Meiji (1868–1912) periods. He did his best to preserve the art of noh, which had lost supporters after the collapse of the Edo shogunate. The excellence of the Ikeda costumes from this period owes much to the aesthetics of Shigemasa. Many costumes in the Ikeda collection display *yūsoku*-style motifs favored by the imperial court as far back as the Heian period (794–1185), thus possibly reflecting friendly relationships between Shigemasa and aristocrats of his time.[7]

In his *Rinchū kenmonshū* (Collection of what Rinchū saw and heard, 1754), author Tokuda Tōzaemon (aka Rinchū), a shite supported by the Tokugawa branch family in Kishū domain (now part of Wakayama and Mie Prefectures), writes that there were many occasions when a patron requested actors to wear a particular costume for a certain performance, as well as suggesting designs and fabrication techniques:

MAIGINU WITH BRANCHES
OF CHERRY BLOSSOMS
Edo–Meiji period, nineteenth century
Hikone Castle Museum, Shiga Prefecture
catalogue 24

Ii Family

**ATSUITA WITH VERTICAL STRIPES AND
TRIPLE-COMMA ROUNDELS (TOMOE)**
Edo period, eighteenth century
Hayashibara Museum of Art, Okayama Prefecture
catalogue 75

Ikeda Family

One day, when the head of the Owari domain was invited to the household of the head of the Kishū domain actors from the four main schools of noh were summoned and the actor Saburōemon was requested to perform *Funa Benkei* (Benkei aboard ship). The daimyo voiced his preference to see Saburōemon wear a black satin-weave (*shusu*) hangire embroidered with white waves a day before the performance was to take place. Embroiderers worked all day and night to prepare the costume. The performance of *Funa Benkei* was superb and greatly admired by the audience.[8]

Patrons frequently chose the colors and designs of costumes for their noh actors. After a successful performance, the costumes became the new standard. *Rinchū hishō gaihen* (Supplementary edition to the secret notes by Rinchū, 1760) confirms such a trend:

It was the daimyo's [Tokugawa Mitsusada] choice to have the actor in *Funa Benkei* wear hangire decorated with waves [cat. 120], but such practice had never taken place before. Anything can be worn these days.

Rinchū kenmonshū also states, "The purple ōkuchi was not fashionable to wear when performing *Teika* until Saburōemon was requested to wear one by his patron. In this way, the daimyo enjoyed making choices for costumes according to his own preferences."

As these examples prove, there were extremely enthusiastic daimyo who were heavily involved in the choice of colors, motifs, and occasionally even techniques used to produce costumes for actors as well as for themselves. This is why daimyo costume collections such as that of the Ikeda family collection exhibit a common aesthetic.

NŌMAI NO ZU
(ILLUSTRATIONS OF NOH DANCES) (detail: *Funa Benkei*)
Edo period, eighteenth century
National Noh Theater, Tokyo
catalogue 120

THE ITSUKUSHIMA SHRINE

Noh performances held at the Itsukushima Shrine have been continuously staged for over four hundred years (fig. 44), ever since noh was recognized as part of a religious ceremony in the late Muromachi period. The shrine owns about 170 noh and kyōgen costumes dating from the Momoyama through late Edo periods. The collection includes a number of items designated by the Japanese government as Important Cultural Properties. These include one karaori noh robe and four kyōgen costumes made from recycled nuihaku noh robes and worn specifically by the actors playing Chinese roles in *Tōsumō* (Chinese sumo) (fig. 43), all dating from the Momoyama period. There are also kosode-style robes (karaori, nuihaku, surihaku, atsuita [cat. 79, p. 132], and noshime), ōsode-style robes (chōken, maiginu, mizugoro-mo, kariginu, happi, sobatsugi, and hitatare), kyōgen suō, and kataginu, as well as headbands and sashes. This collection is outstanding in its variety and quality. Many of the costumes are excellent examples of premodern textile design and are considered irreplaceable.

The Ōnin Wars (1467–1477) brought a temporary halt to the support for noh activities by shogun and daimyo, but shrines and temples continued to stage *kanjin* (subscription) noh. In the Momoyama period assistance from the samurai class resumed, and noh eventually became the official performing art of the military class during the Edo period. Financial backing came both from daimyo and from religious institutions; thus costume orders and production were coordinated through the relations with these two types of patrons.

In 1619, when the Asano clan became head of the Aki domain (now the western part of Hiroshima Prefecture where Itsukushima Shrine is located), noh was placed under the management of the Miyajima magistrate office, and noh actors began to perform in the style of the domain's official noh school, Kita. Religious and secular individuals customarily joined the professional Kita actors for performances at the Itsukushima Shrine. Some of the costumes bestowed upon the actors were ordered and paid for by the Miyajima magistrate office, a fact revealed by twenty-one garments in the shrine's collection that are inscribed with the name of the magistrate.

By the Bunka (1804–1818) and Bunsei (1818–1830) eras, revenue from the shrine's *tomikuji kōgyō* (lottery) provided the funds for noh costumes. Handwritten inscriptions by the magistrate

NOH STAGE AT ITSUKUSHIMA SHRINE,
HIROSHIMA PREFECTURE
figure 44

KYŌGEN NUIHAKU WITH HERONS,
WILLOWS, AND MIST
Momoyama period, late sixteenth–early seventeenth century
Silk plain weave (*nerinuki*) with silk embroidery
and gold leaf stenciled pattern
36 ¼ x 55 ⅛ in. (92.0 x 140.0 cm)
Itsukushima Shrine, Hiroshima Prefecture
Important Cultural Property
figure 43

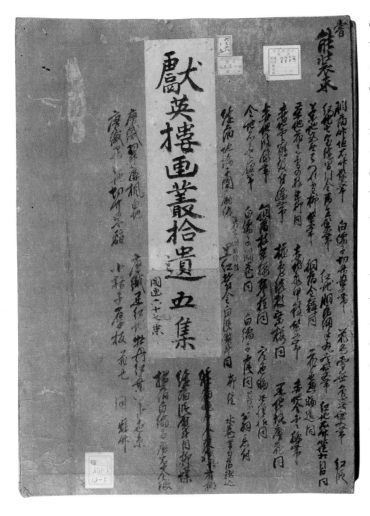

**KEN'EIRŌ GASŌ
(COMPILATION OF GRACEFUL DESIGNS)**
(cover, vol. 5)
Edo period, eighteenth century
Tokyo National Museum
catalogue 122

**ATSUITA WITH LATTICE AND
PAULOWNIA ARABESQUE**
Edo period, eighteenth century
Itsukushima Shrine, Hiroshima Prefecture
catalogue 79

on a number of garments indicate the prosperity of the shrine. From 1797 to 1813 Aoki Inosuke was the thirtieth Miyajima magistrate. During and after his term he had twelve costumes, such as karaori and nuihaku, made and donated to the Istukushima Shrine. From 1814 to 1827 his successor, Itō Han'uemon, ordered eight robes, including surihaku and nuihaku that were given to the shrine. In addition to these kosode-type costumes, there are nineteen robes, including ōsode types such as chōken, maiginu, hitatare, suō, and kataginu, that were stamped on the lining with a square seal in black ink that reads "*tanamori*" (checked by supervisor). These are perhaps inspection marks used for storage during the Bunka and Bunsei eras. Examples with such markings are very important in ascertaining the dates of production. They furthermore suggest that the Itsukushima Shrine costume collection was amassed under the protection and supervision of the local government as well as through contributions from many individuals.

KEN'EIRŌ GASŌ

Though numerous costumes survive from the Momoyama and Edo periods, the development of textile techniques and designs is neither clear nor straightforward. The main reason for this is that only a few garments have documented dates, and most of those are from the late Edo period. There are extant books of hand-drawn color illustrations, however, that present detailed visual data about noh costumes, as well as written performance notes providing information on the relationships between military patrons, noh actors, and their costumes. The *Ken'eirō gasō* (Compilation of graceful designs), a set of illustrated books belonging to the Tokyo National Museum, is an excellent example of how daimyo families had artists document noh costumes and accessories such as masks, fans, and stage props (cat. 122, p. 144–45). Each volume is a folding-style book, approximately 16 1/2 x 11 3/4 inches, with a cover of thick handmade paper (*washi*) colored and strengthened with fermented persimmon juice. (cat. 485, p. 122). The pages of the books are made of thin pale-blue washi, with some pages containing different sizes of attached paper that have additional illustrations of noh costumes, fans, and props.

The title *Ken'eirō gasō* is perhaps derived from the name of a private library belonging to the Tayasu family.[9] The records documenting the heirlooms of the Tayasu family often mention the name Ken'eirō, and thus *Ken'eirō gasō* most likely belonged to the family. The clan must have been involved with the insertion of the illustrations, because many of them have the Tayasu clan seal in red ink.[10]

Notes next to illustrations identify the items, give illustrators' names, and provide dates from 1824 to 1832. The Tayasu clan seal was used regularly on books obtained in the Bunka and Bunsei eras by the clan. These stamp marks were applied not on the books but only on the attached papers, suggesting that it was perhaps the Tayasu clan who commissioned each artist.

In the volumes containing noh costumes, the notes provide costume measurements, techniques, the names of the actors who wore them, and the names and locations of the performances in which they were worn. The handwritten notations extend onto the backs of the pieces of paper, and often the writing on the reverse is more detailed and meticulous than that on the front. Many of the reverse sides have numbers in red ink, and some have *Ken'eirō zushoki* (Record of Ken'eirō illustrations and texts) stamped in red.

These details indicate that the illustrations were not pasted in the book immediately after completion. The numbers were probably used for organizing the papers prior to inserting them in books. The noh costume illustrations often have text written entirely in the Japanese phonetic writing system called *hiragana* rather than in the regular combined Chinese characters (*kanji*) with hiragana, and numbers in black ink on the front sides that differ from the numbers in red ink on the back. These inscriptions of numbers are not consecutive, so they were obviously not made when the sheets of paper were glued on the book pages. The numbers possibly correspond to actual costumes or refer to storage numbers, though their purpose is not certain.

Two groups of *Ken'eirō gasō* volumes are known to exist. One group is in the collection of the Tokyo National Museum, and four volumes are in the private collection of Pierre Kreitmann in Marseilles, France. The Tokyo National Museum books consist of thirteen volumes that were purchased in 1909 by what was then the Teishitsu Hakubutsukan (former name of the Tokyo National Museum).[11] The Kreitmann volumes have the same format as those of the Tokyo National Museum.[12] These volumes were obtained by the owner's grandfather, Louis Kreitmann (1851–1914), who came to Japan as an officer associated with the Japanese military school and lived in Tokyo between 1875 and 1878. Thus the set of *Ken'eirō gasō* was probably divided around 1875, with four volumes acquired by Mr. Kreitmann and the remaining thirteen volumes entering the collection of the Teishitsu Hakubutsukan through other means. The title papers were applied when they were still together as one group; extra sheets of brown paper appearing on the museum's volumes were added by either a previous owner or by the Teishitsu Hakubutsukan. A comparison of the existing volumes in the two collections reveals a lack of continuity, strongly suggesting that more must have existed at one time.[13]

ILLUSTRATIONS OF NOH COSTUMES IN KEN'EIRŌ GASŌ

Noh costumes are realistically illustrated in color, showing both front and back views of the garments and pattern details rendered in actual size. There are also handwritten notations on dyeing and weaving techniques. The detailed illustrations reveal costumes that have been lost or completely unknown. Information such as the name of the owner, the illustration date, the person who donated it to an actor, and the performer who wore it provide information about the relationship between daimyo, noh actors, and noh costumes in the mid-to-late Edo period.[14]

Among the ninety-eight robes illustrated in the Tokyo National Museum volumes, fifty-three are of the kosode type. These include karaori, nuihaku, surihaku, atsuita, and atsuita karaori. The fabric of atsuita karaori robes used for an actor playing a male role is identical to that of a female character's outer robe (karaori), thus the combined name of atsuita karaori is used to differentiate gender. As a consequence, it is difficult to identify an atsuita karaori unless it is clearly documented. Therefore, the atsuita karaori costumes illustrated in *Ken'eirō gasō* are important research resources that scholars are able to use to identify and date other costumes.[15]

There are examples of ōsode-type costumes, such as kariginu, mizugoromo, and chōken, in *Ken'eirō gasō* as well. Others items include fifteen headbands, eighteen sashes, one pair of trousers (*ōkuchi*), one hat (*kakubōshi*), and four unidentified partial illustrations. Among the main noh costumes, noshime of the kosode type, maiginu, happi, sobatsugi of the ōsode type, and hangire trousers are not illustrated. These may have been included in the purported missing volumes of *Ken'eirō gasō*.

THE RELATIONSHIP BETWEEN EXTANT AND ILLUSTRATED NOH COSTUMES

Some of the noh costumes in *Ken'eirō gasō* are identical or quite similar to existing costumes in various museum and private collections. For research purposes this connection is very significant. Generally historical textiles lack background information, making *Ken'eirō gasō* important for the research of noh costumes.

An illustration of a karaori in *Ken'eirō gasō* with a handwritten notation that reads "Karaori with golden Genji cloud and snow-laden camellia design on red background" (cat. 122, p. 136) has the same design and colors as noh robes in the collection of the Los Angeles County Museum of Art (cat. 70, p. 136) and the Hatakeyama Museum of Art in Tokyo. The artisan who painted the illustration in the book most likely saw one of these existing karaori.

Illustrations such as *Ōkuchi with Maple Leaves and Water on a White Ground* (cat. 122, p. 139) and *Kariginu with Chinese Characters, Bird Roundels, and Bamboo Lattice on a Light Green Ground* (cat. 122, p. 143) in the *Ken'eirō gasō* are similar to actual noh costumes now in the collection of the Ii family and housed in the Hikone Castle Museum (fig. 46, p. 139; fig. 47, p. 142).

Information on the relationships between daimyo, noh actors, and extant costumes suggests that the clients ordering costumes were primarily samurai families who were patrons of noh, in particular the Tokugawa clan. Certain notations in *Ken'eirō gasō* imply that more than one owner possessed identical costumes. Another possibility is that a daimyo might have ordered two of the same garment design, one for himself and one for his favorite actor.

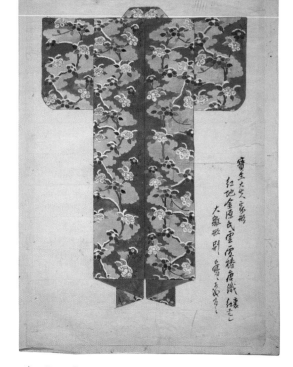

KEN'EIRŌ GASŌ
(COMPILATION OF GRACEFUL DESIGNS)
(illustration of karaori)
Edo period, eighteenth century
Tokyo National Museum
catalogue 122

KARAORI WITH SNOW-LADEN CAMELLIAS
AND GENJI CLOUDS
Edo period, eighteenth century
Los Angeles County Museum of Art, Costume Council Fund
catalogue 70

KARAORI WITH MAPLE LEAVES
AND BAMBOO CURTAIN (MISU)
Edo period, eighteenth century
Eisei Bunko Museum, Tokyo
catalogue 65

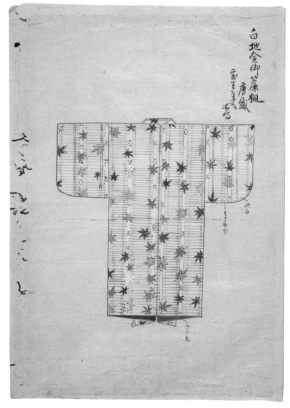

KEN'EIRŌ GASŌ
(COMPILATION OF GRACEFUL DESIGNS)
(illustration of karaori)
Edo period, eighteenth century
Tokyo National Museum
catalogue 122

ŌKUCHI WITH MAPLE LEAVES AND WATER
WORN IN A PERFORMANCE OF TADANORI
figure 45

There are numerous illustrations in *Ken'eirō gasō* that are similar to actual costumes but not identical. The illustration labeled *Karaori with Bamboo Screen and Maple Leaves on White Background* (fig. 122, p. 137) is dated Bunsei 12 (1829) and notes that the head actor of the Hōshō school recieved it after a performance. This implies that it was probably a gift from the shogun or a daimyo. Costumes were specially ordered by daimyo of the purpose of gifts to actors or for their own use. The *Karaori with Maple Leaves and Bamboo Curtain* (cat. 65, p. 137) belongs to the Hosokawa Family. The illustration labeled *Nuihaku with Nandina and Small Birds on Dōhaku Ground* (cat. 122, p. 140) is similar to *Nuihaku with Nandina and Scattered Books* (cat. 57, p. 141), owned by the Metropolitan Museum of Art in New York.

ILLUSTRATION NOTATIONS IN KEN'EIRŌ GASŌ

The extensive detail provided by the handwritten notes in *Ken'eirō gasō* increases its value as a research tool. For example, one notation next to the front view of a nuihaku robe reads:

> Nuihaku with white *tatewaku* [serpentine lines], clouds, and dragon roundels
> > on black silk satin [*shusu*]
>
> Bunka 1 [1804], the year of Kino'e ne [wood rat], made in the third month
> Hōshō
> Bunsei [1818], the year of Hinoto no i [fire boar] tenth month, twenty-third day
> Hitotusbashi household, costume for the performance of *Dōjōji*
> koshimaki
> the same year, tenth month, twenty-sixth day
> drawn by Tamahama
> one of two illustrations.

This means that the illustrated nuihaku was made in 1804 and was worn by the head of the Hōshō school for a *Dōjōji* performance at the estate of the Hitotsubashi clan in 1827. The note substantiates a current rule in noh that the *maeshite* actor in *Dōjōji* wears a black satin nuihaku with roundels draped *koshimaki* style (a robe wrapped around the hips with the upper portion of the garment falling below the waist; fig. 67, p. 210).

ŌKUCHI WITH MAPLE LEAVES AND WATER
Edo period, nineteenth century
Length: 44 1/16 in. (112.0 cm)
Hikone Castle Museum, Shiga Prefecture
figure 46

KEN'EIRŌ GASŌ
(COMPILATION OF GRACEFUL DESIGNS)
(illustration of ōkuchi)
Edo period, eighteenth century
Tokyo National Museum
catalogue 122

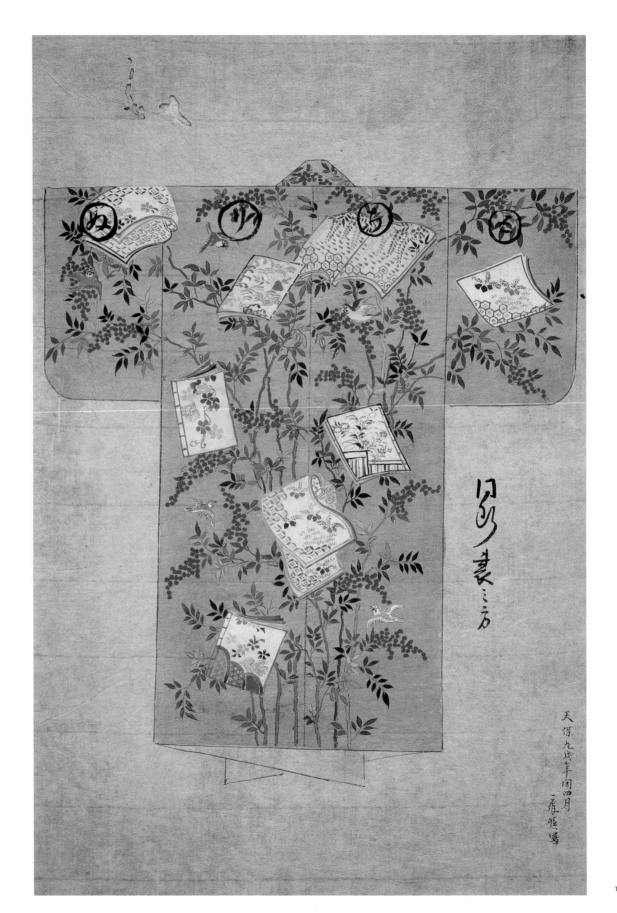

KEN'EIRŌ GASŌ
(COMPILATION OF GRACEFUL DESIGNS)
(illustration of nuihaku)
Edo period, eighteenth century
Tokyo National Museum
catalogue 122

NUIHAKU WITH NANDINA
AND SCATTERED BOOKS
Edo period, eighteenth century
The Metropolitan Museum of Art,
Gift of Mr. and Mrs. Paul T. Nomura,
in memory of Mr. and Mrs. S. Morris Nomura, 1989
catalogue 57

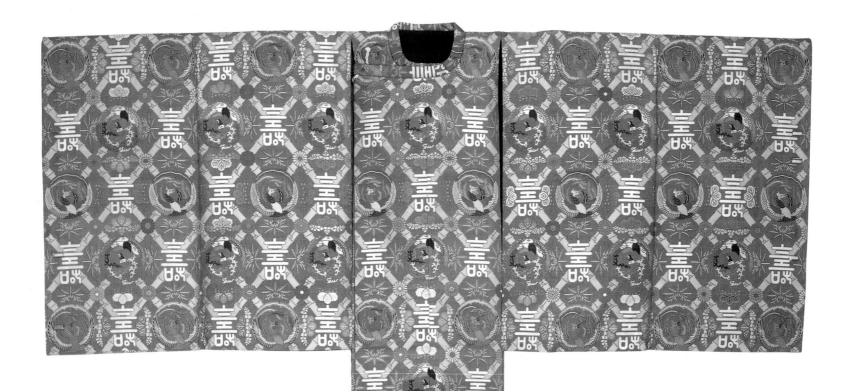

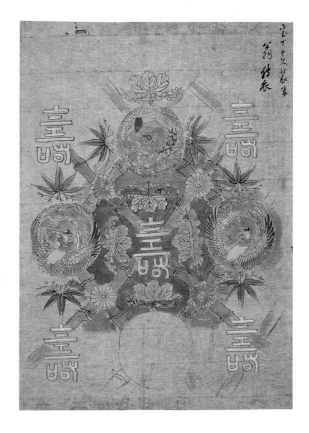

**KARIGINU WITH CHINESE CHARACTERS,
BIRD ROUNDELS, AND BAMBOO LATTICE**
Edo period, 1843
61¼ x 83¾ in. (155.7 x 212.6 cm)
Hikone Castle Museum, Shiga Prefecture
figure 47

**KEN'EIRŌ GASŌ
(COMPILATION OF GRACEFUL DESIGNS)**
(illustration of kariginu design)
Edo period, eighteenth century
Tokyo National Museum
catalogue 122

The karaori costume worn by the principal actor during the first half of the play *Dōjōji* can have different motifs, depending on the noh school. The Hōshō school, for example, wears a karaori with weeping branches of wisteria blossoms or snow-laden camellias, as illustrated and noted in *Kan'eirō gasō*. But another notation brings a different perspective. An illustration of a karaori with pine and wisteria has the name Hōshō Dayū written next to it, but its partial view says "Shōtoku 3 (1713), Mi [year of the serpent] fourth month, fifteenth day, shogun's public speech, the second day of noh performances / karaori with pine, wisteria, and gold pinecone design on red ground, used in *Dōjōji*." This indicates that the Hōshō school once used the pinecone design in addition to the wisteria on their *Dōjōji* karaori costume. If the facts in this note are correct, this karaori was probably made prior to Shōtoku 3 (1713) and would be an example of the standard style of karaori used for *Dōjōji* before the early eighteenth century.

THE IMPORTANCE OF KEN'EIRŌ GASŌ IN EDO-PERIOD HISTORY

The end of the Edo period was a time of great scholarly curiosity, which resulted in the collection and cataloguing of a wide range of items. These initiatives were generally undertaken at the request of daimyo families and reflected the increasing interest in education and knowledge throughout late-Edo society. Such research extended from the natural sciences, including studies of plants and animals, to the social sciences, where attention was paid to historical archives and cultural treasures. *Ken'eirō gasō* is a wonderful example of this intellectual trend and is important in trying to discover the relationships between daimyo families, noh actors, and noh costumes. It is hoped that additional volumes of *Ken'eirō gasō* will be discovered in the future, so that further research will allow a clearer understanding of these dynamics.

Translated by Etsuko Kuroda Douglass

KARIGINU WITH CHINESE CHARACTERS, BIRD ROUNDELS, AND BAMBOO LATTICE (detail)
Edo period, 1843
61¼ x 83¾ in. (155.7 x 212.6 cm)
Hikone Castle Museum, Shiga Prefecture
figure 47

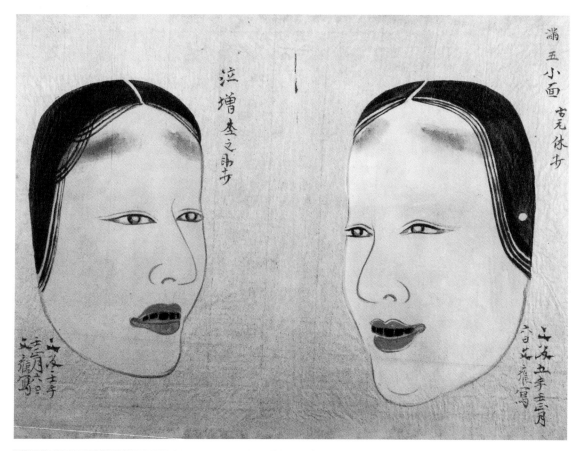

KEN'EIRŌ GASŌ
(COMPILATION OF GRACEFUL DESIGNS)
(illustration of masks)
Edo period, eighteenth century
Tokyo National Museum
catalogue 122

KEN'EIRŌ GASŌ
(COMPILATION OF GRACEFUL DESIGNS)
(illustration of fan paper)
Edo period, eighteenth century
Tokyo National Museum
catalogue 122

KEN'EIRŌ GASŌ
(COMPILATION OF GRACEFUL DESIGNS)
(illustration of stage prop)
Edo period, eighteenth century
Tokyo National Museum
catalogue 122

NOTES

1. Takahama Sugako, "Matsui-ke to nō" (Matsui family and noh) in *Nō men to nō shōzoku* (Noh masks and noh costume), exh. cat. (Kumamoto: Kumamoto Kenritsu Bijutsukan, 1992).

2. Hosokawa Morisada, "Hosokawa-ke no hitobito to nō" (Members of the Hosokawa family and noh), in *Hosokawa-ke no denrai nō men to shōzoku* (Noh masks and robes of the Hosokawa family collection), exh. cat. (Yokohama: Sogō Bijutsukan, 1990).

3. Mori Yoshikazu, "Hikone-han no okakae nō yakusha" (Official noh actors of the Hikone domain), in *Ii-ke denrai no nō men, nō shōzoku* (Noh masks and noh costume of the Ii family collection), (Shiga: Hikone Castle Museum, 1987), 178–80.

4. Ibid.

5. *Ikeda Mitsumasa kōden*, ge, Meiji 31 (The Life of Ikeda Mitsumasa, the last volume, 1899).

6. There is a notation that says, "in our household there are also a number of robes, which were newly made at the time of Sōgen" in "Kazō nō shōzoku dōgu taiyo toriatsukai kisoku" (Rules in loaning and handling noh costume and tools of our collection) by Ikeda Akimasa (1836–1903) in *Ikeda Mitsumasa kōden* (1899).

7. Kirihata Ken, *Okayama bijutsukan no nō shōzoku* (Noh costumes of the Okayama Museum of Art) in *Okayama bijutsukan zō Ikedake denrai nō shōzoku* (Kyoto: Kyoto Shoin, 1986), 69.

8. Ibid., 78.

9. Tayasu was a clan that was started by Tokugawa Munayoshi, the second son of the eighth shogun, Yoshimune, at the location by the Tayasu Gate of the Edo Castle. The Hitotsubashi and Shimizu families along with the Tayasu were called Gosankyō, that followed the three most significant Tokugawa branch families in Owari (Aichi Prefecture), Kii (Wakayama Prefecture), and Mito (part of Ibaragi Prefecture).

10. The Tokyo National Museum has confirmed the seals only on the volumes of their collection.

11. The cover of each volume has a piece of white paper pasted on it with a handwritten title, such as *Ken'eirō gasō, Ken'eirō gasō zokuhen* (sequel), *Ken'eirō gasō zanpen* (remaining volume), *Ken'eirō gasō shū-i* (gleanings), and *Ken'eirō gasō furoku* (appendix) and a brown paper below that indicates the volume number and the number of included illustrations, such as *Shoshū zuga gojūsan-yō* (first volume, 53 illustrations). The space left out of these two pieces of paper is filled with more writing in black ink that appears to be a table of contents.

12. Each title reads *Ken'eirō gasō, Ken'eirō gasō zokuhen* (sequel), and *Ken'eirō gasō shū-i* (gleanings) in black ink. However, none of those owned by Mr. Kreitmann have the brown additional papers that indicate the volume numbers.

13. It is understandable that there is one volume each for *Ken'eirō gasō zanpen* (remaining volume) and *Ken'eirō gasō furoku* (appendix). On the contrary, it seems quite anomalous that there are as many as eleven volumes of *Ken'eirō gasō shū-i* (gleanings) as opposed to the fact that there are only two volumes each for *Ken'eirō gasō* and *Ken'eirō gasō zokuhen* (sequel).

14. The illustrations of the noh costumes and noh accessories in the volumes of the Tokyo National Museum comprise: twenty-eight *chūkei* (fan) and chūkei papers, twenty-five noh costumes, one noh mask in the first volume; thirty-nine noh costumes in the fourth volume; forty noh costumes, twenty-nine noh props in the fifth volume; fifty-five noh masks in the sixth volume; forty chūkei papers in the seventh volume; twenty-two noh props in the ninth volume; one noh mask, one noh theater illustration, ninety-one noh / kyōgen performance illustrations in the twelfth volume. Such a wide range of illustrations is quite helpful in understanding not only noh costumes but also noh art itself. Mr. Kreitmann's volume, *Ken'eirō gasō zokuhen* (sequel) 2 has fifty noh costume illustrations.

15. Atsuita karaori is also mentioned in *Toyotaka nikki* (Diary of Toyotaka) written by Fujita Iuemon Toyotaka, who was an official waki actor for the Kishū Tokugawa clan. It is significant because this diary was written between Genroku 14 (1710) and Hōreki 8 (1758); thus the date of the atsuita karaori production perhaps goes back as early as the first half of the eighteenth century. Furthermore, the atsuita karaori of those days was quite different from what we call atsuita karaori today, though somewhat close to atsuita.

くびゝ

KO NŌ KYŌGEN NO ZU
(OLD NOH AND KYŌGEN ILLUSTRATIONS)
(detail: *Kubihiki*)
Edo period, seventeenth century
National Noh Theater, Tokyo
catalogue 119

KYŌGEN:
A THEATER
OF PLAY

CAROLYN A. MORLEY

Traditionally, comedy is grounded in the physical and material world, in the exuberance of fertility and social renewal portrayed by Mikhail Bakhtin in his well-known study of humor in the marketplace and the carnival.[1] Kyōgen, the classical comedy of Japan, is no exception. Because kyōgen shares its origins with noh in the *shin saragaku* entertainments (short skits and acrobatics) of the twelfth century,[2] and has been performed since the fourteenth century with the noh on a noh stage, kyōgen has come to define its art against that of the noh. The advent of two pivotal figures for the development of noh, Kannami Kiyotsugu (1333–1384) and his son, Zeami Motokiyo (c. 1363–c. 1443), determined the direction noh would take as a drama focused on dance and chant. The earliest texts for noh plays date from this time. Kyōgen, on the other hand, continued to be performed as improvisational comic skits and was not recorded in any form until the *Tenshō* text (1578), a collection of plot summaries. While much of noh is about transcendence of the ordinary, kyōgen brings us tumbling to earth with the abruptness of the thunder god in *Kaminari*, whose fall from the sky injures his hip. The props, masks, robes and even the very bodies of actors that are treated so reverently in the noh become instead the objects of irreverent play: horses whinny and buck their masters to the ground in *Kirokuda*, young maiden demons get into neck-pulling contests with warriors and run away crying in *Kubihiki*, (cat. 119), crabs loom up and pinch the ears of unsuspecting priests in *Kani yamabushi*, monkeys dance and chatter in *Utsubozaru* (cat. 120, p. 149), and foxes sniff at bait and howl at the moon in *Tsurigitsune*.

Though kyōgen acting has undergone a process of refinement over the years (particularly during the seventeenth and eighteenth centuries), the robust and emphatic humor of the body, far from disappearing, became the basis for the artistic conventions of the stage. Transgressive humor associated with the treatment of props and costumes is especially noteworthy. In *Shūron* (A religious dispute), for example, the large woven hats (*kasa*) worn by the priests become bells on which to beat their beads as they leap about the stage, each intent on demonstrating the superiority of his prayers. In *Futari daimyō* (Two daimyo), an irate passerby seizes the luxurious robes of the daimyo, then forces them to bob up and down like dolls at his command. In *Nukegara* (Shedding the demon's shell) the master slips a mask over the sleeping face of his drunk and disobedient servant, who awakens to find himself seemingly transformed into a demon before the mask eventually falls off. (The scene of the servant's frantic alarm is reminiscent of the well-known performance by Marcel Marceau in which he mimes the experience of finding himself stuck in a comic mask.) In each of these examples, the physical world is used playfully to reveal a common humanity beneath society's structures and social distinctions. The daimyo are no greater than the clothing they wear, the priests become confused and begin reciting one another's prayers, and the servant, like Marceau's mime, confuses his outer reflection (the face of a demon) with the inner man.

THE PLAYS

Kyōgen is best known for its repertoire of approximately two hundred and forty *hon-kyōgen* (one-act comic skits). The plays usually require only two to three performers (traditionally male), who take on the roles of *shite* (main actor) and *ado* (secondary actor or actors). In general the plays are identified by their main characters, such as the Daimyo, the Master, the Servant, the Woman, the Bridegroom, the Farmer, the Mountain Priest, or the Blind Man. Their costumes are specific to the character type, but are not identified with any one particular play as is often the case in noh theater. Two thirds of the kyōgen plays focus on the master-servant relationship, reflecting the social system of the medieval and early modern periods. Tarō Kaja, the servant, is the ubiquitous "everyman" with whom almost any audience can identify. Indeed, the irrepressible Tarō Kaja, dressed in the whimsical *kataginu* vest (cat. 38, p. 157), is the character most often associated with kyōgen.

In contrast with the masked noh drama, where music and dance form the basis of the performance, kyōgen is primarily a theater of speech and mime. Masks are infrequently worn; when they are, they are as likely to function as stage props as costumes. The absence of the mask is another reason why kyōgen is considered a "realistic" theater form in spite of its highly choreographed acting and staging. Specific characters, such as animals, some of the secondary female roles, old men and women, and Shinto gods of good fortune, regularly wear masks.[3] Otherwise, the kyōgen actor manipulates his own face as his mask onstage, using various conventions for expressing anger, laughter, surprise, and so forth. Four masks included in this exhibition are the Oto, a young woman with enormous cheeks and a tiny mouth (cat. 98, p. 66), the monkey (cat. 101, p. 150; used in Mibu Temple kyōgen performances but similar to that used in kyōgen for *Utsubozaru* [cat. 120] and others), the fox (used in *Tsurigitsune*, cat. 100, p. 67), and *Sanbasō* (cat. 143, p. 15). Although intentionally comical, they are rendered realistically in order to remind the kyōgen audience of people they might actually know. Indeed, the late Nomura Manzō, a renowned actor and carver, recounted that many of his masks were inspired by the faces of people he would see on the train.[4]

Although the kyōgen of today is as refined and whimsical as the designs on the kataginu vests, comments of Zeami Motokiyo in the early fifteenth century and Ōkura Toraakira in the seventeenth century indicate that medieval kyōgen was a good deal rougher and cruder (factors also evident in the *Tenshō* text). It was probably closer to the type of acting seen in the Mibu kyōgen plays performed three times a year at Mibu Temple in Kyoto and dating back as far as the early fourteenth century.[5] Mibu kyōgen are part of a folk tradition of *dainenbutsu* (Buddhist invocation) plays intended to teach Buddhism. The actors are masked and the plays are done entirely in mime. While today the Mibu kyōgen repertory draws on both kyōgen and noh, evidence of the early didacticism remains. One early seventeenth-century painting, *Rakuchu rakugai zu* (Scenes in and around Kyoto), owned by the Tokugawa

Art Museum), illustrates a Mibu kyōgen performance where the actors, dressed as monkeys, swing from the rafters of the worship hall of the temple. A similar scene can be found in the performance of the Mibu kyōgen play *Kanidon* (Sir crab), based on a well-known folk tale regarding a battle between crabs and monkeys. Although this particular play only dates back to the Meiji period (1868–1912), the monkey mask also appears in a much older Mibu kyōgen play, *Nue* (a play about a fantastic bird, the nue, that is found in the noh repertory as well). In the Mibu kyōgen version, the nue, like the monkeys in *Kanidon*, swings from the beams of the temple. This is the type of desecration of stage space deplored by Ōkura Toraakira in his theatrical criticism, the *Waranbegusa* (Random notes for children, 1651).

The refinement of kyōgen over many years is apparent when comparing the earliest record of one of the monkey plays, *Utsubozaru* (Monkey skin quiver), from the *Tenshō* text , with the version performed today. In contemporary performance a daimyo and his servant, Tarō Kaja, are about to go hunting when they encounter a monkey trainer and his monkey (cat. 120). The daimyo demands that Tarō Kaja kill the monkey in order to use the skin for a quiver. The trainer begs to be allowed to kill his monkey himself. However, the monkey misunderstands his actions as a signal to perform, and begins to mime rowing a boat. The daimyo is so moved by the trainer's anguish and so delighted by the monkey's antics that he gives the monkey his fan, his sword, even his robes. The play ends happily with the daimyo performing alongside the monkey. In contrast, the *Tenshō* version of the play ends with the daimyo, presumably with a rope around his neck, being pulled off the stage by Tarō Kaja, a finale that would never be accepted in a kyōgen performance today. Like the monkeys leaping from the ceiling in the Mibu kyōgen plays, yanking an actor offstage would violate the artistic conventions of the kyōgen.

However much kyōgen has changed, contemporary performances of *Utsubozaru* are still grounded in the physical and material world. Social distinctions are leveled as the daimyo tosses off his beautiful *suō* robe, gets down on the floor, and performs like a monkey. The audience members are invited to identify with the powerful man, who becomes so entranced by the monkey that he loses his sense of self-importance. In a renewal of spirit, the audience laughs not so much at the daimyo as with the playful internal child he represents. While the earlier version of the play offers a far cruder, and in this sense more physical, portrait of the daimyo, the physical and material basis of the humor is

NŌMAI NO ZU
(ILLUSTRATIONS OF NOH DANCES)
(detail: *Utsubozaru*)
Edo period, eighteenth century
National Noh Theater, Tokyo
catalogue 120

SARU (MONKEY) MASK
Muromachi period, fifteenth century
Mibudera, Kyoto
catalogue 101

not lost in current performance. Like the designs for the kyōgen costume, the acting style and humor have become more artistically refined while retaining their roots in everyday life.

OKINA SANBASŌ

The playful element of kyōgen has various guises. Simple comic reversals and revelations predominate, but the earthiness of kyōgen extends beyond plot devices to affect the presentation of the character, his language, and his movement. While most apparent in the hon-kyōgen, this is also evident in the two auxiliary roles for the kyōgen actor: Sanbasō in the ritual performance of *Okina Sanbasō* (a New Year's dance performance dating back to the sarugaku entertainments), and the interlude role (*ai-kyōgen*) within a noh play. In neither of these roles is there an expectation of humor and yet the emphasis on the material world places them squarely within the kyōgen tradition.

In *Sanbasō*, the kyōgen actor performs a fertility dance of rice cultivation and harvest. His robe (cats. 144 and 145, pp. 184 and 185) displays the crane and turtle motif, while his fan displays the crane and pine (cat. 146, p. 185), all symbols of long life. In his opening dance he makes a number of dramatic leaps across the stage, making physical the metaphorical by enacting a crane. These leaps appear to have originated in the crow leaps (*karasu tobi*) in *Yamabushi kagura*, a type of ritual dance performed by mountain ascetics. The two dances of *Sanbasō* are clearly varieties of agricultural dance (*taue*), with a rhythmic up-and-down movement that mimics the planting of rice seedlings. The first dance, *momi no dan*, is performed without a mask and has a kind of brute energy. The second dance, the *suzu no dan*, has an almost electrical charge as the black-masked dancer proceeds to shake the golden Shinto bells of purification (*suzu*, cat. 147, p. 186) as he leaps about the stage. Thus both aspects of kyōgen, the ordinary physical world (rice planting) and the brute energy of a creative force (the fertility god), can be found in the kyōgen dances of *Sanbasō*.

In the first dance a brief exchange takes place between the Sanbasō dancer and the mask bearer (*menbako mochi*). Sanbasō insists that the mask bearer be seated before he begins the final masked dance, while the mask bearer urges the dance to begin first. Their exchange is not so different from the comically mundane exchanges between the characters in a kyōgen skit, and serves to emphasize

KEN'EIRŌ GASŌ
(COMPILATION OF GRACEFUL DESIGNS)
(Illustration of *Sanbasō*)
Edo period, eighteenth century
Tokyo National Museum
catalogue 122

NŌ KYŌGEN EMAKI
(NOH AND KYŌGEN PICTURE SCROLLS)
(detail: *Sanbasō*)
Edo period, eighteenth century
Tokyo National Museum
catalogue 118

the ordinary, as if the actors had stepped out of their expected roles to quarrel. The final dance is performed with the black, laughing elderly man mask (cat. 143, p. 15) that complements the white Okina mask (cat. 137, p. 14) worn by the noh actor in the first half of the performance. The two masks offer the two faces of performance, much like the two dramatic masks of Western theater, the comic and the tragic. Here we have instead the earthy and the sublime.

INTERLUDE KYŌGEN

The second auxiliary role of a kyōgen actor is that of an interlude kyōgen (ai-kyōgen) within a noh play. Here, too, the expectation is not that the actor perform humorously but, rather, convey the immediacy of everyday reality. In the majority of interlude kyōgen, known as *katari-ai* narrations, the actor portrays a "man of the area" who comes forward to retell the story of the noh in plain language as an ordinary man might have understood it. He may also portray, among others, a court messenger or the minor god of a tutelary shrine (in *Kamo*, a tutelary god appears in a *yore mizugoromo* jacket [cat. 14, p. 154; and cat. 16, p. 155] to recite the lineage of the god of Kamo Shrine and to offer a short dance). While the language of the interlude actor is not familiar to today's audience, it appears to be close to the vernacular of the seventeenth and eighteenth centuries, when the interludes were first recorded. In the older ai-kyōgen texts (for example, the seventeenth-century Ōkura school interlude kyōgen text *Jōkyō Matsui bon*) the kyōgen actor's speech is often more detailed than in contemporary performance, endowing it with a degree of verisimilitude not apparent today.

The second major category of ai-kyōgen, known as the *ashirai-ai* (active interludes), consists of interactive roles for the kyōgen within the noh. In *Dōjōji*, for example, the interlude actors are two *nōriki* (ascetics) at a shrine where a new bell is being installed. The head ascetic attempts to dissuade a female dancer (the main character in the noh) from entering the shrine, where women are forbidden, but later relents when she agrees to dance for him. When the bell, the main prop on the stage, crashes dramatically to the ground over the head of the dancer, the interlude actors, until now mesmerized by her dance, are jolted awake and run around in confusion. They add demonstrably to the immediacy of the scene.

Finally, the *kae-ai* (alternative interludes) consist of short, autonomous "plays within plays." Because of their length these are rarely performed, either as part of the noh or independently. An alternative ai-kyōgen for *Kamo*, for example, consists of a rice-planting scene, quite similar to that depicted in the painting of the *taue dengaku* (field music) performance (fig. 4, p. 16) from the middle of the Muromachi period (1392–1568). In the painting a large group of young women (*saotome*) performs the ritual of transplanting the rice seedlings to the left of a group of musicians, the shrine priest, and a black-masked performer. In the ai-kyōgen for *Kamo*, the women (dressed in *kosode*, popular wear in the sixteenth century and later) are performing the annual ritual in celebration of the flooding of the fields. A worker at the shrine (dressed in *kukuribakama*) calls out to them, prompting an exchange to musical accompaniment as the man gently taunts them. While neither Sanbasō nor the ai-kyōgen roles are intended to elicit laughter, they clearly share a foundation in the material and physical world of the common person – the same focus as the kyōgen skits.

The elegant juxtaposition of noh and kyōgen that exists today was not always so seamless. Whether regarding the *Okina Sanbasō*, the interlude kyōgen, or the comic skits performed between the noh dramas, early mentions of comic actors (*okashi*) in the writings of Zeami suggest that they were frequently unreliable, often improvising at whim, and not above crude humor (*Shūdōsho*, 1430).[6] However, the very mention of the comic actor (later to be referred to as kyōgen) both in the comic skits and as an interlude performer, verifies that kyōgen had been performed with the noh at least as far back as the fourteenth century.

EARLY HISTORY

Interestingly, the history of kyōgen costume parallels the development of the relationship between noh and kyōgen. In the sixteenth century, judging primarily from the paintings of noh stages, the comic actor dressed very much like the man on the street, with little attempt to create a costume per se. The depiction of the noh *Hyakuman* (A million) from the Momoyama period (1568–1615) shows the kyōgen actor wearing a solid dark woven jacket (*kitsuke*), no kataginu vest, and *hakama* bound at the calf (*kukuribakama*) with a traditional kyōgen crest. The absence of the kataginu vest and the solid dark color of the *kitsuke* undergarment distinguish the clothing from the kyōgen costume today. From such paintings as this, Kirihata Ken surmises that the kyōgen costume as such did not emerge until early in the Edo period (1615–1868), and even then was probably very much like everyday wear of the period.[7] As the noh theater was formalized under the hand of Zeami (and, later, his son-in-law Konparu Zenchiku, 1405–c. 1470), an awareness of clothing as costume for the noh emerged. This same awareness does not appear to have occurred in kyōgen until the seventeenth century, when a revolution of sorts took place within the kyōgen world: the actors formed schools, recorded their texts, and formalized their acting technique. In other words, kyōgen evolved from a theater of improvisation into a self-conscious acting form. Of course, economic concerns played a large part in the changes in costume as well as staging. Early kyōgen ranked at the bottom of the theatrical hierarchy, and was not likely to obtain the elaborate costumes donated to noh actors by wealthy patrons.

Perhaps because of their marginal status and the improvisational nature of their acting, kyōgen actors were able to adapt easily to the changes taking place during the warfare of the late sixteenth century, garnering large popular audiences in the process. In 1593, the three great generals

YORE MIZUGOROMO
Edo period, eighteenth century
Bunka Gakuen Costume Museum, Tokyo
catalogue 14

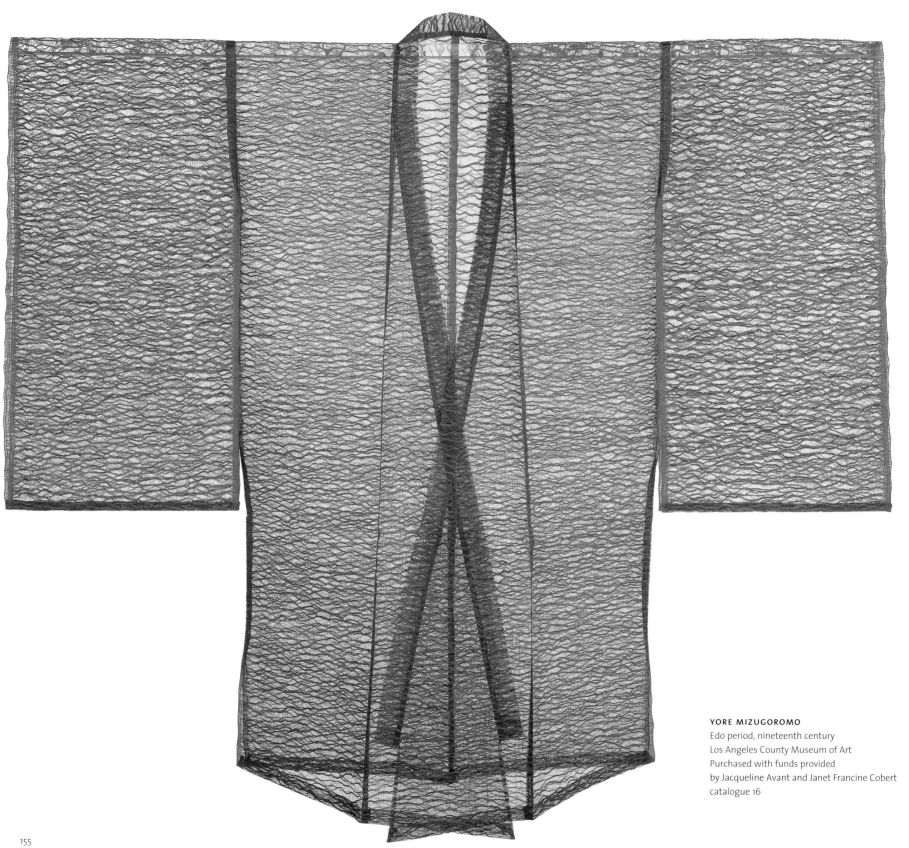

YORE MIZUGOROMO
Edo period, nineteenth century
Los Angeles County Museum of Art
Purchased with funds provided
by Jacqueline Avant and Janet Francine Cobert
catalogue 16

of the day, Toyotomi Hideyoshi (1537–1598, a great aficionado of the noh), Tokugawa Ieyasu (1543–1616), and Maeda Toshiie (1538–1599), performed a kyōgen play entitled *Mimihiki* (Ear pulling), attesting to the growing recognition of kyōgen among amateur performers. Kyōgen actors also crossed over to the newly emerging kabuki entertainment, performing the comic role (*saruwaka*) in kabuki of the period.

However, by the early Edo period, when noh was sanctioned as the official government performance art, the promise of patronage for kyōgen, too, proved a strong impetus toward formalization on every level. Not surprisingly, the names of kyōgen actors start to appear more frequently in documents from the late sixteenth and early seventeenth centuries, with the Ōkura family the first to receive official recognition. Ōkura Toraakira, author of the *Toraakira bon* (1642), the earliest collection of kyōgen plays, as well as a book of criticism, *Waranbegusa*, noted that his grandfather, Toramasa, had the name Tora (tiger) bestowed on him by Lord Nobunaga (Oda Nobunaga, 1534–1582), and that his son (Toraakira's father), Torakiyo, had the patronage of Toyotomi Hideyoshi.

During Toraakira's lifetime the main challenge to his school came from the Sagi school of kyōgen. Toraakira criticizes the Sagi actors in the *Waranbegusa* as vulgar upstarts: "The kyōgen popular today is tasteless. The dialogue is unintelligible, garbled and confused. The lower classes may laugh at facial contortions, mouths hanging open and pop-eyed expressions, but any person of culture would be offended by such vulgar antics. They are no different from the fool [*dōke*] so popular in kabuki."[8] His outrage may have had some foundation, as the theatrical criticism of the day (*Kindai yozayakusha mokuroku*, 1646) noted that one Sagi school actor was jailed for a month after leaping off the stage on a hobbyhorse into an audience that included the shogun's entourage.[9] On the other hand, Toraakira

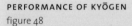

PERFORMANCE OF KYŌGEN
figure 48

KATAGINU WITH RABBITS AND SCOURING RUSH
Edo period, eighteenth century
Toyohashi Uomachi Noh Association, Aichi Prefecture
catalogue 38

also conceded that the Ōkura school was criticized as being too close to the noh in style. The third school of kyōgen to emerge, the Izumi school (which was patronized by a branch of the Tokugawa family and the court in the Kyoto area), published its first text, *Kyōgen rikugi*, in 1646. At the same time as these different schools of kyōgen formed and the texts were recorded, an awareness of costume developed, and kyōgen motifs and dyeing techniques emerged.

Over the next two hundred years, thanks to the patronage of the Tokugawa government, the art of kyōgen was further refined. While Toraakira was critical of Sagi school vulgarity in the seventeenth century, his texts are rougher than the texts of the succeeding century (Ōkura Torahiro's, for example). Not only did the humor in kyōgen become more genteel, but the character types, movement patterns, and stage conventions were regularized. The formalization of kyōgen theater as a whole was accompanied by the development in the late Edo period of distinctive kyōgen kataginu motifs, with large and whimsical designs of radish, rabbits, mosquitoes, household tools, and other common objects and animals. The romanticization of the countryside in kyōgen prints of the period is consistent with other cultural currents of the Tokugawa period seen in *haikai* poetry and *haiga* sketches.

The collapse of the Tokugawa government in 1867–1868 had a decided impact on the kyōgen schools. The Sagi school disappeared altogether, while the individual families of the two remaining schools attempted to establish themselves independently. A century later, kyōgen experienced an unprecedented boom in popularity, due in large part to interest from abroad. Kyōgen acting became known in some circles as the Stanislavsky method of Japanese acting, in spite of the stylization so central to kyōgen. Kyōgen's claim to realism would seem to reside in the familiarity of the plots, the mime, and the language. Kyōgen actors, always more adventurous than those of noh, took roles in productions of works by Samuel Beckett (especially *Waiting for Godot*) and looked for further ways to enrich and modernize their performance, a trend which continues today.

NOTES

1. Mikhail Bakhtin, *Rabelais and His World* (Bloomington: Indiana University Press, 1984).

2. Karen Brazell, ed., *Traditional Japanese Theater* (New York: Columbia University Press, 1998), 7.

3. Aoki Shinji, *Kyōgen men raisan* (In praise of kyōgen masks) (Kyoto: Hōga Shoten, 1981).

4. Nomura Manzō, *Kyōgen geiwa* (Artful talks on kyōgen) (Tokyo: Wanya Shoten, 1981), 117-18: "...a mouth like that one... I'll take that nose, and the eyes from that fellow...Even when I'm riding the train I never get bored. The more crowded the better. I lose myself looking for faces and forget to get off before the door shuts."

5. Inoue Takao, Nishikawa Teruko, and Umehara Takeshi, *Mibu kyōgen no miryoku* (The allure of Mibu kyōgen) (Kyoto: Tankōsha, 1997).

6. Translated in J. Thomas Rimer and Yamazaki Masakazu, *On the Art of the Nō Drama* (Princeton: Princeton University Press, 1984), 170.

7. Kirihata Ken, *Nihon no senshoku* (Japanese textiles), vol. 9, *Kyōgen no shōzoku* (Kyōgen costumes) (Kyoto: Kyoto Shoin, 1993).

8. Ōkura Toraakira, *Waranbegusa* (Random notes for children), in Nishio Minoru, et al., eds., *Yōkyoku kyōgen, kokugo kokubungaku kenkyūshi taisei* (Kyōgen songbook: The complete research history of Japanese language and literature), vol. 8 (Tokyo: Sanseidō, 1977), 517. Based on the *Mukashigatari* (Old tales), his father Torakiyo's work.

9. Yonekura Toshiaki, *Waranbegusa kenkyū* (Research on Waranbegusa) (Tokyo: Kazama Shobō, 1973), 47.

**KAZURAOKE (SEAT AND CONTAINER PROP)
WITH PAMPAS GRASS**
Momoyama period, seventeenth century
Osaka Castle Museum
catalogue 135

SUŌ WITH PINE, BAMBOO CURTAINS (MISU),
PLUM BLOSSOMS, POEM CARDS (TANZAKU),
ROUNDELS, AND SEASHORE LANDSCAPE PICTURE
CARDS (SHIKISHI)
Edo period, nineteenth century
Hayashibara Museum of Art, Okayama Prefecture
catalogue 29

KYŌGEN COSTUMES:
THE FASCINATING
WORLD
OF DYED TEXTILES

KIRIHATA KEN

Designs created by various dyeing methods are the antithesis of the woven designs in noh robes. As opposed to the dignified luxury of the noh robes, kyōgen robes favor a lighthearted simplicity. Those who come face to face with kyōgen costumes, in particular the *suō* (matched outfit of jacket with double-width sleeves and trousers or *hakama*) such as *Suō with Pine, Bamboo Curtains, Plum Blossoms, Poem Cards, and Seashore Landscape Picture Cards* (cat. 29) and *kataginu* (sleeveless jacket) such as *Kataginu with Radish and Mallet* (cat. 33, p. 6), cannot help but be fascinated by them.

Kyōgen is said to be one of the oldest forms of Japanese theater, the elder sibling to noh, and yet evidence testifying to the extent to which kyōgen has been ignored has become commonplace in recent studies. In the words of the historian Kobayashi Seki, kyōgen has endured the "cold-shoulder treatment for the past six hundred years," resulting in a lack of critical research on kyōgen costumes and masks. Little is known about kyōgen costume prior to the Edo period (1615–1868). For noh costumes, we can refer to Muromachi-period (1392–1568) records of garments, including suō worn by warriors, being presented to actors after a performance. Noh costume evolved from these gifts of clothing made to entertainers as, over the centuries, various garment styles of the upper classes were gradually adopted into noh theater. Such luxurious clothing donations were soon to encourage the production of uniquely beautiful noh robes. It would take a great leap of courage to make similar scholarly claims for kyōgen costume. And yet, a glance at the costumes, in particular the suō and kataginu, would suggest that kyōgen costumes evolved in the same way.

What little is known of performance costumes from the mid-Muromachi period has been gleaned from several illustrations in the sixteenth-century painting *Tsukinami fūzoku zu* (Events of the twelve months), belonging to the Tokyo National Museum. In the scene of a rice-planting ceremony (*taue*) a group of musicians and dancers are dressed in red or dark blue sleeveless garments similar to the kataginu (fig. 49). In another vignette a warrior dancing at a banquet wears a black court hat (*kuro tachi eboshi*) and a kataginu with matching long trousers (*naga-kamishimo*). From the Momoyama period (1568–1615) are the illustrated noh songbooks (*utaibon*) with depictions of the noh play *Hyakuman* (A million). The interlude kyōgen actor (*ai-kyōgen*) is shown in a *kitsuke* (solid brown inner robe) and kyōgen hakama (long patterned hakama tied around the calf and falling above the ankle, also known as *kukuribakama*), with scattered yellow roundel crests on a yellow ground. Similar crests would later be known as the kyōgen crest.[1] Significantly, he is not wearing either a naga-kamishimo or a kataginu with *hanbakama* (ankle-length trousers).

The first documented use of the kataginu as a kyōgen costume is from the early Edo period. In the *Ōkura Toraakira-bon* (1642), a book of plays by Ōkura Toraakira (1597–1662), notations refer to the use of kataginu kukuribakama, and *kamishimo* (a matched ensemble of kataginu and hakama). Detailed descriptions for decorative designs of the kataginu, however, are not provided. In the same

**TSUKINAMI FŪZOKU ZU
(EVENTS OF THE TWELVE MONTHS)** (detail: *taue*)
Muromachi period, sixteenth century
Eight-panel folding screen; ink and colors on paper
Each panel: 24$\frac{1}{16}$ ~ 24$\frac{3}{8}$ x 15$\frac{11}{16}$ ~ 16$\frac{5}{8}$ in.
(61.1 ~ 61.8 x 39.9 ~ 42.2 cm)
Tokyo National Museum
figure 49

book there is a reference to the play *Asō* (Lord Asō has his hair fixed), where a kamishimo is described as having the design of a cypress hedge with plovers on a dark indigo ground.[2]

Toraakira is also the author of the *Waranbegusa* (Random notes for children, 1651), an annotated version of the *Mukashigatari* (Old tales, 1651), his collection of his father's teachings. The *Waranbegusa* contains interesting information on kyōgen costumes used during the time of these two actors. It seems that the *shite* (principal-role actor) and *ado* (secondary-role actor) during Toraakira's day were free to wear whatever pleased them, while the musicians dressed in robes with tiny, inconspicuous stenciled paste-resist patterns (*komon*), or robes with a change of pattern on the lower half of the garment. The chorus wore similar outfits decorated with komon patterns on a monochrome ground or with an overall pattern of small motifs. In any case, they wore what was thought to be appropriate for a particular performance. By 1651, however, the musicians were wearing large motifs, and there were incidents where the actors embarrassed one another with an inappropriate choice of costume.[3] Attitudes toward costuming during this period were a subject of great interest to kyōgen audiences. One spectator observed that the costumes used by Toraakira's troupe were gorgeous but too elegant. To this Toraakira replied that he was simply responding to the popular taste for beautiful costumes – no matter how skilled the performance, the audience is not pleased when the costumes are dull.[4] This preference for beautiful costumes seems to have continued at an accelerated pace until the eighteenth century.

Pictorial evidence in the form of handscrolls (*emaki*), painted picture albums (*ekagami*), and woodblock prints are valuable resources for the study of noh and kyōgen costumes. Examples of kyōgen suō and kataginu can be found among the paintings in the seventeenth century *Ko nō kyōgen no zu* (Old noh and kyōgen illustrations) belonging to the National Noh Theater in Tokyo. There is a depiction of an actor in *Hige yagura* (The fortified beard) wearing a suō with a pattern of scattered gingko leaves (cat. 119a). A scene from the play *Tōsumō* (Chinese sumo) shows the Japanese character wearing a kataginu designed with a large white bird flying above a fence (cat. 119b). The bird in flight across the back of the garment and a geometric pattern on the lower part below the belted waist are similar to motifs on the nineteenth-century *Kataginu with Herons and Reeds* (cat. 36, p. 164).

There are a number of examples of mid-Edo period kyōgen suō and kataginu illustrated in *Nō kyōgen emaki* (Noh and kyōgen picture scrolls) belonging to the Tokyo National Museum. The daimyo in *Utsubozaru* (Monkey skin quiver) wears a suō with a large brown sandbar (*suhama*) pattern against a pale blue ground decorated with small hailstones and *nadeshiko* flowers (wild pinks) (cat. 118a). The sandbar is filled with a komon pattern of hailstones and aquatic plants. In *Shidōhōgaku* (Shidōhōgaku the horse) a light blue suō decorated with scattered *koto* bridges (moveable frets) is worn by the master (cat. 118b). Illustrations of kataginu can also be found on the same picture handscroll. The Tarō Kaja in *Shidōhōgaku* wears a kataginu with roundels that has two bars drawn through them on a light green ground (cat. 118b). In *Nabe yatsubachi* (Pots and drums), the drum seller's kataginu has a scattering of water wheels over a striped black ground. Kataginu worn by ai-kyōgen actors are pictured in various scenes of noh plays in *Nō ekagami* (Painted picture album of noh), by Sumiyoshi Jokei (1599–1670). The commoner in *Ataka* wears a light blue kataginu with a komon pattern that resembles piles of firewood (*maki*) (fig. 50).

Painted vignettes in the National Noh Theater's eighteenth-century *Nōmai no zu* (Illustrations of noh dances) include depictions of naga kamishimo. Three examples are worn by villagers in *Yoneichi* (A rice bale taken for a girl). Each naga-kamishimo has a white overall pattern on a plain colored background. There are scattered pine needles on brown, a motif of two parallel bars on gray, and a triangular pattern consisting of three dots on dark indigo. In the scene from *Hagi daimyō* (The bush clover daimyo) the daimyo wears a striking suō with an overall geometric pattern abstractly representing warp beams (*chikiri*) and crests made up of four diamond shapes; the Tarō Kaja wears a kataginu with a set of five white bands along both the upper and lower parts of the vest; and the garden owner wears a naga-kamishimo with an all-over design that resembles sprouts of grass.

For the study of late-Edo-period costume, *Nō ezushiki* (Collection of woodblock prints of noh, 1887) is a good resource. Although its date of publication falls within the Meiji period (1868–1912), we can assume that the prints represent late-Edo-period theater, based on the depiction of the actors with their hair bound in topknots, a style that went out of fashion after the feudal society of the Edo period came to an end. There are, again, examples of both suō and kataginu for the kyōgen plays.

NŌ KYŌGEN EMAKI
(NOH AND KYŌGEN PICTURE SCROLLS)
(detail: *Shidōhōgaku*)
Edo period, eighteenth century
Tokyo National Museum
catalogue 118b

NŌ EKAGAMI
(PAINTED PICTURE ALBUM OF NOH)
(detail: *Ataka*)
Sumiyoshi Jokei (1599–1670)
Private collection
figure 50

KATAGINU WITH HERONS AND REEDS
Edo period, nineteenth century
Shinshiro Honmachi Noh Association,
Aichi Prefecture
catalogue 36

SUŌ WITH WEEPING CHERRY TREE BLOSSOMS
Edo period, eighteenth century
Shinshiro Honmachi Noh Association, Aichi Prefecture
catalogue 27

Suō are shown in *Hagi daimyō*, *Hito uma* (Man into horse), *Awataguchi* (A man poses as a sword), and *Yawata no mae* (The prompted suitor at Yawata). In *Hagi daimyō*, the daimyo's suō is decorated with baskets made of reeds on a black ground, while in *Hito uma*, the suō depicts bottle gourds (*yūgao*) on a shaded (*bokashi*) ground of burnt orange (*kaba iro*). The suō worn by the shite in *Awataguchi* includes crests on a pale blue bokashi ground; in *Yawata no mae* the shite's suō is decorated with rafts and plum blossoms on a light blue ground.

In terms of naga-kamishimo, the *Nō ezushiki* shows Tarō Kaja in *Tsukuzukushi* (The poem fight) dressed in a costume bearing a freehand ink drawing of a sparrow on a light blue ground. In *Yawata no mae*, the ado's garment shows a stream and basket design on a particolored (*somewake*) dyed ground. In *Shidōhōgaku*, the master's kamishimo is decorated with a komon pattern of gingko leaves on a light blue ground. *Shidōhōgaku* also includes Tarō Kaja wearing a kataginu with a large crest (*daimon*) design of three swords and oak leaves on a dark green ground. Other kataginu are illustrated for *Busshi* (The fake sculptor of Buddhist images), where the ado's garment bears a large bamboo design on light blue; *Kamabara* (Unsuccessful suicide with a sickle), in which Tarō Kaja's kataginu is decorated with a large banana leaf pattern on a segmented dyed background (fig. 51); and *Kikazuzatō* (Blind and deaf), which features large centipedes on a dark green ground on the ado's kataginu (fig. 52).

The information gleaned from these important pictorial records allows us to begin to construct the development of the suō and kataginu. The suō was a part of noh costuming from the medieval period, when patrons donated their clothing to actors. A similar path opened up for kyōgen attire as well. The exquisite design sense of the suō commonly worn by the upper classes was eminently suited to theater and was immediately adapted for noh, advancing the development of stage costume. Kataginu, too, were commonly worn in the streets before they were adopted by the theater. From the early Edo period we have records of the musicians and chorus dressed in solid-color robes or in robes with an overall crest design, featuring large design patterns that must have distracted the audience from watching the actors. This suggests that designs other than the komon were appearing freely during this period, dictated by a trend toward gorgeous robes that peaked during the mid-Edo period. According to pictorial documentation of noh performances in this same period, however, the designs on

KATAGINU WITH BANANA LEAVES
IN KAMABARA FROM NŌ EZUSHIKI
Meiji period, 1887
Woodblock print
Private collection
figure 51

KATAGINU WITH CENTIPEDES IN KIKAZUZATŌ
FROM NŌ EZUSHIKI
Meiji period, 1887
Woodblock print
Private collection
figure 52

the kataginu were rather staid, or at least subdued. The dramatic, often playful designs that audiences today have come to associate with kyōgen therefore seem to be a late-Edo period development.

SUŌ

Suō were originally worn by the warrior class and made of plain-weave hemp; those adapted to noh and kyōgen are constructed in the same manner. In noh the suō is worn by a fallen warrior, but in kyōgen the suō is worn by a successful personage of some standing. Kyōgen suō can be divided into two basic categories, according to the size of decorative motifs and the type of dye technique used. Large, beautiful designs in bright colors as seen on *Suō with Pine, Bamboo Curtains, Plum Blossoms, Poem Cards, Roundels, and Seashore Landscape Picture Cards* (cat. 29, p. 160) were designed to catch the eye and express the ebullience of a good-natured character such as a feudal lord (daimyo), a man of fortune, or a bridegroom. The motifs on this particular Edo-period suō are considered lucky omens and hint back to court culture during the Heian period (794–1185). To achieve the placement of such colorful designs against the black ground, the innovative hand-drawn paste-resist dyeing technique known as *yūzenzome* was utilized. In this process, perfected in the eighteenth century by the Kyoto fan painting master Miyazaki Yūzen, a design is outlined with a starch paste that is squeezed through a metal-tipped paper funnel. After the paste has dried, dyes are carefully applied with a brush to the areas inside the paste lines. The fabric is steamed to set the dyes and then rinsed in water to remove the paste. The white thin lines defining the details of the bamboo curtains on this suō are areas where the paste had been applied to resist the dye. The drawn paste-resist yūzenzome technique enabled artisans to express themselves in a freer manner than any previous dye method and allowed actors to order any designs that came to mind.

The second type of suō has minute overall patterns in subdued colors, as seen on *Suō with Weeping Cherry Tree Blossoms* (cat. 27, p. 165). This type is worn by more staid characters such as small landowners (*shōmyō*), dignified farmers whose business takes them to the capital, and father-in-law figures. The difference between the types is so striking that it is tempting to say that they belong to entirely different worlds. The pattern for this second kind of suō is achieved with a cut paper stencil.

**SHOKUNIN TSUKUSHI-E
(VIEWS OF ARTISANS AT WORK)**
(detail: stencil dyers)
Edo period, seventeenth century
Suntory Museum of Art, Tokyo
catalogue 111

SUŌ WITH SCATTERED UMBRELLAS
Edo period, eighteenth century
Toyohashi Uomachi Noh Association, Aichi Prefecture
catalogue 28

**NAGA-KAMISHIMO WITH ABUNDANT
TREASURES**
Edo period, eighteenth century
Hayashibara Museum of Art,
Okayama Prefecture
catalogue 31

Fermented persimmon juice was applied thickly to high-quality handmade paper (*washi*) to ensure the strength of the paper by making it non-absorbent. The design was then cut out of the paper. Although the design motif on the weeping cherry suō resembles pampas grass, here it depicts thin willowlike branches with leaves and tiny flowers that appear to be cherry blossoms. Originally it may have been intended as an amalgamated design, which for simplicity's sake was labeled as weeping cherry. The cut paper stencil of weeping cherry was placed onto the hemp fabric and a paste resist was applied on the cloth through the cut stencil (cat. 111, p. 167). The stencil then was carefully lifted off the cloth and placed in the next position to repeat the process. Once the hemp fabric was sufficiently covered with the stenciled paste resist it was left to dry. The fabric was then dyed. Afterwards, the paste was rinsed off, revealing the design. The size of the stencil paper for this design was quite small, and since over the course of time the stencils were made successively larger and longer (*chūgata*), this pattern is clearly of the old style popular during the early Edo period. The skill evident in filling in the design over the entire surface of the fabric, avoiding the monotony one might expect when a stencil is used repeatedly, is remarkable. The cutting of the stencil was also gracefully done and is another mark of the elegance of the early style. Few such examples of early stencil paste-resist dyeing exist, making this suō very important. The matching long pants (*nagabakama*) indicate that this ensemble was worn for the role of an influential character such as a small landowner or father-in-law. There are many extant suō worn without matching hakama. In such cases, short ankle-length hakama would be worn for such roles as a farmer traveling to the capital on business. This was the formal dress style of Edo-period commoners, when suō were known as *kake suō*.

The attention to detail in laying out the design pattern of *Suō with Scattered Umbrellas* (cat. 28, p. 168) was probably not apparent when the robe was draped on the actor and worn in performance. When spread out so that the repeat pattern of umbrellas is visible in its entirety, however, the design is highly effective. Such care and attention to detail, and the effort made to avoid monotony, are not limited to kyōgen costumes but are characteristic of Japanese arts as a whole. The umbrella pattern takes as its subject an article familiar in everyday life; as such it is a very suitable design for a kyōgen costume. In addition, viewers would be familiar with the popular kyōgen play about umbrellas, *Suehirogari* (An umbrella instead of a fan). On the one hand, as a costume for a man of good fortune who appears in a play laden with images of good fortune, it may seem overdone and lose its appeal. On the other hand, that the message of good fortune delivered by the image of the umbrella is reinforced by the diamond-shaped abstract snowflake crest (*yukiwa*) is notable (cat. 28). In the center, over the dandelion depicted within the crest, is the Chinese character (*kanji*) for "big." This would appear to be one of the kanji found in the name of the person who ordered the robe, or a personalized crest such as found on kabuki costumes.

SUŌ WITH SCATTERED UMBRELLAS
(detail: crest)
Edo period, eighteenth century
Toyohashi Uomachi Noh Association,
Aichi Prefecture
catalogue 28

NAGA-KAMISHIMO

The combination of a kataginu and matching long hakama is known as a naga-kamishimo. The naga-kamishimo is worn by characters of a status slightly greater than that of Tarō Kaja (the servant) but not so important as a small landowner. These would include such characters as the Master, the Uncle, and so forth. In the waki kyōgen plays featuring the household Shinto gods, and in plays of celebration, the naga-kamishimo may be worn regardless of the character type in order to emphasize the celebratory nature of the play. The emphasis is on the dignity of the character, and the stencil-dyed design expresses this most effectively. In a typical stencil-dyed textile the background is a solid dark color while the design is reversed in white. Although the naga-kamishimo is not as dignified as the suō, it is still a costume worn by a character with some status.

Naga-kamishimo with Abundant Treasures (cat. 31, p. 169) has a particularly remarkable design. First, the striking background was paste-resist dyed into large forms known as *matsukawabishi* (pine-bark lozenge). The selection of small motifs is known as *takarazukushi* (abundant treasures) and were drawn in ink and then painted with pigment. The celebratory meaning of the takarazukushi, which originated in China, was respected in Japan, and by the early Edo period various Japanese treasures were added to the design. The back of this robe, for example, displays ink drawings of Japanese woven straw raincoats, woven umbrellas, treasure pouches, pine, bamboo, and mandarin oranges. Small shoulder drums are also found on the matching hakama. Because the ink lines are delicately drawn with a limited use of crimson, the design never becomes too ostentatious and remains suitable for kyōgen. The design is appropriate for the supplicant in a waki kyōgen play such as *Fuku no kami* (The god of happiness) or *Daikoku renga* (Daikoku and the poets).

KATAGINU

Without question, the charm of kyōgen costume ultimately lies in the kataginu. The design of the kataginu expresses volumes about the character wearing it – usually the feudal servants, Tarō Kaja and Jirō Kaja, as well as other characters that move actively around the entire stage. Though the kataginu is designed like a painted picture, it is not made simply to be admired as a painting: its basic function as a stage costume is always stressed. Clearly a great deal of consideration went into the design of the kataginu for effective use onstage. For example, since it is worn over a robe and short hakama, the front panels are arranged to hang evenly down the front of the hakama. In the back the kataginu hangs over the hips and is fastened tightly with a cotton sash (*koshiobi*), which is tied in the front and hangs down in a double layer with three crests for decoration. The pictorial motif on the back of the kataginu would be divided at the hips by a belt when worn. With this in mind, the composition was designed in two parts, upper and lower.

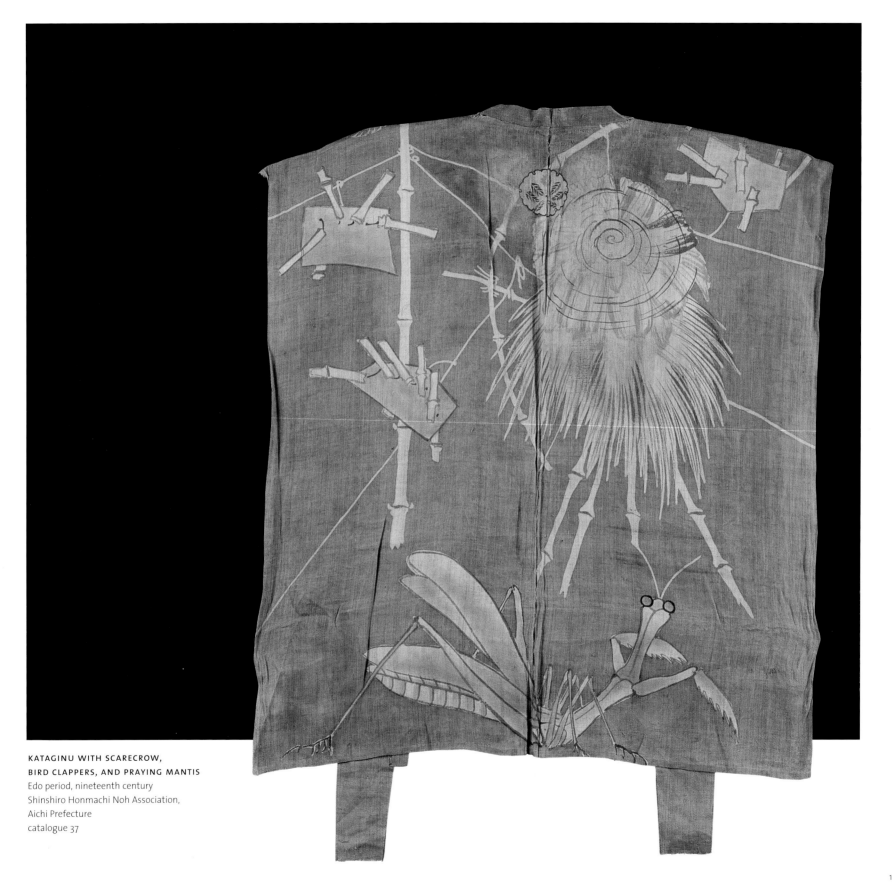

KATAGINU WITH SCARECROW,
BIRD CLAPPERS, AND PRAYING MANTIS
Edo period, nineteenth century
Shinshiro Honmachi Noh Association,
Aichi Prefecture
catalogue 37

KATAGINU WITH WATERFALL AND CHERRY BLOSSOMS
Edo period, seventeenth–eighteenth century
Eisei Bunko Museum, Tokyo
catalogue 34

**KATAGINU WITH TRIPLE-COMMA (TOMOE)
SAILS AND TATTERED FENCE**
Edo period, nineteenth century
Hayashibara Museum of Art, Okayama Prefecture
catalogue 35

The motifs for kataginu come from every possible source, and are beautifully realized. Changes in nature and the atmosphere of the seasons are expressed through depictions of seasonal grasses, flowers, and trees. Fruits and vegetables represented include peaches, chestnuts, radishes (cat. 33, p. 6), and turnips. Animals include dogs, rabbits (cat. 38, p. 157), monkeys, and bats.[5] Birds, even birds that rarely appear in other Japanese designs such as the crow, are used for kataginu. Insect designs are difficult to incorporate on clothing, but they are used on kyōgen kataginu without hesitation. The praying mantis pictured on *Kataginu with Scarecrow, Bird Clappers, and Praying Mantis* (cat. 37, p. 172) and other small creatures such as snails are meant to surprise and delight. Fish and shellfish motifs are also numerous. The crab in the satirical play *Kani yamabushi* (Crab and the mountain priest), for example, relates to a crab spirit whose appearance deflates the arrogance of a mountain priest. Not surprisingly, scenery is also used to beautiful effect, such as a full moon rising over an autumn field,[6] smoke rising from salt kilns, or views of villages with grass-thatched huts. Annual events also provide a rich source of images: the sacred Shinto rope decorated with new green leaves for the New Year, a sardine head and holly for the spring equinox, orange blossoms and the cuckoo for the summer, bamboo poles decorated with rhododendron and azalea flowers for folk festivals, and Gion Temple amulets and arrowroot for the Gion Festival. Even simple utensils, such as spear sheaths, gargoyle roof tiles, coins, and so forth, are used as motifs. Finally, geometric designs like circles, rectangles, or triangles may also appear on the front of kataginu. Altogether, the array of design possibilities appears to be limitless. It is noteworthy, however, that mythical subjects such as the Chinese lion, dragon, and phoenix, which often appear on noh robes, are not selected for kyōgen costumes. This suggests that the design motifs are meant to reflect the heart and spirit of kyōgen.

The techniques for applying patterns to the hand-woven hemp kataginu are no different from those used on the suō. Paste-resist techniques are frequently used. White resist patterns (*shiroage*) stand out best against a dark blue ground. After paste is applied to areas of the cloth intended to remain white, the fabric is immersed in indigo dye. A red oxide or dark black ink may be added to highlight certain parts of the design (cat. 34, p. 173). Color may be applied to the white areas, or it can be added with the paste-thread technique. Both are yūzenzome techniques requiring a skillful hand or brush; the resulting subtlety of the color is suitable for hemp and for kyōgen as well. Sometimes the white paste-resisted areas are employed like a painter's canvas. Pigments used for hand-drawn motifs include cinnabar, red ocher, and iron oxide. Green, indigo, and dark red watercolors are also used. Mineral pigments not employed are green (copper) rust and lapis lazuli. In the examples of designs drawn directly onto reserved white areas, it is likely that well-known artists were consulted. Finally, small designs created by a stencil are especially noteworthy. In some, a paste-resist is employed first, and the white areas are then dyed using a stencil cut in small designs. When the ground color is complex, however, this takes a great deal of time. Other than the small pattern, there are middle-sized stencil designs such as those on the suō. These robes are very valuable as evidence of early modern stencil dye techniques.

In *Kataginu with Triple-Comma Sails and Tattered Fence* (cat. 35, p. 173), once belonging to the Ikeda clan of Bizen (now Okayama Prefecture), the comparative narrowness of the shoulders indicates that it is in the older style that was popular during the early Edo period. It is prized for the wonderfully playful rendering of the boat sails in round shapes that look like commas. The sharp outline of the matsukawabishi-shaped crest was clearly meant to contrast with the curves of the abstract boat sails. The right shoulder is covered in a cloud, while at the hem is the tattered fence, offering a striking contrast of curved and straight lines. Although the attraction of kyōgen designs is said to lie in their realism and down-to-earth quality, there are designs that do not fit this description, and this is one example. The fact that this kataginu, with its narrow shoulders, is tailored in an earlier style suggests that a nonrealistic quality may be characteristic of an older style. What is thought of as typical kyōgen design seems to have flourished in the late Edo and modern periods.

The examples presented here demonstrate that designs for kataginu are numerous and varied. Not only are scenes of town life depicted, but also lively scenes of life in the countryside, indicating the presence of kyōgen actors in both locations. The most important aspect of a kyōgen kataginu design is that first it surprises the audience, and in the next instant moves them to laughter.

Translated by Carolyn A. Morley

NOTES

1. The kyōgen crest, a snowflake with a dandelion within, is the most common one for kyōgen robes where individual crests are not used. The design is particularly appropriate for a popular theater like kyōgen. Just how the crest was chosen is not clear. However, one might theorize that the sound of the word for dandelion, *tanpopo*, echoes the sound of the shoulder drum (*kotsuzumi*) used in noh. Moreover, when this tender wildflower is cut and put in water, the end of the cut stem curls inward, creating the shape of a miniature drum. Since the dandelion comes up through the snow in early spring, the crest can be seen as both the surface of a shoulder drum and as a snowflake. Scattered spots around the crest, known as snow powder, add further credence to the theory.

2. However, this costume was intended for a celebratory New Year's performance, and the robes were meant to be worn with a court hat (*eboshi*), so a suō would probably have been more appropriate.

3. At the time, the word "kamishimo" was written with the characters for "above" and "below" rather than the character used today. Therefore, it is difficult to determine that the upper garment is the same as what is later referred to as the kataginu. If we just consider the characters for "above" and "below," then the suō would seem to be the more obvious choice. However, for our purposes I use it to refer to the kataginu exclusively.

4. Toraakira seems to have decided that if costumes were too realistic it would be difficult to appear before government officials.

5. Bats are usually avoided in Japanese design, but there is one extant kataginu with an imposing figure of a bat with spread wings.

6. This particular scene hints at something hidden within an atmosphere overflowing with emotion. There is a depth that goes beyond the visual pleasure in the uniqueness and surprising boldness of the design. One is reminded of the play *Tsukimizatō* (A blind man goes moon viewing), which is about the instability of human life, subject to the betrayal of trust. However, at the end of the play we are not overwhelmed by a feeling of distrust, but rather are buoyed up by feelings of lightness. These feelings, found in this remarkable design of the moon rising over the autumn fields, are the source of the depth and breadth in kyōgen. Kataginu of this type were probably common at the outset of the early modern period or early Edo period.

KO NŌ KYŌGEN NO ZU
(OLD NOH AND KYŌGEN ILLUSTRATIONS)
(detail: *Dōjōji*)
Edo period, seventeenth century
National Noh Theater, Tokyo
catalogue 119

THE STAGING OF NOH: COSTUMES AND MASKS IN A PERFORMANCE CONTEXT

MONICA BETHE

A noh play unfolds through transformation; this is most often realized in changes of costume, accompanied by shifts in music and dance style. In *Okina* a man becomes a god through the donning of a mask. In *Dōjōji* a dancer turns into a revengeful snake through exchanging a mask and shedding a robe. In *Tadanori* what seemed an old man is revealed to be the ghost of a young warrior. The change of costume often occurs during a short interlude (*ai*) between two acts, in the first of which the main character appears simply to be a local person with knowledge of the area but in the second reveals him/herself to be a ghost, god, or demon. Even some one-act plays that do not follow this formula include transformations: in *Matsukaze* a young woman dons the robe of her lover and is possessed by his spirit; in *Hagoromo* a similar robing restores celestial powers to a moon maiden.

Most noh center on a single main character, the *shite*. It is this role that undergoes transformation, and by extension it is the costumes for this role that embody the changes in the play. The elements of the costume – a combination of inner robes, overgarments, and bifurcated skirts, as well as masks, fans, and other handheld objects – were established over time. The outfits, imitative of street attire of the sixteenth century, are role-defined, and similar roles in different plays can be costumed identically.[1] Within the limitations of prescribed garment types, however, the variety of pattern and color combinations available presents a wide spectrum of possibilities to an actor preparing for a performance. It is the actor himself (there being neither director nor costume designer) who selects the costume, following guidelines set by tradition. In his choice he seeks to evoke the distinct character of the play, the mood that emerges from the flow of the text, and the style of the music and movement. The costume must be appropriate in particular ways. There should be no spring flowers in a play set in the fall. Color should reflect age (i.e., red for the young, no red for older figures). Social status should be conveyed by the tailoring and in the color of the collars. The mood of the play should be evoked through the color, size, and density of pattern, and the inclusion or exclusion of gold. Few costumes are intended to be "read" in the sense that their patterns carry specific meanings, though inappropriate imagery is avoided, and some plays, like *Okina* and *Dōjōji*, have prescribed design patterns.

Noh plays take an average of an hour and a half to perform, kyōgen plays around twenty minutes.[2] A day's program is generally made up of a number of noh and kyōgen performed in alternation. Early records list as many as seventeen plays in a day.[3] The renown actor, playwright, and theorist Zeami Motokiyo (c. 1363–c. 1443) suggested ordering these according to the principle of *jo ha kyū*, which entails a slow beginning, a developmental section, and a fast-paced finale requiring concentrated skill.[4] By the eighteenth century a system was established whereby each play was placed within a numbered category, and a program was constructed by presenting plays in numerical order. A full program would begin with the ritual piece *Okina*, followed by five noh and four kyōgen, and end with a brief return to jo in the form of a light congratulatory piece. Today the principle of arrangement

PERFORMANCE OF OKINA
AT THE GOLDEN PAVILION, KYOTO
figure 53

CATEGORY	DEITY	JAPANESE NAME	MODE	PLAY	PLAYWRIGHT/PERIOD
OKINA			CELEBRATORY	*Okina*	*(thirteenth century or earlier)*
FIRST		(WAKI NOH)	CONGRATULATORY	*Kamo*	ZENCHIKU *(1405–c. 1470)*
SECOND	WARRIOR	(SHURA NOH)	NARRATIVE	*Tadanori*	ZEAMI (C. *1363–c. 1443)*
THIRD	WOMAN	(KAZURA NOH)	LYRICAL	*Hagoromo*	UNKNOWN *(fourteenth–fifteenth century)*
FOURTH	MISCELLANEOUS	(ZATSU NOH)	DRAMATIC	*Dōjōji*	UNKNOWN *(late-fifteenth century)*
FIFTH	DEMON	(KIJIN NOH)	DYNAMIC	*Kumasaka*	UNKNOWN *(mid- or late-fifteenth century)*
			FELICITOUS	*Shōjō*	UNKNOWN *(fifteenth century)*

TOYOKUNI SAIREI ZU
(CEREMONY AT THE TOYOKUNI SHRINE FESTIVAL)
Edo period, seventeenth century
Pair of six-panel screens; ink and colors on paper
Each 65⅞ x 138⅞ in. (167.2 x 352.6 cm)
Tokugawa Art Museum, Nagoya
figure 54

remains the same, though many programs present only one, two, or three noh with one kyōgen.

The representative plays from each category discussed here cover the major costume types, as well as a spectrum of different playwrights from various stages in the development of noh.

OKINA

Okina celebrates peace on earth, fertility, harmony, and long life. Solemnity and ritual pervade the first section, during which the white-faced, smiling Okina (cat. 137, p. 14) dances. The second section, where the black-faced Sanbasō (cat. 143, p. 15) dances, exudes energy. Ritualistic and solemn, *Okina* is performed on celebratory occasions, particularly on New Year's Day. In addition, *Okina*-related pieces are performed in shrines throughout Japan during festivals for the new year, spring planting, and fall harvest.[5] Many of these folk versions preserve aspects of early performance that provide important insights into practices that predate noh. A performance of *Okina* lent authority to such occasions as the Toyokuni Shrine Festival (fig. 54, p. 179). The piece was also accorded special importance by the Tokugawa shogunate when it adopted noh as the official entertainment for state occasions.

Several aspects of the performance of *Okina* set it apart from standard noh plays: Ritual dominates over drama, so the piece lacks narrative interaction. Important moments take place offstage, out of sight of the audience. The donning of the mask, on the other hand, is done onstage in full view. The masks have attached eyebrows (horsehair for Sanbasō, rope pompoms for Okina) and detached chins lashed on with cord ties. The chorus sits behind the instrumentalists rather than at their side. There are three *kotsuzumi* (shoulder drum) players rather than one, and they play without the *ōtsuzumi* (hip drum) during the Okina (noh) section. The Sanbasō (kyōgen) section follows seamlessly from the Okina section and mimics its structure.

Okina as performed today begins backstage with a religious ritual.[6] The masks are set on an altar as embodied forms of deities (*shintai*). The performers gather to worship them and be purified (fig. 55), then the masks are placed in a special box (cat. 138). The young man playing the role of mask bearer carries the box down the covered passageway, or "bridge," that leads onto the empty stage, bows, and retires to upstage left. Zeami stipulates that the mask bearer be played by a handsome young man, preferably a youth, but warns that a childlike appearance would be inappropriate for someone carrying a laden box. The box carrier, he states, should be dressed in a tall lacquered hat (*eboshi*) and matched suit (*hitatare*).[7]

Then the man who will subsequently play Okina enters and bows downstage center. The musicians, dancers, and chorus enter and take positions. A young unmasked performer, Senzai, steps to the center and praises the reign of "eternal prosperity," relating it to the tortoise and crane from the legendary mountain of Hōrai and to an inexhaustible waterfall that never diminishes even under

OKINA PRE-PERFORMANCE CEREMONY
figure 55

DONNING OF THE OKINA MASK
figure 56 a, b

OKINA MASK BOX
Edo period, eighteenth century
Museum of Noh Artifacts, Sasayama, Hyōgo Prefecture
catalogue 138

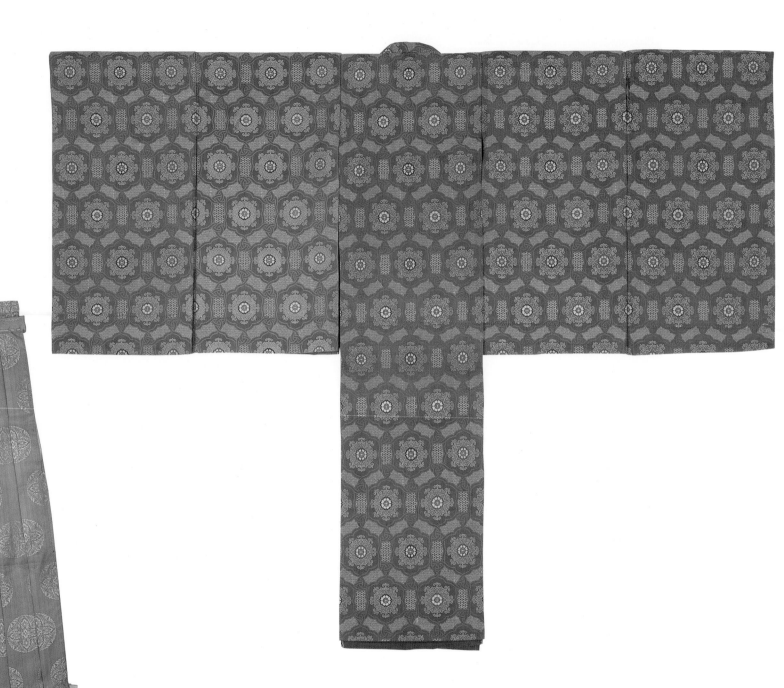

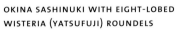

OKINA SASHINUKI WITH EIGHT-LOBED
WISTERIA (YATSUFUJI) ROUNDELS
Edo period, eighteenth century
Bunka Gakuen Costume Museum, Tokyo
catalogue 140

OKINA KARIGINU WITH LINKED HEXAGONS
AND FLORAL MEDALLION PATTERN (SHOKKŌ)
Edo period, eighteenth century
Fujita Museum of Art, Osaka
catalogue 139

KOSHIOBI (SASH) WITH EIGHT TREASURES
Edo–Meiji period, nineteenth century
Hikone Castle Museum, Shiga Prefecture
catalogue 141

OKINA FAN WITH MOUNT HŌRAI
Edo period, nineteenth century
Toyohashi Uomachi Noh Association, Aichi Prefecture
catalogue 142

PERFORMANCE OF OKINA
figure 57

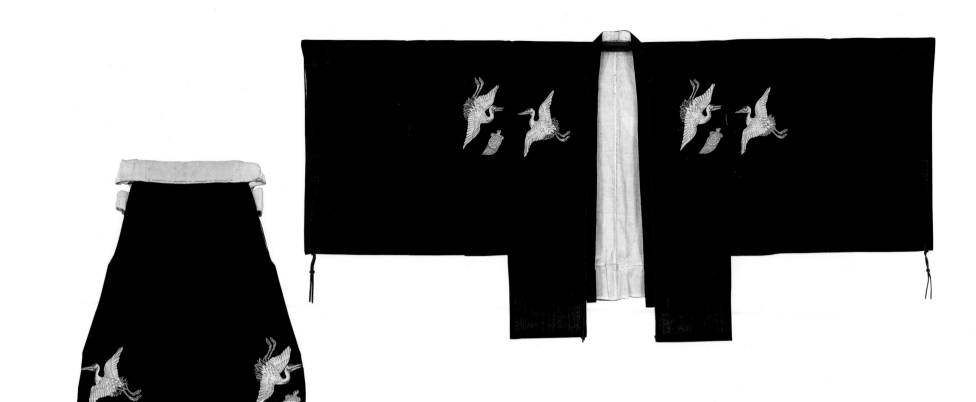

SANBASŌ HITATARE AND HAKAMA
WITH CRANES AND TORTOISES
Edo period, nineteenth century
Private collection
catalogue 144

PERFORMANCE OF SANBASŌ
figure 58

**SANBASŌ HAKAMA WITH CRANES,
TORTOISES, AND PINE**
Edo period, eighteenth century
Fujita Museum of Art, Osaka
catalogue 145

**SANBASŌ FAN WITH CRANES,
TORTOISES, PINE, BAMBOO, AND WATER**
Edo period, eighteenth century
Tokyo National Museum
catalogue 146

a relentless sun. He then dances, purifying the stage by stamping and twirling his long sleeves to mark out the cardinal directions and chase away evil.

During the latter part of this dance, the actor performing the role of Okina unobtrusively takes a mask from the box in front of him, bows to it in reverence, and places it on his face. An attendant ties the cords at the back of his head (fig. 56, p. 181). This reverential masking is identical with the one that happens in front of a mirror just offstage in a standard noh performance. The fact that it occurs in front of the audience creates a visible distinction between the man who walked onstage, and the god-figure of Okina.[8] It emphasizes that the audience is also taking part in the sacred ritual. Okina then stands at center stage with his arms stretched out to the side (fig. 57, p. 183). The chorus chants "Let us celebrate our lord," and after invoking the crane and tortoise as symbols of long life, ends with "Under heaven all is at peace, the world safe."

Okina then performs the "heaven, earth, and man" dance. Slowly he advances to the downstage right corner. Each step is articulated by three measured movements: sliding the foot forward flat along the surface of the stage boards, tilting the foot up using the heel as a fulcrum, and replacing the toes to the ground while shifting the weight onto the foot. The steps interact rhythmically with the unmetered beats and calls of the three kotsuzumi players, who sometimes play in unison and some-times in alternation with each other.[9] At the downstage right corner the actor stamps, while looking up to indicate heaven. Next he moves to the downstage left corner, where he looks down to indicate earth. Then, upstage center, he twirls his sleeve around his raised arm to indicate man (fig. 57, p. 183). Okina's symbolic action has established harmony in the universe. The final text ends with a mantralike repetition of "peace for ten thousand years."

Finished with the role, the actor playing Okina takes off his mask, returns it to the box, bows at center stage, then exits.[10] At this point the ōtsuzumi drummer takes his seat, and the actor playing Sanbasō is called up to perform the kyōgen's lighter recapitulation.[11] As with the more solemn first half, there are two dances, one unmasked, the other masked, and the donning of the mask is a part of the stage ritual. The first dance, *momi no dan*, awakens the earth. Using the stage as a drum, the dancer stamps out complex rhythms, punctuating them with wild calls similar to those emitted by the drummers. His traversal of the stage includes vigorous leaps and sleeve manipulation. Then he dons a black mask and takes up a *suzu* (bell tree, cat. 147). The second dance, *suzu no dan*, mimics the planting and harvesting of rice. Sanbasō crisscrosses the stage, shaking the suzu to call forth life energy. The momentum increases through repetition, bolstered by trills on the flute and quick strokes on the large and small hand drums. Suddenly, the excitement ceases. The mask is removed, the dancer departs, and the musicians and chorus prepare for the next play.

The white-masked Okina is dressed in the *kariginu* (cat. 139, p. 182) and *sashinuki* (cat. 140, p. 182) of the noble class, lending him a dignity and authority commensurate with his role as peacemaker. The unmasked Senzai and black-masked Sanbasō both wear matched suits of bast fiber, *hitatare* (cat. 144, p. 184), typical of samurai garb and suggesting ties with agriculture. While the woven patterns on Okina's garments follow ancient court designs, the paste-resist patterns on Senzai's and Sanbasō's suits represent the crane and tortoise mentioned in the play. The actors' headgear also indicates the different status of the respective roles. The black lacquered *Okina eboshi* is tall and rounded, with an indented front section and white cording that forms a cross. Sanbasō's tall black lacquered *kensaki eboshi* (spearhead hat) is shaped like an unequal pentagon and fits squarely on the head.

Pictorial evidence suggests these costumes were already standard in the sixteenth century.[12] Little is precisely known about earlier costuming, though Zeami's son records in the *Sarugaku dangi* that the costume for Okina should avoid being ostentatious, that the performer should give an impression of modesty (thus gold-brocaded *kinran* is rarely seen), and that one of the basic colors should be used.[13] As kariginu are most prominent among the limited number of Muromachi-period (1392–1568) noh robes still extant, it is possible that already in Zeami's time kariginu were worn for the Okina role.

OKINA

ROLE	MASK	COSTUME
Menbako: mask-box carrier	unmasked	hitatare
Senzai: stage purifier	unmasked	kamishimo hitatare with large cracked-ice pattern; can be brown, black, or blue and usually includes crane and tortoise motif as a mon (crest) decoration
Okina: old man/god	Okina	underrobe (*kitsuke*)
		kariginu with shokkō pattern
		sashinuki with large round or oblong medallions
		white (or other color) figured satin (koshiobi)
		Okina hat (eboshi)
		fan with Hōrai motif
Sanbasō: earth god	Sanbasō	atsuita with facing cranes on a red ground
		kamishimo hitatare with cranes and tortoises on a black or dark blue ground
		hat (tate eboshi)
		fan with Hōrai motif

PERFORMANCE OF KAMO
figure 59

KASUGA WAKAMIYA ONMATSURI EMAKI
(FESTIVALS AT KASUGA WAKAMIYA SHRINE) (detail)
Edo period, eighteenth century
Kasuga Taisha, Nara Prefecture
catalogue 116

KAMO (ALSO YAHATE KAMO OR YAWATE KAMO)

This first-category "deity" play is concerned with the power of water. Wakeikazuchi, the Thunder God, appears in a brief climactic finale to perform a rain dance. He stomps out the sounds of thunder, and swishing paper streamers appear as flashing lightning. The rain will bring a rich harvest and is a welcome blessing after the summer's heat. The function of *Kamo* to call forth rain was evident already in the first recorded performance in 1515, when it began a program of seventeen plays celebrating "the joy of rain."[14]

Leading up to the final thunderstorm are celebrations of water as pure, clear, and sacred, to be dipped and offered to the gods. The water flows in rivers that travel over time and space, bearing the source of life, cleansing the heart as well as the body, and evoking the world of green growth and luxuriant shade.

The play opens with priests traveling from Muro to Kyoto to visit the Kamo Shrine. The lower shrine, Shimogamo, houses the Mother Goddess, and the upper shrine, Kamigamo, standing at the foot of the city's northern hills, is home of the Thunder God.[15] On their arrival at the lower shrine, the priests notice an arrow with white feathers stuck into the sand of the riverbank. This scene is depicted in the *Kasuga Wakamiya onmatsuri emaki* (Festivals at Kasuga Wakamiya Shrine, cat. 116) as an outdoor performance at the annual firelight noh at Kōfukuji in Nara.

The priests inquire about the significance of the arrow from two approaching women who carry buckets on their way to the river to dip water for a sacred offering. In reply to the priests' questions they relate the story of the shrine.

Once in the hamlet of Kamo there lived a woman of the Hata clan. Morning and evening she came to the riverside and drew water to dedicate to the deity. One day a white-feathered arrow came floating down the stream and lodged in her pail. She scooped it up, brought it home, and stuck it in the eaves of her hut. Then unexpectedly she became pregnant and bore a son. When the boy was three, people gathered to ask who his father was. He pointed to the arrow, which turned into lightning, rose into the heavens, and became the deity Splitting Thunder. The mother also became a goddess.[16]

The white-feathered arrow bears deeper implications as well: the women imply that it extols the military aristocracy ruling Japan at the time. The theme of honoring the government's capacity to keep peace and harmony runs through all first-category plays.

The arrow stands downstage center as a stage prop (as seen in a *Kamo* performance, fig. 59, p. 188). The framework supporting it is reminiscent of the conical sand formations that stand in the upper Kamo Shrine. In the second act similar imagery occurs for the hand prop held by the Thunder God (cat. 118), a purification stick with white folded paper streamers at its tip.

Before the women leave they intimate that they themselves are gods and beg the priests to wait for the disclosure of a miracle. An *ai-kyōgen* interlude (a kyōgen actor performing within a noh) bridges the first act with the revelation of the god in the second act. Today the most common interlude involves a subsidiary god of the shrine entertaining the priests with a lighthearted dance to instrumental accompaniment. The *ai* wears a bearded Noborihige mask, tall hat (*zukin*), and plain-colored *mizugoromo*. Originally, however, a kyōgen play called *Onda* (also *Taue*) was commonly inserted. Since this play presents the act of planting rice, it is thematically tied to *Kamo*.

The second act begins when the Mother Goddess appears in a flowing *chōken* robe, her long loose hair topped by a crown with quivering gold pendants. Embracing everyone in the world as her children, she guards the land and performs a graceful dance to lilting flute and drums. Then, kneeling close to the front of the stage, she dips her fan into the cool refreshing waters in an act of purification and renewal.[17] Suddenly the ground begins to shake, and the Thunder God appears, guardian

NŌ KYŌGEN EMAKI
(NOH AND KYŌGEN PICTURE SCROLLS)
(detail: *Kamo*, acts 1 and 2)
Edo period, eighteenth century
Tokyo National Museum
catalogue 118

of the capital and protector of the bonds between lord and subject. Momentarily transfigured to earthly shape so he may save sentient beings, he stamps and rushes about, zigzagging across the stage. He becomes dew and lightning and rain, swinging his sleeve high over his head, or flailing his streamers and stomping out rhythms. Heralding the ripening of grain, he waves the Mother Goddess away, then pierces the clouds and mist to ascend the heavenly path.

One of the challenges of the shite role in *Kamo* is enacting the contrast between the gentle role of the woman in the first act and the masculine vigor of the Thunder God in the second. The costumes and masks of the first act are elegant and restrained. The patterns on the *karaori* (cat. 149, p. 192) robe worn by the shite are ornate, while her companion wears somewhat simpler garb. The shite's Zō-onna mask (cat. 148, p. 191) has a cool beauty reserved for roles of deities; her companion wears the standard full-cheeked Ko-omote (cat. 162, p. 202). In contrast, the costume for the Thunder God (cat. 153, p. 192; cat. 152, 154, 155, p.193) should flash with his swift, sharp movements. Dark grounds with large gold or silver patterns work best. His gold Ōtobide mask (cat. 151, p. 191), with its large red tongue and bulging eyes, is offset by a flaring headpiece of shaggy red hair topped by a small black lacquer crown (*tōkanmuri*).

Konparu Zenchiku (1405–c. 1470), the son-in-law of Zeami, is thought possibly to have based *Kamo* on an earlier *dengaku* (field music) piece performed during another annual festival at Kamo.[18]

KAMO

ROLE	MASK	COSTUME
waki: priest from Muro Shrine	unmasked	plain mizugoromo
		plain noshime
wakizure: his servants	unmasked	plain mizugoromo
		plain noshime
shite: woman	Zō-onna	karaori without red
tsure: woman	Ko-omote	karaori with red
ai: subsidiary god	Noborihige	mizugoromo
		underrobe (kitsuke)
		zukin cloth headgear
nochizure: Mother Goddess	Ko-omote	chōken
		surihaku
		ōkuchi
nochijite: Thunder God (Wakeikazuchi)	Ōtobide	atsuita
		kariginu
		hangire
		tōkanmuri crown

KAZURAOBI (HEADBAND) WITH TRAILING BRANCHES OF CHERRY BLOSSOMS
Edo period, eighteenth century
Eisei Bunko Museum, Tokyo
catalogue 150

ZŌ-ONNA MASK
Deme Zekan (d. 1616)
Edo period, eighteenth century
Toyohashi Uomachi Noh Association, Aichi Prefecture
catalogue 148

ŌTOBIDE MASK
Momoyama–Edo period, seventeenth century
Toyohashi Uomachi Noh Association, Aichi Prefecture
catalogue 151

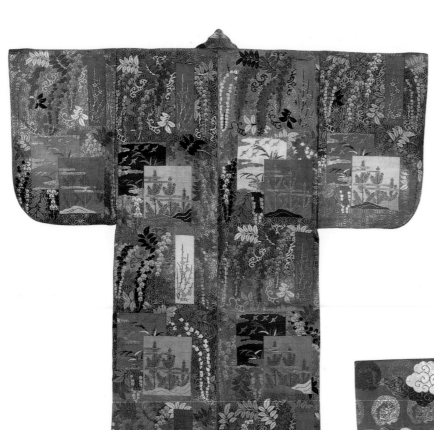

KARAORI WITH FLAX, WISTERIA,
PICTURE PAPERS (SHIKISHI), AND POEM
CARDS (TANZAKU)
Edo period, eighteenth century
Tokyo National Museum
catalogue 149

ATSUITA WITH DRAGON ROUNDELS
AND AUSPICIOUS CLOUDS
Edo period, eighteenth century
Hayashibara Museum of Art, Okayama Prefecture
catalogue 153

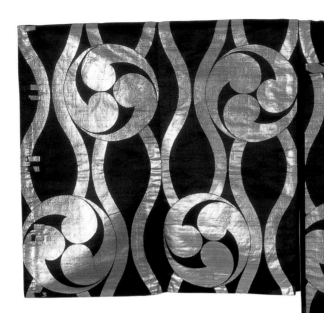

KOSHIOBI (SASH) WITH SWIRLING CLOUD CRESTS
Edo–Meiji period, nineteenth century
Hikone Castle Museum, Shiga Prefecture
catalogue 155

**KARIGINU WITH INVERTED COMMA
ROUNDELS (TOMOE) AND SERPENTINE LINE
PATTERN (TATEWAKU)**
Edo period, eighteenth century
Hayashibara Museum of Art, Okayama Prefecture
catalogue 152

**HANGIRE WITH STYLIZED LIGHTNING
AND TRIPLE COMMA CLOUD ROUNDELS (TOMOE)**
Edo period, nineteenth century
Noda Shrine, Yamaguchi Prefecture
catalogue 154

PERFORMANCE OF TADANORI
figure 60

TADANORI

Tadanori is named after a poet-courtier and warrior of the Taira (also Heike) clan who died in the Battle of Ichinotani on Suma Beach in 1184. Typical of the second category of warrior pieces (*shura* noh), it is based on episodes from narratives such as *Tales of the Heike* and *Gempei seisuiki* (The rise and fall of the Genji and Heike), telling of the demise of the Heike and the rise of the Genji, who became the first ruling shoguns.[19]

A battle scene with mimetic dance forms the highlight of warrior plays. The narrative mode dictates that the shite play all the roles. In *Tadanori* he begins as the title character, then briefly acts two roles simultaneously by also playing his own slayer. At times he switches between the two, but certain actions – crossing the arms above the body, or crossing the legs and twirling while sinking to the ground – represent two figures grappling with each other. He then returns to the dramatic present as the ghost of Tadanori. Angled stance, swift advances, sword-plunges, grappling, slaying and being slain – all make for a vivid dramatization that is more mimetic than most noh dance. Nonetheless the symbolism still relies on a fluid abstraction: crossed arms indicate two people wrestling; bodies twirl and sink to plummet from their horses; the drop of a hand means that it was sliced off; and a raised fan tilted down toward the head signifies the head being severed from behind. To facilitate active swordplay, the right sleeve of the outer jacket (chōken or *happi*) is slipped off, rolled up, and tucked into the belt at the back (fig. 60).

Artistry, however, is at least as much the topic of *Tadanori* as is bravery in battle. Indeed, Zeami may have created this category precisely with the intention of transforming the bombastic demonstrativeness of earlier battle pieces into aesthetic expressions of the human presence behind the warrior.[20] In his *Fūshikaden* Zeami suggests, "If you take a famous character from the Genji or the Heike and bring out the connection between him and poetry or music, then – so long as the play itself is well written – it will be more interesting than anything else."[21]

Tadanori is about a poet and his poem, but as the piece unfolds and circles back to itself, the way imagery can in a well-wrought poem, the play itself becomes an enactment of the poem at its center. The theme of Tadanori's poem is the blossoming cherry, so beautiful that it invites one to spend the night under it. Though the cherry tree is not represented physically on stage, its implied presence dominates the performance.

The traveling priest who opens the play has cast aside the world, which implies rejecting the attractions of beauty, yet he soon finds himself drawn to a cherry tree on Suma Beach. An old man arrives and sets an offering branch in front of the tree, for it is a memorial to the Battle of Ichinotani. When the priest requests shelter for the night, the old man replies that the cherry tree would make a fine lodging and its flowers a perfect host. Indeed, he continues, a man buried under it composed the poem:

Traveling late,
I lodge beneath this tree
Tonight, the blossoms will serve as host[22]

The priest recognizes the poem as Tadanori's, then agrees to pray for his soul. He rests under the tree and awaits a dream.

After an interlude, the ghost of Tadanori appears in battle array. He relates Tadanori's last hours and how, after he was slain, a paper inscribed with the poem was found tied to one of his arrows. Turning to the priest, the ghost claims himself to be the cherry tree, to have acted as host, and that the priest's passing the night there has actualized the poem.

The unity of the piece reaches farther than this imagery, for the priest is actually a follower of Tadanori's mentor, the renowned poet Fujiwara no Shunzei (1114–1204).[23] As Tadanori narrates in the second part, he secretly returned to Kyoto before his final battle to plead with Shunzei that one of his poems be included in an Imperial anthology, guaranteeing his recognition as a skilled poet. In fact, Shunzei did include a poem of his in the *Senzaishū*, but omitted Tadanori's name.[24] It would have been impossible to have thus honored a member of the defeated Heike clan.[25]

Just as Tadanori went to talk with Shunzei, so he now returns from the realm of the dead to plead with Shunzei's disciple to attribute the poem to him. His spirit cannot rest with the knowledge of this slight. The proof that Tadanori was indeed the author comes when the poem is read and the priest, and audience, experience it. Thus the priest, who has renounced the world, is drawn into a worldly encounter. Tadanori, through the priest's promise to relay his message to Shunzei's son and poetic heir, is released from his attachment and can find enlightenment.

The first act is dominated by the figure of the old man, poor yet devoted, gathering wood from the mountains.[26] It is drawn in subdued tones, and the costumes are simple: plain colors, slender lines, plain-weave textures. The old man's mask is a plainer version of a type seen in cat. 85, p. 59, his mizugoromo a plain-weave version of that in cat. 15, p. 233, and his *noshime* similar to the one in cat. 58, p. 247 (only without the midriff stripes). It mirrors the priest's garb except in the headdress.

The second act by contrast evokes a warrior's power as well as a courtier's elegance. The draping of the chōken, bound at the waist with one sleeve off, facilitates swordplay, though the diaphanous broad sleeve billows with the flow of the movements as it is flipped or twirled around the arm. Its gossamer lightness reminds us of the transience of the Heike clan.[27]

KOSHIOBI (SASH) WITH PAULOWNIA CRESTS
Edo–Meiji period, nineteenth century
Hikone Castle Museum, Shiga Prefecture
catalogue 160

ŌKUCHI WITH PINE, SEASHELLS,
AND FANS IN FLOWING WATER
Edo period, eighteenth century
Hikone Castle Museum, Shiga Prefecture
catalogue 159

KARAORI WITH BOAT SAILS, PINE TREES,
ABSTRACT PINE-BARK LOZENGES (MATSUKAWABISHI),
AND LINKED HEXAGON PATTERN (KIKKŌ)
Edo period, eighteenth century
Tokyo National Museum
catalogue 158

CHŌKEN WITH BUTTERFLIES
Edo period, eighteenth century
Hayashibara Museum of Art, Okayama Prefecture
catalogue 157

CHŪJŌ MASK
Iseki Kawachi Daijō Ieshige (d. c. 1646)
Edo period, seventeenth century
Toyohashi Uomachi Noh Association,
Aichi Prefecture
catalogue 156

TADANORI

ROLE	MASK	COSTUME
shite: old man	Waraijō or Asakurajō	light blue collar
		plain noshime or with small checks (kitsuke)
		plain mizugoromo
		satin koshiobi
		walking stick
		faggots/branch
waki: priest	unmasked	cloth hat (sumibōshi)
		plain noshime (kitsuke)
		mizugoromo
		satin koshiobi
		fan with ink painting (sumi-e)
		prayer beads
wakizure: priests	unmasked	same as waki
nochijite: ghost of Tadanori	Chūjō or Imawaka	warrior wig (kurotare)
		warrior's hat (nashiuchi eboshi)
		white sweat band (hachimaki)
		white collar with light blue or red
		karaori or nuihaku
		white, colored or patterned ōkuchi
		chōken or happi
		embroidered koshiobi
		sword
		warrior fan (shura ōgi)
		arrow with poem paper

SHURA ŌGI (WARRIOR FAN) WITH SETTING SUN AND OCEAN WAVES
Edo period, eighteenth century
Hikone Castle Museum, Shiga Prefecture
catalogue 161

HAGOROMO

Early one gentle spring morning a fisherman finds a wonderful robe of feathers slung over a pine. "What a prize," he thinks, and is about to take it home when he is stopped by a beautiful woman who claims it is hers and that without it she cannot fly back to the moon, where she dwells. The rustic fisher responds by clinging more tenaciously to the robe, hoping it will become a national treasure. Frustrated and depressed, the maiden loses her celestial demeanor as she wilts into the mire of human emotions. Finally compassion blooms in the crude heart of the fisher. He promises to return the robe if she will dance for him. She agrees, but needs the robe to dance. When he doubts her intention to keep her promise she admonishes him, saying that such lack of faith belongs to the mortal world and is unheard of in heaven. Humbled, he hands over the robe (fig. 61), which she dons onstage. She then performs the beautiful "Rainbow Skirts and Feather Mantle Dance" (fig. 62).[28]

A straightforward presentation of a universal folktale, *Hagoromo* has a direct appeal.[29] The luminous beauty of the moon maiden and her transfixing dance create an uplifting, joyous tone. The piece opens with the marvels of a gentle spring dawn that moves even the sensibilities of the lowly fisherman:

> Spring has touched the pine woods,
> Wave on wave washes the shore
> As mists rise, and the moon
> Loiters in the plains of Heaven;

PERFORMANCES OF HAGOROMO
figure 61 and 62

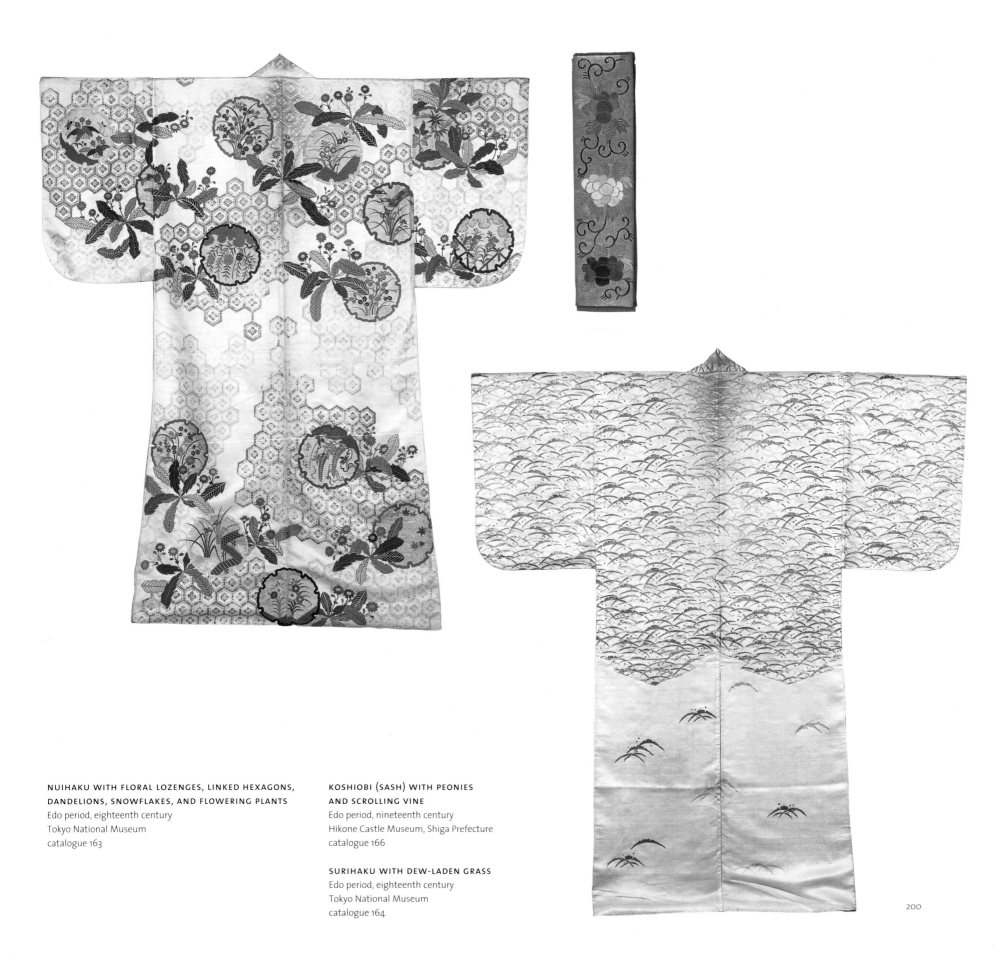

NUIHAKU WITH FLORAL LOZENGES, LINKED HEXAGONS,
DANDELIONS, SNOWFLAKES, AND FLOWERING PLANTS
Edo period, eighteenth century
Tokyo National Museum
catalogue 163

KOSHIOBI (SASH) WITH PEONIES
AND SCROLLING VINE
Edo period, nineteenth century
Hikone Castle Museum, Shiga Prefecture
catalogue 166

SURIHAKU WITH DEW-LADEN GRASS
Edo period, eighteenth century
Tokyo National Museum
catalogue 164

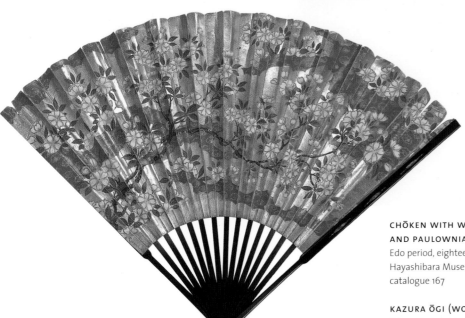

CHŌKEN WITH WEEPING WISTERIA
AND PAULOWNIA ARABESQUES
Edo period, eighteenth century
Hayashibara Museum of Art, Okayama Prefecture
catalogue 167

KAZURAOBI (HEADBAND) WITH PHOENIXES
AND MANDARIN ORANGE BLOSSOMS
Edo–Meiji period, nineteenth century
Hikone Castle Museum, Shiga Prefecture
catalogue 165

KAZURA ŌGI (WOMAN'S FAN) WITH CHERRY BLOSSOMS
Edo period, eighteenth century
Tokyo National Museum
catalogue 169

Even for such as we,
Beauty to transport the heart with keen [delight][30]

The place is Suruga Bay, nestled under the soaring Mount Fuji in present-day Shizuoka Prefecture. The pine groves, seascape, and mountainous backdrop form recurring images that retain a specificity yet transcend and transform the locale. As the moon maiden dances, she is drawn to the beauties around her, and wishing to linger awhile declares heaven and earth to be essentially one: The gods who created both upper and lower realms live on in their imperial offspring, protectors of peace. The Songs of the East (traditional music with reputedly mythological origins) are voiced by celestial instruments that welcome earthly souls to paradise. Scattered blossoms and swirling snow magically descend from above, along with gifts the moon maiden showers upon mankind. Yet her swirling sleeves transport her upward, slowly at first, and then with ever greater momentum. The fisher, and we in the audience, follow mesmerized as

The celestial feather mantle,
Windborne, floats on down the shore
Above the pine woods of Mio,
The moors of Ukishima,
Mount Ashitaka, Fuji's soaring peak,
And, mingling with the mists,
Fades into the heavens,
Lost forever to view.[31]

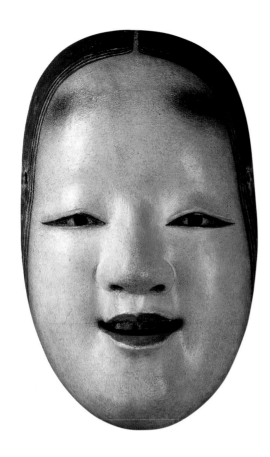

KO-OMOTE MASK
Ōmiya Yamato Sanemori (d. 1672)
Edo period, seventeenth century
Hikone Castle Museum, Shiga Prefecture
catalogue 162

The moon maiden's dance consists of four parts, two accompanied by singing and two by instrumental passages. Of the latter, the *jo no mai* (quiet dance) establishes the mood of the play. The overall rhythm of the dance, which is accompanied by the stick drum (*taiko*), is more lively than the same dance in many third-category plays. In this slow, lilting piece both melody and movement flow subtly and gracefully, with restraint, in suspended euphoria. The dancer begins with stamping timed to the drummer's calls[32] then circles and zigzags across the stage, marking key musical shifts with changes in fan attitude, stamping, or sleeve manipulation (fig. 62, p. 199). Gradually, the tempo increases until the music and movement reach full momentum and the moon maiden appears, "a wonder in scent and hue," with her train sweeping, swaying, and rustling.

Hagoromo is considered a third category ("woman") play primarily because of the jo no mai. A highly feminine dance, jo no mai (as opposed to similar instrumental dances with faster pace or more dynamic force) appears in the majority of the third-category plays and epitomizes the lyrical mood of *yūgen*, or grace. Yet there are many aspects of *Hagoromo*, including the character of the yūgen it expresses, that distinguish it from standard third-category pieces. While yūgen is generally seen as a subtle, mysterious beauty – associated with court ladies, perhaps expressed by a glint of gold in a darkened room – the yūgen in *Hagoromo* is more buoyant and joyous. Third-category plays tend to be built around a classical poem or a court tale, like *The Tales of Ise* or *Tale of Genji*, but *Hagoromo* derives its story from folklore. While the standard play of this type features ghosts of refined women retelling their love trials in a dream vision to an anonymous traveling priest, *Hagoromo* presents a celestial being interacting in the dramatic present with a fisherman with the improbable name of Hakuryō (White Dragon).[33]

Hagoromo's use of the dramatic present is probably the reason the piece was initially grouped with the fourth category, in which the device is more common. It has alternatively been placed at the end of the program, in the fifth-category slot, because of its buoyant final dance in an even rhythm (*ōnori*) to taiko accompaniment, which expresses a kind of rejoicing similar to *Shōjō* (discussed later). In variant form it can also be performed in place of a first-category deity play, since its shite is a celestial being, and its text extols the peace of the imperial reign. Nevertheless, already in the mid-Edo period it appeared most commonly as a third-category piece.[34]

Beautiful, flowing dance, well-paced plot, and familiar story all make this a highly accessible noh and account for its enduring popularity. Neatly constructed, seamlessly integrating Chinese and Japanese poems with accessible imagery, the piece is a small gem. Its simplicity recommends it as a beginner piece, and it is a great favorite for amateur performances. It is never trite, however, and in performance can be truly transfixing.

The standard performance uses a cubical bamboo frame, placed at center front, with a diagonal crossbar supporting a fresh-cut pine branch on which a chōken representing the feather mantle is draped. For variant performances this prop is dispensed with, and the chōken is laid on the third pine placed at the side of the bridgeway. In the standard performance, the moon maiden wears a gold-colored crown (*tengan*, cat. 168) with delicate dangling ornaments and topped with a crescent moon. In variations the figure on top is either a phoenix with spreading wings and fanning tail, or a large white lotus flower.

Other versions of the play incorporate alternative costumes as well as changes in music, dance, and text. Some have the moon maiden float along the bridge and rise beyond the mountains while the chorus is still singing. The fisherman stands watching her leave and performs the final stamping in place of the shite.

Hagoromo has also inspired the creation of chōken to evoke the image of the feather mantle. The Fujita Museum of Art owns one, reputedly hand-painted by the Rinpa school artist Ogata

TENGAN (HEAVENLY CROWN)
Edo period, eighteenth century
Hikone Castle Museum, Shiga Prefecture
catalogue 168

Kōrin, depicting facing phoenixes spead over the double-width sleeves, tails flowing gracefully behind them. A central phoenix with arabesque tail circles down towards scattered paulownia sprigs (fig. 63). The Tokugawa Art Museum owns a chōken with a single large phoenix whose body fills the back panel; its wings are spread across both sleeves, which are woven in shades of green, red, blue, brown, and gold (fig. 65). A robe used today by the Kongō school has large feathers cascading down from the shoulders (fig. 64). Though bird motifs are not specifically prescribed, they are often chosen for their appropriateness.

The chōken, whether standard or specially designed for the role, plays an important part in the stage action. The fisher finds it draped over the pine tree, takes it into his arms (hoarding it from the maiden), and finally hands it over to her graciously. His interaction with the garment reflects his changes in feeling, from avarice to selfishness to compassion. To dress in the mantle, the actor retires to the stage attendants' spot, kneels, and allows the attendants to drape it over his shoulders. They tack the back of the collar to the undergarments, slide his arms though the broad sleeves, arrange the front panels so they loosely cross each other, and tie the ornamental cords in a large bow knot that rests at chest level. All the while the flute plays a "costume-changing melody" in unfixed rhythm. Once draped, the mantle completes the identity of the moon maiden, and as she dances, the large diaphanous sleeves move in ever broader sweeps, until the feather sleeves indeed seem to "billow, coil, and turn," and finally fly off into the sky.

HAGOROMO

ROLE	MASK	COSTUME
shite: moon maiden	Zō-onna	woman's wig (kazura)
	or Waka-onna	kazuraobi with red on gold ground
	or Ko-omote	crown with ornament (tengan)
		two white collars
		surihaku
		nuihaku with red in koshimaki style
		koshiobi with red on gold ground
		woman's fan (kazura ōgi)
		chōken or maiginu
waki: Hakuryō	unmasked	dark blue collar
		striped noshime (kitsuke)
		white ōkuchi (optional)
		mizugoromo
		koshiobi with embroidered crests
		man's fan (otoko ōgi)
		prayer beads

**CHŌKEN WITH HAND-PAINTED PHOENIXES
ON RED GROUND**
Ogata Kōrin (1658-1716)
Edo period, eighteenth century
Colors on silk
38 3/4 x 50 1/2 in. (98.5 x 128.4 cm)
Fujita Museum of Art, Osaka.
figure 63

CHŌKEN WITH PHOENIX ON GOLD GROUND
Taishō period, twentieth century
Colors and gold leaf on silk
42 7/8 x 89 3/4 in. (109.0 x 228.0 cm)
Kongō Household/ Kongō Noh Theater, Kyoto.
figure 64

CHŌKEN WITH PHOENIX ON PURPLE GROUND
Edo period, nineteenth century
Silk gauze weave with silk and gold-leaf paper
supplementary wefts
40 9/16 x 81 1/2 in. (103.0 x 207.0 cm)
Tokugawa Museum of Art, Nagoya
figure 65

DŌJŌJI

Riveting, concentrated movement and protracted stage tension followed by a dramatic leap into a bell as it descends over the actor make *Dōjōji* one of the most technically demanding noh (fig. 66). Many actors perform it only once in their life, as a proof they have mastered the skills of the art.[35] The telepathic timing of isolated drum calls in coordination with individualized foot movements in the section called the *ranbyōshi* (disordered beat), requires numerous rehearsals, as opposed to the single rehearsal prior to a standard noh performance. The bell prop, a large frame covered with damask and hung from a special pulley hooked to the ceiling over the stage, takes six to eight stage attendants to hoist and lower. Precise timing is of utmost importance. A diary entry from 1592 mentions the breaking of the bell rope and that injuries during performances of *Dōjōji* were "common events since long past."[36]

Like *Kamo*, *Dōjōji* is based on a well-known legend,[37] and like *Tadanori*, the action of the play grafts a future onto the original story. *Dōjōji* begins with the hanging of the bell. This is a solemn affair executed by the stage attendants in some schools, and a comic preface performed by the kyōgen actors in others.[38] Then the abbot of Dōjōji Temple (*waki*) announces that he has restored the temple bell and warns the temple servants (ai) not to let a woman on the premises.

A little later a woman dancer appears and manages to gain entry by agreeing to perform a dedicatory piece for the bell. "What harm could that do?" argue the servants, secretly wanting to watch her. She dons a tall dancer's hat (*eboshi*). Retreating onto the bridge for a moment, she stares at the bell, then enters the stage to rapid stick-drum beats and begins to stamp out the rhythm. Her feet trace out triangles as her body moves in sudden bursts, often minutely and at odd angles between long pauses.

BELL SEQUENCE IN A PERFORMANCE OF DŌJŌJI
figure 66

The tension rises as the solo kotsuzumi drummer punctuates the dance with strident calls and sharp beats. She goes round and round, repeating the same steps. This has been interpreted as climbing toward the belfry and also as tracing out snake scales (represented as triangles). During the ranbyōshi's forty minutes of live-wire intensity the servants fall into a hypnotic sleep and do not wake even when the chorus sings of the founding of the temple and of the sinking moon striking the bell. The dancer speeds into a quick whirl around the stage (*kyū no mai*):

Up to the bell she stealthily creeps
Pretending to go on with her dance.
She starts to strike it [*swings fan arm back and forth like a bell hammer*]
This loathsome bell, now I remember it!
        [*unfastens hat, strikes it off with her fan, and stands under the bell*]
Placing her hand on the dragon-head boss,
She seems to fly upward into the bell [*stamps, then leaps up as bell comes down*][39]

        The clatter wakes the servants, who eventually discover the cause. Fearing criticism, each tries to get the other to report the incident. The quarrel provides welcome comedy. On hearing the news the abbot calls the priests together and tells them the background story: An ascetic would regularly stop at a man's house on his way to Kumano Shrine. The daughter of the host was led to believe that one day she would marry the ascetic. When this did not happen, she went to his bedroom to ask him when the day would be. Shocked, he escaped to Dōjōji Temple and begged for protection. They hid him in the bell.

        Meanwhile, the girl ran after him, faster and faster. When she found her way blocked by the swollen river, she turned into a snake, swam across, searched the temple, spotted the bell, and wound herself around it in seven coils (fig. 19, p. 56). Spitting flames, she lashed the bell with her tail until the bronze grew so hot that the man inside was roasted.

        Now, the abbot continues, they will exorcise the serpent-woman with the power of the sacred texts. Busily rolling their prayer beads, they call on the strong guardian kings (*myō-ō*) and pray for the serpent's salvation. The bell rises slightly and swings a bit, then lowers. They pray more fervently, and the bell makes sounds of its own (in actuality, the shite strikes cymbals inside it). The bell begins to sway, then rises to reveal a figure with a horned mask (cat. 174, p. 213; cat. 96, p. 54) and long tresses. She sheds the robe she had earlier wrapped around her midriff, and with her demon wand (a cloth-covered stick with bow at the end), she strikes at the priests.

ONI ŌGI (DEMON FAN) WITH PEONY
Edo period, eighteenth century
Hikone Castle Museum, Shiga Prefecture
catalogue 173

**KARAORI WITH WEEPING CHERRIES AND
ABSTRACT PINE-BARK LOZENGES (MATSUKAWABISHI)**
Edo period, eighteenth century
Hikone Castle Museum, Shiga Prefecture
catalogue 171

NUIHAKU WITH DECORATIVE ROUNDELS
Edo period, nineteenth century
Toyohashi Uomachi Noh Association, Aichi Prefecture
catalogue 175

SURIHAKU WITH TRIANGULAR SCALE PATTERN (UROKO)
Edo period, nineteenth century
Kyoto National Museum
catalogue 176

To erratic drum accompaniment the serpent-woman and the priests advance and retreat across the stage. At one dramatic moment she winds her body around the pillar that separates the bridge and the stage. With a sharp jerk of her head that makes her round metallic eyes flash, she raises the wand high (fig. 67). The priests call on the dragons of all directions and colors; she falls back. Then, vomiting fire toward the bell, the serpent-woman leaps into the river (offstage) to cool her burning body. She will never return.

Dōjōji is a late play, dating probably from the early sixteenth century. It is a recasting, possibly by Konparu Zenpō (1454–c. 1532), of an earlier play, *Kanemaki* (Bell coiling), which has been tentatively attributed to Kanze Kojirō Nobumitsu (1435–1516).[40] The first recorded performance was in 1536,[41] and it quickly became incorporated into the canon. The oldest noh stage extant, the north stage at Nishihonganji in Kyoto (constructed around 1595), was already equipped with a built-in pulley hook for the bell.[42] *Dōjōji* eliminates from *Kanemaki* a lengthy discussion of the founding of the temple and of the Buddhist profundities, and substitutes the ranbyōshi and the dramatic entrance into the bell. Stage effects take precedence over religious proselytizing, a process that foreshadows trends seen in subsequent theater forms, such as kabuki. The text is highly prosaic.

The costume change within the bell prop is another feat of virtuosity in this piece. All the articles needed are neatly stored on shelves within the bell by the actor himself and must not fall down while the bell is being manipulated. In total darkness the actor, who in other plays passively allows others to dress him, must change his mask, slip off at least the upper half of his outer garment, clash the cymbals, and replace them on a shelf. If he performs a variant using long trailing bifurcated skirts and red headpiece, he must slip off two garments, slip on the skirts, and cover himself with the woven, not the embroidered, of the two discarded garments.

The costumes for *Dōjōji* are more precisely prescribed than those for most noh plays. Each school has its own tradition of fabric patterns and fans: for example, abstracted, coiled spools in red among weeping cherries for the Kanze school (cat. 171, p. 208), and diamond arrays of facing cranes for the Kita school (similar to those seen on the left shoulder of cat. 80, p. 250). All schools use interlocking triangles for the *surihaku* underrobe (cat. 176, p. 209) that lies hidden under a karaori in the first

PERFORMANCE OF DŌJŌJI
figure 67

act, but is exposed to signify snake scales in the second. All also use a black or dark blue *nuihaku* with flower roundels (cat. 175, p. 209), folded down at the waist in *koshimaki* (waist-wrap) style.

The mask traditions have some latitude, for the woman can be represented either as a young woman with a mask like Ōmi-onna (cat. 170, p. 212) or as a middle-aged woman wearing Fukai or Shakumi (cat. 92, p. 63). The horned Hannya mask (cat. 174, p. 213; cat. 96, p. 54) worn in the second act would conventionally have a light-colored forehead and red cheeks, though any number of variations are possible.

As a piece about madness engendered by jealousy, *Dōjōji* is representative of one type of fourth-category plays, which tend to be dramatic presentations set in the present time (rather than remembered time). Other types of fourth-category plays include lost-child plays, suffering-ghost plays, and plays with unmasked shite.

DŌJŌJI

ROLE	MASK	COSTUME
waki: head priest of Dōjōji	unmasked	cloth headgear with gold (sumibōshi)
		white twill underrobe (kitsuke)
		white ōkuchi
		purple mizugoromo
		white undecorated koshiobi
		small sword
		plain gold fan
		prayer beads
wakizure: sub-priests	unmasked	cloth hat (sumibōshi)
		plain noshime
		white ōkuchi
		mizugoromo
		damask koshiobi
		fan with ink painting (sumi-e)
		prayer beads
ai: temple servants	unmasked	noshime underrobe (kitsuke)
		mizugoromo
		kukuribakama
shite: shirabyōshi dancer	Ōmi-onna, etc.	women's wig (kazura)
(Kanze school)	Fukai, etc.	kazuraobi with gold scale triangles
		white and red, or two whites collars
		surihaku with scale triangles
		nuihaku with embroidered rounds on black ground draped in koshimaki style.
		koshiobi with scale triangles
		karaori with red draped in tsubo-ori style
		dancers hat (mae-ori eboshi)
		demon fan (oni ōgi)
nochijite: snake figure	Hannya	demon wig (nagakazura)
		kazuraobi with gold scale triangles
		surihaku with scale triangles
		nuihaku with embroidered rounds on black ground draped in koshimaki style.
		karaori with red
		red wand

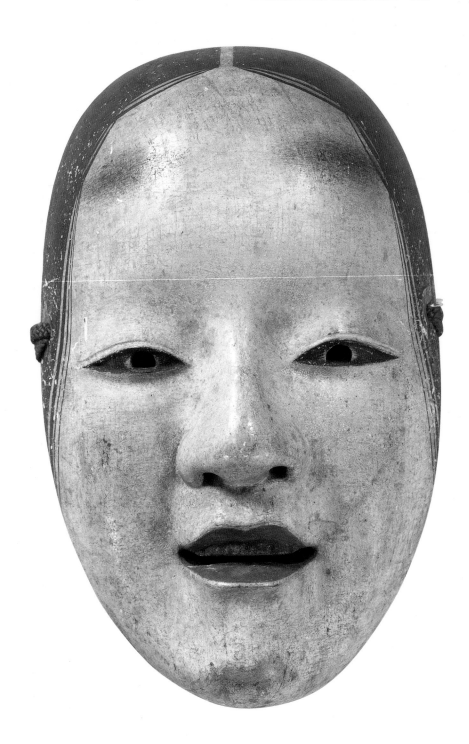

KAZURAOBI (HEADBAND)
WITH TRIANGULAR SCALE PATTERN (UROKO)
Edo–Meiji period,
eighteenth–nineteenth century
Hikone Castle Museum, Shiga Prefecture
catalogue 172

ŌMI-ONNA MASK
Attributed to Zōami
Momoyama period, sixteenth century
Tokyo National Museum
catalogue 170

HANNYA MASK
Attributed to Hannyabō
Muromachi period, fifteenth–sixteenth century
Eisei Bunko Museum, Tokyo
catalogue 174

KUMASAKA

Slight, agile, elegant, and ingeniously clever at masterminding a battle, Minamoto Yoshitsune, younger brother of the first ruling shogun, is one of Japan's most beloved heroes. The historical figure quickly became legendary and appears in most of the tales about the late-twelfth-century wars between the Taira and the Minamoto clans. In particular, the *Gikeiki* (Tales of Yoshitsune) relates his life and the story of his encounter with the bandit Kumasaka.

After a childhood of being held hostage in a mountain temple, Yoshitsune (known in boyhood as Ushiwaka-maru) escaped at the age of sixteen to accompany a gold merchant on his way to the Northeast. There he planned to ask Minamoto sympathizers to lend him an army so he could take revenge on the Taira for having destroyed his family. On the way, bandits attack the gold merchant. Ushiwaka fends them off with his small waist-sword and puts an end to the life of the greatest of them all, Kumasaka Chōhan.

This portion of the story is dramatized in two noh plays, *Eboshi ori* and *Kumasaka*, both fifth-category plays filled with lively action and the victory of good over evil.[43] *Eboshi ori* (The hatmaker) is episodic and evolves chronologically in the dramatic present (*genzai*) noh. It begins with Ushiwaka purchasing a hat (eboshi) for his coming-of-age ceremony, whereupon he is recognized by the hatmaker's wife, who knew his half brothers. It then portrays the gold merchant stopping at an inn, the bandits preparing for attack, and finally the encounter between the bandits and Ushiwaka. Typical of late plays, numerous characters (a minimum of nine) engage in dramatic interaction, and technical feats provide much of the attraction. In contrast, *Kumasaka* is a dream play (*mugen*) noh wherein the

CHŌREI BESHIMI
Deme Yūkan (d. 1652)
Edo period, seventeenth century
Toyohashi Uomachi Noh Association, Aichi Prefecture
catalogue 178

ghost of the bandit Kumasaka begs prayers from a passing priest and relates his fateful encounter with Ushiwaka as a religious confession. Only two people appear onstage, a priest from the capital and the ghost of Kumasaka, first disguised as a fellow priest. The band of brigands and Yoshitsune himself appear only as evoked by the text and suggested by Kumasaka's wild slashing of his halberd. Narrative recounting as opposed to dramatic action is a feature *Kumasaka* shares with *Tadanori* and most second-category plays derived from war tales. This method of presentation focuses on the psyche of the vanquished bandit: his defeat provokes self-reassessment and religious awakening.

The first act of *Kumasaka* is subdued. Priest encounters priest, both dressed in simple, plain-color robes. They confront each other with Buddhist logic: To say a prayer for someone one must know his name, says the priest from the capital. The other priest counters that the benefit of prayer extends to all, without distinction. In parley of shorter and shorter lines they come to agree that prayers can be for all those who seek them, even the trees and grasses.

When the priest from the capital enters the other's hut (shown by shifting positions, without a prop), he finds in it no Buddhist altar, but rather the remnants of fighting apparel. The disguised priest confesses he was a bandit until his encounter with Ushiwaka. He then justifies his ways by alluding to the swords, arrows, and lances used by Buddhist figures to ward off the evils of attachment and delusion. Employing the logic of Zen, he argues that good and evil are not always what they appear to be, and concludes, "Delusion and enlightenment are in the mind, so become the master of your mind, lest your mind master you." As he bids goodnight, he recedes, and with him the hut vanishes. The priest from the capital is left in the shadow of the pine tree. The priest questions a local person and hears for the first time the name Kumasaka, learning how he turned into a bandit and how he met his end. The priest then performs services for the soul of Kumasaka.

In contrast to the sober tone of the first act, the second act has a dynamic energy. Dressed in voluminous, dark, but flashy garb with his head wrapped in cloth, Kumasaka carries a long halberd. His power is conveyed by his dynamic Chōrei Beshimi mask (cat. 178), with its clenched mouth and wide-set round eyes. Kumasaka's ghost is torn between the bandit's urge to raid and remorse at taking others' possessions. The priest asks him to recount his story, continually prodding him for details. As Kumasaka names his companions, the priest begins to tell the story with him. Their identities merge, outwardly opposite but spiritually joined in recounting what is really a tale of Ushiwaka's heroism. The chorus narrates how the many bandits threw torches and attacked, only to be outdone by the fleet-footed Ushiwaka, who seemed to be everywhere and nowhere at once. Seeing this, Kumasaka decides to retreat, but thinks better of it, hoping to use his magic arts to prevail.

Action takes over. Kumasaka wields his halberd in figure-eight patterns. He raises it high, plunges, backs, circles; everywhere he strikes he meets only air. In the darkness Ushiwaka has leapt

PERFORMANCE OF KUMASAKA
figure 68

**HAPPI WITH DRAGON ROUNDELS
AND ABSTRACT LIGHTNING**
Edo period, nineteenth century
Toyohashi Uomachi Noh Association, Aichi Prefecture
catalogue 179

HANGIRE WITH STYLIZED WAVE AND FLAMING DRUM
ROUNDELS AND GEOMETRIC PATTERN
Edo period, nineteenth century
Noda Shrine, Yamaguchi Prefecture
catalogue 181

KOSHIOBI (SASH) WITH TEMPLE GONG (UNPAN) CRESTS
Edo–Meiji period, nineteenth century
Hikone Castle Museum, Shiga Prefecture
catalogue 182

ATSUITA WITH CLOUDS AND TRIPLE COMMA
ROUNDELS (TOMOE), ARROW SCREENS,
AND TRIANGULAR SCALE PATTERN (UROKO)
Edo period, nineteenth century
Tokyo National Museum
catalogue 180

CHŌHAN ZUKIN (CLOTH HEADGEAR)
Edo period, eighteenth century
Hayashibara Museum of Art, Okayama Prefecture
catalogue 183

over and ducked under the blows, hit from behind, never himself hurt but always inflicting pain. Kumasaka discards his sword. With all ten fingers stretched in aggressive anticipation he prepares to wrestle but ends up running around in circles, grabbing at thin air. Ushiwaka is like "flashing rays, lightning, or moon on water, seen, but impossible to grasp." Wounded again and again, Kumasaka weakens till he is "like the dew and frost on the moss at the foot of pine." He pleads to the priest for release in the other world, and his ghost fades into the pine shadows.

As in *Tadanori* a single tree dominates the scene. It is the marker of the nameless haunted tomb, the spot where the priest spends the night, the mass grave of the bandits, and the symbol of Kumasaka's hope for salvation. Unlike Tadanori, however, here the shite is not a warrior-courtier but a crude bandit. Kumasaka lacks the elegance tempering strength that is more typical of second-category plays.

The costume for the role of Kumasaka is similar in *Eboshi ori* and *Kumasaka*. The bold patterns on dark grounds can be gaudy, and those in the happi (cat. 179, p. 216) need not harmonize with those in the *hangire* (cat. 181, p. 217) or *atsuita* (cat. 180, p. 217). Illustrations of noh from the Edo period show blue and brown grounds with either huge motifs of wheels or circles, or else dense patterns within patterns, often forming circles. Generally the right sleeve of the happi is slipped off the shoulder, folded, and tucked into the sash at the back to give free play to the arm when manipulating the long halberd. An alternative is to hike up both sleeves, exposing more of the atsuita and mimicking the shape of Japanese armor. The special *chōhan*-style cloth cap (*zukin*, cat. 183) is used only for this role.

KUMASAKA

ROLE	MASK	COSTUME
waki: traveling priest	unmasked	cloth hat (sumibōshi)
		reddish-yellow collar
		plain noshime
		mizugoromo
		damask koshiobi
		fan with ink painting (sumi-e)
		prayer beads
shite: priest	unmasked	cloth hat (sumibōshi)
		light yellow collar
		plain noshime
		mizugoromo
		damask koshiobi
		prayer beads
shite (act 2): Kumasaka	Chōrei Beshimi	chōhan zukin headgear
		blue collar
		atsuita without red
		hangire
		happi
		koshiobi with embroidered crests
		halberd

SHŌJŌ

Shōjō celebrates with song and dance the joys of drink. A short congratulatory piece, it radiates gaiety and warmth. The final word of the play, "medetakere" (joyous), sums up its auspicious mood (*shūgen*). *Shōjō* shares with *Okina* and many of the first-category plays the themes of prosperity and long life. It lacks, however, their formality and slow pace. For this reason, instead of being an opening play, its standard place is as a conclusion to the program, a return to the auspicious mood of the opening but in a lighter vein, allowing the audience to leave feeling uplifted. Today many programs end with the chorus chanting the last two lines of *Shōjō* as a final felicitation.[44] This placement of *Shōjō* seems already to have been prevalent in the mid-sixteenth century, and scholars have suggested that the piece may have been composed expressly as a final shūgen piece.[45]

The story is so simple it has been dismissed by some as merely an excuse for a previously existing dance to be incorporated into noh: In China, a wine merchant in the town of Yōzu at the foot of Gold Money Mountain relates that every day a somewhat strange customer comes to buy wine: no matter how much he drinks, his face never changes color. Asked his identity, he replies, "A shōjō of the sea." The wine merchant now waits for him at Shinnyō Bay. Under the moonlight, accompanied by "bridging music" (*watari byōshi*), a red figure appears. "Never grow old," he says, "with medicine called Chrysanthemum Water [wine]." He then drinks, sings, and dances to music and chanted text. He revels in praise for wine: it lengthens life, bonds friendships, fights the cold, inspires poetry, and aids sleep. He mimes drinking and finally, stumbling and groggy, lies down to dream of an inexhaustible fountain of wine (or perhaps it is real and he has granted it to the merchant).

A version of *Shōjō* no longer in the repertory called *Shōjō no mae* (First act of *Shōjō*) suggests that originally the piece was probably a two-act play and only later contracted into a one-act form.[46] This version includes a section where the shōjō defines himself: "I am not a Buddha, nor am I a sentient being. For a while being and nonbeing were skimmed over; that is to say, I could be man or beast, or something from the six realms of existence. Thus you could call me human, or an I-don't-know-what. I just live in the white waves of the sea and am called a shōjō." On the noh stage the character Shōjō is portrayed as a red-faced ageless youth, dressed in red from head to foot (cat. 120), but legends

NŌMAI NO ZU
(ILLUSTRATIONS OF NOH DANCES) (detail: *Shōjō*)
Edo period, eighteenth century
National Noh Theater, Tokyo
catalogue 120

PERFORMANCE OF SHŌJŌ
figure 69

ŌKUCHI WITH CHRYSANTHEMUMS
AND WATER
Edo period, eighteenth century
Tokyo National Museum
catalogue 187

KARAORI WITH CHRYSANTHEMUMS
AND WAVES
Edo period, eighteenth century
Bunka Gakuen Costume Museum, Tokyo
catalogue 185

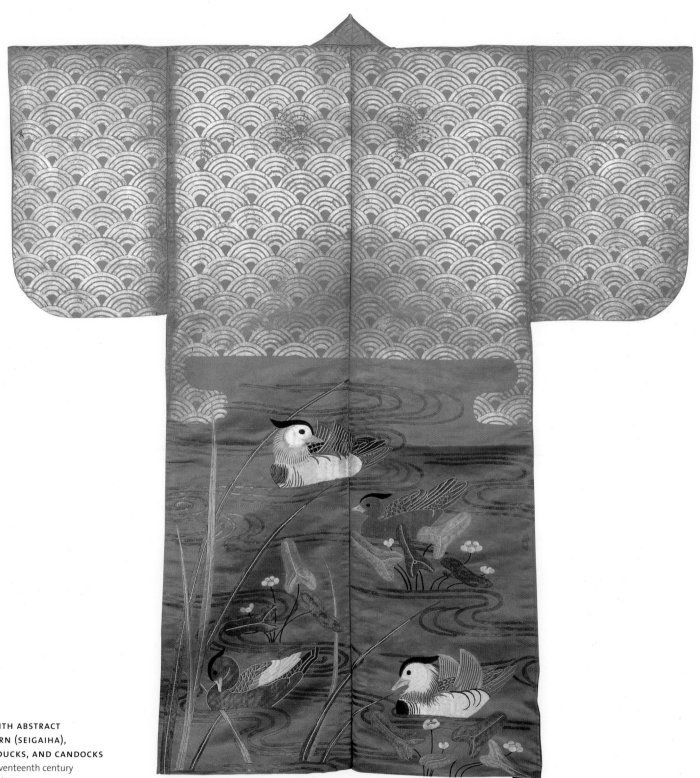

**NUIHAKU WITH ABSTRACT
WAVE PATTERN (SEIGAIHA),
MANDARIN DUCKS, AND CANDOCKS**
Edo period, seventeenth century
Tokyo National Museum
catalogue 186

221

and stories describe him as anything from an owl or talking animal to a monkey caught for his blood (which is used to dye fur). All the stories agree that he loves to drink. All proclaim the medicinal value of wine,[47] include an inebriated dance where Shōjō stumbles, and have Shōjō strike up a friendship with a wine merchant.

The noh scholar Kanai Kiyomitsu has researched the play by finding precursors in folk performances.[48] He found that in certain festivals in Tottori Prefecture the role of Shōjō as a path-clearer at the beginning of the shrine performance is similar to the role of the god Sarutahiko (Monkey Field, a pathfinder or traveler's god, with long red nose and high *geta* sandals) in other festivals. Both begin the program by chasing away evil spirits . Both perform a stumbling dance, which he feels enacts the subservience of the natives to new lords of the domain. When this preexisting Shōjō dance was incorporated into the noh for entertainment, Kanai argues, it was translated into a Chinese setting.

Whatever its origins, by the sixteenth century variations of *Shōjō* were being performed for different occasions. Some had multiple Shōjō figures, including one with a wife shōjō and another using a huge jug prop (fig. 69, p. 219), but the most popular of all was *Midare*, or the Disheveled Shōjō, which replaces the standard instrumental dance with a special *midare* dance involving syncopated rhythms, lilting music, and complex dance steps. While the standard *Shōjō* is quite an easy piece, the disheveled version requires special advanced instruction and uses a different costume and fan.

Although Shōjō is definitely male, he is dressed in a colorful, floral karaori, a garment generally associated with female roles. This indicates his agelessness and nonhuman aspects. A wide variety of red karaori are possible, and imagery from the play, like running water and chrysanthemums,

SHŌJŌ FAN WITH
CHRYSANTHEMUMS
AND WATER
Edo period, nineteenth century
Hikone Castle Museum, Shiga Prefecture
catalogue 190

SHŌJŌ

ROLE	MASK	COSTUME
waki: wine merchant	unmasked	blue collar
		atsuita
		white ōkuchi
		sobatsugi
		koshiobi with embroidered crests
		man's fan (otoko ōgi)
shite: Shōjō	Shōjō	red head-piece
		red and gold kazuraobi
		two red collars
		red surihaku
		red ōkuchi
		red embroidered koshiobi
		red karaori draped in tsubo-ori style
		young boy's fan (warabe ōgi)

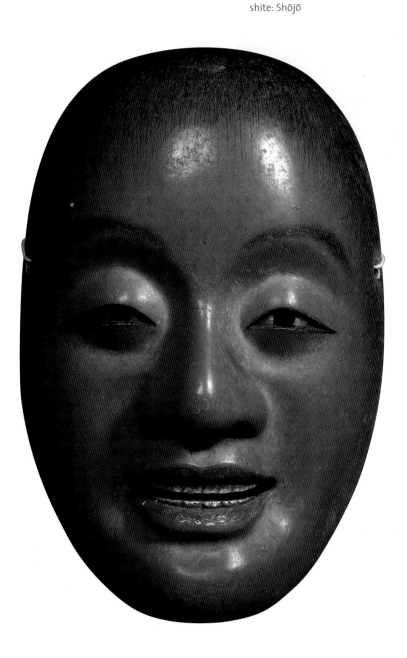

KOSHIOBI (SASH) WITH CHRYSANTHEMUM CRESTS
Edo period, nineteenth century
Noda Shrine, Yamaguchi Prefecture
catalogue 188

SHŌJŌ MASK
Ōmi Kodama Mitsumasa (d. 1704)
Edo period, seventeenth century
Ishikawa Prefectural Museum of Art
catalogue 184

would be most appropriate (cat. 185, p. 220). The karaori is draped in *tsubo-ori* (tucked-waist) style over broad pleated pants (*mon ōkuchi*, cat. 187, p. 220) and an underrobe of satin with a stenciled repeat pattern in gold or silver leaf (*surihaku*) and a red ground. (The garment shown in cat. 186, p. 221 is actually a nuihaku, but only the upper half would be exposed under the karaori. This is in surihaku style, with a stylized wave pattern suggesting the sea habitat of Shōjō.) A red sash (cat. 188, p. 223) and headpiece with cascading red hair (cat. 189, p. 225) complete the outfit. The fan used in *Shōjō* is used also by youths possessing the elixir of eternal life, such as Dōji in *Kikujidō*, and has chrysanthemums floating in running water on a red ground (cat. 190, p. 222).

The noh described in this essay are only a few from the approximately 250 in the canon as it exists today. They represent a spectrum of literary and performance styles and hypothetically could constitute a full day's program. The progression followed here moves from formal, slow opening pieces (*Okina* and *Kamo*), through very human narrative and poetic pieces (*Tadanori* and *Hagoromo*), to dramatic and dynamic demonstrations of technique (*Dōjōji* and *Kumasaka*). This is the progression of jo ha kyū and return to jo mentioned earlier, which informs not only the arrangement of pieces, but also every aspect of performance. The dancer conforms his movements to cycles of restraint and acceleration. The drummers begin their patterns and musical sections slowly, but gradually speed up, only to slow again, like waves gaining momentum till they crash at the shore, recede and reform. Different renditions of this cyclical progression make for different styles of performance. The lyrical women's pieces flow gently, suspended ends merging with the new beginnings. The dynamic, masculine noh, on the other hand (particularly the fighting scenes), progress in spurts. Energy is held back until it cannot help but burst forth, then the quick movements end in sharply delineated stances.

Although the outline of noh action often seems simple, many of the plays tap deep cultural experiences. Their poetic diction and symbolic abstraction help make them universal. The texts presume a Shinto-Buddhist world, the figures can seem to be slow-moving dolls, and the music often strikes the newcomer as a weird conglomeration of sounds. But as the performance progresses and the viewer settles into the alternate time-space of the noh universe, all the elements unite on a different level. In a good performance everything fits and is felt. Noh is immediately grasped in a flow of imagery, sound, and action linked by associations rather than logical deductions. Each of the plays discussed here, embodied by the costumes and masks that outfit them, presents a different view of the mysteries of life and a mirror of something inside each of us.

HEADPIECE
Edo period, nineteenth century
Tokyo National Museum
catalogue 189

PERFORMANCE OF SHŌJŌ
figure 70

NOTES

1. For example, the warrior-courtiers Tadanori and Kiyotsune (in noh plays of the same names) might wear exactly the same costume and mask, though one fought to his death while the other committed suicide.

2. The longest noh, such as *Obasute* or *Ōmu Komachi*, take two and a half hours, the shortest, *Shōjō*, a little over half an hour. Short kyōgen, like *Kuriyaki*, take about five minutes.

3. Obviously the plays took less time to perform in the fourteenth century than they do today. Increasing concentration on technical finesse led to a gradual slowing due to fuller rendering of the performance.

4. Zeami's first discussion of the ordering of plays in a program appears in his *Fūshikaden* (*Kadensho*), in the question-and-answer section. Various translations have been made into western languages; the most readily available appears in J. Thomas Rimer and Yamazaki Masakazu, *On the Art of the Nō Drama* (Princeton: Princeton University Press, 1984). The relevant section is on p. 21.

5. Some of these, like the Okina at Hiyoshi Shrine, Shiga Prefecture, and the *Shikisanban* at Kasuga Shrine firelight festivities are performed by professional noh actors and have a tradition reaching back to the fourteenth century. Others, like the *Okinamai* at Naratsuhiko Shrine, Nara Prefecture, are performed by villagers and exhibit different forms from the standard practice of the modern professional noh troupes. Some, like the *Shikisanban* at Shimiyoshi Shrine in Hyōgo Prefecture use the Okina masks, but not the standard text or movement. Yet others, such as the *Okinamai* in *Yudate kagura*, *Yamabushi kagura*, and *Nōmai* do not use the Okina masks (but rather old-men's masks without detached chins) and follow their own scenario, but do share with noh Okina the themes of long life, fertility, prosperity, and harmony.

6. For a fuller description of the details of the Okina performance see my article, "Okina: An Interview with Takabayashi Kōji," in the 1984 *Mime Journal*: "Nō / Kyōgen Masks and Performance," compiled by Rebecca Teele. The Shinto aspects of the Okina performance may reflect Edo-period practice and not reach back to Zeami's time, as suggested by Noel Pinnington in his essay, "Invented Origins: Muromachi Interpretations of Okina Sarugaku," *Bulletin of the School of Oriental and African Studies* (University of London) 61, part 3 (1998): 492–518.

7. *Sarugaku dangi* in Omote Akira, *Zeami Zenchiku* (Iwanami Shoten, 1974), 272. Translated in J. Thomas Rimer and Yamazaki Masakazu, *On the Art of the Nō Drama: The Major Treatises of Zeami* (Princeton: Princeton University Press, 1984), 224; Erika de Poorter, *Zeami's Talks on Sarugaku: An Annotated Translation of the Sarugaku Dangi*, with an Introduction on Zeami Motokiyo; Japonica Neerlandica, vol. 2 (Amsterdam: J. C. Gieben, 1986), 114.

8. Interpretations of the relationship between the god in the mask and the performer vary from the donning of the mask as being seen as a possession of the actor by the god, to the actor performing as an instrument of the god, to suggesting the mask is merely symbolizing for the audience that which is godly within the actor.

9. In the screens depicting the Toyokuni Festival *Okina* performance where the role of Okina is multiplied, with representatives from all four schools, the Tokugawa Art Museum copy shows eight kotsuzumi players, while the earlier Toyokuni Shrine version shows sixteen.

10. This present-day practice seems to stem from Zeami's time, since in the *Sarugaku dangi* under "Okina" Zeami states, "When the actor portraying Okina has finished his dance, he should remove his mask, straighten his costume, bow facing the audience, and then exit" (Omote, 293).

11. The structural repetition in lighter mode seen in the kyōgen section follows a tradition of imitation (*modoki*) seen in the bugaku performance of Ama-Ninomai and in many folk pieces, such as *Yamabushi kagura* and *Nōmai*. Though performed by a kyōgen player, the effect should not be comic, as already Zeami warns (*Sarugaku dangi*, in Omote, 273; Rimer, 225; de Poorter, 116).

12. Sixteenth- and early-seventeenth-century depictions of *Okina* include, in addition to those already mentioned, two scenes on the *Tsukinami fūzokuzu byōbu* from the Tokyo National Museum, one depicting Okina entering the *torii* gate of Kasuga Shrine during the Onmatsuri rites, the other showing a dengaku performance with Okina and Sanbasō dancing simultaneously while people plant rice. Sanbasō dressed in white matched suit appears in the *Yūgakuzu byōbu* (Screens of various amusements), an early seventeenth-century piece at the Tokugawa Art Museum.

13. Omote, 293–4.

14. Itō Masayoshi, *Yōkyokushū ge* (Anthology of noh songs, third volume) (Tokyo: Shinchōsha, 1988), 498.

15. Originally Kamo Shrine owned much of the Shinchōsha area now occupied by the city and its gods still preside over the city, keeping the peace and ensuring prosperity through providing rain for a bountiful harvest. Every year a grand festival spanning the first two weeks of May is conducted to plead for the goodwill and cooperation of these Kamo deities. Gifts and prayers are presented from the emperor himself, horse races and competitive archery contests are held, and the imperial daughter residing within the shrine as vestal virgin priestess, *Sai-in*, conducts purification ceremonies involving ritual hand-washing (*mitarashi*) in a small branch riverlet that runs through the shrine. This Kamo Festival, also referred to as Aoi matsuri, has lived in the Japanese awareness as a central event of the year since the days of the *Tale of Genji* a thousand years ago. The festival forms an unstated, but undeniable background for the play.

16. My translation of *Kamo* appears in Karen Brazell, ed., *Traditional Japanese Theater* (New York: Columbia University Press, 1998), 44-60.

17. The mother goddess's water-dipping scene in act 2 replays the purification dipping that takes place in act 1 as well as the *misogi* purification ceremony in the Kamo festival.

18. Other sources include old records of the Kyoto area (*Yamashiro Fudooki*), *Kamo Engi* (Tales of the Kamo Shrine), and *Hatashi Honkechō* (Notes on the Hata family). Interestingly the mother goddess, Hata Toyohime, belongs to the same Hata family who were the original sarugaku players and ancestors of the Konparu line.

19. Kami Hiro, in his article in *Kanze* (March 1976), discusses the various sources of Tadanori, including differing versions of the *Tales of the Heike*.

20. Zeami is responsible for the majority of the second-category plays. In the *Fūshikaden* (chapter 2), he warns that warrior plays should be tempered by elegance, such as would be appropriate for roles of the warrior-courtiers of the *Tales of the Heike*, and should avoid both being too rough in style and too dancelike. In creating his warrior style, Zeami was perhaps responding to the aesthetic of his first patron, the shogun Ashikaga Yoshimitsu, who fostered the concept of *bumbu*, where the ideal warrior was seen as excelling in both artistic and martial skills.

21. Thomas Blenman Hare, *Zeami's Style* (Stanford: Stanford University Press, 1986), 185.

22. A discussion of *Tadanori* and the final dance appears in Bethe and Brazell, *Dance in the Noh Theater*, vol. 2, East Asia Papers no. 29 (Ithaca: Cornell China-Japan Program, 1982), 44–67.

23. Shunzei was not only a great poet and famous anthologizer, but also a teacher of poetry. His son Teika compiled the *Shinkokinshū* and the *Hyakunin isshu*, and set the poetic standards for the medieval period.

24. The poem that was actually included in the *Senzaishū* is not this cherry poem but another.

25. Many other examples of expunging the Taira accomplishments in music, art, and poetry exist.

26. The association of salt-making with Suma Beach also appears in *Matsukaze*.

27. An alternative outfit that the actor could choose to evoke more closely the image of armor substitutes an unlined happi draped with both sleeves hiked up and tucked in at the shoulders. Deep primary colors are a common choice for robing *Tadanori* and other warrior plays. There is no need to follow the text explicitly, though *Tales of the Heike* has Tadanori in dark blue while *Genpei Seisuiki* has him in crimson red. The choice of a happi is more common for more military warrior plays, like *Yashima*.

28. That was the origin, according to the noh text, of the *Surugamai* part of *Azuma Asobi* (Songs of the East, still performed in certain shrines today).

29. Royall Tyler in *Japanese Nō Dramas* (London: Penguin, 1992), 96–107, summarizes the various legends that inform the playwright.

30. Translation: ibid., 101.

31. Ibid., 101.

32. Timing minor foot movments to the drums occurs also in Okina's "Heaven, Earth, and Man" dance and, differently, in the *ranbyōshi* of *Dōjoji*. Here the timed steps and stamps are related to ritualistic stamps (*henbai*) used to chase away evil spirits in yin-yang ceremonies.

33. Both Tyler and Kenneth Yasuda in *Masterworks of the Nō Theater* (Bloomington and Indianapolis: Indiana University Press, 1989), 133–75, discuss the implications of this name.

34. *Hagoromo* is not the only piece which proved hard to categorize. The distinctions are particularly blurred for plays that seem like they belong to the third category because they are about a beautiful woman (*Yuya*); or include *jo no mai*, even though they are, like *Yuya*, in present time (typical of the fourth category); or are, like *Yūgyō yanagi*, and *Saigyōzakura*, about male figures.

35. Tsumura Reijirō, in his article "*Dōjoji*: Preparations for a Second Performance" (Teele, ed., *Mime Journal*, 1984: 104–13), says "the critical evaluation of [the actor's] first performance is of such importance that it can dominate the course of his professional life. This is because it is impossible to successfully perform *Dōjoji* without a full mastery and understanding of all the essential elements of his craft—noh chant, dance, music, masks, and costumes." The tremendous taxation of physical strength and stamina during the performance and the great expense of paying for the many stage attendants and the extra rehearsal times at particularly high rates are major deterrents to performing *Dōjoji* frequently, though recently there has been something of a boom in *Dōjoji* productions, probably due to it its being so dramatically compelling.

36. Quoted in Ito vol. 2, 489–94.

37. Sources of the story include *Dōjoji engi emaki*, etc.

38. Kanze and Hōshō actors hang the bell in solemn silence, while the Kita, Kongō, and Konparu schools give the job of hanging the bell to the kyōgen actors, who ham it up with unsuccessful attempts.

39. Translation by Donald Keene, *Twenty Plays of the Nō Theater* (New York: Columbia Unversity Press, 1970), 237–52; and Brazell, 193–206.

40. *Kanemaki* has been recently reconstructed for performance. It is also still performed in Yamabushi kagura, nōmai, and Kurokawa nō, along with *Dōjoji* by other troupes, and this reflects the sixteenth century, when both plays were in the repertory.

41. First performance: 1536 at Ishiyama Honganji, as recorded in *Shōnyo shōnin nikki*.

42. It is unclear when the bell prop was first devised, but records suggest that in the beginning *Dōjoji* used a kosode garment to represent the bell.

43. While *Eboshi ori* is generally attributed to the sixteenth-century Miyamasu, about whom little is known, Kumasaka's authorship is unknown. The Konparu family records from the early sixteenth century suggest Miyamasu, while the Kanze family records of about the same time mention the possiblity of Konparu Zenchiku, or at least someone in the Konparu family.

44. The other common closure song at the end of a program comes from the first-category play *Takasago*.

45. See Itō Masayoshi, 458. Other plays composed as felicitous end-pieces are *Shakkyō* (The stone bridge) and *Sagi* (The heron).

46. Ito, 456–57, contains a text of *Shōjō no mae*.

47. Other pieces with similar references to the benefits of wine (referred to as "chrysanthemum water") include *Kikujidō*, *Makurajidō*, and the dengaku piece Kikusui.

48. Kanai Kiyomitsu, (Nō no kenkyū (Studies of noh) (Tokyo: Yōhōsha, 1939), 353–61.

CHECKLIST OF THE EXHIBITION

COSTUMES

Noh costumes are classified according to tailoring, weave structure, design patterns, and use. Three broad groups differentiated by tailoring and use are: *ōsode* (or *hirosode*) – outer garments with broad sleeves open at the cuff; *kosode* – kimono-style garments with wrist-length box sleeves sewn up at the outer edge to leave only a small opening for the cuff; and *hakama* – pleated pants or bifurcated skirts. Various accessories include hairbands (*kazuraobi*), sashes (*koshiobi*), headgear, wigs, and fans.

Further classification of the broad-sleeved outer garments, many of them descendants of Heian and Kamakura-period garments worn by the nobility and military aristocracy, depends for the most part on details of tailoring. Each has a characteristic shape with set proportions. Each type of broad-sleeved garment has one or more typical weave structures and one or more typical design layouts. These jackets and cloaks include *kariginu, happi, sobatsugi, mizugoromo, chōken, maiginu, hitatare, suō,* and *kataginu.*

Kosode are all of one cut, with slight variation over time. The noh kosode garments are classified according to decorative technique. Those made from soft, pliant textiles, like satin, are worn as undergarments or combined to form outfits. These include the undecorated white *haku*; the *surihaku*, decorated with designs done in metallic leaf; the *nuihaku*, decorated with embroidery and metallic leaf; and the *noshime,* a plain-weave silk of solid colors or bands of colors. Kosode with pictorial weft patterning (*karaori, atsuita,* and *atsuita-karaori*) are distinguished from each other by ground-weave structure, design motifs, and use.

Pleated pants may be broad and stiffened in the back, like the plain-color *ōkuchi* and the brocaded *hangire,* or softer and either tied at the ankle, like the *sashinuki* and the *kyōgen kukuribakama,* or extra long so they trail behind the wearer (*nagabakama*). (MB)

Ōsode
KARIGINU

A broad-sleeved, round-collar outer garment worn by ministers, gods, goblins, and courtiers, the noh kariginu is a variation on a garment worn by the Heian aristocracy as informal wear and by the military aristocracy of later centuries as formal wear.

Tailoring: This three-quarter-length garment has single-width central panels. Cords at the base of the round collar fasten an overlapping front panel in place. Double-width open sleeves with round braided cords laced into their cuffs are stitched to the center panels at the back shoulder area, leaving the front of the sleeves free.

Textile characteristics: Lined (*awase*) kariginu come in many weave structures, though most typical is lampas, with a satin or twill ground weave and gold- or silver-leaf paper supplementary weft patterning in plain weave. Some have patterns in colored silk wefts (*nishiki*) on a satin or twill ground. Figured satin (*donsu*), double weave (*fūtsū*), and embroidery are other decorative possibilities. Old examples are often made of textiles imported from China or modeled on Chinese imports. Unlined (*hitoe*) kariginu are sheer, either gold pattern on simple gauze (*rokin*), or gold-leaf or multicolored patterning on plain gauze (*sha*). Some have a structural pattern woven into the plain gauze ground (*monsha*). Unpatterned kariginu for more rustic roles can be made of gauze, plain weave (*shike*) or loose plain weave with displaced threads (*yore*).

Typical colors and patterns: Lined kariginu are often white, or dark colors like indigo, green, or deep red, with gold or silver patterns, often large-scale. Unlined kariginu of patterned gauze tend to be blue, green, cream, or white, and many have patterns reminiscent of the Heian nobility (*yūsoku mon'yō*). Plain-weave kariginu are often dull green or brown. (MB)

KARIGINU DRAPING AND ROLES:
STRONG GOD

Kamo
Kariginu over hangire
tōkanmuri crown
Ōtobide mask

MINISTER

Tsurukame (waki)
Kariginu over ōkuchi,
eboshi hat
No mask

GOBLIN

Kurama Tengu
Kariginu over hangire
ōtokin hat
feather fan
Ōbeshimi mask

COURTIER

Tōru
Kariginu over sashinuki
shokanmuri crown
Chūjō mask

KARIGINU (LINED) WITH HERONS AND REEDS

① *Momoyama period, sixteenth century*
Dark blue silk satin weave with silk embroidery and gold leaf
55 ½ x 62 ³/₁₆ in. (141.0 x 158.0 cm)
Neo Kasuga Shrine, Gifu Prefecture
Important Cultural Property
catalogue 1, p. 70, p. 81 (detail)

KARIGINU (LINED) WITH LIONS AND FLOWERS

② *Momoyama period, sixteenth century*
Brown silk warp and cotton weft satin weave with cotton and gold-leaf paper supplementary weft patterning (ōdon)
54 ⅛ x 76 ⅛ in. (139.4 x 194.0 cm)
Seki Kasuga Shrine, Gifu Prefecture
Important Cultural Property
catalogue 2, p. 75

KARIGINU (UNLINED) WITH PEONY ARABESQUES

① *Edo period, eighteenth century*
Dark blue silk gauze weave with silk and gold-leaf paper supplementary weft patterning (kenmonsha)
69 ³/₁₆ x 79 ⅝ in. (175.8 x 202.2 cm)
Tokyo National Museum
catalogue 3

This unlined kariginu has a plain gauze weave ground with discontinuous supplementary weft patterning in gold and many different colors of silk, using a technique known as "Korean brocade" (*chōsen nishiki*). The Uesugi family, important warlords of the sixteenth century, originally owned this kariginu. (MB)

KARIGINU (UNLINED) WITH BAMBOO

② *Edo period, eighteenth century*
Green silk gauze weave with gold-leaf paper supplementary weft patterning (rokin)
68 ½ x 84 ¼ in. (174.0 x 214.0 cm)
Hayashibara Museum of Art,
Okayama Prefecture
catalogue 4

NOTE: Because of their sensitivity to light, many objects in the exhibition will be exchanged for others at the halfway point, indicated in the checklist as follows: ① first half; ② second half Objects not marked are displayed throughout the entire duration.

NŌSHI

A long courtier's jacket with broad cloth bands at the hemlines joining front and back panels, the nōshi is the same cut as formal Heian court uniforms (*hō*) but without the color restrictions. Basically a court garment, it is sometimes worn in the noh for courtier roles as a substitute for the kariginu.

Tailoring: Like the kariginu, the nōshi has double-width, open-cuffed sleeves, single-width body panels, a round collar and front overlapping panel tied at the right side of the neck. Unlike the kariginu, it has no decorative cords, but does have bands of cloth at the hemline, similar to those on the happi, but broader.

Textile characteristics: Lined (*awase*) nōshi tend to be figured twills (*aya*), while unlined (*hitoe*) are generally simple gauze (*sha*) with patterning.

Colors and patterns: Court motifs (*yūsoku mon'yō*) like linked concentric diamonds and flower roundels are standard. (MB)

NŌSHI DRAPING AND ROLES:

COURTIER

Nōshi over sashinuki
and nuihaku
shōkanmuri crown
Chūjō or Imawaka mask

NŌSHI WITH PHOENIXES AND CLOUDS

Edo period, nineteenth century
Silk gauze weave with gold-leaf
stenciled patterns (inkin)
64 ½ x 79 ½ in. (163.8 x 202 cm)
Private collection
cataogue 5, p. 74

This unlined, gauze weave summer *nōshi* differs from standard court garments in having larger, more pictorial pattern motifs, as is suitable for the stage. Rows of large phoenixes with swirling tail feathers alternate with rows of smaller cloud formations. Staggering the placement of the figures in the rows and combining large and small motifs this way has its roots in the *karahana* design brought to Japan from China in the seventh and eighth centuries. (MB)

HAPPI

An outer garment worn by warriors, demons, and bandits, the happi has double-width open sleeves joined at the shoulder to body panels, which are connected at the hem by means of cloth bands. The happi was created specifically for the noh and first appears in written records in the early Edo period.

Tailoring: A three-quarter length garment with two body panels edged at the neck and front with a straight collar, the happi has double-width, square, open sleeves. The cloth bands that join the front body to the back are considerably narrower than those on the nōshi.

Textile characteristics: Lined (*awase*) happi can have a variety of weave structures, many identical with those used to make kariginu. Gold, silver, or colored weft plain-weave patterning on a satin ground is standard, but twill grounds also exist. Unlined (*hitoe*) happi are made of sheer weaves, such as simple gauze (*ro*) or plain gauze (*sha*) with gold or silver woven patterns; occasionally happi have stenciled or painted designs.

Typical colors and patterns: Lined: bold patterns, often geometric or suggestive of Chinese imagery, on white, blue, green, purple, brown, or black grounds. Unlined: plain or patterned with arabesques, insects, flowers, or *yūsoku mon'yō* designs derived from court garments on white, blue, or purple grounds. (MB)

HAPPI DRAPING AND ROLES:

REVENGEFUL WARRIOR GHOST

Funa Benkei
Happi with sleeves hiked up
over atsuita
and hangire
Ayakashi mask

GOOD DEVIL

Nomori
Happi over hangire
tōkanmuri crown
Kobeshimi mask

CHINESE SPRITE

Kikujidō
Happi with right sleeve off
over atsuita
and hangire
Dōji mask

HAPPI (LINED) WITH LEAVES

①*Edo period, nineteenth century*
White silk satin lampas weave with gold-leaf paper
supplementary weft patterning (kinran)
41¾ x 79 in. (106.0 x 200.6 cm)
Noda Shrine, Yamaguchi Prefecture
catalogue 6

Large leaves seem to float down through the air like golden flakes. Reversing the direction of the pattern on the right sleeves alleviates the repetitiveness of the pattern and adds to the sense of the leaves being buffeted in a strong wind. (MB)

HAPPI (LINED) WITH FLOWERS ON BROKEN LATTICE

②*Edo period, nineteenth century*
Green silk satin lampas weave with gold-leaf
paper supplementary weft patterning (kinran)
42⅛ x 77 1/16 in. (107.0 x 196.0 cm)
Noda Shrine, Yamaguchi Prefecture
cataogue 7

HAPPI (UNLINED) WITH CHERRY BLOSSOMS

①*Edo period, eighteenth century*
Green silk gauze weave with gold-leaf
stenciled pattern (inkin)
39 11/16 x 74⅝ in. (100.8 x 189.6 cm)
Hayashibara Museum of Art,
Okayama Prefecture
cataogue 8

The unostentatious quiet of this unlined happi sets it apart from many others. The randomly scattered cherry blossoms are few, rendered by stenciling adhesive onto the gauze fabric and then laying gold foil on the areas that have been stenciled. This differs from the standard technique of weaving in the design, and creates a more solid gold surface. Time, however, has worn away most of the gold, which flakes off easily due to abrasion. (MB)

HAPPI (UNLINED) WITH COMPOSITE FLOWERS (KARAHANA)

②*Edo period, eighteenth century*
Blue-green silk gauze weave with gold-leaf paper
supplementary weft patterning (kinsha)
39 1/16 x 78 9/16 in. (99.2 x 199.6 cm)
Tokyo National Museum
cataogue 9

This happi is a good example of one used for warrior-courtier roles in second category plays (*shura* noh), where the actor would have a choice of wearing either an unlined happi or a chōken. In either case the right sleeve is rolled up and tucked away, exposing the kosode-style undergarment and giving full play to the right arm for manipulating a sword. Of the two types of garment, the happi is the more masculine. Elegance combined with strength can be seen in the gold flowers, whose form is a side view of a popular Chinese floral pattern known as *karahana*. (MB)

SOBATSUGI

Also known as a *sodenashi*, or "sleeveless," this long vest is similar to a lined happi, (except for the lack of sleeves) and can substitute for it, or be worn for roles of Chinese figures.

Tailoring: The straight front panels have no overlap, but are edged with a narrow collar that runs almost down to the hem of the knee-length garment. The front panels are joined at the bottom to the back panels with narrow strips of cloth. All sobatsugi are lined.

Textile characteristics: Gold, silver, or colored weft-patterning is woven on a satin or twill ground, often in lampas weave (*kinran*, *ginran*, or *nishiki*). Some are patterned with embroidery.

Typical colors and patterns: Sobatsugi that are worn to represent armor for warrior roles tend to have bold gold patterns on white, blue, olive, purple, brown, or black-blue grounds, while those used for Chinese roles often have denser Chinese patterns, or jewels.

SOBATSUGI DRAPING AND ROLES:

MALICIOUS GOD

Kinsatsu
Sobatsugi over atsuita and ōkuchi
wakanmuri crown
Tenjin mask

SOLDIER

Youchi Soga (tsure)
Sobatsugi over noshime and ōkuchi
sweatband
halberd
No mask

CHINESE WOMAN

Kureha
Sobatsugi over a kosode garment
Young woman's mask

CHINESE LOW-RANKING OFFICIAL

Kyōgen
Sobatsugi over a kosode garment
and momohiki pants
No mask

SOBATSUGI WITH STONE PAVEMENT PATTERN (ISHIDATAMI) TREASURES
① AND BUDDHIST IMPLEMENTS

Edo period, eighteenth century
Blue, purple, green, yellow, and white satin
or twill lampas weave with silk and gold-leaf
paper supplementary weft patterning (kinran)
42 1/8 x 25 9/16 in. (107.0 x 65.0 cm)
Tokyo National Museum
catalogue 10

② SOBATSUGI WITH CLOUDS AND TREASURES

Edo period, nineteenth century
Dark blue silk twill lampas weave with gold-leaf
paper supplementary weft patterning (kinran)
42 13/16 x 33 1/4 in. (108.8 x 84.4 cm)
Toyohashi Uomachi Noh Association,
Aichi Prefecture
catalogue 11

Bold gold designs on a dark ground typify costumes used for strong characters and appear on happi, kariginu, and hangire as well as on sobatsugi like this one. The dynamic impact of the glitter against darkness makes this sobatsugi suitable for representing a warrior's armor. The staggered rows of large linked diamonds, symbolizing treasures, and the trailing clouds evoke Chinese imagery, which in the Japanese sensibility is considered masculine. (MB)

MIZUGOROMO

The most ubiquitous of the outer garments, the mizugoromo is an overcoat worn by male and female, young and old, priests and laymen. Draped loose, it becomes a coat for old women, traveling or working women, shrine priestesses and nuns; belted it forms an outer jacket for old men, monks, workingmen (fishers, woodsmen, hunters), ghosts, Chinese old men, and gods in the guise of youths. Belted over bifurcated skirts (*ōkuchi*) mizugoromo are worn by high priests, *yamabushi* priests, dignified old men, and ghosts suffering in hell. The mizugoromo is purely a stage costume, having been created sometime before the early-Edo period specifically for the noh.

Tailoring: Unlike other outer garments with broad, open-cuffed sleeves, the mizugoromo has sleeves made from a single width of cloth. A three-quarter length garment like the maiginu, the mizugoromo has flared lapels (*okumi*) adding width to the front panels. The sleeves are sewn to the main panels from the shoulders to about halfway down the sides, and are left unattached. This allows for freedom of movement. No tassels or cords decorate the mizugoromo.

Textile characteristics: Mizugoromo exhibit a variety of plain weave types. Some are balanced weave of raw silk warp and weft; *shike* are a solid color woven with silk of uneven thickness for the weft; *shima* have warp stripes; *sha* are plain gauze; and *yore* appear ragged, having displaced wefts. The *yore* are woven with a spaced weft that is later displaced by combing areas together after the cloth is taken off the loom.

Typical colors and patterns: Most mizugoromo are plain color: white, gray, black, brown, light brown, green, purple, red, blue, or yellow. Some are striped and have two or three colors arranged vertically. Very occasionally one finds stenciled patterns in a restricted area, like along the hem of the main panels. (MB)

MIZUGOROMO DRAPING AND ROLES:

WORKING WOMAN OR TRAVELING WOMAN,
OLD OR YOUNG

Matsukaze
Mizugoromo draped in koshimaki style
Young woman's mask

NUN, OHARA GOKŌ, ACT 2

Mizugoromo over karaori draped in kinagashi style with nun's headgear
Young or middle-aged woman's mask

TRAVELING MONK

Tadanori (waki)
Mizugoromo over noshime (kitsuke)
No mask

YAMABUSHI PRIEST

Ataka
Striped mizugoromo with pompoms over ōkuchi
tokin hat
No mask

DIGNIFIED OLD MAN, TAKASAGO, ACT 1

Mizugoromo over checked atsuita and ōkuchi
Kojō mask

GHOST IN HELL

Kayoi Komachi
Mizugoromo over noshime (kitsuke) and ōkuchi
Yase-otoko mask

MIZUGOROMO WITH HACHIJŌ STRIPES

① *Edo period, eighteenth century*
Multicolored silk plain weave
44⁵/₁₆ x 69¹⁵/₁₆ in. (112.5 x 177.6 cm)
Tokyo National Museum
catalogue 12

    The striped silk textile of this mizugoromo
was woven on the island of Hachijō.
The colors were produced from natural
dyes derived from native plants. (SST)

MIZUGOROMO WITH STRIPES

② *Edo period, eighteenth century*
Green and white silk plain weave
40³/₄ x 57¹/₂ in. (103.5 x 146.0 cm)
Hikone Castle Museum, Shiga Prefecture
catalogue 13

    The evenly spaced stripes, though somewhat
exceptional, create a forceful impression
and thus suit roles such as the followers
of Benkei in the play *Ataka*. Yamabushi
priests always wear stripes along with their
pompoms (*suzukake*) and small round
lacquer hats. (MB)

YORE MIZUGOROMO

① *Edo period, eighteenth century*
Dark green silk plain weave
with displaced wefts (yore)
42¹⁵/₁₆ x 63³/₄ in. (109.0 x 162.0 cm)
Bunka Gakuen Costume Museum, Tokyo
catalogue 14, p. 154

    The irregular, ragged impression created by
the displaced wefts makes yore mizugoromo
suitable for roles of the poor and destitute,
like old women and suffering ghosts. (MB)

YORE MIZUGOROMO

② *Edo period, nineteenth century*
Gray silk plain weave with displaced wefts (yore)
43¹¹/₁₆ x 61¹³/₁₆ in. (111.0 x 157.0 cm)
Noda Shrine, Yamaguchi Prefecture
catalogue 15

YORE MIZUGOROMO

Edo period, nineteenth century
Light brown silk plain weave
with displaced wefts (yore)
50 x 57 in. (127.0 x 144.8 cm)
Los Angeles County Museum of Art
Purchased with funds provided by Jacqueline
Avant and Janet Francine Cobert; M.2002.71.2
catalogue 16, endsheets and p. 155

11

10

12

13

15

CHŌKEN

A gossamer, loose outer robe, the chōken is worn primarily by women performing long instrumental dances, but also by elegant men, children, and warrior-courtiers. In the last case, the chōken replaces an unlined happi.

Tailoring: Double-width sleeves with open cuffs and tassel cords (*tsuyu*) attached to the outer corner are sewn to the two center, free-falling panels (*migoro*) edged by a narrow collar (*eri*). Long, braided (*maru-uchi*) cords sewn at the chest with a bow formation are tied for women's roles and tucked into the belt for men's roles.

Textile characteristics: Simple gauze (*ro*) with supplementary patterning in gold or silver, or plain gauze (*sha*) possibly with structural pattern (*monsha*, *kinsha* if gold), or plain-weave raw silk with embroidery or appliqué. Alternative methods of applying pattern are painting, stenciling, or freehand gold leaf application.

Typical colors and patterns: Ground colors include white, crimson, purple, light and dark blue, green, yellow, and brown. Cords are red, yellow, purple, or green. Design construction tends to be either an overall pattern (like arabesques, flowers, grids, birds, and trees) or large crests above (three at the back and two on the front) with smaller scattered motifs below. (MB)

CHŌKEN DRAPING AND ROLES:

ANGEL

Hagoromo
Chōken over koshimaki
kanmuri crown
Zō-onna or Ko-omote mask

COURT LADY

Nonomiya
Chōken over red ōkuchi
and surihaku
Young woman's mask

WARRIOR-COURTIER

Tadanori
Chōken over ōkuchi and
atsuita-karaori
nashiuchi eboshi hat
Chūjō mask

CHILD

Kantan (child actor)
Chōken over ōkuchi
No mask

CHŌKEN WITH WISTERIA, FOLDED PAPERS (NOSHI) AND PRIMROSES

①*Edo period, eighteenth century*
Blue silk gauze weave with silk and gold-leaf paper supplementary weft patterning (rokin)
46⁷/₈ x 81⁷/₈ in. (119.0 x 208.0 cm)
Fujita Museum of Art, Osaka
catalogue 17, p. 23

The upward movement of the small, scattered primroses balances bouquets of drooping wisteria. The folded papers that hold the wisteria suggest a celebratory occasion. (MB)

CHŌKEN WITH WEEPING WILLOW AND SWALLOWS

②*Edo period, eighteenth century*
Green silk gauze weave with gold-leaf paper supplementary weft patterning (rokin)
50¹¹/₁₆ x 84⁷/₈ in. (128.8 x 215.6 cm)
Toyohashi Uomachi Noh Association,
Aichi Prefecture
catalogue 18, p. 79

The veil of young willow branches and returning swallows forms a variation on the "crest and hem" design. (MB)

CHŌKEN WITH FLOWER BASKETS, MAPLE LEAVES, AND DANDELIONS

①*Edo period, eighteenth century*
Yellow-gold silk gauze weave with silk and gold-leaf paper supplementary weft patterning (rokin)
40⁹/₁₆ x 81⅛ in. (103.0 x 206.0 cm)
Eisei Bunko Museum, Tokyo
catalogue 19

Solid gold grounds are rare in chōken. Here the rather large maples scattered all over the garment confuse the crest effect of the flower baskets. (MB)

CHŌKEN WITH PICTURE CARDS (SHIKISHI) AND POEM PAPERS (TANZAKU)

②*Edo period, eighteenth century*
Purple silk plain weave with gold-leaf paper supplementary weft patterning and appliqués of silk plain weave with gold-leaf paper weft patterning
41⁵/₁₆ x 83⁷/₁₆ in. (105.0 x 212.0 cm)
Eisei Bunko Museum, Tokyo
catalogue 20, p. 124

This atypical chōken is constructed out of thin plain-weave silk, a denser weave than the standard gauze. The patterning techniques are also nonstandard, being applied to the finished cloth rather than woven in. Although the overall design follows the "upper-crest, lower scattered motifs" layout, here the crests are light and small, while the rectangles of picture cards and poem papers appear heavy with their gold grounds. The overall effect is one of luxury, as might be worn as an outer garment by a court lady, like Lady Rokujō in *Nonomiya*. (MB)

CHŌKEN WITH WEEPING WILLOWS

①*Edo period, eighteenth century*
Green silk figured gauze weave (monsha) with gold-leaf paper thread embroidery
41⁵/₁₆ x 81⅛ in. (105.0 x 206.0 cm)
Hayashibara Museum of Art,
Okayama Prefecture
catalogue 21

The painterly grace of the embroidered sparse trees with small, freshly budding leaves creates a stunning elegance suitable for courtiers and young warriors. (MB)

CHŌKEN WITH INSECTS AND LATTICE PATTERN

②*Edo period, eighteenth century*
Blue-black and white silk gauze weave with gold-leaf paper threads (hirakinshi) and gold-leaf paper wrapped silk thread (yorikinshi) embroidery (rokin)
43½ x 81⅛ in. (110.5 x 206.0 cm)
Fujita Museum of Art, Osaka
catalogue 22

Despite the repetition of model forms for the bell crickets, and pine crickets embroidered in gold against a blue-black sky, great variety is achieved by altering the embroidery thread and stitch. The insects done in gold-wrapped thread couched onto the surface appear to be outside the lattice, which possibly represents bars of an insect cage. Those insects done in gold-wrapped threads or in flat gold-leafed paper strips embroidered into the gauze structure appear to be inside the cage. Its almost pristine condition suggests that this garment was rarely or never worn. (MB)

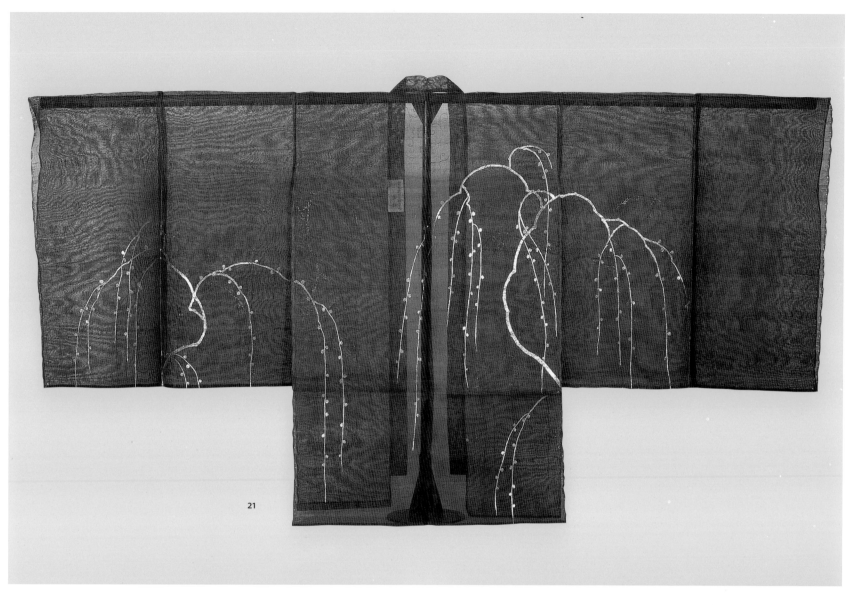

21

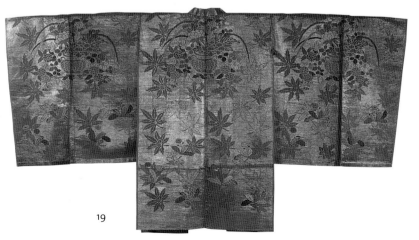

19

22

MAIGINU

A gossamer robe, worn by women who perform a long instrumental dance, created specifically for the noh some time in the early Edo period. In impression similar to the chōken, the maiginu differs in both tailoring and draping.

Tailoring: The longish main panels (*migoro*) have side seams connecting front to back in the lower portion. The double-width open-cuffed sleeves attached at the shoulder have no cords or tassels. Overlapping lapels (*okumi*) are sewn to front panels in most cases.

Textile characteristics: Weave structures and patterning techniques are the same as for chōken.

Typical colors and patterns: Overall patterns covering the complete garment predominate: arabesques (*karakusa*), vertical serpentine lines (*tatewaku*), grids, roundels, and floral patterns on purple, red, gray, white, or varicolored grounds; some crest designs. (MB)

MAIGINU DRAPING AND ROLES:

DRAGON GIRL

Ama
Maiginu over colored ōkuchi
dragon crown
Deigan mask

WIFE OF DRUM PLAYER, FUJI

Fujidaiko, Umegae
Maiginu over koshimaki
torikabuto headdress
Fukai or Ōmi-onna mask

MAIGINU WITH BUSH CLOVER, CHRYSANTHEMUM, AND PEONY ROUNDELS

① *Edo period, eighteenth century*
Dark green silk gauze weave with gold-leaf paper supplementary weft patterning (rokin)
51 9/16 x 83 7/16 in. (131.0 x 212.0 cm)
Fujita Art Museum, Osaka
catalogue 23, p. 128

A trailing arabesque fills the whole surface of this maiginu. At intervals, somewhat to the right and left of center, flowers and leaves form wreaths within the swerving vines. The three types of flowers appear to be randomly distributed and the wreaths to contain some variation, making for a truly free-flowing design The gold strips used as thread are made from Japanese paper with thin gold leaf pasted to its surface. The gold paper is cut with a knife into thin strips, leaving the top edge uncut. Once the gold paper is rolled up with another paper, the top portion is cut off and the individual strips can be pulled out as needed. They are passed through the shed by hooking them with a flat bamboo stick. When the entire garment is woven and off the loom, the parts of the strips that do not show as pattern but run along the back of the cloth are shaved off with a razor, so they do not show through the gauze. (MB)

MAIGINU WITH BRANCHES OF CHERRY BLOSSOMS

② *Edo period, nineteenth century*
Light blue silk gauze weave with silver-leaf paper supplementary weft patterning (rogin)
51 5/8 x 86 1/8 in. (131.2 x 218.8 cm)
Hikone Castle Museum, Shiga Prefecture
catalogue 24, p. 128

The overall balanced pattern of sprigs placed in rows of alternating directions has a simple uniformity found more often in maiginu than chōken. (MB)

MAIGINU WITH HYDRANGEA CRESTS AND STYLIZED CLOUDS

① *Edo period, eighteenth century*
Purple silk plain weave with silk and gold-leaf supplementary weft patterning
51 3/16 x 59 1/16 in. (130.0 x 150.0 cm)
Fisei Bunko Museum, Tokyo
catalogue 25

The tailoring is typical of maiginu, but the design and weave structure are atypical. Hydrangea branches curl into almost perfect rounds forming crests that bridge seams, yet are perfectly matched. The simplified symmetry of the clouds rendered in flat masses has an almost modern abstraction. The gold on a solid plain-weave ground creates an opaque density. (MB)

MAIGINU WITH YOUNG PINES ON ABSTRACT SNOWFLAKE PATTERN (YUKIWA)

② *Edo period, eighteenth century*
Purple silk gauze weave with silk and gold-leaf paper supplementary weft patterning (rokin)
58 1/4 x 84 1/4 in. (148.0 x 214.0 cm)
Noda Shrine, Yamaguchi Prefecture
catalogue 26, p. 78

Partial abstract snowflakes (*yukiwa*) are arranged in an overall pattern similar to an abstract wave pattern (*seigaiha*) symbolizing longevity. The young pines depicted here in gold on a purple ground suggest potentiality and are often gathered at the New Year for a special ceremony. The evergreen pine remains fresh even in the winter snow. (MB and SST)

23

25

HITATARE

Matched lined suits of hemp worn by the military class. The pleated pants can be either trailing extra-long nagabakama, or ankle-length hanbakama. The jacket worn without matching pants is known as a *kakehitatare*.

Tailoring: The noh hitatare with open-cuff double-width sleeves and short main panels is similar to formal samurai wear of the Edo period, except for its decoration and the flat rather than round cords attached at the chest and bottom corners of the sleeves. Strips of plain cloth reinforce the collar lapels and the sides of the pants.

Weaving and techniques: Plain-weave hemp with paste-resist patterns. Rice powder is mixed into a thick paste and applied either freehand through a funnel (*tsutsugaki*) or using a stencil (*katazome*) to protect areas from absorbing dye. Extra colors are often brushed or stamped on.

Colors and patterns: Overall patterns, crests along the jacket top and below the knee. Tortoises and cranes are common, particularly for costumes worn in *Okina* by Sanbasō and Senzai. Ground colors include black, indigo, brown, and green. (MB)

HITATARE DRAPING AND ROLES:

SAMURAI OFFICIAL

Hitatare over noshime
nashiuchi eboshi hat
No mask

SUŌ

Matched unlined suits of hemp worn by the military class.

Tailoring: Noh suō are basically unlined hitatare and correspond to samurai suō of the Edo period. Suō differ from hitatare in having crests at the chest and upper back but no decorative sleeve cords and generally cloth chest cords.

Weaving and techniques: Plain-weave hemp is the base for stenciled paste-resist patterns (see hitatare).

Colors and patterns: Small overall patterns (*komon*) are common, often with divided areas of different patterning on green, dark blue, gray, or brown grounds. Some have stripes. (MB)

SUŌ DRAPING AND ROLES:

ORDINARY MAN

Suō over noshime
No mask

SUŌ WITH WEEPING CHERRY TREE BLOSSOMS

(1) *Edo period, eighteenth century*
Indigo hemp plain weave
*with stenciled paste-resist (*katazome*)*
Suō: 33 7/8 x 78 3/8 in. (86.0 x 199.0 cm);
nagabakama length: 59 13/16 in. (152.0 cm)
Shinshiro Honmachi Noh Association,
Aichi Prefecture
catalogue 27, p. 165

Stylized weeping cherries form a dense texture of pattern. The stencil has been reversed in every other panel to give an impression of movement and variety. The dandelions in snowflake crests form a light counterpoint to the otherwise dark outfit. (MB)

SUŌ WITH SCATTERED UMBRELLAS

(2) *Edo period, eighteenth century*
Indigo hemp plain weave
*with stenciled paste-resist (*katazome*)*
Suō: 32 3/8 x 44 2/5 in. (82.2 x 112.8 cm);
nagabakama length: 60 7/8 in. (154.6 cm)
Toyohashi Uomachi Noh Association,
Aichi Prefecture
catalogue 28, p. 168

The pairs of open and closed umbrellas scattered over the ground are clearly a stencil design. Where the sleeves join the garment the design is reversed, as was done when stencils were first used in dyeing, suggesting that this is an early robe. (KK)

SUŌ WITH PINE, BAMBOO CURTAINS (MISU), PLUM BLOSSOMS, POEM CARDS (TANZAKU), ROUNDELS, AND SEASHORE LANDSCAPE PICTURE CARDS (SHIKISHI)

(1) *Edo period, nineteenth century*
*Black hemp plain weave with colors and freehand paste-resist (*tsutsugaki and yūzenzome*)*
Suō: 32 1/16 x 79 15/16 in. (81.5 x 203.0 cm);
nagabakama length: 51 9/16 in. (131.0 cm)
Hayashibara Museum of Art, Okayama Prefecture
catalogue 29, p. 160

Various seashore and spring motifs are arranged in a free-flowing design. The large spirals represent whirlpools. Nearby lies the sandy beach, pine groves, and fishing buoys off the shoreline. On the upper-right sleeve, plum branches are in full bloom. Elegant bamboo curtains suggest a party of nobles, including women, having an early spring flower-viewing party. The many rectangular decorative papers that lie scattered in the middle section of the garment suggest the poems composed for the occasion. (MB)

SUŌ WITH BAMBOO

(2) *Edo period, eighteenth century*
Black hemp plain weave with pigments
*and paste-resist (*tsutsugaki*)*
Suō: 29 15/16 x 75 9/16 in. (76.0 x 192.0 cm);
nagabakama length: 59 1/16 in. (150.0 cm)
Shinshiro Honmachi Noh Association,
Aichi Prefecture
catalogue 30, p. 238

The variations in the sizes of the bamboo in the forest are illustrated in an interesting manner. The design is drawn in starch paste, and the thin white lines, known as "paste threads" because they resemble thin threads, require a specialized technique. Dyeing this textile in four distinct colors required repeated application of rice paste to protect the lighter areas. Although bold in design, the colors of brown and indigo give an subtle overall impression. (KK and MB)

NAGA-KAMISHIMO

Matched unlined suit with sleeveless jacket and long pleated pants of hemp worn by the military class.

Tailoring: Basically this is a suō with the sleeves cut off. The front panels are pleated so they converge into a broad band that is tucked into the pants.

Weaving and techniques: Plain-weave hemp is the base for stenciled paste-resist patterns (see hitatare).

Colors and patterns: Crests stand at the shoulder and center back; overall patterns or divided areas with pictorial figures on indigo, gray, brown, and green. (MB)

NAGA-KAMASHIMO DRAPING AND ROLES:

TOWNSMAN

Naga-kamishimo
over a kosode garment
No mask

NAGA-KAMISHIMO WITH ABUNDANT TREASURES (TAKARAZUKUSHI)

(1) *Edo period, eighteenth century*
*Parti-colored hemp plain weave with ink, pigment, and stenciled and freehand paste-resist (*katazome *and* yūzenzome*)*
Top: 26 3/16 x 25 3/16 in. (66.5 x 64.0 cm);
nagabakama length: 63 9/16 in. (161.5 cm)
Hayashibara Museum of Art, Okayama Prefecture
catalogue 31, p. 169

NAGA-KAMISHIMO WITH VERTICAL SERPENTINE LINE PATTERN (TATEWAKU)

(2) *Edo period, eighteenth century*
*Black hemp plain weave with stenciled paste-resist (*katazome*)*
Top: 26 9/16 x 22 3/16 in. (67.5 x 56.4 cm);
nagabakama length: 56 1/8 in. (142.6 cm)
Hayashibara Museum of Art, Okayama Prefecture
catalogue 32, p. 238

Originating from ancient China, the vertical serpentine line pattern (*tatewaku*) is an abstract representation of rising steam or vapor. During the former Han dynasty the concept of spiritual energy, *ki*, formed the basis for the understanding of heaven and earth. A light, warm energy was said to have risen up and created the heavens and the sun. Tatewaku is the visualization of this concept of energy, and in this sense must be regarded as celebratory as well. By the early modern period, when this robe was made, the original meaning of the design had been lost. (KK)

30

32

KATAGINU

Sleeveless jackets of unlined hemp are created specifically for the stage and worn by commoners and servants in kyōgen plays.

Tailoring: Basically the top vest of the kamishimo, the front panels are pleated so they converge into a broad band that is tucked into the pants.

Weaving and techniques: Plain-weave hemp is the base for paste-resist patterns (see hitatare).

Colors and patterns: From small stenciled repeats to bold hand-drawn oversized vegetables and pictorial scenes, the designs are various, but always include crests depicting shepherd's purse flowers inside snowflakes. (MB)

KATAGINU DRAPING AND ROLES:

ORDINARY KYŌGEN MAN, SERVANT, BANDIT (ACTIVE)

Fumiyamadachi
Kataginu over ankle-bound kukuribakama
No mask

ORDINARY KYŌGEN MAN OR SERVANT

Busshi
Kataginu with standard hakama
No mask

KYŌGEN MESSENGER

Kataginu with right sleeve off over ankle-bound kukuribakama
No mask

KATAGINU WITH RADISH AND MALLET

①*Edo period, nineteenth century*
Hemp plain weave with ink
*and paste-resist (*tsutsugaki)
29 1/8 x 26 7/8 in. (74.0 x 68.2 cm)
Eisei Bunko Museum, Tokyo
catalogue 33, p. 6

> The Chinese name for the radish is *ra fuku*. The reading for the character for good fortune is also "fuku." Radish often appears in designs with mice and therefore results in the following flow of images: radish – mice – rice – Daikokuten (a household god of good fortune) who always carries a mallet. (KK)

KATAGINU WITH WATERFALL AND CHERRY BLOSSOMS

②*Edo period, eighteenth century*
Blue hemp plain weave with pigment
*and paste-resist (*tsutsugaki)
30 7/8 x 25 13/16 in. (78.5 x 65.5 cm)
Eisei Bunko Museum, Tokyo
catalogue 34, p. 173

> Cherry blossoms tumble over a waterfall with waves and water bubbles at the base of the waterfall. The gentleness of spring is evoked by the pleasant rhythm of falling water and the cherry blossoms reversed in white and detailed with rouge pigment. The unique characteristics of this vest suggest a date from early Edo period. (KK)

KATAGINU WITH TRIPLE COMMA (TOMOE) SAILS AND TATTERED FENCE

①*Edo period, eighteenth–nineteenth century*
Dark brown hemp plain weave
with pigments and paste-resist
29 5/8 x 21 7/16 in. (75.2 x 54.5 cm)
Hayashibara Museum of Art, Okayama Prefecture
catalogue 35, p. 173

> This kataginu once belonged to the Ikeda clan of Bizen. The comparative narrowness of the shoulders indicates that it is in the older style that was popular during the early Edo period. It is prized for the wonderfully playful rendering of the boat sails in round shapes that look like commas. The sharp outline of the lozenge-shaped crest was clearly meant to contrast with the curves of the abstract boat sails. The right shoulder is covered in a cloud, while at the hem is a tattered fence, offering a striking contrast of curved and straight lines. Although the attraction of kyōgen designs is said to lie in their realism and down-to-earth quality, there are designs that do not fit this description, and this is one example. The fact that this kataginu, with its narrow shoulders, is tailored in an earlier style suggests that a nonrealistic quality may be characteristic of an older style. What is thought of as typical kyōgen design seems to have flourished in the late Edo and modern periods. (KK)

KATAGINU WITH HERONS AND REEDS

②*Edo period, nineteenth century*
Brown and green hemp plain weave with ink,
*pigments and paste-resist (*tsutsugaki)
30 11/16 x 27 7/8 in. (77.9 x 70.8 cm)
Shinshiro Honmachi Noh Association, Aichi Prefecture
catalogue 36, p. 164

> Three herons were resisted in white with details skillfully drawn in ink. The reeds are suggested by a white design against a green ground. The traditional kyōgen crest is depicted. (KK)

KATAGINU WITH SCARECROW, BIRD CLAPPERS, AND PRAYING MANTIS

①*Edo period, nineteenth century*
Green hemp plain weave with colors
*and paste-resist (*tsutsugaki)
29 5/16 x 27 3/4 in. (74.5 x 70.5 cm)
Shinshiro Honmachi Noh Association, Aichi Prefecture
catalogue 37, p. 172

> The scarecrow standing in a field with bird clappers suggests the presence of sparrows descending on a ripening autumn field. The scarecrow's bow and arrow have been so effective, however, that there is no sign of a bird. So accurately are they realized, the movement and loud noise of the clappers can almost be seen and heard. The lines spreading out around the composition accentuate the clamor, as does the angle at which the feet of the bamboo poles have been placed. A large praying mantis reigns over the events. (KK)

KATAGINU WITH RABBITS AND SCOURING RUSH

②*Edo period, eighteenth–nineteenth century*
Black hemp plain weave with ink
*and paste-resist (*tsutsugaki)
30 5/16 x 24 9/16 in. (78.4 x 62.4 cm)
Toyohashi Uomachi Noh Association, Aichi Prefecture
catalogue 38, p. 157

> The combination of rabbits and scouring rush has been a common motif for centuries. Scouring rush, stiff and veined, was used by artisans to polish their crafts and here suggests the idea of the rabbits polishing their teeth. By shifting the subject to humans, the meaning becomes one of polishing the self, or praising effort and condemning laziness. The straight lines of the rush form a pleasing contrast with the roundness of the rabbits. (KK)

Kosode
SURIHAKU

A soft silk kosode-style undergarment with patterns in gold or silver leaf worn primarily by women.

Tailoring: The box-sleeved garment with a lining of white, purple, red, or dark blue.

Weaving and patterning techniques: While Momoyama-period surihaku are mostly made from plain-weave silk with glossed wefts (*nerinuki*), Edo-period ones tend to be satin (*shusu*), warp-faced twill (*aya*) or figured satin (*donsu* or *rinzu*). Stencils are cut to create a pattern that is repeated over all or part of the garment. Adhesive is applied through the stencil onto stretched cloth. Before the adhesive dries, metal pounded to a thin foil is laid on the cloth and pressed gently. After drying, the excess gold or silver leaf is brushed away and kept for other uses.

Colors and patterns: Geometric designs like rice field patterns (*ajiro*), fence interlace (*kakine*), abstract waves (*seigaiha*), and interlocking triangles (*uroko*) are common, also more-flowing designs like dew-laden grass, flower sprigs, or swirling water. Some surihaku are entirely covered with pattern, but as draping styles expose only the upper portion of the garment, often only that part is fully patterned. White predominates, also light blue, red, or yellow grounds, or horizontal color bands. Surihaku with small amounts of embroidery are called *nui-iri surihaku*. (MB)

SURIHAKU DRAPING AND ROLES:

WOMAN OF LOCALE

Nonomiya
Surihaku shows at neck under the karaori in kinagashi draping
Standard young woman's mask, middle-aged woman's mask

MADWOMAN OR WOMAN DOING LABOR

Hanjo
Surihaku shows over right side under karaori in nugisage draping
Young woman's mask, or masugami

JEALOUS WOMAN, ALSO USED FOR MANY WOMAN'S ROLES

Aoi no ue, Dōjōji, Izutsu, Kakitsubata
Surihaku exposed on upper torso with nuihaku in koshimaki below
Hannya mask

SURIHAKU WITH PICTURE CARDS (SHIKISHI) AND GRAPEVINES

① *Momoyama period, sixteenth century*
Purple silk plain weave (nerinuki) with gold-leaf stenciled patterns
40 ⁷/₈ x 37 ¹⁵/₁₆ in. (103.9 x 96.4 cm)
Tokyo National Museum
Important Cultural Property
catalogue 39, p. 90

> Although this costume is for a child actor the elegant design and technical virtuosity make it one of the finest examples of suri-haku. Grapevine motifs are often depicted on Momoyama- and Edo-period textiles. (NI)

SURIHAKU WITH PAULOWNIA, CHERRY BLOSSOMS, AND WATER PLANTAINS

② *Momoyama period, sixteenth century*
Silk plain weave (nerinuki) parti-colored (somewake) in red-orange and white with gold- and silver-leaf stenciled patterns, cinnabar and ink
55 x 47 ¹¹/₁₆ in. (139.7 x 121.2 cm)
Seki Kasuga Shrine, Gifu Prefecture
Important Cultural Property
catalogue 40

> Within the woven red color blocks, clouds in pine-bark lozenge (*matsukawabishi*) formations along with water plantains, paulownia, cherry blossoms, and maple leaves are drawn with gold ink and outlined with cinnabar. The clouds have black ink shadow lines. The white blocks have vertical serpentine lines (*tatewaku*) and a gold-leaf stenciled lattice with chrysanthemums, plums, bell flowers, water plantains, and orange flowers drawn with wavy ink lines in a style similar to that of early *tsujiga-hana* (sixteenth-century stitch-and-bind dyed textiles with gold stenciling and ink drawing). This is one of the oldest surviving noh costumes. (MB)

SURIHAKU WITH AUTUMN GRASSES

Edo–Meiji period, eighteenth–nineteenth century
White silk satin weave with silver-leaf stenciled patterns
39 x 56 ¼ in. (99.1 x 142.9 cm)
Los Angeles County Museum of Art,
Costume Council Fund; M.90.39
catalogue 41, p. 91 (detail)

> This luminous white robe is embellished with silver-leaf stenciled patterns of delicate sprigs of bush clover (*hagi*), hemp agrimony (*fujibakama*), balloonflower (*kikyō*), and pampas grass (*susuki*). The silver leaf has tarnished in an array of colors just as autumn foliage changes colors. Autumnal motifs such as these have been popular since the Heian period. The short length and undecorated hem of this robe are abbreviations common in noh undergar-ments. (MB and SST)

SURIHAKU WITH ABSTRACT MOUNTAIN PATH PATTERN (YAMAMICHI)

② *Edo period, 1812*
Light red silk plain weave with gold-leaf stenciled pattern
57 ¹³/₁₆ x 54 in. (146.8 x 137.2 cm)
Ishikawa Prefectural Museum of Art
catalogue 42

> The cut paper stencil used to create the wavy abstract mountain path motifs was reversed left and right so as to match the paths at the garment's seams. (MB)

SURIHAKU WITH ABSTRACT WAVE PATTERN (SEIGAIHA) AND MAPLE LEAVES

① *Edo period, eighteenth century*
Silk figured satin (rinzu) with silver- and gold-leaf stenciled patterns, colors, and ink
56 ½ x 57 ½ in. (143.5 x 146.0 cm)
National Noh Theater, Tokyo
catalogue 43

> This distinctive surihaku has painted maple leaves on the stenciled abstract wave pattern, popularized during the Genroku era (1688–1704). The maple leaves were built into the stencil pattern, but the *yūzenzome*-style shaded coloring gives the sense of great variety. Each leaf is outlined in ink with stems rendered in silver ink. Key-fret patterns (*sayagata*) woven into the figured silk satin are revealed in the leaves' white centers. (MB)

SURIHAKU WITH WILD PINKS ON WICKERWORK PATTERN (AJIRO)

② *Edo period, eighteenth century*
White silk satin weave with silk embroidery and silver-leaf stenciled patterns (nui-iri surihaku)
58 ⅜ x 53 ¹⁵/₁₆ in. (148.4 x 137.0 cm)
Hayashibara Museum of Art,
Okayama Prefecture
catalogue 44

> Small and dainty wild pinks with tassel petals line pathways forming three rows of horizontal zigzags. Between the rows lies an expanse of silver-leaf stenciled wickerwork pattern made up of squares composed of six vertical lines next to six horizontal lines arranged in a checkerboard pattern. The half-tarnished silver leaf reflects a spectrum of subtle colors. Soiling along the neck and flaking at the waist area attest to this having been a favored costume of its previous owners, the Ikeda family. Embroidery has been left off the center front section, an area that would be hidden when the costume was worn. (MB)

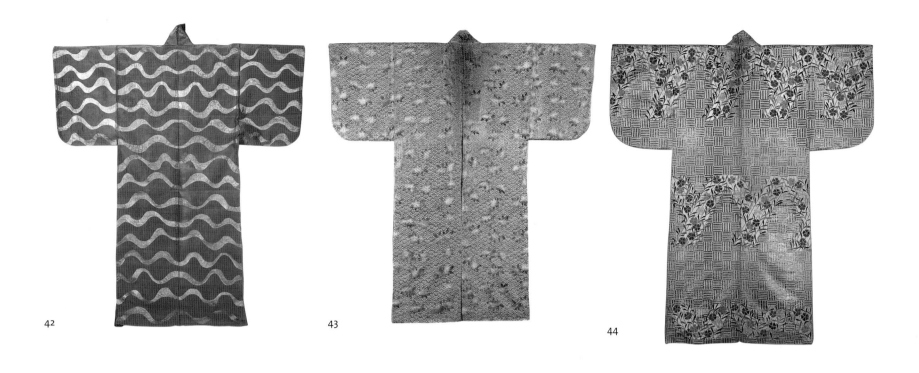

42   43   44

40   41

NUIHAKU

A soft silk kosode-style garment worn by women and young men and decorated with embroidery and gold- or silver-leaf stenciled designs.

Tailoring: Usually nuihaku are lined with white, red, or purple plain-weave silk.

Techniques: Weaves and metallic-leaf designs are similar to surihaku. Embroidery stitches changed over time. Long parallel stitches across the obverse with only tiny stitches on the back (*watashi nui*) characterize the Momoyama-period garments. Edo-period embroidery seeks greater pictorial realism and textural variety and employs long and short stitch, satin stitch, stem stitch, and overlay stitch.

Colors and patterns: Grounds include solid white, red, blue, yellow, light browns, purple, and black, as well as bands or blocks of color dyed after weaving. While some nuihaku, particularly early ones, are densely embroidered over the whole garment, others have decoration only in defined areas, or sparsely arranged over the whole. Shoulder and hem compositions are particularly suited to wearing the garment folded at the waist in *koshimaki*-style draping. Solid gold grounds (*dōhaku*) are reserved for aristocratic roles. (MB)

NUIHAKU DRAPING AND ROLES:

JEALOUS WOMAN, ALSO USED FOR MANY WOMAN'S ROLES

Aoi no ue, Dōjōji, Izutsu, Kakitsubata
Nuihaku draped in *koshimaki* stye slipped off the shoulders and folded down at the waist
Hannya mask /
young woman's mask

GHOST OF A WOMAN / SPIRIT OF A PLANT

Izutsu / Kakitsubata
Nuihaku draped in *koshimaki* style under *chōken*
Young woman's mask

WARRIOR-COURTIER

Atsumori, Tadanori
Nuihaku (*kitsuke*) worn under *chōken* with *ōkuchi*
Jūroku or Chūjō mask

BLIND BOY / YOUNG BOYS

Yorobōshi
Nuihaku under *mizugoromo*
Yorobōshi mask

NUIHAKU WITH SCATTERED FANS AND SNOW-LADEN WILLOW BRANCHES

① *Momoyama period, sixteenth century*
Silk plain weave (nerinuki) with silk embroidery and gold leaf
52 13/16 x 44 1/4 in. (134.1 x 112.4 cm)
Tokyo National Museum
Important Cultural Property
catalogue 45, p. 87

The wavy sand bar border (*suhama*) that delineates the *katasuso* (shoulder and hem) pattern was popular from the Kamakura through Momoyama periods. The combination of green and white of the willows as well as the red and yellow of the fans typifies the Momoyama-period color scheme, as do the dense stitches running only over the surface. (MB)

NUIHAKU WITH SNOW-LADEN WILLOW BRANCHES AND ABSTRACT PINE-BARK LOZENGES (MATSUKAWABISHI)

② *Momoyama period, sixteenth–seventeenth century*
Silk plain weave (nerinuki) parti-colored (somewake) in red and white with silk embroidery
53 1/8 x 44 3/16 in. (134.9 x 112.2 cm)
Seki Kasuga Shrine, Gifu Prefecture
Important Cultural Property
catalogue 46, p. 86

Although this robe is categorized as a nuihaku there is no trace of gold leaf, only multicolored silk embroidery thread depicting stylized willow trees over an abstract pine-bark lozenge pattern. The tree trunks are detailed in a manner similar to Momoyama-period lacquer. (SST)

NUIHAKU WITH SNOW-LADEN REEDS AND BIRDS

① *Momoyama period, sixteenth century*
Silk plain weave (nerinuki) with silk embroidery and gold and silver leaf
55 7/8 x 47 1/4 in. (142.0 x 120.0 cm)
Hayashibara Museum of Art,
Okayama Prefecture
Important Cultural Property
catalogue 47, p. 82 and 80 (detail)

Inspired by imported Ming embroidery that utilized gold thread between flower and bird motifs, the Japanese placed gold or silver leaf in the negative areas between the embroidery. Artisans in Japan did not have the technical expertise to produce gold thread (*kinshi*) until the seventeenth century. (SST)

NUIHAKU WITH SNOW-LADEN PLANTAIN

② *Momoyama period, sixteenth–seventeenth century*
Silk plain weave (nerinuki) parti-colored (somewake) in red and white with silk embroidered appliqués and gold- and silver-leaf stenciled pattern
57 13/16 x 48 13/16 in. (146.8 x 124.0 cm)
Hayashibara Museum of Art, Okayama Prefecture
catalogue 48, p. 27

Embroidered during the Momoyama period this bold snow-laden plantain was probably salvaged from a worn-out garment and appliquéd onto this robe at a later date. A gold-leaf stenciled pattern covers the base fabric, which has been dyed in blocks of red and white. The robe once belonged to the Ikeda daimyo family of Bizen (now Okayama Prefecture). (SST)

54

53

NUIHAKU WITH LILIES AND OXCARTS

① *Momoyama period, sixteenth century*
Brown silk plain weave (nerinuki) with silk
embroidery and gold-leaf stenciled patterns
54 5/16 x 49 3/16 in. (137.9 x 125.0 cm)
Tokyo National Museum
Important Cultural Property
catalogue 49, p. 88

While the predominant technique of long
embroidery stitches passing over the surface
leaving only tiny dots of stitches on the
reverse (ura-nuki) is typical of Momoyama-
period embroidery, the fine, short stitches
seen in the oxcarts foreshadow trends that
were to become popular in the seventeenth
century. (NI)

**NUIHAKU WITH GRASSES, POEM PAPERS
(TANZAKU), SERPENTINE-LINE PATTERN
(TATEWAKU), PLANK BRIDGES,
AND SNOW-LADEN WILLOW BRANCHES**

② *Momoyama period, sixteenth century*
Silk plain weave (nerinuki) parti-colored
(somewake) in red and white with silk embroidery
and gold-leaf stenciled patterns
54 3/16 x 46 7/16 in. (137.6 x 118.0 cm)
Tokyo National Museum
Important Cultural Property
catalogue 50, p. 83

A design of alternating blocks of color
filled with a myriad of patterns was popular
in the Momoyama period. This nuihaku
formerly belonged to the Mōri clan that
controlled the Aki domain (now western
Hiroshima prefecture). (NI)

**NUIHAKU WITH SCATTERED CRESTS
OF WILD CHERRIES AND SCROLLS**

① *Momoyama period, sixteenth–seventeenth century*
Silk figured twill on plain-weave (saya) parti-
colored (somewake) in red, dark brown, and white
with silk embroidery, gold ink and gold-leaf
stenciled patterns
51 15/16 x 42 1/8 in. (132.0 x 107.0 cm)
Hayashibara Museum of Art, Okayama Prefecture
Important Cultural Property
catalogue 51, p. 89

The combination of ground colors and
the small-scaled embroidery and stenciled
gold-leaf patterns on this robe is consistent
with fashionable nuihaku kosode worn
by samurai women in the Keichō and
Kan'ei eras. (SST)

**NUIHAKU WITH SCROLLING CLEMATIS
VINES, EULALIAS, AND SCATTERED FANS**

② *Momoyama period, sixteenth–seventeenth century*
Silk plain weave (nerinuki) parti-colored (some-
wake) in dark brown and red with silk embroidery
and gold-leaf stenciled patterns
52 1/4 x 51 3/16 in. (132.7 x 130.0 cm)
Tokyo National Museum
catalogue 52, p. 85

Made of two different textiles, this is
a good example of the sixteenth-century
katamigawari (split body) design layout.
The left sleeve and right body panel have
large fans filled with Momoyama-period
embroidery over a gold-leaf stenciled
pattern of dew-laden grasses. The right
sleeve and left body panel have small
clematis arabesques embroidered on a
ground whose near-black color is associated
with the Keichō era. The tailoring of the
garment in its present form was probably
done in the early Edo period, after weaving
widths became somewhat narrower and
sleeves were made the same width as the
body panels. (MB)

**NUIHAKU WITH FLOWERS AND GRASSES
OF THE FOUR SEASONS**

① *Edo period, eighteenth century*
Silk plain weave parti-colored (somewake)
in bands of blue, green, red, and white
with silk embroidery and gold- and silver-leaf
stenciled patterns
54 1/2 x 53 1/8 in. (138.5 x 135.0 cm)
Nomura Art Museum, Kyoto
catalogue 53, p. 243

One of a variety of metallic-leaf stenciled
patterns that include dew-laden grasses,
flower-filled lozenges, misty haze, key-frets
(*sayagata*), abstract waves (*seigaiha*), and
water is placed within each horizontal
band. Several seasons are alluded to by the
embroidered clumps of bellflowers and
primroses scattered on the upper half of
the robe and irises on the lower half. (SST)

**NUIHAKU WITH CHRYSANTHEMUMS
AND KEY-FRET PATTERN (SAYAGATA)**

② *Edo period, eighteenth century*
Silk satin weave parti-colored (somewake) in red
and white with silk embroidery, and gold-leaf
stenciled patterns
54 3/4 x 52 3/8 in. (139.0 x 133.0 cm)
Noda Shrine, Yamaguchi Prefecture
catalogue 54, p. 243

The parti-colored (*somewake*) dyed horizontal
stripes of this robe are covered with a gold-
leaf stenciled interlocking key-fret pattern
called *sayagata*. Side-views of long-petal
embroidered chrysanthemums (*rangiku*) lie
scattered at various angles. The balanced,
light arrangement of the design as well as
the use of a variety of embroidery stitches
typifies mid-Edo-period embroidery. (MB)

**① NUIHAKU WITH PINE TREE ON STONE
PAVEMENT PATTERN (ISHIDATAMI)**

Edo period, eighteenth century
Silk plain weave parti-colored (somewake) in
red, blue, and white with silk embroidery and gold-
and silver-leaf stenciled pattern
59 7/16 x 53 9/16 in. (151.0 x 136.0 cm)
Hayashibara Museum of Art, Okayama Prefecture
catalogue 55, p. 245

The realistically embroidered pine tree
on the back of this robe resembles the lone
pine tree depicted on the back wall of
a noh stage. Similar standing tree (*tachiki*)
motifs, rising up from the hem and
branching out across the back, were used
on eighteenth-century fashionable kosode.
The gold- and silver-leaf checkered pattern
resembling stone pavement is canted to
correspond with the stitch and dyed
(*nushime shibori*) diagonal stripes. (SST)

NUIHAKU WITH BIRDS IN FLIGHT

Edo period, eighteenth century
Silk satin weave with silk embroidery
and gold leaf (dōhaku)
57 1/2 x 52 3/8 in. (146.0 x 133.0 cm)
Eisei Bunko Museum, Tokyo
catalogue 56, p. 245

The solid gold-leaf ground (*dōhaku*) on six-
harness satin of this nuihaku places it
as especially high ranking, and suggests a
mid-Edo-period date. Gorgeous birds of
many colors – swallows, sparrows, peacocks,
and long-tailed varieties – appear to be
twisting and turning in the air. Feathers and
plumage are detailed in tiny embroidery
stitches aiming toward realism. Overlay
stitches add graphic outlines. This nuihaku
would probably be worn as the lower half
of an ensemble draped *koshimaki* style. (MB)

**NUIHAKU WITH NANDINA
AND SCATTERED BOOKS**

Edo period, eighteenth century
Silk satin weave with silk embroidery
and gold leaf (dōhaku)
61 1/4 x 56 in. (155.6 x 142.2 cm)
The Metropolitan Museum of Art
Gift of Mr. and Mrs. Paul T. Nomura, in memory
of Mr. and Mrs. S. Morris Nomura, 1989
catalogue 57, p. 141

The design motif of plants with scattered
books and their placement on this noh robe
can also be found on fashionable kosode
of the same period. A nearly identical
design can be found in the pattern book
Ken'eirō gasō (Compilation of graceful
designs, cat. 122, p. 140). (NI)

55

56

NOSHIME

A plain-weave kosode-style garment worn mostly by less exalted men, sometimes by old women.

Weaving characteristics: Raw silk warp and glossed weft form a plain-weave structure, sometimes with textural element added by varying the thickness of the threads. In the Edo period noshime were standard garb worn under matched suits like suō and hitatare, and the term could refer to a wide variety of textiles.

Colors and patterns: Solid dark blue, brown, purple, green, or tan, or horizontal bands of contrasting solid colors with checks. One common form is to leave the waist area white (*koshiaki*), or give it checks on a white ground. Stripes and bands of color are considered higher-class than solid-color noshime. (MB)

NOSHIME DRAPING AND ROLES:

TRAVELING PRIEST

Waki in many plays,
i.e. *Izutsu*
Plain noshime
of brown or dark blue
under mizugoromo
sumibōshi headgear
No mask

TRAVELING PRIEST

Taema (wakizure)
Plain noshime
under mizugoromo
and ōkuchi
sumibōshi headgear
No mask

SERVANT

Noshime under kamishimo
with nagabakama

MILITARY MAN

Fujito (waki)
Noshime under hitatare
No mask

NOSHIME WITH HORIZONTAL BANDS

① *Edo period, eighteenth century*
Green, yellow and white silk plain weave
54 15/16 x 53 7/8 in. (139.5 x 136.8 cm)
Itsukushima Shrine, Hiroshima Prefecture
catalogue 58

NOSHIME WITH HORIZONTAL STRIPES

② *Edo period, eighteenth century*
Green, yellow and indigo silk plain weave
58 9/16 x 53 15/16 in. (148.7 x 137.0 cm)
Eisei Bunko Museum, Tokyo
catalogue 59

KARAORI

Lavishly brocaded with feminine designs, the karaori is a kosode-style garment worn as a main garment, an overgarment, or an undergarment, usually by women, occasionally by men or sprites.

Tailoring: The karaori box sleeves are sewn to the main panels, rounded slightly at the outer edge, and sewn up to form a small cuff. While Momoyama karaori sometimes have extra-broad panels and half-width sleeves, Edo-period pieces have sleeves and main panels of equal widths.

Weaving characteristics: Supplementary float patterning in many colors of silk floss is woven in discontinuous shots into a ground weave of 2-to-1 twill of raw silk warp and weft. When the pattern includes gold-leaf paper strips, they are generally held in place by a more spaced twill than the ground twill.

Ground colors: Red, white, purple, blue, brown; solid or in alternating blocks. To create the alternating blocks, the warp is resist (ikat) dyed before dressing the loom.

Patterns: Flowers predominate. Usually one design contains ten to fourteen different colors. (MB)

KARAORI DRAPING AND ROLES:

WOMAN OF PLACE

Nonomiya / Kamo: act 1
Karaori draped in kinagashi style with spread-out collar but snug around the hips
Woman's mask

MADWOMAN OR WOMAN LABORING

Hanjo / Semimaru
Karaori draped in nugisage style with the right sleeve slipped off
For madwoman roles the actor carries a bamboo branch
Masugami mask

WOMAN OUT IN THE WORLD

Dōjōji: act 1
Karaori draped in tsubo-ori style with the karaori hiked up and tucked in at the waist over koshimaki (surihaku with nuihaku folded down at the waist)
Ōmi-onna or middle-aged woman's mask

NOBLE WOMAN / SPRITE

Sōshiarai Komachi / Shōjō
Karaori draped in tsubo-ori style with karaori hiked up and tucked in at the waist over ōkuchi
Young woman's mask / Shōjō mask

WARRIOR-COURTIER

Tadanori: act 2
Karaori worn as an undergarment for elegant male roles with chōken over ōkuchi
Chūjō mask

KARAORI WITH CHRYSANTHEMUMS, PAULOWNIA, AND LATTICES, WITH WILLOW BRANCHES AND PAULOWNIA CRESTS

① *Momoyama period, sixteenth century*
Silk twill weave on ikat-dyed (kasuri) warp in alternating blocks of red and white with silk supplementary weft patterning
55 1/8 x 46 7/8 in. (140.0 x 119.0 cm)
Hayashibara Museum of Art, Okayama Prefecture
Important Cultural Property
catalogue 60, p. 109, p. 110 (detail)

This kosode karaori gives an elaborate impression in combining the design of alternating blocks of white and red and the narrow body and sleeves, the form unique to the robes of the Momoyama period. The blocks in red are a woven plaid, in addition to the burgeoning branches of willow tree and the paulownia crests woven in uki-ori, a weaving practice in which the supplementary weft draws patterns on a 5/1 twill weave ground. On the contrary, the patterns in the white blocks, chrysanthemums and the paulownia crests, have been woven by using a typical weaving technique of the Momoyama-period karaori. It arranges one rectangular design unit consisting of a chrysanthemum branch and a crest, which is repeated twice across the textile width. Likewise, this unit is repeated up and down the length of the textile. In detail, a pair of chrysanthemums, widely called *omotegiku* ("front" chrysanthemum) and *uragiku* ("back" chrysanthemum) nestle into each other; this is also a popular design of karaori made in the Momoyama period. In terms of the overall design, the bold alternating blocks suggest the juxtaposition of two seasons, the willow tree in spring and the chrysanthemum in autumn, each woven in contrasting techniques. Such laborious technique marks the extraordinary quality of this robe. (KS)

KARAORI WITH CHRYSANTHEMUM, PAULOWNIA, AND WEEPING CHERRY TREE BLOSSOMS

② *Momoyama period, sixteenth century*
Silk twill weave with ikat-dyed (kasuri) warp
in alternating blocks of red and white
with silk supplementary weft patterning
57 ¼ x 57 ½ in. (146.5 x 146.0 cm)
Tokyo National Museum
catalogue 61, p. 112

This karaori has alternating white blocks with sweeping cherry branches and red blocks with chrysanthemums and paulownia combined with an abstract mountain path pattern of zigzags. The flowers of chrysanthemum and paulownia are often used as family crest motifs. Both crest motifs have been emblems for the imperial family since Emperor Gotoba (reigned 1185–1198) and became the most prestigious crests of the warrior class since Emperor Godaigo (reigned 1318–1339) bestowed them on the shogun Ashikaga Takauji. In the Momoyama period, Toyotomi Hideyoshi (c. 1537–1625) used the crests without exception. A similar robe with a design of chrysanthemum and paulownia flowers scattered along with a mountain lane was a gift from Hideyoshi to Mōri Terumoto (1553–1625). The combination of an evergreen tree and seasonal flower such as cherry blossoms shown on this robe is a conventional design as recorded in *Ren'chū kyūki* (The old record inside the bamboo curtain) of the Muromachi period. The up-and-down repeating pattern throughout the length of the fabrics, most obviously seen in the white blocks, is characteristic of Momoyama period karaori. There is a design of a trunk of willow tree similar to the cherry trunk of this robe, which indicates the establishment of a stylized pattern. This robe has been retailored into a slimmer garment. (KS)

KARAORI WITH SNOW-LADEN MANDARIN ORANGE TREES

① *Momoyama period, sixteenth century*
Silk twill weave with silk supplementary
weft patterning
56 ¹¹/₁₆ x 48 ⁷/₁₆ in. (144.0 x 123.0 cm)
Kyoto National Museum
Important Cultural Property
catalogue 62, p. 120

With red in its design, this karaori would be used for a role of a young woman. However, there is no historical record attesting to whether it was made for the noh stage or was originally a fashionable kosode, which is common for Momoyama-period karaori.

Composed of two patterning units throughout the width, with the vertical, reciprocal patterning throughout, indicates the exemplary style of the Momoyama period. Each unit consists of the branches of snow-laden mandarin orange and lozenge-shaped flowers with snowflakes. The evergreen mandarin orange trees symbolize longevity. Snow, which covers everything in white, signifies purity. (KS)

KARAORI WITH CHRYSANTHEMUMS AND TRIANGLES FILLED WITH STONE PAVEMENT PATTERN (ISHIDATAMI)

② *Edo period, seventeenth century*
Silk twill weave with silk
supplementary weft patterning
58 ¹¹/₁₆ x 48 ¹³/₁₆ in. (149.0 x 124.0 cm)
Itsukushima Shrine, Hiroshima Prefecture
catalogue 63, p. 116

The meticulous detailed pattern of chrysanthemums amid a ground pattern of triangles, covering the entire surface, is typical of Edo-period-style karaori. Each triangle is made up of fine squares in a popular pattern known as *ishidatami* (stone pavement).

The weaving technique of layering patterns can be traced back to *futaeorimono*, a kind of textile highly appreciated by Heian courtiers. The technique instantly became popular when Kazuko, a daughter of the second Tokugawa shogun Hidetada, ordered furnishings covered with such textiles as part of her trousseau for her marriage to Emperor Gomizuno-o. Unlike the monochrome ground of futaeorimono, this karaori has been patterned using multicolored silk. Yet the rich coloring of Edo-period karaori is more somber than Momoyama robes. The arrangement of the two adjoining chrysanthemums on this robe is reminiscent of Momoyama style. The technique of warp threads that secure the patterning weft floats and integrate with the design (*mon toji*), as seen on the petals of the chrysanthemums, becomes more sophisticated in the Edo period. (KS)

58

59

KARAORI WITH BAMBOO CURTAINS (MISU), PICTURE CARDS (SHIKISHI), POEM PAPERS (TANZAKU) AND BUSH CLOVERS

① *Edo period, eighteenth century*
Silk twill weave with ikat-dyed (kasuri) warp
in alternating blocks of green and red with silk and
gold-leaf paper supplementary weft patterning
57⅞ x 54⅝ in. (147.0 x 138.8 cm)
Tokyo National Museum
catalogue 64, p. 121

The woven depiction of bush clovers rising toward the sky intersecting with poem papers falling toward the ground contrasts with the bamboo curtains woven on subtle alternating blocks of color. (NI)

KARAORI WITH MAPLE LEAVES AND BAMBOO CURTAIN (MISU)

② *Edo period, eighteenth century*
Silk twill weave with silk and gold-leaf paper
supplementary weft patterning
58¼ x 58¼ in. (148.0 x 148.0 cm)
Eisei Bunko Museum, Tokyo
catalogue 65, p. 137

The woven motifs of maple leaves scattered on a bamboo curtain allude to the court culture of the Heian period. Bamboo curtains were made to screen out sunlight and were often depicted in paintings showing the nobility trying to maintain privacy. It is possible to associate the robe with the chapter "Momijiga" (Maple leaves) in the Heian-period novel *Tale of Genji*, written by Murasaki Shikibu. *Mutsura*, a noh play based on this chapter, takes place in the village of Mutsura, where there is an evergreen maple tree amid colorful autumn leaves. One day a Buddhist priest comes to the tree to say prayers; the maple tree immediately turns into a beautiful woman who dances along with the prayers. This robe would appropriately embody the story. (KS)

KARAORI WITH AUTUMN GRASSES

① *Edo period, eighteenth century*
Silk twill weave with ikat-dyed (kasuri) warp
in alternating blocks of brown and light blue
with silk supplementary weft patterning
60⅛ x 56⅜ in. (152.7 x 143.2 cm)
Tokyo National Museum
catalogue 66, p. 100

This karaori does not have the color red in its design and is therefore called *ironashi*. *Zenpō zōdan*, written by the actor Konparu Zenpō (1454–c. 1532), records that "it is quite interesting to see the use of ironashi robes in the plays *Ugetsu* (The moon and the rain) and *Mutsura* (The village Mutsura)." Presumably Zenpō refers to karaori robes worn by the supporting role of an old woman in *Ugetsu* and the leading role of a village woman in *Mutsura*. It is typical that an elderly woman wears an ironashi robe. Yet it would be odd to see the leading role of a young woman in *Mutsura* wearing anything but a robe with the color red (*iroiri*).

On the other hand, an ironashi robe with the design of autumn grasses would be properly worn for the play *Kinuta* (The fulling block), in which a wife in a small village beats a cloth on a wooden block night after night, waiting for the return of her husband. The design and muted colors of this karaori successfully convey the mental state of this wife during a lonesome, tranquil autumn night. (KS)

KARAORI WITH AUTUMN GRASSES

② *Edo period, eighteenth century*
Silk twill weave with ikat-dyed (kasuri) warp
in alternating blocks of blue, red, and off-white
with silk supplementary weft patterning
59⁷⁄₁₆ x 56⁷⁄₁₆ in. (151.0 x 146.6 cm)
Kyoto National Museum
catalogue 67, p. 113

This karaori uses the color red (*iroiri*) in the woven design of autumn grasses. As Lady Izumi, one of the renowned female poets of the Heian period, once wrote, "Spring is all about flowers in bloom, autumn is the season to feel the pathos of nature" (*mono no aware*). In Japanese aesthetics, autumn grasses symbolize such pathos. They are also small and refined and therefore perfect motifs to represent femininity, especially in second category woman (*onna*) plays or third category wig (*kazura*) plays, where the leading role is a beautiful young woman. (KS)

ATSUITA-KARAORI WITH PAPER MULBERRY LEAVES ON WOVEN FENCE PATTERN

① *Edo period, eighteenth century*
Silk twill weave with ikat-dyed (kasuri) warp
in alternating blocks of green and white with silk
and gold-leaf paper supplementary weft patterning
59⅝ x 56³⁄₁₆ in. (151.45 x 142.8 cm)
Tokyo National Museum
catalogue 68

This karaori has a raised design motif of paper mulberry leaves with a background pattern of a woven fence on alternating color blocks of green and white. The leaves of the paper mulberry tree are deeply related to Tanabata, the star festival celebrated on the seventh day of the seventh month of the traditional lunar calendar. The legend tells of a husband, Star Altair (Ken'gyu-sei), and wife, Star Vega or Weaver Princess (Shokujo-sei), separated by the Milky Way, who can only meet once a year on that day. A mulberry leaf serves as a ship for Altair to cross the Milky Way. For that reason, on the date of the festival it became popular to write a poem on a leaf, or to make a ball out of paper mulberry leaves tied with branches, and dedicate it to the stars. Therefore this robe would be an appropriate costume for the play *Kureha* (Weaver from China). (KS)

KARAORI WITH AUTUMN GRASSES AND BUTTERFLIES

② *Edo period, eighteenth century*
Silk twill weave with ikat-dyed (kasuri) warp in
alternating blocks of white and green with silk and
gold-leaf paper supplementary weft patterning
58¹⁄₁₆ x 52¾ in. (147.5 x 134.0 cm)
Ōtsuki Seiinkai, Osaka
catalogue 69, p. 96

At first glance, the design seems to be the normal alternating color blocks, and yet the patterns of grasses and butterflies were created with total disregard of these blocks. Here the bold blocks serve merely as a background, rather than in Momoyama-period robes of the same type that emphasize the contrasting blocks.

Woven motifs include chrysanthemums, pampas grass, and butterflies. Chrysanthemums were originally imported from China, where they were greatly esteemed. The chrysanthemum is an emblem of longevity as well as of autumn. The sentiment of autumn has been further heightened on this robe with pampas grass, which was described by Sei Shōnagon in *Makura no sōshi* (The pillow book) as "the extensive beauty of the autumn field." Woven with multicolored silk and gold-leaf paper threads, the chrysanthemums give a feeling of magnificence, while the delicate pampas grass adds a tranquil and plaintive feeling to the robe. (KS)

KARAORI WITH SNOW-LADEN CAMELLIAS AND GENJI CLOUDS

Edo period, eighteenth century
Silk twill weave with silk and gold-leaf
paper supplementary weft patterning
59¹⁄₁₆ x 55⅛ in. (150.0 x 140.0 cm)
Los Angeles County Museum of Art,
Costume Council Fund; M.2002.71.1
catalogue 70, p. 136

Camellias have long been highly regarded as sacred as well as embodying the joys of spring. In fact, the Chinese written character for camellia combines the ideograms for tree and spring. Popular belief has it that if camellias bloom in autumn or winter it is an omen of an abundant crop, which may be the reason for the depiction of snow-laden camellias on this robe. (KS)

68

ATSUITA

The standard undergarment for male roles, atsuita range from simple checks to gorgeously brocaded designs. Tailoring is kosode-style, similar to the karaori.

Weaving characteristics: The ground weave tends to be a six-harness twill, and the supplementary patterning, when there is any, is done with discontinuous multicolored glossed weft, in a technique similar to that used for karaori.

Ground colors: red, white, purple, blue, browns; solid or in alternating color blocks. To create the alternating blocks, the warp is tie-dyed before dressing the loom.

Patterns: checks, linked hexagons, concentric diamonds, and circles, as well as Chinese-derived patterns, like temple gongs, dragons in clouds, and Chinese lions with peonies. (MB)

ATSUITA DRAPING AND ROLES:

OLD MAN

Takasago: act 1
Atsuita (kitsuke)
under mizugoromo
and ōkuchi
Kojō mask

OLD CHINESE MAN

Tenko: act 1
Atsuita (kitsuke)
under mizugoromo
Akobujō mask

WARRIOR GHOST

Funa Benkei: act 2
Atsuita (kitsuke)
under happi
with sleeves tucked under
Ayakashi mask

OLD WOMAN OF THE HILLS

Yamamba: act 2
Atsuita draped in tsubo-ori
style tucked up at the waist
over hangire
Yamanba mask

ATSUITA WITH POEMS

① *Edo period, seventeenth century*
Silk twill weave with silk and gold-leaf paper thread
supplementary weft patterning
56⁵⁄₁₆ x 52⁵⁄₁₆ in. (143.0 x 132.8 cm)
Tokyo National Museum
catalogue 71, p. 85

Six poems from the *Wakan rōeishū* (Japanese and Chinese poems for singing), an anthology compiled by Fujiwara Kintō around 1013, are skillfully woven to appear handwritten in an asymmetrical compositional style known as *chirashigaki* (scattered writing). The robe belonged to the Konparu family of noh actors. (SST)

ATSUITA WITH SNOW-LADEN WILLOW AND DEW-LADEN GRASSES, PAULOWNIA, CHRYSANTHEMUM, WISTERIA, AND PLUM BLOSSOMS

② *Momoyama period, seventeenth century*
Silk twill weave with silk supplementary
weft patterning
54⁵⁄₁₆ x 60⁹⁄₁₆ in. (138.0 x 153.8 cm)
Tokyo National Museum
catalogue 72, p. 250

The two center panels have similar color schemes but different motifs: spring willows holding lingering snowflakes on the left side and mixed autumn and spring flowers on the right. Having two different materials or patterns, known as "split body" (*katamigawari*) design, was popular in the Momoyama period. At that time kosode tended to have wide central panels and narrow sleeves, so it is possible that the sleeves seen here were added later when the garment was remade to accord with Edo-period tastes. Typical of some Momoyama-period weaving, the pattern repeat is short and only half the width of the fabric, and the weft floats have no intermediate binding warps (*toji*) holding them in place. (MB)

ATSUITA WITH LIONS AND CONCENTRIC LOZENGE PATTERN

① *Edo period, seventeenth century*
Silk twill weave with silk supplementary
weft patterning
52³⁄₈ x 52³⁄₄ in. (133.0 x 134.0 cm)
Shinshiro Honmachi Noh Association,
Aichi Prefecture
catalogue 73, p. 250

Wonderfully detailed lions with curly manes and fluffy tails prance in rows over a background of concentric lozenges. Apparently the design was intended specifically for the undergarment of the fox god in the noh *Kokaji*, where the animal deity teaches a swordsmith the secrets of his art. The dark colors as well as the slightly narrow and more rounded sleeves suggest a Keichō era (1596–1615) date, when the kosode form was changing from Momoyama to Edo style. The Shinshiro Shrine preserves old costumes such as this one, as well as a tradition of noh and kyōgen performance styles. (MB)

ATSUITA WITH FLOWERS IN LINKED HEXAGONS (KIKKŌ) AND WISTERIA ROUNDELS

② *Edo period, seventeenth century*
Silk twill weave with silk supplementary
weft patterning
46¹⁄₁₆ x 50¹⁄₄ in. (117.0 x 127.6 cm)
Tokyo National Museum
catalogue 74, p. 92

The raised weft patterning (*e-nuki*) of wisteria roundels is executed in a relatively loose manner with multicolored silk threads. Lack of gold-leaf paper supplementary wefts indicates a seventeenth-century date. (NI)

ATSUITA WITH VERTICAL STRIPES AND TRIPLE-COMMA ROUNDELS (TOMOE)

① *Edo period, eighteenth century*
Silk twill weave with silk supplementary
weft patterning
53¹⁵⁄₁₆ x 53³⁄₁₆ in. (137.0 x 136.0 cm)
Hayashibara Museum of Art,
Okayama Prefecture
catalogue 75, p. 129

The simple bold design of blocks of straight vertical stripes alternating with contrasting blocks of swirling circular triple-coma roundels startles with its fresh modernity. While the stripes follow a consistent repeat of red, green and white, a playful variation of browns, reds, yellows, blues and greens appears in the roundels. (MB)

ATSUITA WITH WEEPING CHERRY TREE BRANCHES ON VERTICAL STRIPES

② *Edo period, eighteenth century*
Silk twill weave on ikat-dyed (kasuri) warp
in blue, red, brown, white, green and yellow
with silk supplementary weft patterning
58¹¹⁄₁₆ x 54⁵⁄₁₆ in. (149.0 x 139.6 cm)
Hayashibara Museum of Art,
Okayama Prefecture
catalogue 76, p. 250

Trailing branches of tiny cherry blossoms, a favorite motif of the Ikeda family, add the bright texture of a multicolored background. Narrow breadths of warp threads have been dyed in blocks of blue and red, brown and white, or green and yellow, then arranged in rows that form blocks of alternating color. Variation in block size makes for a wonderful play of color, mostly lost from sight when the garment is worn under a broad-sleeved jacket and tucked into pleated pants. (MB)

ATSUITA WITH PAULOWNIA CRESTS AND TEMPLE GONGS (UNPAN) ON LINKED HEXAGONS (KIKKŌ)

① *Edo period, eighteenth century*
Silk twill weave with silk supplementary
weft patterning
56¹⁄₈ x 57¹⁄₂ in. (142.5 x 146.0 cm)
National Noh Theater
catalogue 77, p. 93

Large temple gongs and other medallion-like figures scattered over an overall geometric pattern typify atsuita made for strong male roles, including strong gods, warriors, bandits, and demons. The vibrant colors and bold patterns mix well with the bold designs of many happi and hangire. When worn under gauze garments, like chōken and unlined happi, a sense of masculinity is added to the more gentle impression of the gossamer outer garment. (MB)

**ATSUITA WITH CHINESE
LION-DOGS (SHISHI)**

②Edo period, eighteenth century
*Silk twill weave with silk supplementary
weft patterning*
54 1/2 x 53 9/16 in. (138.5 x 136.0 cm)
Tokyo National Museum
catalogue 78, p. 94, 95 (detail)

Two types of lion-dogs (*shishi*) are seen
romping on this atsuita. Larger, squat ones
face right, turning their heads to look back
at the pouncing lions behind them. Most
of the pouncing lions face left, as if chasing
their companions, though the one on
the left back sleeve has been reversed. The
one spanning the center back required
tremendous effort to weave, for the pattern
had to be displaced in two portions of
the warp, which necessitates restringing
the pattern just for that section. The
theme of romping lion-dogs makes reference to the Bodhisattva Manjusri (*Monju
bosatsu*) who rides a lion-dog. The noh
Shakkyō (Stone bridge) has lion-dogs playing
among the peonies in Manjusri's Pure Land.
This atsuita is noteworthy for having the
large lion-dog motif set against a plain
ground. (MB)

**ATSUITA WITH LATTICE
AND PAULOWNIA ARABESQUE**

①Edo period, eighteenth century
*Silk twill weave on ikat-dyed (kasuri) warp
in bands of green and white with silk
supplementary weft patterning*
57 1/8 x 51 9/16 in. (145.7 x 131.0 cm)
Itsukushima Shrine, Hiroshima Prefecture
catalogue 79, p. 132

The sharp, clean lines of this multicolored
plaid pattern on a white ground appear
to meld softly into an ikat-dyed green
horizontal band patterned with paulownia
arabesques. (MB)

**ATSUITA WITH FACING-CRANE LOZENGES,
LATTICE, AND PAULOWNIA CRESTS**

②Edo period, nineteenth century
*Silk twill weave on ikat-dyed (kasuri) warp
in alternating blocks of brown, green, and white
with silk supplementary weft patterning*
58 1/8 x 54 1/2 in. (148.2 x 138.4 cm)
Ishikawa Prefectural Museum of Art
catalogue 80

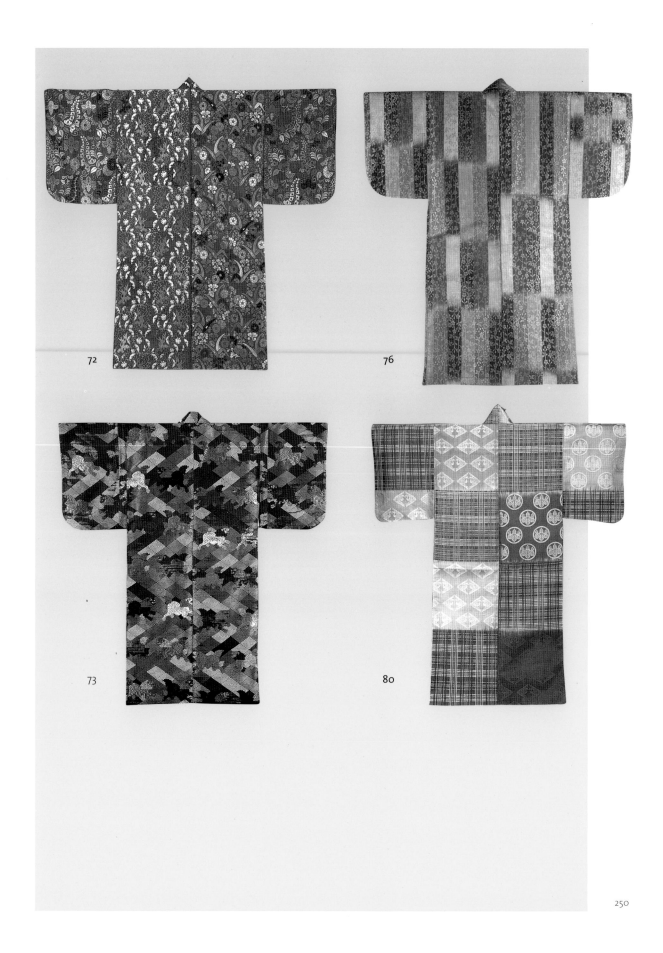

72

76

73

80

Hakama
ŌKUCHI

A type of broad stiff pleated pants (hakama; also referred to as divided skirts) with large hump in the back, ōkuchi are worn by high-class women, priests, warriors, and ministers. Ōkuchi are also worn like crinolines under other types of pleated pants to add body and bulk.

Tailoring: Four large pleats and a slightly flared cut make for a full front, woven with raw silk, while the back consists of two broad, stiff panels tightly woven with ribs (*uneori*) created by alternating thick and thin wefts. A sash made of the front panel material is attached to the top of the front and back panels. Cords laced through a breadth of the center top back panel can be pulled tight to form a pleated hump that is held up by a Y-shaped wood brace inserted in the tied sash at the actor's back.

Colors and patterns: Solid colors are the norm, with white predominant, and red used often for high-class women. Other colors are purple, green, brown, and dark and light blue. Some ōkuchi have discrete, subdued patterns, like shells, waves, or small flowers. (MB)

ŌKUCHI DRAPING AND ROLES:
YAMABUSHI PRIEST

Ataka
White ōkuchi
with striped mizugoromo
No mask

GOD IN THE GUISE OF AN OLD MAN

Takasago
White ōkuchi with plain
mizugoromo
Kojō mask

FIGHTING WOMAN, DANCING WOMAN

Tomoe
Red ōkuchi with chōken
Young woman's mask

WARRIOR-COURTIER

Tadanori
Ōkuchi with chōken,
right sleeve off,
and kosode garment
Chūjō mask

HANGIRE

Brightly patterned broad stiff pleated pants (hakama; also referred to as divided skirts) with large hump in the back that are worn by high-class warriors, demons, bandits, and strong gods. While ōkuchi were incorporated into noh from everyday wear, hangire were invented for the noh.

Tailoring: Similar to the ōkuchi, except that the belt sash is of a different cloth, generally white silk, and the back panels are made of the same material as the front and then stiffened by inserting straw mats between the face and lining fabrics.

Textile characteristics: Most common is a satin ground with gold or silver brocading (*kinran*) in a lampas weave.

Colors and patterns: Bold, geometric patterns against strong colors; dark blue, purple, green, red, brown, black, and white are common. Sometimes overall designs, such as huge waves, are used. (MB)

HANGIRE DRAPING AND ROLES:
MALICIOUS OLD MAN

Koi no omoni
Hangire with happi
and atsuita
Akujō mask

STRONG GOD

Kamo
Hangire with kariginu
Ōtobide mask

REVENGEFUL GHOST OF WARRIOR

Funa Benkei
Hangire with happi, sleeves
hiked up,
and atsuita
Ayakashi mask

SASHINUKI

Courtier's pantaloons bound at the ankle. These pleated pants are essentially the same as those worn by the nobility with nōshi and kariginu.

Tailoring: Sashinuki have six pleats in front and a large pleat in the back, but no stiffener. To make up for their slimmer cut and to add bulk, ōkuchi are worn under the sashinuki.

Textile characteristics: Most common is a twill ground with either weft-float or twill patterning.

Colors and patterns: Court patterns, like medallions of eight-lobed wisteria (*yatsufuji*) or linked birds (*toridasuki*) are common on purple or light blue grounds. (MB)

SASHINUKI DRAPING AND ROLES:
HEIAN COURTIER

Unrin'in: act 2
Sashinuki with kariginu
Chūjō mask

NAGABAKAMA

Long, trailing pleated pants, often forming the bottom part of a matched suit, and worn by the military class.

Tailoring: Nagabakama are basically long versions of the standard men's hakama. They have six, sometimes eight, front pleats and one large back pleat. Waistband sashes are attached to the top of the front and back. Side seams begin at mid-thigh.

Textile characteristics: Generally, plain-weave hemp.

Colors and patterns: paste-resist designs are dyed on blue, black and brown grounds. Small repeat patterns (*komon*) might be stenciled on, or larger patterns drawn freehand. (MB)

NAGABAKAMA DRAPING AND ROLES
ORDINARY MALE

Nakabakama
as part of suō suit
No mask

MASKS
Male

KASSHIKI (ACOLYTE) MASK
Muromachi period, sixteenth century
Pigment on Japanese cypress wood (hinoki)
8 3/8 x 5 3/16 in. (21.3 x 13.1 cm)
Seki Kasuga Shrine, Gifu Prefecture
catalogue 81, p. 42

With bangs across the forehead and dimples enhancing the cheeks, Kasshiki masks represent attractive teenage boys working as acolytes in Zen temples. Their red-lipped smiles, long loose hair, and almond eyes with almost rectangular pupil openings resemble the iconography of women's masks.

Kasshiki masks are classified by the shape of their bangs: straight across the forehead for "large" ones; narrow at the top and fanning out for "medium" ones; narrower and hardly spreading for "small" ones. This mask, despite its early date, is a good example of the medium type in everything but the color of the teeth, which normally are black. A bright eagerness seems to come from the eyes, tersely modeled cheeks, and curling lips. The finely brushed eyebrows twisting upward above the nose bridge and flaring out to the sides add a delicate sensitivity.

Youngest of the male masks, Kasshiki are worn in *Kagetsu*, *Tōgan Koji*, and *Jinen Koji* for roles featuring the performance of the lighthearted cuckoo (*kakkō*) dance, where the actor mimes beating a drum tied to his waist. (MB)

WAKAI OTOKO (YOUNG MAN) MASK
Muromachi period, sixteenth century
Pigment on Japanese cypress wood (hinoki)
7 3/4 x 5 1/2 in. (19.7 x 14.0 cm)
Seki Kasuga Shrine, Gifu Prefecture
catalogue 82, p. 61

This mask has the delicate features of an aristocrat: eyebrows painted high on the forehead, creases at the upper nose bridge, gently curled lips exposing blackened upper teeth (a cosmetic custom), and a flat black rim at the top of the forehead marking the rim of a courtier's hat. Similar features define the Chūjō mask (cat. 156, p. 197), though in a more fully defined, mature form. Due to discoloration and defoliation, only portions of the pinkish coloring remain. Crumbling of the prime coat has exposed portions of the smoothed wood surface. Bits around the eyes and lips have chipped off.

Although initially roles of grown young men were played unmasked, those representing ghosts of courtiers, warriors, and lovers came eventually to be masked. Exactly when is unclear, but examples such as this one help to define the time. Two carved inscriptions appear on the back. One reads "Hōshō Dayū," probably indicating a one-time owner or donor, or the man who verified the attribution: "Tatsuemon." In the *Sarugaku dangi*, Zeami praises the carver Tatsuemon as creating masks that "anyone can wear without much difficulty." If this attribution is correct, the mask would date from the first half of the fifteenth century, evidence that young-men's masks were being made before the end of Zeami's life. (MB)

HEITA MASK
Deme Zekan (d. 1616)
Momoyama–Edo period, seventeenth century
Pigments on Japanese cypress wood (hinoki)
8 x 5 5/8 in. (20.3 x 14.3 cm)
Toyohashi Uomachi Noh Association,
Aichi Prefecture
catalogue 83, p. 60

Stories accompanying this sole middle-aged-man's mask emphasize its use for roles of victorious warriors, such as Yoshitsune in *Yashima*, and the vanquisher of northern barbarians, Sakanoue no Tamuramaro, in *Tamura*. Vigor and self-confidence radiate from the ruddy skin color, the thick eyebrows that swerve upward paralleled by the full mustache, and the round, downward-turned eyes. These features contrast with those of the Chūjō mask (cat. 156, p. 197).

This mask is a good example of the mature form of its type. The care for detail seen in the minute brushwork and layered base colors shows the hand of the founder of the Ōno Deme line, Zekan Yoshimitsu (d. 1616), whose brandished seal on the back reads "First under Heaven: Zekan." (MB)

JŌ (OLD MAN) MASK
Nanbokuchō period, 1369
Pigment on Judas tree wood (katsura)
8 3/8 x 5 7/8 in. (21.2 x 14.9 cm)
Nagataki Hakusan Shrine, Gifu Prefecture
Important Cultural Property
catalogue 84, p. 8, 58

The somewhat distorted features of this old-man's mask reflect its early date, when noh had not yet been perfected and the sarugaku masks had a rural flavor. Still it already has certain characteristics that were to become standard. Its size approximates the human face. Remnants of white in the crevices, red on the lips, and black on the teeth follow what was to become standard coloring. The holes along the rim of the forehead as well as on the chin indicate places where hair was implanted and correspond to later forms of old-men's masks (cat. 85, p. 59). The absence of ears and stylized wrinkles, however, are more similar to Okina masks (cat. 137, p. 14). The choice of Judas wood rather than cypress also sets this mask apart.

This Jō mask is one of twenty-some masks used in religious rites at Nagataki Temple and Hakusan Shrine in Gifu Prefecture and housed at the shrine since the Meiji period, when Shinto and Buddhism were split. One of the earliest noh masks, its roughly hewn, unpainted back bears a donation inscription from 1369, the year after Zeami was born. (MB)

KOJŌ MASK
Edo period, eighteenth–nineteenth century
Pigment on Japanese cypress wood (hinoki)
with hair
7 1/2 x 6 in. (19.1 x 15.24 cm)
The Metropolitan Museum of Art,
Rogers Fund, 1925
catalogue 85, p. 59

In the first act of the god plays *Takasago*, *Yumiyawata*, and *Naniwa*, Kojō is used to represent an old man who later becomes a god. Ears and implanted beard hair characterize all old-men's masks, while a painted (rather than implanted) mustache and a single row of teeth indicate the higher dignity of the Kojō mask. The realistic rendition of the wrinkles on this standard example contrasts with the stylization on Okina masks.

An alternative name for the mask, Koujijō, derives from the name of a fifteenth-century carver, Koushi Kiyomitsu, credited with inventing the mask and known for his skill in making masks of old men. (MB)

YASE-OTOKO MASK
Deme Zekan (d. 1616)
Momoyama–Edo period, seventeenth century
Pigment on Japanese cypress wood (hinoki)
7 11/16 x 5 15/16 in. (19.5 x 15.2 cm)
Toyohashi Uomachi Noh Association,
Aichi Prefecture
catalogue 86, p. 51

Yase-otoko represents a ghost suffering in hell either for having taken life, such as the hunter in *Utō* and the fisher in *Akogi*, or from being obsessed with unfair treatment, like the fisher in *Fujito* and the lover Fukakusa no Shōshō in *Kayoi Komachi*. A mere skeleton, with sunken eye sockets, downturned mouth, and limpid hair, the face seems bloodless but for the intensity of the metallic eyes highlighted with vermilion. Zekan's Yase-otoko follows the standard, with hair only at the sides and not across the forehead, as on the earlier mask, owned by Mitsui Bunko (fig. 15, p. 50). A comparison with the female counterpart, Yase-onna (cat. 90, p. 51), reveals the angular masculinity of the mask. (MB)

AKUJŌ (EVIL OLD MAN) MASK
Muromachi period, sixteenth century
Pigment on wood with hair
8 1/16 x 6 5/8 in. (20.4 x 16.8 cm)
Oyama Shrine, Ishikawa Prefecture
catalogue 87, p. 49

Akujō masks represent fierce old men, like the angry spirit of the gardener who was mocked to death in *Koi no Omoni* and the strong gods appearing in *Tamanoi* and *Naniwa*. Larger than many noh masks, the face of Akujō harbors ill feeling, appropriate to its name.

This Muromachi-period version of Akujō is important for understanding the development of demon masks in general and Akujō masks in particular. It lacks the lower teeth, red tongue, and bulging central vein of later Ōakujō masks; rather the iconography, with side veins and slightly open mouth, seems closest to the "eagle-nose" or Washibana Akujō masks, though the overall expression of this piece seems more human and less stylized than later versions. A carved inscription on the back of the forehead written in a combination of *katakana* (Japanese square syllabary) and *kanji* (Chinese characters) reads, "Made by Yamato / Hikai (higaki) Moto / Shichirō." Presumably this is the same man who made the young-woman's mask from Katte Shrine in Nara. (MB)

BESHIMI MASK
Chigusa Saemon Dayū
Muromachi period, 1413
Pigment on Japanese cypress wood (hinoki)
8 5/16 x 6 1/8 in. (21.1 x 15.6 cm)
Naratsuhiko Shrine, Nara Prefecture
catalogue 88, p. 47

There are two main types of clenched-mouth masks. Larger ones have a rectangular construction, bulging eyes set in deep sockets, and a mouth that curls up. Smaller ones are oval, with smaller metallic eyes popping out under raised eyebrows, and a mouth that curls down. This mask comes from a formative period and cannot be easily classified. Most conspicuously, the heavy upper eyelids and irregular curve of the lower eyelids differ from later masks, the clenched lips extend in a straight line, and it lacks ears. Despite the paper pasted over the forehead, the gesso (*gofun*) primer and cypress base are standard, though most of the coloring has flaked off, leaving only an indication of the original tan and the vermilion in the furrows.

A carved inscription records the name of Chigusa, one of two carvers mentioned by Zeami for whom there is solid evidence, and the date 1413, which makes this the oldest dated demon mask made specifically for noh. The smooth back of the mask is painted with lacquer, which probably was applied at a later date. (MB)

KOTOBIDE MASK
Muromachi period, 1475
Pigment on Japanese cypress wood (hinoki)
8 7/16 x 5 7/8 in. (21.5 x 15.0 cm)
Nagataki Hakusan Shrine, Gifu Prefecture
Important Cultural Property
catalogue 89, p. 47

Tobide masks, with their bulging eyes and wide-open mouths, form the "ah" element in the "ah, un" demon pairs. While large Ōtobide (cat. 151, p. 191), meant to represent gods, have a rectangular construction, ears, and round gold eyes, the small ones, like this, have an oval construction, no ears, and smaller, less deeply set eyes. These are worn for animal spirits, such as the fox spirit in *Kokaji* (Small smith), the murderous stone spirit in *Sesshōseki* (Death rock), and the miraculous jewel-granting fish in *Kappō*. Stemming from the formative period, this mask's mouth lacks the standard red tongue.

Much of the primer and red paint has crumbled away, exposing the wood base, and the metal inserts for eyeballs have fallen off, but one can still make out the high crescent eyebrows and broad, upward-sweeping mustache. The back has been carved smooth and left in plain wood. An ink inscription dates the mask to 1475, shortly after the death of Konparu Zenchiku. (MB)

Female

YASE-ONNA
Edo period, seventeenth century
Pigment on Japanese cypress wood (hinoki)
8 3/8 x 5 11/16 in. (21.3 x 14.5 cm)
Oyama Shrine, Ishikawa Prefecture
catalogue 90, p. 51

The Yase-onna mask, representing the suffering spirit of a woman who dies from a problematic love relationship, has a gaunt passivity, yet also a haunting grace. Unlike the Yase-otoko mask (cat. 86), with its sharp edges and haggard look, the Yase-onna mask has smooth, rounded-off edges that give the bony face a fluid softness. Here one finds no gold inserts in the eyes, no red highlights, but instead calm, almost rectangular pupil openings. Unlike the peppered hair of the Rōjō mask, Yase-onna has black hair (in death one is ageless) with looping strands starting a few millimeters from the central part. In *Teika* and *Motomezuka* it is worn for women hounded by love and suffering in hell. This example from Oyama Shrine is a good rendition of the standard form. (MB)

RŌJO (OLD WOMAN) MASK
Momoyama period, sixteenth century
Pigments on Japanese cypress wood (hinoki)
8 1/8 x 5 11/16 in. (20.6 x 14.4 cm)
Hikone Castle Museum, Shiga Prefecture
catalogue 91, p. 63

Rōjo is the mask of an aged yet beautiful woman, such as the hundred-year-old poetess Ono no Komachi who, though reduced to rags, retains a sharp, sensitive mind, or the aged sage in *Higaki*. The sunken cheeks and hollow eye sockets reflect advanced years and at the same time reveal inner elegance. Only an occasional crease lines the clear skin. The mask has a quiet sobriety apparent in the downcast eyes and the gently open mouth.

The Ii family dates this mask to the Momoyama period, when mask types were essentially set, but various refinements in painting techniques, particularly the adding of patina (*furubi*), were being developed. Here the light skin has darkened areas highlighting the bone structure. A few loose strands of the black and white hair fall across the broad forehead and cheeks in multiple thin strands looping over each other in three units, a pattern not found on all Rōjō masks. The general mask type is attributed to the fifteenth-century carver Himi Munetada and is used by all five schools for noh of the highest rank, performed only by experienced actors over the age of sixty. (MB)

SHAKUMI MASK
Deme Chōun Yasuyoshi (d. 1774)
Edo period, eighteenth century
Pigments on Japanese cypress wood (hinoki)
8 1/8 x 5 9/16 in. (21.3 x 14.2 cm)
Toyohashi Uomachi Noh Association,
Aichi Prefecture
catalogue 92, p. 63

Shakumi is one of two types of noh masks representing middle-aged women, the other being Fukai. These roles feature women torn by separation from a loved one, either a husband or a child. Heavy eyelids, downcast eyes, a nearly frowning mouth, and tense cheek muscles all express suffering and age. Unlike most women's masks, Shakumi has strands of hair emerging not from the central hair part but several millimeters away from it: three strands of hair are crossed by two, and then four, with one thicker than the others.

Reputed to have been invented by Tatsuemon, a contemporary of Zeami, this mask type is well represented here by a piece attributed to the eighteenth-century carver Deme Chōun. It bears two red inscriptions and an insignia attesting to its having been owned by the Komparu school.

DEIGAN (GOLD-PAINTED EYES) MASK
Edo period, seventeenth century
Pigments on Japanese cypress wood (hinoki)
8 3/16 x 5 5/16 in. (20.8 x 13.5 cm)
Toyohashi Uomachi Noh Association,
Aichi Prefecture
catalogue 93, p. 52

The name of the mask refers to the gold-painted eyeballs, which hint that the figure is more than human, for gold eyes are associated with the highest of five types of vision in Buddhist theology. Gold-rimmed teeth peep out from thin lips whose soft corners neither smile nor frown. A soft gray tinges the flesh color. Thin eyebrows appear mid-forehead, and the parted hair has three loose strands running down the side of the face, joined by two more above the cord holes.

Originally the Deigan mask was worn for roles of enlightened women in *Ama* (The diver) and *Taema*. In the late Muromachi period it began to be used also in *Aoi no ue* for the jealous spirit of Lady Rokujō, who transforms into a Hannya figure. This mask typifies the standard form. Although it bears no inscription, the back has been finished smoothly and then painted with black lacquer. (MB)

WAKA-ONNA (YOUNG WOMAN) MASK
Muromachi period, 1469
Pigment on Japanese cypress wood (hinoki)
8 1/16 x 4 7/8 in. (20.5 x 12.4 cm)
Rinnōji, Tochigi Prefecture
catalogue 94, p. 64

Rinnōji boasts at least six women's masks inscribed with dates between the fifteenth and seventeenth centuries that together outline a progression of sophistication, this being the earliest. The inscription on the unpainted back indicates that it was donated by the actor Tsuruwaka Dayū in 1469. The somewhat lopsided perimeter, wide-set eyes, and thin lips have a rustic simplicity that contrasts with the subtle contours of the mature style seen in Ko-omote (cat. 162, p.202). In particular, the gouged-out, rounded corners of the smiling lips and the unrealistic dimples speak of an intermediate stage.

Although much of the soft prime coat on this mask has crumbled off, enough remains to suggest that the painting followed what was to become standard iconography: black hair parted at the center and flowing down the sides of the face; vermilion-enhanced lips; fine eyebrows brushed high on the forehead; and tiny strokes added inside the eyes. The edge of the top rim on the left side of the mask is badly damaged. (MB)

HASHIHIME MASK

Edo period, seventeenth century
Pigment on Japanese cypress wood (hinoki)
8 1/4 x 5 9/16 in. (21.0 x 14.2 cm)
Oyama Shrine, Ishikawa Prefecture
catalogue 95, p. 53

The Hashihime mask is worn by a woman who painted her face with red designs, placed candles on her head, and marched off to murder her husband, in bed with another woman. As a halfway stage between the Deigan mask, whose gold eyes give just a hint of superhuman power, and Hannya, a mask of jealousy in the form of a snake, Hashihime is frighteningly human. Bedraggled hair, long eyebrow furrows shooting upward, sharply chiseled eyes with metallic inserts, and two rows of metallic teeth expose her malignant intentions. Unlike many Hashihime masks, which are white (human) on the forehead and red (demonic) below the eyes, this one has a single color as an overall base. Originally made for *Hashihime* (The princess of the bridge), which is no longer extant, the mask is today used exclusively for the noh *Kanawa* (The iron crown). (MB)

HANNYA MASK

Iseki Jirōzaemon Chikamasa
Muromachi period, 1558
Pigment on Japanese cypress wood (hinoki)
8 7/16 x 6 3/8 in. (21.4 x 16.2 cm)
Museum of Noh Artifacts, Sasayama, Hyōgo Prefecture
catalogue 96, p. 54

This horned, malevolent snake figure is of a slightly older style than the mature form seen in the Eisei Bunko Hannya mask (cat. 174, p. 213). Hannya masks come in three colorings: red, white (generally used for the spirit of Lady Rokujō in *Aoi no ue*) and white above with red below (commonly used in *Dōjōji*). The peeling paint on this mask reveals that it was probably originally a red Hannya (typically used for the ogre woman in *Adachigahara / Kurozuka*), and then repainted white (more appropriate for *Aoi no ue*). Flaking has also disclosed the carver's inscription on the front of the mask. This sheds light on the identity and style of early carvers of the Iseki family, who painted over their inscriptions, but also carved diamonds representing the "well" in the first character of their name on the backs of their masks.

Here the name and abode of the carver, Iseki Jirōzaemon Chikamasa, run across the forehead, while the date 1558 is inscribed along the side. Chikamasa's father, Chikanobu, was a student of Sankōbō, the alleged teacher of the founders of all three main mask carving families of the Edo period, Ōmi Iseki, Ōno Deme, and Echizen Deme. The Iseki line reached its pinnacle in Chikamasa's grandson, Kawachi Ieshige (d. 1645) (cat. 156, p. 197). (MB)

YAMANBA MASK

Momoyama-Edo period, seventeenth century
Pigments on Japanese cypress wood (hinoki)
8 x 5 3/4 in. (20.3 x 14.6 cm)
Toyohashi Uomachi Noh Association, Aichi Prefecture
catalogue 97, p. 53

Yamanba, the play for which this mask was specifically made, is about a half-demonic old woman who roams the mountains and encounters her impersonator, a dancer. By experiencing her own dance, she tries to define herself as good, or at least beyond distinctions between good and evil. Yamanba's enigmatic personality, enlightened and demonic, human and supernatural, is apparent in the wide variety of masks used to represent the role.

Here the ruddy, weather-beaten face balances power, wisdom, and age (expressed in the salt-and-pepper hair), with flashing, demonic eyes and drawn lips exposing gold teeth. The arched eyebrows have not been shaven as for an upper-class woman, but follow the bone structure (similar to the eyebrows of the elfin Shōjō mask seen in cat. 184, p. 223).

The small peg in the middle of the forehead is for securing a cloth hat (zukin, cat. 183, p. 218). Yamamba does not wear such a hat, so the peg indicates that this mask may have also been used for the role of the warrior Yorimasa, who does. (MB)

Kyōgen

OTO MASK

Muromachi period, fifteenth century
Pigment on Japanese cypress wood (hinoki)
8 3/8 x 6 1/8 in. (21.3 x 15.5 cm)
Seki Kasuga Shrine, Gifu Prefecture
catalogue 98, p. 66

Feminine beauty gets a comic interpretation in kyōgen. The rustic young woman depicted here is meant to appear so gross that the young man in *Nikujūhachi*, who has asked the deity to send him a wife, runs away in horror after unveiling his bride. Behind this facade, however, one senses a spunky, unaffected young woman with a good sense of humor.

This mask is perhaps the oldest of its type still extant. Unfortunately much of the paint has flaked off the front, leaving only a suggestion of what the eyebrows and hair must have looked like. The mask has been carved to an even, somewhat heavy thickness and carefully finished on the back side. Under a black lacquer coat, traces can be made out of round chisel marks, both horizontal and vertical. (MB)

SHIOFUKI (SALT BLOWER) MASK

Edo period, eighteenth century
Pigment on Japanese cypress wood (hinoki) with hair
7 1/2 x 6 1/16 in. (19.0 x 15.3 cm)
Eisei Bunko Museum, Tokyo
catalogue 99, p. 66

Shiofuki is a variant of the kyōgen mask Usobuki (Empty blower). The face stares with rounded eyes at its own lips, pursed as if whistling. Kyōgen masks are allowed a freedom for individualistic expression, so this type includes masks with eyes focused up or to the sides and with varying shapes of puckered lips, but all have implanted hair whiskers and wrinkles. Whistling masks are used for weak characters, such as dead men, scarecrows, ants, fish, and insects. In the kyōgen *Kazumō* (Wrestling with a mosquito) a sheet of paper rolled up to form a long tube is inserted in the orifice to form the mosquito's stinger. (MB)

KITSUNE (FOX) MASK

Muromachi period, fifteenth century
Pigment on paulownia wood (kiri)
8 x 5 1/2 in. (20.3 x 14.0 cm)
Naratsuhiko Shrine, Nara Prefecture
catalogue 100, p. 67

Although the fox deity of Inari shrine guards the rice fields and brings affluence, other foxes transform into beautiful women and attempt to trick or beguile. Several kyōgen feature foxes, but perhaps the best-known and surely the most technically demanding is *Tsurigitsune* (Fox trapping). Here a fox disguises himself as a priest and lectures the hunter on the evils of trapping. Unconvinced, the hunter enticingly baits his trap. Reappearing in a full-body fox outfit and fox mask, the fox cannot resist the temptation, gets temporarily caught, but manages to escape the hunter.

Renditions of the fox mask vary from realistic to suggestively abstract, like this one, with a simplicity of construction and absence of detailing that convey only the fox essence. The lower jaw is carved separately and attached with a cord so that it can open and shut. Traces of earth yellow indicate the overall coloring, darkened with black on the sides and highlighted with red in the nose and mouth holes. The number 18 on the inside of the mouth gives no clue to dating, but the general style and use of paulownia wood rather than cypress suggest the mid-Muromachi period. (MB)

SARU (MONKEY) MASK

Muromachi period, fifteenth century
Pigment on Japanese cypress wood (hinoki)
8 1/16 x 5 3/4 in. (20.4 x 14.6 cm)
Mibudera, Kyoto
catalogue 101, p. 150

Monkeys appear in a number of kyōgen plays, both as performing creatures, as in *Utsubozaru* (Monkey skin quiver), and as wild animals, as in *Sarumuko* (Monkey groom). This mask, however, was not made for a standard kyōgen, but for performances at Mibu Temple of special prayer plays known as *nenbutsu kyōgen*. Particularly in the early years, these performances featured monkey acts, and it may be that the present mask was made to be used in the now-lost play *Saru* (Monkey) as a part of Mibu sarugaku recorded as having been performed during the Bunmei era (1469–1487). Its thick carving, three-dimensional realism and immediacy of expression suggest that it could in fact date from that time and set it apart from standard monkey masks, with their flattened faces and etched wrinkle patterns. (MB)

MASK-MAKING TOOLS

Most noh masks are carved from Japanese cypress (*hinoki*). A block without knots and well drained of sap is preferable (fourth row, farthest left). After establishing the center line, the carver saws off the corners of the block to approximate the perimeter of the mask and then saws horizontal slits into the wood above and below the nose (fourth row, second from left). Next using a mallet (*kizuchi*, first row, left) and chisel (*nomi*, third row, far right) he lops off the excess wood around the nose. Using a variety of curved and flat knives (*tō*; in tool pouch, third row, right) he whittles down the wood so that the basic features emerge (fourth row, third from left). He then hollows out the back. Working alternately on the front and back, he thins and refines the mask till the general features are set. He opens holes for the eyes, nostrils, and mouth with a hand drill (next to the ruler in the tool pouch, third row, right). On the back of the mask he hollows out conical forms around the eye holes, triangular indentations for the nose, and a cavity for the mouth. The eye openings for female masks are rectangular, for men slightly curved, and for demons round. A good mask is thin and light, but sturdy.

Although a master carver may take only a day to get this far, he is likely to take weeks or even months to finish the carving. His art lies in modeling the subtle contours of the mask so the play of light and shadow on the mask as it turns and tilts will bring to life a spectrum of shifting expressions. While thus refining the details, the carver will often hold the mask at a distance and slowly move it in imitation of the movements and angles of the actor. Once he is satisfied with the carving (fourth row, third from right), he will prepare the primer. He grinds calcium carbonate (*gofun*, second row, bag at left) in a pestle and mortar (*suribachi*, second row, right) and mixes the powder with animal glue (*nikawa*, second row, third from left) to form a smooth, thick primer, which he paints over the mask using a flat brush (third row, fourth group from right). After several layers of primer have dried, he sands them smooth and applies more (fourth row, second from right). To the last layer(s) of primer, he adds color, generally an earth yellow (*ōdo*, third row, far left), sometimes mixed with red (*shu*, cinnabar, third row, far left, bottom). He does not sand the last layer, so the brushstrokes become part of the texture of the face. Finally he paints in the features of the mask with thin-tipped round brushes (third row, fourth group from left): black (*sumi*) for the hair and to outline the eyes; dilute black applied in many tiny strokes for the eyebrows and inside the eyeballs; black, white, or gold for the teeth; and a shade of red for the lips. To give the mask greater depth and variation in skin hue, an antiquing solution (*furubi*) of dilute soot is applied around the edges and on prominent areas, like the nose and chin. Finally the mask is buffed with a soft cloth to bring out the sheen latent in the primer.

To make the metallic inserts for eyeballs or teeth, the metal sheet is cut to size with scissors (*kanakiribasami*, third row, third from right). The pieces are shaped with a round-tipped hammer (third row, second from left) using a shaping block of hard wood (first row, far right). The edges are trimmed and the metal insert is glued in place. Honing stones are used for sharpening the knives and chisels (second row, middle left). (MB)

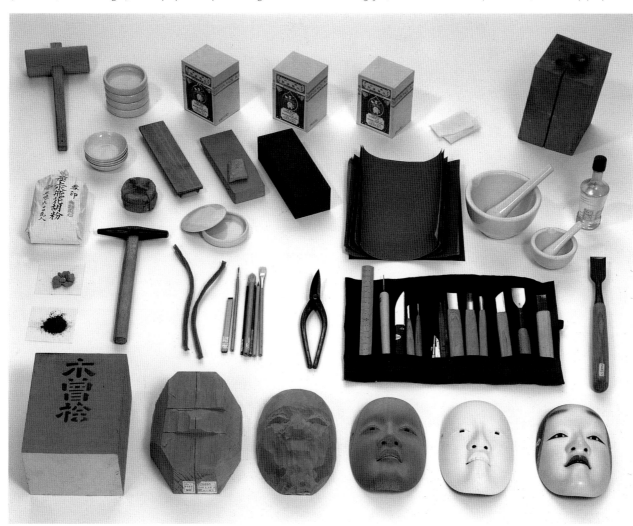

MASK-MAKING TOOLS
Various media and dimensions
Tsubouchi Memorial Theatre Museum,
Waseda University, Tokyo
catalogue 102

WEAVING TOOLS

A piece of cloth begins with the making of thread, which in the case of noh costumes is either silk or bast (mostly hemp). Good silk depends on well-tended strains of silkworms, which feed on mulberry leaves. In the Momoyama period, when the earliest costumes in the exhibition were made, much of the silk yarn was imported from China, but by the mid-Edo period Japan was producing large quantities of its own. The long silk fibers are reeled from the cocoons to form skeins of raw unglossed silk thread (*kiito*), still covered with the protective gum spit out by the silkworm. For many noh costumes raw silk, which is strong and resilient, is used for warp threads and for ground wefts. The soft, glossy threads used to form the pattern wefts have had their protective layer of gum removed (*neriito*). The threads are then dyed. In the Edo period vegetable dyes such as safflower, indigo, madder, grasses, and acorns were used to produce a palette of colored threads.

According to Yamaguchi Akira, an expert on reproducing Edo costumes, a single karaori usually contains ten to fourteen different colors. The deftness with which these limited hues are combined creates a sense of infinite variety. The dyed threads are wound onto frame spools (*waku*), from which they can be smoothly pulled during the measuring of the warp threads. One way of transferring the thread is to set the skein loop so it encircles the three upright poles of the *tatari*, and then pass the thread end over a suspended bamboo pole and onto the frame spool. Next a stick tapered at both ends is placed into the center of the spool to be wound (*teburi*) and twirled by lightly shaking the hand. The freehand guides the thread as it unravels (see cat. 112, p. 77; cat. 111, p. 123). A more efficient late-Edo invention for winding frame spools is the *wakumaki*. The measured warps are set on the loom, passed through heddles (which pull the threads up or down to form the ground weave and pattern) and through slats in a reed (*osa*) with a sleying tool (*ito tōshi*), and then tied to the front beam of the loom. When a ground of alternating blocks is woven (as shown on the back loom in cat. 111, p. 77; cat. 112, p. 123), the measured warp is resist-dyed (ikat / *kasuri*) to form blocks of more than one color.

The same back loom is also used for weaving complex weft-patterned textiles, like the karaori and atsuita, using two sets of heddles, one for weaving the ground, operated by foot peddles, and the other for weaving the pattern, operated from above by a boy seated on a ledge. This type of loom is called a *sorabiki*. The loom shown in the front (cat. 111, cat. 112) is for weaving plain-weave cloth, such as the noshime. A similar loom, with the warp tied to the waist of the weaver for better tension control, would be used for weaving the bast-fiber fabrics of the kataginu, kamishimo, and hitatare. The thread for these is made by stripping the inner skin from the hemp stalk and splitting it into narrow long tapes, which are then ply-joined into a continuous thread.

Weaving the weft threads into the warp forms the fabric. The weft is wound onto small bamboo spools with a bobbin winder (*kudamaki*), as shown in the center front of the screen (cat. 111, cat 112). The bobbins are slipped into shuttles (*hi*) that are passed through the shed made by raising or lowering the warp threads. Large shuttles cross the whole width of the cloth, while the small shuttles are passed through the pattern shed only in the areas where their color appears. (MB)

KASE (SKEINS OF SILK THREAD)
Heisei Period, twentieth century
Silk, unglossed (kiito) and glossed (neriito)
a): 11 7/16 x 2 3/4 in. (29 x 7 cm);
b): 8 11/16 x 2 3/16 in. (22 x 5.5 cm)
Private collection
catalogue 103

TATARI (SKEIN HOLDER) WITH BŌ (POLE), KASE (SKEIN OF SILK THREAD), AND TEBURI (HANDHELD FRAME SPOOL WINDER)
Meiji–Taishō period, nineteenth–twentieth century
Wood and silk thread skein
a): 31 7/8 x 24 1/8 x 5 1/2 in. (81 x 61.2 x 14 cm);
b): 31 7/8 x 14 3/16 x 5 1/2 in. (81 x 36 x 14 cm);
c): 43 5/16 x 3/4 in. (110 x 2 cm);
d): 8 11/16 x 2 3/16 in. (22 x 5.5 cm)
Private collection
catalogue 104

ŌWAKU (FRAME SPOOLS)
Taishō period, twentieth century
Wood and silk thread
3 15/16 x 4 1/8 x 5 7/8 in. (10 x 10.5 x 15 cm) each
Private collection
catalogue 105

WAKUMAKI (FRAME SPOOL WINDER)
Shōwa period, twentieth century
Wood, bamboo, and leather
9 1/16 x 20 1/16 x 15 1/16 in. (23 x 51 x 38.3 cm)
Private collection
catalogue 106

KUDAMAKI (BOBBIN WINDER / SPINNING WHEEL)
Meiji period, nineteenth century
Wood, bamboo, and leather
a): 24 5/8 x 42 5/16 x 11 1/4 in. (62.5 x 107.5 x 28.5 cm);
b): 11 1/16 x 1 3/8 in. (28 x 3.5 cm)
Private collection
catalogue 107

OSA (REEDS)
Taishō–Shōwa period, twentieth century
Bamboo, wood, cotton thread, and paper
a): 3 3/4 x 1 3/8 in. (9.5 x 3.5 cm);
b): 3 1/16 x 16 1/4 in. (7.7 x 41.3 cm);
c): 3 1/4 x 16 1/4 in. (8.2 x 41.3 cm)
Private collection
catalogue 108

ITOTŌSHI (SLEY)
Shōwa period, twentieth century
Metal
6 3/8 x 1 3/8 in. (16.2 x 3.5 cm)
Private collection
catalogue 109

HI (SHUTTLES)
Taishō–Shōwa period, twentieth century
Wood, bamboo, metal, porcelain, rabbit fur, and human hair
a): 5 3/4 x 13/16 in. (14.6 x 2.1 cm);
b): 5 3/8 x 15/16 in. (13.7 x 2.3 cm);
c): 8 7/16 x 1 3/16 in. (21.4 x 3 cm);
d): 9 15/16 x 1 5/16 in. (25.0 x 3.3 cm);
e): 10 7/8 x 1 5/16 in. (27.6 x 3.4 cm)
Private collection
catalogue 110

104   106   107

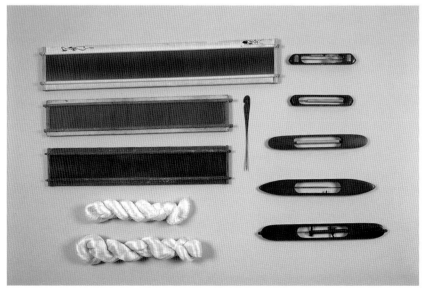

108   109   110
103

PAINTINGS
Artisans at work

**SHOKUNIN TSUKUSHI-E
(VIEWS OF ARTISANS AT WORK)**

Edo period, seventeenth century
Pair of six-fold screens: ink and colors on paper
43 ⅞ x 123 ⅛ in. (111.5 x 312.6 cm) each
Suntory Museum of Art, Tokyo
catalogue 111, p. 80, 123, 167 (all details)

**SHOKUNIN TSUKUSHI-E
(VIEWS OF ARTISANS AT WORK:
WEAVERS AND DYERS)**

② *Edo period, seventeenth century*
*Two from set of twelve framed panels:
ink and colors on paper*
Paper size: 23 ⅝ x 19 ¹¹/₁₆ in. (60.0 x 50.0 cm) each
National Museum of Japanese History, Sakura,
Chiba Prefecture
catalogue 112, p. 77 (detail)

Painted screens depicting artisans are from a composition type formalized in the late Momoyama or early Edo period. The significance of family industry to the economy had been deepening since the Muromachi period; by the Edo period the importance of a person's function within society had become key. Artisans were one of four classes in Edo society (in order: samurai, farmer, artisan, merchant), and they took pride in the service they performed. Merchants especially were dependent on craftspeople for their goods, and often adorned their homes with these paintings. (HG)

Performance

KAN NŌ ZU (WATCHING NOH)

① *Edo period, c. 1607*
*Eight-fold screen: ink, colors,
and gold on paper*
41 ¹⁵/₁₆ x 167 ⅝ in. (106.5 x 425.5 cm)
Kobe City Museum
catalogue 113, p. 10 (detail)

This screen was painted in remembrance of a visit by Emperor Goyōzei to Toyotomi Hideyoshi's mansion at Jūrakudai. Despite its early-Edo-period date, the screen has a Momoyama flavor in figure and costume style as well as the manner of painting trees and flowers. Sudden shifts of scale, a mark of the late Muromachi through Momoyama periods, cause landscape elements to vary dramatically in proportion.

The central section shows a performance of *Okina* on a makeshift stage in the garden of a wealthy house. Okina wears a green kariginu with red binding cords and tassels, light sashinuki and a tall Okina *eboshi* hat. The mask is barely perceptible. His bent-over posture may indicate a moment in the instrumental dance of "Heaven, Earth, and Man," since the flute and three drums are playing. The lord of the house and high-ranking personages watch from behind bamboo curtains in the neighboring building. Ladies in waiting sit on the verandah or on carpets in the garden. Among the people milling around the garden are women veiled by kosode draped over their heads, and foreigners in European garb. Despite the liberties taken with perspective and placement of figures, great care was given to the depiction of

the garments, which exhibit fashions typical of the early seventeenth century that strongly influenced the styles of noh costumes. (MB and HG)

**EN NŌ ZU BYŌBU NANIWA
(SCREEN DEPICTING THE NOH NANIWA)**

② *Edo period, seventeenth century*
Six-fold screen: ink, colors, and gold on paper
28 ¹¹/₁₆ x 48 ¼ in. (72.8 x 122.6 cm)
Museum of Noh Artifacts, Sasayama,
Hyōgo Prefecture
catalogue 114

By contrast with cat. 113, p. 10, the style of this screen is clearly of the Edo period. Groups and forms have been simplified, with a large expanse of the screen given to the noh performance and its setting. The audience consists entirely of women and children, a rare occurrence that may indicate the commemoration of a specific performance.

The artist has depicted the shite's entrance in the second act, when the tsure is dancing on stage. By depicting the shite on the bridge, the artist illustrates a typical use of diagonal spacing in noh choreography, where one figure is upstage right and another downstage left. The use of the bridge for observation expands the performance area, which is usually focused on the stage alone. The costumes are typical of those worn today, showing that the basic rules had already been set by the late seventeenth century. Likewise the instumentalists are sitting in their standard positions, with the two hand-drummers seated on stools facing the audience. (HG)

NOH PLAY: FUNA BENKEI

② *Edo period, c. 1660*
Six-fold screen: ink, colors, and gold on paper
41 ¹⁵/₁₆ x 18 in. (106.6 x 45.7 cm) each
Indianapolis Museum of Art, Gift of the Alliance of the Indianapolis Museum of Art
catalogue 115

A celebratory day during which the play *Funa Benkei* is performed is the subject of this screen. At center, a climactic moment in the play is depicted, as the great warrior heroes Yoshitsune and Benkei face the ghost of Taira Tomomori amid the waves. Tomomori brandishes a halberd and, hoping to drown Yoshitsune, approaches the heroes and oarsman in their boat. While Yoshitsune opts to stand and fight, Benkei wisely calls upon the Five Great Luminous Kings, who defeat Tomomori and his band of warrior ghosts, casting their angry souls upon the water. This play was popular for festive events because of the number of actors and extent of the action.

To the right of the stage and audience areas is a group of gentlemen with attendants seated on red cloths before a stream. Sake is being floated downstream in cups placed on lotus leaves, a traditional celebratory activity. The samurai facing the stage are probably the patrons of the performance. On two sides are rooms for female observers, who are separated from the male company both by architecture and by clouds. Costumes, hairstyles, and the curving silhouettes of stream and foliage help to date this screen. (HG)

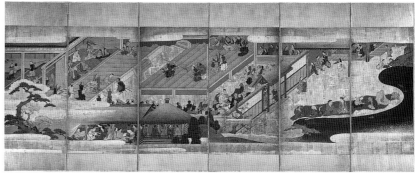

KASUGA WAKAMIYA ONMATSURI EMAKI (FESTIVALS AT KASUGA WAKAMIYA SHRINE)

Edo period, eighteenth century
One handscroll from set of three:
ink, colors, and gold on paper
14 ¹⁵/₁₆ x 1086 ⁷/₁₆ in. (38.0 x 2759.5 cm)
Kasuga Taisha, Nara Prefecture
catalogue 116, p. 188

Even before Zeami's time, the god of the subsidiary Wakamiya Shrine was taken out and carried down to a grassy area close to the main *torii* gate for the Honorable Festival, Onmatsuri, yearly functions of Kasuga Shrine and its associated temple, Kōfukuji. The noh actors from the four Yamato schools (the predecessors of the modern schools) participated in the main rituals beneath the sacred pine, as well as performing full noh in front of the temporary shrine and in the Wakamiya Shrine. In the spring they also performed by firelight in front of the south gate of Kōfukuji. All these functions continue today, though the south gate has burned down. (MB)

KANJIN NŌ ZU (SUBSCRIPTION NOH PERFORMANCE)

①*Meiji period, 1896*
Unbound album: ink and colors on paper
10 ¹³/₁₆ x 15 ⅛ (27.0 x 38.4 cm)
Research Archives for Japanese Music
at Ueno Gakuen University, Tokyo
catalogue 117

This album provides an intimate look at activities in and around the staging of subscription noh performances. Details include the construction of the temporary stage and seats, dressing rooms, eating areas, and actors making an entrance from the green room. (MB)

NŌ KYŌGEN EMAKI (NOH AND KYŌGEN PICTURE SCROLLS)

Edo period, eighteenth century
Two handscrolls from set of three:
ink and colors on paper
14 ½ x 1321 in. (36.9 x 3355.2 cm) each
Tokyo National Museum
catalogue 118, p. 18, 19, 21, 26, 35, 151, 163, 189 (all details)

Probably by a painter of the Sumiyoshi school, the three handscrolls entitled *Nō kyōgen emaki* depict 51 noh and 21 kyōgen. As a resource on the staging of noh in the early Edo period, they are invaluable, for they depict scenes within neatly sketched stages (including a portion of the bridge connecting the stage to the curtained-off dressing area). Viewed from above and at a slight angle, the stages are shown in Japanese-style reverse perspective, parallel lines widening towards the back. Posts and railings appear thin, the veranda on stage left for the chorus is very narrow, and the pine tree on the back wallboards (*kagami ita*) is absent. Unlike the boards on a modern stage, those behind the musicians run vertically rather than horizontally. Each staged scene sits in a misty cloudbank of gold and is labeled with the play's title in flowing inked characters. (MB)

KO NŌ KYŌGEN NO ZU (OLD NOH AND KYŌGEN ILLUSTRATIONS)

Edo period, seventeenth century
Ink and colors on paper
17 ⁵/₁₆ x 23 ⁷/₁₆ in. (44.0 x 59.5 cm) each
National Noh Theater, Tokyo
catalogue 119, p. 33, 146, 162, 176 (all details)

One scene depicts the shite's appearance at the beginning of the second act of *Dōjōji* (p. 176). In response to the priests' concerted prayers, the bell first resounds, then sways, and finally rises to reveal a snake figure dressed in white surihaku and koshimaki with a red-ground triangle pattern. The gaping mouth and bulging eyes of the mask are visible, though the bell hides its horns. The green cloth covering the bell contrasts nicely with the reds, browns, and gold that

dominate the rest of the painting. More common today would be a purple damask covering. The musicians are shown intensely concentrating on the action as they accompany the contest of wills with shifting drum and flute patterns. At the upper right one can just make out someone pulling on the bell rope. A number of aspects are simplified: the chorus has been reduced to three; the chorus verandah (which on a modern stage juts out to the right) and the front steps were either absent or ignored; and the bridge, set at a steeper angle than became standard, disappears into the vagaries of glittering mist. (MB)

NŌMAI NO ZU (ILLUSTRATIONS OF NOH DANCES)

Edo period, eighteenth century
Pair of handscrolls: ink and colors on paper
a) 12 ⅜ x 215 ½ in. (31.4 x 547.3 cm);
b) 12 ⁷/₁₆ x 200 ¹¹/₁₆ in. (31.6 x 509.8 cm)
National Noh Theater, Tokyo
catalogue 120, p. 22, 130, 149, 219 (all details)

The *Nōmai no zu* is a handscroll showing scenes from various noh set against a misty gold background. As the stage is not delineated, the perimeters of the acting area are only vaguely defined, but the general space relationships between the figures are true to life. Costumes are depicted with special attention to pattern detail, making this a good source for trends of the mid-Edo period. (MB)

117

Treatise

ROKURIN ICHIRO HICHŪ (SECRET NOTES ON THE SIX CIRCLES, AND THE ONE DEWDROP)

Konparu Zenchiku (1405–c. 1470)
Muromachi period, 1466
Handscroll: ink and colors on paper
13⁵/₁₆ x 202³/₁₆ in. (33.8 x 513.5 cm)
Hōzanji, Nara Prefecture
catalogue 121, p. 30

Rokurin ichiro hichū (Secret notes on the six circles and the one dewdrop) is the title given to two treatises on the religio-aesthetic character of noh (and in a broader sense, of poetry) by the important fifteenth-century actor, playwright, and dramaturge Konparu Zenchiku. The circles and dewdrop of the title are figures in a schematic understanding of aesthetics and performance that Zenchiku elaborated on the basis of his extensive studies of Buddhism, neo-Confucianism, and Shinto. In a series of texts he created a network of relations between diverse religious and philosophical concepts, and individual classical poems (*waka*) and types of noh performance. At an early stage he presented his scheme to two eminent intellectuals of the day, the Buddhist priest Shigyoku and the statesman Ichijō Kaneyoshi, for their commentaries. Thereafter he elaborated the system in seven more treatises. This treatise, the last in the series, is in Zenchiku's own hand, though restored.

The most immediately appealing characteristic of this piece is the combination of its fluid calligraphy and the delicate illustrations, in gold ink, which accompany the text. Each image is preceded by an explanation of the religio-philosophical concepts it is intended to represent, which is then followed with a number of waka poems and textual references. The illustrations reveal the schematic nature of a system Zenchiku began developing perhaps as many as two decades earlier. Though not always readily understandable, it is certainly one of the most intriguing and complex of medieval Japanese aesthetic projects. (TH)

BOOKS
Design book

KEN'EIRŌ GASŌ (COMPILATION OF GRACEFUL DESIGNS)

Edo period, eighteenth century
Set of books: ink and colors on paper
16⁹/₁₆ x 11¹³/₁₆ in. (42.0 x 30.0 cm) each
Tokyo National Museum
catalogue 122, p. 133, 136, 137, 139, 140, 143, 144, 145, 151

Prop book

NŌ TSUKURIMONO DŌGU ZU (ILLUSTRATED BOOK OF NOH PROPS)

Edo period, eighteenth century
Book: ink and color on paper
10¹¹/₁₆ x 8 in. (27.3 x 20.4 cm)
National Noh Theater, Tokyo
catalogue 123, p. 260

With the increasing canonization of noh performance, it became necessary to specify in detail how dances were to be performed, how music was to be played, how characters were to be costumed, what masks were to be worn for what roles, and so on. In this context, booklets explaining the construction of stage props for noh were written, and this is a beautifully illustrated example.

The largest inscriptions on each page generally give the title of a play, and the rest of the text provides explanations about how the item(s) pictured are to be constructed, sometimes general, sometimes with precise measurements and other specifications. (TH)

Songbooks

ZENPŌ UTAIBON SUMIDAGAWA (ZENPŌ'S SONGBOOK "SUMIDA RIVER")

Konparu Zenpō (1454–c. 1532)
Muromachi period, fifteenth century
Handscroll: ink on colored paper
with under-designs in powdered mica
of silver or pale green
Nogami Memorial Institute for Noh Studies at Hōsei University, Tokyo
catalogue 124, p. 31

Noh songbooks with vocal notation, termed *utaibon*, date from the days of Zeami himself. It was rare for noh texts to be written out for transmission in the fifteenth and early sixteenth centuries. Professionals of the day seem to have preferred oral transmission. During subsequent centuries, when amateurs took up noh chanting,

utaibon became more common. In this context, the utaibon changed from scroll to booklet, and increasingly became a work of art in its own right.

This example, an utaibon in the hand of Konparu Zenpō, head of the Konparu troupe in the early sixteenth century, is an early example of such a book mounted onto a handscroll. One of several extant examples in Zenpō's hand, this booklet contains the texts of the play *Sumidagawa* (Sumida River). The text is written in a fluent cursive script primarily with phonetic *kana*, with only occasional *kanji*. Musical notation takes the form of small dots and hooks placed to the right of the words of the text.

The Konparu troupe enjoyed the ardent patronage of Toyotomi Hideyoshi, and seems to have been the first troupe to have its libretti printed with movable type, following Hideyoshi's introduction of movable type to Japan from his military adventurism in Korea. (TH)

NŌ UTAIBON (NOH SONGBOOKS) WITH RHYTHMIC NOTATIONS

Momoyama period, 1584
Three books: ink and color on paper with mica
8⁷/₁₆ x 6¹/₁₆ in. (21.5 x 15.7 cm) each
Noda Shrine, Yamaguchi Prefecture
catalogue 125, p. 260

Rather different in character from the other noh songbooks or utaibon in the exhibition, this booklet is intended for transmission within a family of professional ōtsuzumi players. In addition to the texts of twenty-four passages from noh plays, this booklet contains rhythmic notation in red for the ōtsuzumi.

The notation here is consistent in general terms with notation used later in the tradition to indicate the way in which the sung text is to be related to the beats of the drums. The relationship is rather complex, in that the typical verse line of twelve syllables is to be correlated with an eight-beat musical measure. When the relationship is predictable and regular, drum notation can simply indicate the name of a specific drum-pattern to be played along with the given phrase, but in many cases it is preferable to spell out more precisely where the beats fall by aligning syllables of the text with indications of a specific beat, as we see here. (TH)

NŌ UTAIBON (NOH SONGBOOKS)

Hon'ami Kōetsu (1558–1637);
published by Suminokura Soan (1571–1632)
Edo period, seventeenth century
Twelve bound volumes; cover: ink on colored paper
with under-designs in powdered mica;
text: printed ink on paper
9⁷/₁₆ x 7¹/₁₆ in. (23.9 x 18 cm) each
Agency for Cultural Affairs, Tokyo
catalogue 126, p. 38–40

The so-called Kōetsu utaibon, named for the remarkably innovative Hon'ami Kōetsu (1558–1637) represent the pinnacle of aesthetic achievement in the production of noh libretti. Kōetsu had been patronized by Toyotomi Hideyoshi in the late sixteenth century, and with the change of government in the early seventeenth century, he garnered the patronage of Tokugawa Ieyasu as well, eventually securing land northeast of Kyoto where he founded an artist's colony for the production of fine tea ware, exquisite books, paintings, and screens.

The twelve books included in the exhibition are all noh plays based on the texts and musical notation of the Kanze troupe, the favored troupe of the Tokugawa shogunate. These utaibon show not only innovation in the use of movable type, but an important revival in papermaking technology that reintroduced mica printing on fine paper, a practice which had been introduced into Japan from China several centuries earlier, but had not been in use since the Heian period (794–1185). (TH)

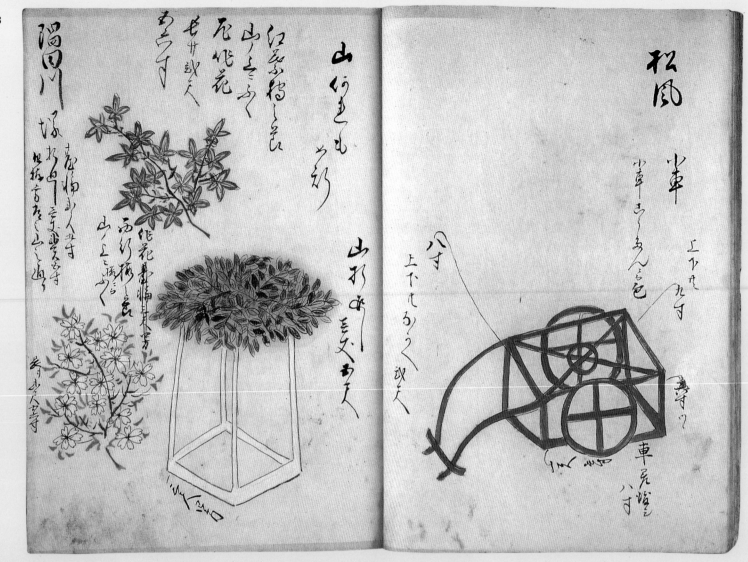

123

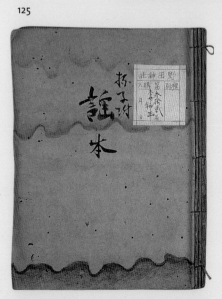
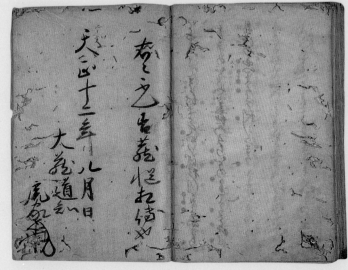

125

MUSICAL INSTRUMENTS

NŌKAN (FLUTE) KNOWN AS "YAEGIKU"

① *Edo period, seventeenth century*
Lacquer on bamboo
Length: 15 ⁹/₁₆ in. (39.5 cm)
Eisei Bunko Museum, Tokyo
catalogue 127, p. 262

NŌKAN (FLUTE) KNOWN AS "HOKKYO" AND CASE WITH AUTUMN GRASSES

② *Edo period, seventeenth century*
*Flute: lacquer on bamboo; case: lacquer on wood with gold powder (*takamakie *and* nashiji*)*
Flute length: 15 ¼ in. (38.8 cm);
case: 15 ½ x 1 ⁵/₁₆ in. (39.3 x 3.3 cm)
Eisei Bunko Museum, Tokyo
catalogue 128, p. 262

The flute used in the noh ensemble, the *nōkan*, is a bamboo transverse flute wrapped with a binding, usually of wisteria or birch bark and subsequently lacquered, red or reddish brown on the inside and around the mouth and finger holes, and black on the bark binding. It is not constructed of a single piece of bamboo, but rather of several pieces carefully joined. The closed end of the flute is stopped with beeswax, weighted, and capped with a decorative disk, the *kashiragane*, sometimes of gold and/or silver. Old and celebrated nōkan are often named, usually in relation to the design used on the disk.

The nōkan ranges over more than two octaves. Pitch can be altered by the player's embouchure as well as by fingering, but as the notes rise in pitch overall, they characteristically go somewhat flat. The highest pitches of all, known as *hishigi*, are shrill and penetrating, and serve an important role in cuing actors backstage.

In contrast with this shrill whistling, the nōkan is also capable of playing quiet, contemplative melodies, which are used to great effect as entrance or exit music, as preludes to dance, and during costume changes. The instrument is played at specific points during the chanted parts of a noh play, simultaneously with the drums but in alternation with the voice, and it has the sole melodic role in the instrumental dances (*mai* and *hataraki*), usually performed during the last part of a play. (TH)

KOTSUZUMI (SMALL HOURGLASS DRUM) WITH PEONIES

Edo period, seventeenth century
*Lacquer on wood with gold powder (*takamakie, e-nashiji, hiramakie*), horsehide, gold paper, and silk cords*
Drum core: 9 ⁵/₁₆ x 4 in. (25.3 x 10.2 cm)
Los Angeles County Museum of Art,
in honor of Shizu Shimoda from the Hiroshi Shimoda Family; M.89.134.1
catalogue 129, p. 262

KOTSUZUMI (SMALL HOURGLASS DRUM BODY) WITH AQUATIC MOTIFS

Momoyama–Edo period, seventeenth century
*Lacquer on wood with gold powder (*makie *and* e-nashiji*)*
Drum core: 9 ⅞ x 4 in. (25.08 x 10.16 cm)
Los Angeles County Museum of Art,
gift of Julia and Leo Krashen; M.84.103.1
130, p. 32

The kotsuzumi is the smallest of three drums used in the noh ensemble, consisting of an hourglass-shaped, hollowed-out cherrywood body, two horsehide drumheads, each stretched over an iron ring, and a long hempen rope, dyed orange, which is used to tie the two heads together. The body is lacquered on the outside, often with gold and/or silver *makie* designs.

The performer holds the instrument in the left hand over the right shoulder, gripping the ropes that hold the heads to the body. The right hand is used to strike the frontal head of the drum, and the sound varies considerably, depending on where it is struck. The kotsuzumi is considered the most sensitive, even lyrical, Japanese drum, and is widely used outside of noh as well. It is deployed during the greater part of any given noh performance, played in carefully designed patterns which interlock with the drumbeats of the ōtsuzumi (and with the *taiko* as well, in those plays in which a taiko is used). Drum calls – "yo," "ho," "iya," and the like – ejaculated by the drummers are an indispensable element in all the drum music of noh. These calls originally served to maintain agreement among the drummers about where the beat is, but they have a role reaching beyond mere time-keeping, and can be strikingly expressive. (TH)

ŌTSUZUMI (LARGE HOURGLASS DRUM BODY) WITH WIND AND THUNDER GODS

① *Edo period, seventeenth century*
*Lacquer on wood with gold powder (*makie*)*
11 ¼ x 4 ½ in. (28.5 x 11.5 cm)
Museum of Noh Artifacts, Sasayama,
Hyōgo Prefecture
catalogue 131, p. 32

ŌTSUZUMI (LARGE HOURGLASS DRUM BODY) WITH DAIKON RADISH

② *Momoyama–Edo period, seventeenth century*
*Lacquer on wood with gold powder (*e-nashiji, hiramakie, harigaki*)*
11 x 4 ⅛ in. (28.0 x 10.5 cm)
Suntory Museum of Art, Tokyo
catalogue 132, p. 262

The ōtsuzumi (also known as the *ōkawa*) is the larger of the two hourglass-shaped drums used in noh. Like the kotsuzumi, it consists of a hollowed-out cherrywood body, two horsehide drumheads, and a long hempen rope tying the heads together. The wooden body is lacquered like the kotsuzumi and may have gold and/or silver makie designs.

In a full-fledged noh performance, the ōtsuzumi and kotsuzumi drummers sit on folding stools while they perform, but when playing for kyōgen performance or for recital pieces, they sit on their knees onstage. The performer holds the ōtsuzumi with the left hand over the left knee by the ropes. The right hand is used to strike the frontal head of the drum, which faces to the performer's right, and it produces a sharp and loud thwack at important points in the eight-beat rhythmic "measure," or a softer wooded click, usually in preparation for a thwack later on. The ōtsuzumi is not capable of the range of sound that the kotsuzumi makes, but it performs a more prominent structural role in noh music patterns.

It is important that the drumheads on the ōtsuzumi be kept as dry as possible, so that they produce the hard wooden sound desired among noh performers. To keep them in optimal playing condition, they are heated over a charcoal brazier before performance, and in long performances may be replaced with a "freshly baked" instrument. The kotsuzumi, on the other hand, is considered most responsive when played in rather humid conditions. This paradox is considered to produce a dynamic tension in the music of noh. (TH)

127

128

129

132

TAIKO (STICK DRUM BODY) WITH DECORATIVE ABSTRACT FLOWERS OF POUNDED RICE (MOCHI-BANA)

① *Muromachi period, 1450*
Lacquer on wood with gold flecks (fundame)
5 9/16 x 10 1/4 in. (14.2 x 26.0 cm)
Eisei Bunko Museum, Tokyo
catalogue 133

TAIKO (STICK DRUM) WITH FANS

② *Edo period, eighteenth century*
Lacquer on wood with gold powder
and silver flecks (makie)
5 3/4 x 10 1/2 in. (14.5 x 26.7 cm)
Eisei Bunko Museum, Tokyo
catalogue 134

The taiko is a stick drum, unlike the two hourglass-shaped drums used in noh. The body is generally made of *keyaki* (zelkova) or *sendan* (Japanese bead tree) wood, and consists of a broad cylinder with a slight convex curve. The drumheads of the taiko are made of cowhide stretched over an iron hoop, and the outer rim of each head is lacquered. The two heads are tied over the body with an orange hempen rope. The top head has a small circle of deerhide glued to the center on both the surface and under-side, at the point where the drumsticks strike it. The taiko is set into a drum stand and placed on the floor before the per-former, who sits on his knees. It is struck with two large drumsticks, each about an inch and a quarter in diameter.

The taiko is used in only about a third of the plays commonly performed, almost always in the last part of the play, where it has important roles in the entrance music and dances of certain kinds of shite. The patterns used in taiko drumming are more minutely spaced within the standard eight-beat measure than those of the ōtsuzumi and kotsuzumi. When the three drums are played in ensemble, the taiko takes the lead in determining rhythm and pace.

The so-called mochi-flower design is emblematic of late Muromachi period lacquer style. Its simplicity and dynamism, clearly forecasting the coming fashion of the Momoyama period, combine with a limited range of techniques, red for twine, and *fundame* (densely packed gold flecks) for mochi flowers against a black ground.

The drum with a design of scattered fans (cat. 134) shows the revived appreciation for complex technique that took hold during the Edo period. This design in lacquer dates back at least to the Kamakura period (1185–1333), but the casual ease and elegance with which these fans are arranged mark the composition as a product of the peaceful Edo period (1615–1868). Silver flecks used to embellish forms and create mist add contrasting color to the predominant gold makie. (TH and HG)

133

134

ACTOR PROPS

KAZURAOKE (SEAT AND CONTAINER PROP)
WITH PAMPAS GRASS

(1) *Momoyama period, seventeenth century*
Lacquer on wood with gold powder (makie)
17 11/16 x 11 1/8 in. (45.0 x 28.3 cm)
Osaka Castle Museum
catalogue 135, p. 159

KAZURAOKE (SEAT AND CONTAINER PROP)
WITH WEEPING CHERRY BLOSSOMS

(2) *Momoyama period, sixteenth century*
Lacquer on wood with gold powder
(e-nashiji, hiramakie, harigaki)
16 1/4 x 10 3/8 in. (42.5 x 26.4 cm)
Kyoto National Museum
catalogue 136

One of the few props used on the noh stage,
the *kazuraoke* acts as a stool for the shite.
Sometimes placed center stage, this stool
can be sat upon or used, especially in kyōgen,
to represent an object, such as a bucket
from which water is scooped. The shite can
also use it while waiting to come onstage.

Very few kazuraoke survive; the ones
here are decorated with simple, bold designs
in the so-called Kōdaiji makie style of the
Momoyama period. The design of weeping
cherry blossoms is clearly laid out in gold
against black. Also employed is the *harigaki*
technique, whereby a pin is drawn across
a wet lacquered area to create a line within
a form.

Dew-speckled pampas grass (cat. 135,
p. 159) of the fall season and cherry blossoms
of early spring were appropriately poetic
motifs, both poignantly transitory in nature.
They were not, however, tied to specific
literary references, which would have
required deeper learning than the samurai
had at this time. (HG)

136

COSTUME ENSEMBLES

Okina
CELEBRATORY

OKINA (OR HAKUSHIKIJŌ) MASK
Nanbokuchō period, fourteenth century
Pigment on Japanese cypress wood
(hinoki) with hemp
7⁷⁄₁₆ x 6⁷⁄₁₆ in. (19.0 x 16.4 cm)
Nyū Shrine, Nara Prefecture
catalogue 137, p. 14

Age is viewed with reverence in Asia, and masks representing old men carry a special dignity. Okina is both a mask of an old man and of a god. Like the more realistic old men's masks used in other noh plays (cat. 85, p. 59; cat. 84, p. 58) the Okina mask has implanted beard and is lined with wrinkles. Unlike other old-men's masks however, the Okina mask smiles joyfully and his stylized wrinkles form patterns. Rather than painted eyebrows, the Okina mask has hemp-cord pompoms flayed out and fuzzed and glued above the eyes (no longer on the Nyū mask). The detached chin (*kiri-ago*) has been tied to the cheeks with hemp cords passed through small holes at the edges of the mouth. As the actor speaks and moves, the chin jiggles slightly. In contrast to the fluidly changing expressions of most noh masks, the abstract features of the Okina mask remain smiling all the time.

The Nyū mask is comparatively large for an Okina mask. Three deeply incised wrinkles spread across the broad forehead and sweep down in a curve to the upper eyelids. Thin crescent openings form the smiling eyes. The tension in the arc of the eyes characterizes this mask and leads into the terse, deep curved wrinkles on the cheeks. Of the numerous old Okina masks, this one stands out for its strikingly vivid expression. Carved from Japanese cypress, it is painted with a white prime coat seemingly mixed with small amount of mica to give it a slight glitter. The back is neatly chiseled with no surface treatment. The carved inscriptions on the back reading, "Nyū Shrine" and "Treasure number seven" are later additions, as is probably the hemp beard implanted on the chin. (MB)

OKINA MASK BOX
① *Edo period, eighteenth century*
Lacquer on wood with gold powder
(makie and nashiji)
14¹⁄₈ x 10¹⁵⁄₁₆ x 9¹⁵⁄₁₆ in. (35.8 x 27.8 x 25.2 cm)
Museum of Noh Artifacts, Sasayama,
Hyōgo Prefecture
catalogue 138, p. 181

An Okina mask would be carried onstage within this box. The box is decorated with family crest of the Hyūga Date family – on the face the melon/tree/hermitage crest, and on the lid the "10 day" crest. Designs are applied in various *makie* (sprinkled gold) techniques including *nashiji* (literally, pear skin), widely sprinkled large flakes covering the background, and for the family crests *hiramakie*, with tiny flakes densely sprinkled on the surface plane of the lacquer to create the look of an unmodulated gold surface. The lacquer artisan left areas in reserve (*kakiwari*) to indicate spaces between design segments of the crests. A fine line of makie follows the inside edge of the quatrefoil melon form for extra embellishment.

The box shape, straight-sided with tightly rounded corners and a slightly mounded lid, show a conservative manner of construction. An exquisitely crafted loop handle and plate hint at daimyo-level patronage for this box. The clear and simple forms of the makie design would have been easily readable by the audience, showing a wish for recognition on the part of the patron. (HG)

OKINA KARIGINU WITH LINKED HEXAGONS AND FLORAL MEDALLION PATTERN (SHOKKŌ)
① *Edo period, eighteenth century*
Silk twill weave with supplementary
silk weft patterning (nishiki)
64⁹⁄₁₆ x 83⁷⁄₁₆ in. (164.5 x 212.0 cm)
Fujita Museum of Art, Osaka
catalogue 139, p. 182

The densely interlocking patterned weave creates an ambience of the ancient and eternal. *Shokkō* (Shuchiang, an area near Chengtu in Szechwan province, China) referred initially to textiles with a compound warp pattern (*tatenishiki*) on a red ground imported from China during the seventh century. Later versions manufactured in Ming China using weft-patterning techniques and a supplementary warp for tying down the pattern threads were among the textiles imported to Medieval Japan. The design of Ming shokkō was based on a grid composed of large octagons linked by smaller squares at the cardinal points. Variations and embellishments included the insertion of Tang-style floral medallions and intricate patterning of compositional elements. Both types of variation can be seen in this piece, which sets Tang flower medallions within linked hexagons with connected knot patterns at the corners. At the center of each flower lie eight small white petals set around a core with white dot and backed by a dark ground. Around these petals spreads an eight-pointed snowflake with brown ground. The sides of the linked hexagons contain rectangles articulated with small patterning. To retain the impact of the original octagons and squares while translating the pattern into linked hexagons, the vertical rectangles within the hexagons have a lattice of tiny hexagons, while the angled sides contain an interlace of "y" figures. This textural variance invites the eye to roam from link to link. The contrast of light and dark within each flower lends a depth and brightness that enlivens the geometric regularity of the design. (MB)

OKINA SASHINUKI WITH EIGHT-LOBED WISTERIA (YATSUFUJI) ROUNDELS
① *Edo period, eighteenth century*
Silk twill weave with silk
supplementary weft float patterning (monori)
57¹⁄₂ x 26³⁄₄ in. (146.0 x 68.0 cm)
Bunka Gakuen Costume Museum, Tokyo
catalogue 140, p. 182

The sashinuki worn by Okina can range in color from darker purples and greens to lighter tans, white or light blue, such as those of the Bunka Gakuen Costume Museum. Typical of Japanese pants (hakama), they are constructed of pleated front and back panels joined three-quarters of the way up at the sides and along the inseam. While the back has wide pleats, the front has six narrower pleats. Sashinuki are meant to be worn over stiff ōkuchi. The legs of the sashinuki, which are bound at the ankles by means of bands of cloth inserted at their lower edge, must be tailored long to compensate for the extra bulk of the undergarment.

Since sahinuki were standard clothing for the nobility of the Heian period, they are typically fashioned from silks woven with court patterns (*yūsoku mon'yō*), such as white weft-float patterns (*mon ori*) on a plain color ground. Floral rounds, oblongs, and diamonds predominate. Here the wisteria rounds have an internal geometric construction. White fills a circle, in which negative lines define a central four-petal flower set in a cross composed of arcs. Small points run down the center of the cross and mark the rim of the circle at even intervals. (MB)

KOSHIOBI (SASH)
WITH EIGHT TREASURES

① *Edo–Meiji period, nineteenth century*
Silk twill weave with silk supplementary
weft patterning
2 15/16 x 94 1/8 in. (7.5 x 239.0 cm)
Hikone Castle Museum, Shiga Prefecture
catalogue 141, p. 183

> The dense pattern of scattered treasures
> is woven with many binding threads so that
> it is tightly worked into the ground, in a
> style typical of many fabrics imported in the
> mediaeval period and used for bags for
> tea caddies and mounting paintings. (MB)

OKINA FAN WITH MOUNT HŌRAI

① *Edo period, nineteenth century*
Ink, colors, and gold leaf on paper
with bamboo ribs
Length: 13 7/8 in. (35.0 cm)
Toyohashi Uomachi Noh Association,
Aichi Prefecture
catalogue 142, p. 183

> The elements of the design on the fan used
> by Okina depict the legendary mountain of
> Hōrai, a motif drawn from the libretto. This
> floating island somewhere in the Eastern
> Sea lures Daoist ascetics in search of an elixir
> of everlasting life. The association with
> longevity provides the auspicious aura and
> makes depictions of Mount Hōrai ubiquitous
> on celebratory occasions, such as New Year
> and marriage ceremonies. On the mountain
> island grow the evergreen pine of constancy,
> the resilient bamboo, and the early-
> blossoming plum. Long-lived cranes come
> to rest here, building nests to nurture their
> young. Aged sea tortoises with flowing
> tails also breed on the sandy beaches.
>
> The Toyohashi fan shows the mountain
> rise off the back of a giant tortoise. As
> evening approaches a crane sweeps towards
> the spreading branches of a central pine
> silhouetted against a golden sky with a hint
> of red underpaint. The undulating gradated
> lines that fill the lower third of the fan arc
> suggest a powerful ocean. (MB)

Sanbasō

SANBASŌ (OR KOKUSHIKIJŌ) MASK

Muromachi period, fifteenth century
Pigment on camphor or Japanese
cypress wood (hinoki)
6 13/16 x 5 11/16 in. (17.3 x 14.5 cm)
Nyū Shrine, Nara Prefecture
catalogue 143, p. 15

> In construction the Sanbasō mask is very
> similar to the Okina mask. Both have
> detached chins (kiri-ago), broad foreheads
> lined with three wrinkles that curl around
> the eyebrows down to smiling crescent
> eyes, and rounded cheeks lined with semi-
> circular wrinkles. What distinguishes
> Sanbasō is the black color, the thinner beard,
> a hair mustache, and hairy eyebrows that
> flare outward. Although this mask has lost
> all the hair, one can still see the holes where
> it was implanted. The wonderful smile
> that seems to flow from its wrinkled nose
> and then to circle in on itself in the curves
> of the eyes and lips forms a contrapuntal
> pattern with the abstract lines of the
> surrounding wrinkles. Joy and vigor aptly
> express the energy of this Sanbasō, freely
> executed in the style of early masks. (MB)

SANBASŌ HITATARE AND HAKAMA
WITH CRANES AND TORTOISES

② *Edo period, nineteenth century*
Hemp plain weave with ink, pigment,
and paste-resist (tsutsugaki)
jacket: 38 3/4 x 83 7/8 in. (98.5 x 213.0 cm);
hakama: 61 1/4 x 26 in. (155.6 x 66 cm)
Private collection
catalogue 144, p. 184

> The standard color for Sanbasō's costume
> is black, though other colors, such as dark
> blue, are used on certain occasions. Sea
> tortoises with long flowing tails and cranes,
> both symbols of long life and inhabitants
> of the mystic island of Mount Hōrai,
> appear in the standard spots for placing
> crests. Two cover the right and left chest;
> three line the upper back spanning the
> center seam and the sleeve seamos,
> and two decorate the hakama where the
> side seams begin. The cranes face each
> other, one swooping down from the sky,
> the other flying up to meet it. (MB)

SANBASŌ HAKAMA WITH CRANES,
TORTOISES, AND PINE

② *Edo period, eighteenth century*
Hemp plain weave with pigment
and paste-resist (tsutsugaki)
Length: 59.45 in. (151.0 cm)
Fujita Museum of Art, Osaka
catalogue 145, p. 185

> These hitatare hakama have, in addition to
> the standard cranes and sea tortoise,
> another auspicious symbol of long life and
> constancy: the pine that never changes
> color. The white paste-resisted areas delin-
> eating the pine appear fresh and tactile
> against the black ground. For the crane and
> tortoise additional green, red, blue, gray,
> and yellow have been painted into areas
> carefully outlined in white with resist
> paste. In a few areas, such at the base of
> the crane's neck, one can find shading from
> one color to another (here gray to red),
> a technique that typifies yūzen dyeing. The
> hitatare matching jacket has been lost. (MB)

SANBASŌ FAN WITH CRANES, TORTOISES,
PINE, BAMBOO, AND WATER

② *Edo period, eighteenth century*
Colors, ink, and gold leaf on paper
with bamboo ribs
Length: 13 7/8 in. (35.2 cm)
Tokyo National Museum
catalogue 146, p. 185

> Sanbasō's fan is similar to the fan used by
> Okina. An image of Mount Hōrai is
> appropriate, but the upper edges form
> triangular colored blocks rather than the flat
> gold ground seen on many fans used by
> Okina. Different kyōgen actors follow slightly
> different traditions concerning Sanbasō
> fans: while the Nomura family of the Izumi
> school uses one fan with red edge triangles
> for both dances, the Shigeyama family of
> the Ōkura school uses two different fans.
> For the first mominodan they use a fan like
> that shown here with blue edge triangles,
> while for the suzunodan they use a fan with
> red. This fan shows two cranes gracefully
> circling toward a lone pine backed by
> swirling water. The bottom portion of the
> pine lies hidden behind a broad gold strip
> that runs along the lower edge of the
> fan, suggesting but not defining the place
> as Mount Hōrai. (MB)

BELL TREE (SUZU)

② *Edo period, 1699*
Metal and wood
14 1/2 x 4 3/8 in. (37.0 x 11.0 cm)
The Metropolitan Museum of Art, New York
The Crosby Brown Collection of Musical
Instruments, 1889. (89.4.94)
catalogue 147, p. 186

> The bell tree used by Sanbasō in the second
> half of Okina are typical of shrine bells
> carried by shrine maidens (miko) when they
> perform kagura dances. Shaking objects
> to make them jingle activates latent forces
> and thus aids fertility, in this case the grow-
> ing of rice. Such handheld sticklike objects
> also function as pathways for the gods
> to descend, and are known as torimono.
>
> Eleven small bells with internal
> clappers and fluted middles hang along a
> spiraling metal rod that is set into a stick
> handle. A metal disk sits at the junction
> between rod and handle. Both the upper
> and lower portion of the handle bear
> decorative metal trappings, and a braided
> cord dangles from its base. During the
> dance, the bells are given sharp, rhythmic
> shakes that make them jingle in a confusion
> of pitches. (MB)

Kamo
CONGRATULATORY; FIRST CATEGORY

ZŌ-ONNA MASK

Deme Zekan (d. 1616)
*Momoyama–Edo period,
sixteenth–seventeenth century*
Pigment on Japanese cypress wood (hinoki)
8⁵/₁₆ x 5³/₈ in. (21.1 x 13.6 cm)
Toyohashi Uomachi Noh Association,
Aichi Prefecture
catalogue 148, p. 191

The reserved, cool expression of the Zō-onna mask is seen as a mark of unearthly elegance. This is a fine example: the slightly open lips and the narrow eyes neither smile nor frown. Thin eyebrows line the upper regions of a high forehead and complement the subtle modeling. The cheeks, less full than those of other young-women's masks, are smooth, unmarked by dimples or the creases and prominent bones of older faces. A faint blush heightens their color, though the consistently horizontal brush-strokes with which the white *gofun* finish coat has been applied work to flatten their contours. The loose strands at the fringe of the parted hair start from the top as two, are interrupted by a loop of two others, and stream down the side in a set of three.

Zō-onna is used by all schools for roles of celestial women, such as the moon maiden in *Hagoromo* and the deity disguised as a village in the first act of *Kamo*. The original model mask (*honmen*) is reputed to have been created by the dengaku player Zōami, a contemporary of Zeami known for the subtle beauty of his dance and favored by the shogun Ashikaga Yoshimochi.

The back of the Toyohashi mask has been painted deep brown. The carved insignia at the upper left is a square with rounded corners, containing four characters that read "Deme Zekan." Both the horizontal tool marks and the insignia are characteristic of other masks by the skillful progenitor of the Ono Deme line, Zekan Yoshimitsu (d. 1616), making it highly likely that the insignia is original. (MB)

**KARAORI WITH FLAX, WISTERIA,
PICTURE PAPERS (SHIKISHI),
AND POEM CARDS (TANZAKU)**

② *Edo period, eighteenth century*
*Silk twill weave with ikat-dyed (kasuri) warp
in alternating blocks of red and brown with silk
and gold-leaf paper supplementary weft patterning*
62 x 54¹³/₁₆ in. (157.4 x 139.2 cm)
Tokyo National Museum
catalogue 149, p. 192

The village woman who appears as shite in the first act of *Kamo* and who turns out to be a deity in disguise wears a karaori "with red." Her costume should be more elegant than that of her companion, but otherwise there is no specific stipulation. This karaori is particularly rich in ornamentation. The density of the surface weft float pattern all but obscures the alternating blocks that form the ground. The colors of the ground blocks are close rather than contrasting or complementary, and the hazy shift from one block to the other helps form a cohesive ground that consolidates the pattern confusion into a harmonious whole. The ground blocks appear as negative/positive versions of each other: the starlike inter-locking pattern known as *asa no ha* (hemp leaf) is rendered in gold lines on the red-brown ground and in red lines on gold in the "red" ground area. Each ground color block covers three-quarters of the whole pattern unit, which consists of two sections: two square papers with a long wisteria to their right, and a single poem strip to the right of center set among five large wisteria trellises. In tailoring the garment the extra width of the cloth has been taken up differently in different panels so as to shift the center of the pattern and create the effect of greater variety than is actually in the woven textile.

Karaori can be draped in several ways, but the most common for figures appearing in the first act of a play is kinagashi style. For this the karaori is wrapped snugly around the legs, bound at the waist with a koshiobi sash, and opened in a broad V over the chest. (MB)

**KAZURAOBI (HEADBAND)
WITH TRAILING BRANCHES
OF CHERRY BLOSSOMS**

② *Edo period, eighteenth century*
*Silk satin weave with silk embroidery
and gold-leaf stenciled pattern*
1⁹/₁₆ x 99³/₅ in. (4.0 x 253.0 cm)
Eisei Bunko Museum, Tokyo
catalogue 150, p. 190

Kazuraobi hairbands are used to hold the wig hair in place and add a decorative touch. They are tied at the back of the head in a cross-shaped knot, their long ends dangling down the black tresses. As with the belt sashes (koshiobi), only the exposed middle section and ends are decorated. The middle portion runs around the forehead, under the mask, in an aesthetic that reminds the spectator that the actor is masked. (In country performances, like at the village of Kurokawa in Yamagata prefecture, the kazuraobi is placed over the mask forehead, blending the mask into the costumed figure more realistically than in standard performances.)

The kazura obi worn by the shite in the first act of *Kamo* should be elegant and refined. Red is stipulated, to go with the youthful mask. Flowers and gold-leaf sten-ciled mist add luster. The blue, black, and white cherry buds and blossoms fall in two willowy strings. Most of the embroidery is satin stitch and outline stitch. (MB)

ŌTOBIDE MASK

*Momoyama–Edo period,
seventeenth century*
*Pigment on Japanese cypress
wood (hinoki)*
8¹/₈ x 6¼ in. (20.6 x 15.9 cm)
Toyohashi Uomachi Noh Association,
Aichi Prefecture
catalogue 151, p. 191

The name Tobide ("bulging eyes") describes the large round eyeballs covered with metal that characterize this mask of a strong god. A gaping mouth in a large jaw exposes a red tongue and two sets of well-formed teeth. The cavities that flank the flaring nostrils form the middle tier in a row of oval hollows, with the eye sockets above and the mouth below. The thin black line across the top of the head marks where a lacquer cap would sit on the forehead, though generally a shaggy red headpiece would be worn, obscuring the upper area of the face. The entire face is painted with gold, on top of which wispy eyebrows, mustache, and hair are drawn in thinly brushed ink.

Tobide-style masks were among the earliest type of noh mask to develop. Their open mouths form the sound "ah," reminiscent of paired "ah-un" guardian figures in temples. The Toyohashi Ōtobide mask is a fine example of the mature form as it developed over time. Explosive energy and surprise seem to burst from it, making it particularly appropriate for a role like the Thunder God in *Kamo*.

Although the mask bears no identify-ing insignia, the back is hollowed out and finished with the finesse of a first-class carver. The general style suggests a date not later than the seventeenth century. (MB)

KARIGINU WITH INVERTED COMMA ROUNDELS (TOMOE) AND SERPENTINE-LINE PATTERN (TATEWAKU)

② *Edo period, eighteenth century*
Silk twill lampas weave with gold-leaf paper supplementary wefts (kinran)
62 3/16 x 79 1/2 in. (158.0 x 202.0 cm)
Hayashibara Museum of Art, Okayama Prefecture
catalogue 152, p. 193

The Thunder God who heralds a downpour in the second act of *Kamo* should wear a lined (*awase*) kariginu with dynamic design. In this garment three rows of large tomoe, circles composed of three interlocking commas, are imposed on a background lattice of vertical serpentine lines. The latter tatewaku motif belongs among designs associated with the imperial court (*yūsoku mon'yō*) and thus bears an aura of authority. It has been interpreted as expressing the climbing spirit (*ki*) of good omen. The former pattern appears often on end tiles of temple buildings and on drumheads, whose sound recalls that of thunder. Its form recalls that of the double-comma yin-yang design, the sacred *magatama* comma-shaped jewel, and also dragon claws. It, too, was associated in ancient China with the theory of mind/spirit. The swirling motion of the locked heads and mutually enclosing tails of the commas has a dynamic force that interrupts the vertical sway of the background tatewaku lines, almost like eddies in a swift-flowing river.

The kariginu used in noh is a slightly altered version of a garment by the same name that was worn as informal attire by the Heian courtiers and later adopted as formal wear by the military aristocracy. The round collar and broad front overlap are similar to (but not identical with) the construction of men's formal court wear. The front section is belted at the waist in such a way that extra yardage is given to the upper portion, which loosely folds over itself, hiding part of the lower portion. This draping method explains why the bottom row of tomoe is placed so far from the other rows. Cords strung through the cuffs of the double-width sleeves were originally to gather the sleeves at the wrist, but in noh they are purely decorative, their tassels hanging from the sleeve edges and their colors adding a finishing touch. (MB)

ATSUITA WITH DRAGON ROUNDELS AND AUSPICIOUS CLOUDS

② *Edo period, eighteenth century*
Silk twill weave on ikat-dyed (kasuri) warp in alternating blocks of red and green with silk supplementary weft patterning
59 13/16 x 55 7/8 in. (152.0 x 142.0 cm)
Hayashibara Museum of Art,
Okayama Prefecture
catalogue 153, p. 192

The Thunder God of *Kamo* dwells among the clouds, making them a particularly appropriate motif for his garments. Two different styles of cloud formations alternate in this atsuita. Each cloud cluster contains bright and dark clouds, good and bad weather, rendered in a variety of color combinations. The white billows and trailing tails stand out prominently, while the other clouds, excepting the black ones, blend with the overall color scheme of reds and greens. While these clouds are woven with long floats that allow the glossed silk to expand and form a solid surface, the rows of dragon rounds have been woven with narrowly spaced warp ties that bind them into the structure of the fabric. This creates a layered effect, with the clouds foregrounding the dragons, a reversal of the standard arrangement. The blocks of complementary colors that form the twill were created by resist-dyeing the warp before setting it on the loom and then matching the weft colors while weaving. The slightly blurred edges of each block result from the impossibility of lining up the pre-dyed warps perfectly. (MB)

HANGIRE WITH STYLIZED LIGHTNING AND TRIPLE COMMA CLOUD ROUNDELS (TOMOE)

② *Edo period, nineteenth century*
Silk satin lampas weave with gold-leaf paper supplementary weft patterning (kinran)
36 1/4 x 18 1/8 in. (92.0 x 46.0 cm)
Noda Shrine, Yamaguchi Prefecture
catalogue 154, p. 193

Below his kariginu, the Thunder God wears bulging bifurcated skirts (hangire) with dynamic patterns. Hangire are typically woven with the same techniques as the lined kariginu. Gold-leaf thread patterning is held in place by a separate warp, whose color will enhance the gold but be virtually invisible. As a result, the areas of gold appear like unbroken surfaces, not dissimilar to gold leaf pasted directly on the cloth, as is done on surihaku, though they are effectively bound into the structure of the textile. Here the abstractly rendered bolts of lightning flash between clouds forming three-comma tomoe, suggesting at once the source of rain and the roar of the thunder through their similarity to drumheads.

The pleats in the front of the hangire are tacked in place and held by the long sash sewn on to the top edge. When the hangire is put on, the front is set in place first, then the sashes are wrapped around the hips and tied in back. The back pleat is created just before donning the costume by tying cords laced through holes slightly below the upper edge. This large pleat creates the characteristic hump over the back side and is held in place by setting it on a wooden frame in the shape of a tuning fork that is slipped between the body and the already-tied front-panel sashes. The back sashes are then tied in front of the belly of the actor with a knot that appears like a cross. (MB)

KOSHIOBI (SASH) WITH SWIRLING CLOUD CRESTS

② *Edo–Meiji period, nineteenth century*
Silk satin weave with silk embroidery
2 15/16 x 103 7/16 in. (7.4 x 262.8 cm)
Hikone Castle Museum, Shiga Prefecture
catalogue 155, p. 193

Koshiobi belt sashes are used to hold garments in place. In the costume for the Thunder God in *Kamo*, the koshiobi secures the kariginu, tucking up its front panel, so the upper portion falls loosely over the chest, and pulling in the back panel so it lies snugly over the hump created by the hangire. The central portion of the sash is soft cloth, while the two decorative ends enclose a stiff interfacing. Stipulations as to which koshiobi should be used in a particular play tend to be generalized. For *Kamo* they read, "embroidered crest koshiobi." In the Ii family example, three swirling clouds facing in alternating directions have been embroidered in black glossed silk. Used in combination with the other garments selected here for *Kamo*, the cloud motif echoes motifs in the hangire and the atsuita. (MB)

Tadanori
NARRATIVE; SECOND CATEGORY

CHŪJŌ MASK
Iseki Kawachi Daijō Ieshige (d. 1645 or 1657)
Edo period, seventeenth century
Pigment on Japanese cypress wood (hinoki)
7 15/16 x 5 7/16 in. (20.1 x 13.8 cm)
Toyohashi Uomachi Noh Association,
Aichi Prefecture
catalogue 156, p. 197

Representing a mature courtier-warrior, Chūjō is the standard mask for many of the warrior plays, and is also worn by noblemen enjoying the elegance of Heian life, such as in the play *Tōru*. A faint smile, gentle almond-shaped eyes, and quizzical furrows softening the area above the nose lend the mask a delicacy also apparent in the cosmetics of blackened teeth, caterpillar eyebrows, and faint mustache. The straight black line at the top of the forehead marks where the courtier's cap would rest. Below it a small wooden nail helps keep in place the white sweatband that is worn for warrior pieces, obscuring the area above the eyes. The effect is a stronger, more masculine expression.

A fine example of the style of Iseki Kawachi Daijō Ieshige (d. 1645 or 1657), this mask has both strength and delicacy. Kawachi is looked upon as one of the finest carvers of the Edo period. By his time old model masks were recreated, rather than new masks being invented. Few of the copyists managed the depth and subtlety of Kawachi. New painting techniques are apparent in this Chūjō mask, where a flush of pink is barely perceptible in the cheeks and antiquing has given the facial contours greater fullness. The back of the mask has been elegantly finished, with shallow tool marks following the contours and a light brown coat. Above the left eye a burn insignia reads, "Tenka ichi Kawachi." The title he was given, First under Heaven, was instigated by the military mastermind Toyotomi Hideyoshi to award excellence in art and was later adopted by the Tokugawa. (MB)

CHŌKEN WITH BUTTERFLIES
①*Edo period, eighteenth century*
Silk gauze weave with gold-leaf paper supplementary weft patterning (rokin)
37 x 73 5/8 in. (94.0 x 187.0 cm)
Hayashibara Museum of Art, Okayama Prefecture
catalogue 157, p. 197

Butterflies were the symbol of the Heike clan, and thus appropriate for Tadanori to wear on his garments. Here three types of butterflies stand in staggered rows. The bright gold shimmers against the gossamer green ground. The gauze weave used here is standard for many Edo-period gauzes: three shots of plain weave followed by one row where adjacent warps interlace to form openwork. The loose ends of the gold paper threads have been shaved close after the yardage was taken off the loom.

For a warrior role, the chōken is draped with the right sleeve slipped off the arm. To do this, the robe is first put on with both arms in the sleeves. After centering the chōken, it is tacked to the atsuita under it at the neck. Next, the loose front and back panels are bound to the body of the actor at his waist using a koshiobi sash tied in front. The back of the chōken lies against the upper body and rises over the hump formed by the ōkuchi, while the front panels are brought straight down to the waist and then smartly folded so they flare to the sides. The decorative cords attached to the collar of the chōken, rather than being tied at the chest as they are for female roles, are knotted to the koshiobi. A sword is then slung at the right side of the actor by means of a braided cord that is tied in an elaborate knot to the left of center. Finally the right sleeve is slipped off his arm, stretched out, folded in triangles, and then rolled up and tucked into the koshiobi at the back. The right portion of the atsuita undergarment is thereby left exposed. (MB)

KARAORI WITH BOAT SAILS, PINE TREES, ABSTRACT PINE BARK LOZENGES (MATSUKAWABISHI) AND LINKED HEXAGON PATTERN (KIKKŌ)
①*Edo period, eighteenth century*
Silk twill weave with ikat-dyed (kasuri) warp silk and gold-leaf paper supplementary weft patterning
59 1/4 x 57 1/2 in. (151.7 x 146.0 cm)
Tokyo National Museum
catalogue 158, p. 196

Behind beach pines sails blow in a gusty wind. Jagged diamond and hexagon lattices fill in the intermediary space, appearing here like sand, and there like ocean. Since the design lacks the floral motifs typical of many karaori, it has a somewhat masculine flavor appropriate for warrior roles; the garment could be classed as an *atsuita-karaori*. Given the context of the play, in an undergarment for Tadanori the design could be interpreted as the imperial boats sailing off from Suma Beach, leaving Tadanori and a number of other Heike warriors featured in noh plays stranded on land to face the enemy.

Deft control of color variation creates an overall image out of the pattern repeats. While color contrast predominates above, colors that blend with the ground are more prevalent below. The dark sails in each row draw the eye downward. The ground is worked in colors and gold on red with three block repeats forming a suggestion of a dangawari pattern: jagged diamond lattice (*matsukawabishi*, pine bark lozenge), starred hexagon lattice, and plain hexagon lattice (*kikkō*). The dominant colors of the lattices repeat: dark red, light red in staggered rows.

The shape and measurements of this karaori, with the narrower loom width and slight flare at the bottom, are standard for the mid-seventeenth century and later. The weave, with comparatively short weft floats held down by incidental warps (*toji*) that form patterns within the sails and delineate the branches of the pines, typifies techniques of the eighteenth century and later, but lacks the outlining that characterized many nineteenth-century karaori patterns. (MB)

ŌKUCHI WITH PINE, SEASHELLS, AND FANS IN FLOWING WATER
①*Edo period, eighteenth century*
Silk plain-weave lampas with glossed silk and gold-leaf paper supplementary weft patterning (kinran)
Length: 45 3/8 in. (115.2 cm)
Hikone Castle Museum, Shiga Prefecture
catalogue 159, p. 196

The standard ōkuchi bifurcated skirts for the role of Tadanori are plain white, but since his final battle is on the seashore, a seaside design is not inappropriate. Here, open and closed clamshells and fans shift about in the shallow surf that swirls in small eddies on the sands. While the front of the ōkuchi is woven with weft patterning on a plain-weave ground, the back panels have a stiff rib weave produced by using very thick wefts, actually bundles of silk threads used as a single element, that give the garment a stiff shape. The skirts are stored flat, but in preparation for putting them on, silk cords are threaded through holes in the back panels and pulled tight to form a deep pleat that creates the characteristic bulge in the back. Broad white sashes attached to the upper edge of the front and back are used to tie the garment onto the actor. The dressing process is identical with that of hangire. (MB)

KOSHIOBI (SASH) WITH PAULOWNIA CRESTS
①*Edo–Meiji period, nineteenth century*
Silk satin weave with silk and gold-leaf paper wrapped silk thread embroidery
2 9/16 x 92 1/2 in. (6.5 x 235.0 cm)
Hikone Castle Museum, Shiga Prefecture
catalogue 160, p. 195

Paulownia flowers rise from large three-pointed leaves with decorative arabesque tendrils tying them into a vertical row of three. Meticulous embroidery, using mostly short and long and satin stitch, delineates the design. Line stitch is used to outline the leaves and flowers, while an over-stitch forms the veins of the leaves. The subtle browns and off-greens are combined differently for each repetition.

Having three crestlike patterns placed above each other in a row is one standard design for koshiobi. (Other examples include cat. 155, p. 193, and cat. 188, p. 223.) Intimate motifs, such as flora and fauna, are appropriate though not required for the role of a courtier-warrior like Tadanori. (MB)

SHURA ŌGI (WARRIOR'S FAN) WITH SETTING SUN AND OCEAN WAVES

① *Edo period, eighteenth century*
Ink, colors, and gold leaf on paper
with lacquered bamboo ribs
Height: 13⅞ in. (35.1 cm)
Hikone Castle Museum, Shiga Prefecture
catalogue 161, p. 198

A red sun sinks behind huge splashing blue waves against a gold-leaf ground. This image catches the mood of the heroic defeat suffered by the members of the Heike clan, the last of whom died in the naval battle of Dannoura, with many drowning themselves in preference to being killed by a nameless soldier. Warrior plays about victorious heroes use a fan showing a red sun rising behind a pine tree. Some warrior fans have both images, one on each side. The frothy waves on the Ii family fan splay up in wild breakers that frame the blood red orb. To the right an ocean eddy spirals inward in gradated shades of blue. The strong primary colors and flat opaque paints follow the Yamato-e school traditions of native Japanese painting using earth pigments. Fans are categorized in part by the color of their ribs: plain or lacquered. These are black lacquered. (MB)

Hagoromo
LYRICAL; THIRD CATEGORY

KO-OMOTE MASK
Ōmiya Yamato Sanemori (d. 1672)
Edo period, seventeenth century
Pigment on wood
8⅜ x 5¼ in. (21.2 x 13.4 cm)
Hikone Castle Museum, Shiga Prefecture
catalogue 162, p. 202

Ko-omote, or "Little Face," is the youngest of the masks of young women. "Little" not only suggests her naiveté but also refers to the size of the triangle formed between the pupils of the eyes and the base of the nose. That the eyes are set closer together than on most other masks makes the face appear a bit plump. The full cheeks and lips curl into a smile, echoed in upward-swerving eyes with a bright, open expression. The broad, somewhat square forehead sports thick caterpillar eyebrows and balances a square chin. Black locks parted in the middle run down the face in broad bands. Loose strands of hair framing the face are suggested by scratching out three white lines with widening spacing. This technique contrasts with the method of denoting side hair on all other young-women's masks, where the separate strands are carefully painted in along the side of the solid bands (cat. 94, p. 64 and cat. 170, p. 212).

Ko-omote masks are worn for supporting tsure roles, such as the companion and the mother goddess in *Kamo*, but they are also used by the Kita and Konparu schools for shite roles, such as the mistress of the well in *Izutsu* and the moon maiden in *Hagoromo*. Other schools distinguish between the human-ghost role and the celestial-being role by choosing (depending on school tradition) the masks Waka-onna, Fushiki-zō, or Magojirō for the former and the Zo-onna mask, with its more impassive expression, for heavenly maidens.

This mask, from the Ii collection, is attributed to Yamato Sanemori of Ōmiya (d. 1671), a disciple of the great early-Edo master Kawachi. The finely balanced curves and muted shading in the painting tell of a master's hand. (MB)

NUIHAKU WITH FLORAL LOZENGES, LINKED HEXAGONS, DANDELIONS, SNOWFLAKES, AND FLOWERING PLANTS

② *Edo period, eighteenth century*
Silk figured satin weave with silk embroidery
and gold- and silver-leaf stenciled patterns
56⁵⁄₁₆ x 52¹⁄₁₆ in. (143.0 x 132.2 cm)
Tokyo National Museum
catalogue 163, p. 200

Large snowflake frames enclosing embroidered sprays of various flowers lie scattered over the shoulder and hem portions of this kosode garment. Between them and often overlapping in portions are oversized dandelions that have been embroidered in vivid colors. The stenciled background of linked hexagons (*kikkō*) forms irregular masses of gold and silver suggesting a cracked-ice pattern. The combination of the chilly background and the warm colors of the embroidered plants aptly suggests the emergence of spring, the season in which *Hagoromo* is set. Many embroidery stitches were used to create the varied textures of the plants.

Leaving the waist bare has practical advantages, since this area of the garment gets the most wear from folding and tying, especially when the upper half is folded down at the waist in *koshimaki* style, as it is for *Hagoromo*. It also harks back to sixteenth-century design systems known as *katasuso* (shoulder and hem; cat. 45, p. 87 and cat. 46, p. 86). The suggestion of a diagonal line running from left shoulder to right hem, however, is a remnant of seventeenth-century streetwear styles, and here is muted by an overall horizontal balance, typical of styles that became more prominent in the eighteenth century. (MB)

SURIHAKU WITH DEW-LADEN GRASS

② *Edo period, eighteenth century*
Silk satin weave with gold- and silver-leaf
stenciled patterns
60¹⁄₁₆ x 57¹⁄₁₆ in. (152.5 x 145.0 cm)
Tokyo National Museum
catalogue 164, p. 200

Only the upper half of this surihaku has been decorated, as the lower half lies hidden beneath other garments. Gold and silver (tarnished black and copper color) blades curve over each other to form a rippling sea of grass. The graceful lines form an elegant, refined design suggestive of poetic imagery. The jagged borderline between dense patterning above and almost bare white ground below forms a "pine bark lozenge" (*matsukawabishi*) partition, reminiscent of Momoyama-period design constructions (see ground pattern in cat. 46, p. 86).

When worn as a part of a koshimaki outfit, the entire upper portion of the surihaku is exposed, and the combination produces a two-part suit. In *Hagoromo*, after the chōken has been donned, the surihaku is almost entirely covered. Only a hint of the glitter of gold and silver shines through the gossamer weave of the outer garment. (MB)

KAZURAOBI (HEADBAND) WITH PHOENIXES AND MANDARIN ORANGE BLOSSOMS

② *Edo–Meiji period, nineteenth century*
Silk satin weave with silk embroidery
and gold leaf (dōhaku)
1½ x 97⅛ in. (3.9 x 247.3 cm)
Hikone Castle Museum, Shiga Prefecture
catalogue 165, p. 201

Kazuraobi, or hairbands, are long narrow strips of plain color silk with decorated stiffened areas at the two ends and in the middle, where the band is tied around the forehead. The same motifs decorate all three areas. Here long-tailed birds fly in graceful swerves, their tails trailing at an angle behind them. Birds and flowers are executed precisely in varied colors. As with the koshiobi sash, the gold ground of the kazura obi, made by applying gold leaf to the red cloth, accords with the celestial status of the moon maiden in *Hagoromo*. (MB)

KOSHIOBI (SASH) WITH PEONIES AND SCROLLING VINE

②*Edo period, nineteenth century*
Silk satin weave with silk embroidery
and gold leaf (dōhaku)
2⁵/₈ x 93³/₄ in. (6.7 x 238.1 cm)
Hikone Castle Museum, Shiga Prefecture
catalogue 166, p. 200

When dressing a figure in koshimaki style, the nuihaku is first donned over the surihaku and secured at the waist with the koshiobi. Then the upper portion is slipped off the actor's shoulders and neatly folded at the waist so the sleeves hang down over the hips. Only a portion of the koshiobi remains visible under the folds of the garment. The elegance and celestial status of the moon maiden in *Hagoromo* requires that she wear accessories with gold grounds, while her ageless beauty is expressed by the inclusion of red. Here three peonies, the Chinese symbol of feminine beauty, have been embroidered in varied colors and joined by trailing arabesque tendrils. Long and short stitch fills the broad peony petals in solid color. Satin stitch defines the leaves, with overlay stitch for their veins, and outline stitch is used to create the curling tendrils. (MB)

CHŌKEN WITH WEEPING WISTERIA AND PAULOWNIA ARABESQUES

Edo period, eighteenth century
②*Silk gauze weave with gold-leaf paper*
supplementary weft patterning (rokin)
41⁵/₁₆ x 80⁵/₁₆ in. (105.0 x 204.0 cm)
Hayashibara Museum of Art,
Okayama Prefecture
catalogue 167, p. 201

The feather robe so necessary for the moon maiden in *Hagoromo* to fly back to her celestial abode has no stipulated color or design, though red and white are favorites. Here the wisteria suggest spring and their long flower clusters are reminiscent of feathers. In a typical "crest and hem" layout, the upward movement of the paulowina flowers counterbalances the downward sway of the wisteria blossoms. (MB)

TENGAN (HEAVENLY CROWN)

②*Edo period, eighteenth century*
Metal, paper, colors
3⁵/₁₆ x 5⁹/₁₆ in. (8.4 x 14.1 cm)
Hikone Castle Museum, Shiga Prefecture
catalogue 168, p. 203

A gilt bronze circlet with filigree mounds rising from it forms the central portion of this celestial crown. Delicate filigree pendants are suspended from four spots, and a closed crescent moon cushioned on a cloudbank rises from a support at the back. The two side projections, also placed at the back, correspond to similar forms on black lacquer crowns and indicate status. In overall conception this crown harks back to early gold crowns found in Tumulus period (third to sixth century) grave sites and in Three Dynasty period artifacts in Korea. It also resembles the gilt canopies with dangling pendants that hang above Buddhist statues.

The crown is secured to the head by braided cords threaded through holes at the base of the circlet. As the dancer moves, the swaying gold pendants glitter. For *Hagoromo* the crown is worn over a wig tied in a low ponytail at the nape of the neck, but for the role of the Mother Goddess in *Kamo* a similar crown sits on open hair cascading down the shoulders. (MB)

KAZURA ŌGI (WOMAN'S FAN) WITH CHERRY BLOSSOMS

②*Edo period, eighteenth century*
Colors and ink on paper
with lacquered bamboo ribs
Length: 13⁹/₁₆ in. (34.5 cm)
Tokyo National Museum
catalogue 169, p. 201

The face side of this fan shows ladies in Chinese costume gathering under a giant tree. Such colorful depictions of court scenes, generally taken from Chinese sources, are the most common decoration for women's fans and set the tone of elegance associated with third-category women's plays. The reverse side of this fan has delicate cherries whose pinkish white stands out against the muted tones of the background landscape. Cherry blossoms epitomize the soft, hazy beauty of the beginning of warm weather in the spring. As the moon maiden waves her fan in dance patterns the blossoms on the fan seem to become the text: "swept by storm winds that scatter blossoms like swirling snow." The bamboo slats that form the spine of this fan are painted with black lacquer. (MB)

Dōjōji
DRAMATIC; FOURTH OR FIFTH CATEGORY

ŌMI-ONNA MASK

Attributed to Zōami
Momoyama period, sixteenth century
Pigment on Japanese cypress
wood (hinoki)
8¼ x 5¼ in. (20.9 x 13.3 cm)
Tokyo National Museum
catalogue 170, p. 212

High eyebrows, hair parted in the middle with loose strands along the edge, a slight smile, and full cheeks are characteristics of all masks in the "young woman" category. The Ōmi-onna mask represents someone older than the Ko-omote mask (cat. 162, p. 20), but not as remote as Zō-onna (cat. 148, p. 191). Heavy eyelids lend the Ōmi-onna mask an atmosphere of mystery. Two free strands of hair run from the center part, then two more curve out at about the level of the eyebrows. Three more, one thicker, line the sides. Although discoloration from sap and from general handling has left spots on the mask, the balanced features, supple contours, and polished painting all bespeak a master artist. The back side shows shallow chisel marks going with the contours. The gold paint inscription, validated by seals of the fifth and seventh carvers in the Ōno Deme line, reads, "The work of Zōami." Zōami was an actor, living about the same time as Zeami. He was known for the lyrical beauty of his dances and for having created the Zō-onna mask type. Although the attribution is unlikely, the mask is a fine example, and from its style probably dates from the mid-to-late sixteenth century. (MB)

KARAORI WITH WEEPING CHERRIES AND ABSTRACT PINE-BARK LOZENGES (MATSUKAWABISHI)

①*Edo period, eighteenth century*
Silk twill weave with silk and gold-leaf paper
supplementary weft patterning
57⁷/₁₆ x 54³/₄ in. (145.9 x 139 cm)
Hikone Castle Museum, Shiga Prefecture
catalogue 171, p. 208

In Dōjōji, the standard karaori worn as an outer robe, folded and bound at the waist in tsubo-ori style, by the Kanze school has weeping cherry branches on a gold ground and large spools of thread scattered as a foreground. Here jagged diamonds with mist substitute for the spools. Gold-leaf paper cut into narrow strips has been woven into the red ground. The formalized cherry branches run in stiff vertical lines but show dexterous use of color and internal variation. Each of the five vertical branches of leaves, flowers, and buds has the same progression pattern but in opposing orientation for the second, fourth, and fifth strings. Typical of late-Edo karaori is the outlining of the cherry blooms with contrasting color: red against white, purple against yellow. The weaving unit is deceptively long, for it comprises two large diamonds and two small ones; one-and-a-half units cover the total length of the back. The result of their zigzag placement is that the small diamonds seem to travel from the lower right of the garment back diagonally across and up to the left shoulder. Simple as the pattern may appear, it required a far more ambitious loom setup than many earlier karaori. (MB)

KAZURAOBI (HEADBAND) WITH TRIANGULAR SCALE PATTERN (UROKO)

① *Edo–Meiji period, eighteenth–nineteenth century*
Silk satin weave with silk embroidery
and gold-leaf stenciled pattern
1½ × 99³/₁₆ in. (3.8 × 252.0 cm)
Hikone Castle Museum, Shiga Prefecture
catalogue 172, p. 212

On this kazuraobi the uroko scale pattern has been divided into horizontal color blocks of blue, red, green, white, and purple. Four rows of each color are embroidered to form one block. As with the surihaku and the koshiobi, the alternate triangles are stenciled gold leaf. The undecorated portions of the hairband, used for tying a bow knot at the back of the head, are woven in red silk. (MB)

ONI ŌGI (DEMON FAN) WITH PEONY

① *Edo period, eighteenth century*
Ink, gold and colors on paper with lacquered
bamboo ribs
Length: 13⅝ in. (34.6 cm)
Hikone Castle Museum, Shiga Prefecture
catalogue 173, p. 208

Each of the noh schools has its own regulations for the appropriate fan to use for *Dōjōji*. The Kanze school uses a "demon" fan with one large peony against a red ground. The petals of the peony on this fan have pink bases that spread toward white, frilly edges. The tips of the veined leaves peep out from the edges. A thin gold arabesque fills the entire red ground. The peony was associated with female beauty in China, but the large scale of this one suggests the lust of the woman in *Dōjōji*. The fan ribs have been painted with black lacquer. (MB)

HANNYA MASK

Attributed to Hannyabō
Muromachi period, fifteenth–sixteenth century
Pigment on Japanese horse chestnut wood (tochi)
8¼ × 6¹³/₁₆ in. (21.0 × 17.3 cm)
Eisei Bunko Museum, Tokyo
catalogue 174, p. 213

In *Dōjōji*, the shite in the second act is vengeful jealousy incarnate. The mask used to represent this emotional state is the horned, snakelike Hannya, which combines human pathos and animalistic traits. The parted black hair with straggly wisps, faint eyebrows high on the forehead, and bony nose appear human, while the horns, round metallic eyes, large gold fanged teeth,

and gaping mouth suggest animalistic ferocity. Tilt the mask forward and the overhang above the eyes casts a pained shadow, but jerk the mask to right or left in a movement called *omote o kiru* and the eyes appear to jump, the fangs to flash, and the horns to await attack. With its fully fleshed cheeks and deep furrows above the eyes joining a sharp nose ridge, this mask deftly balances the two aspects, fully embodying the pathetic and the fearsome.

The Hosokawa family, who own the mask, attribute it to Hannyabō, though this is unverified. Little is known of Hannyabō except that he lived in Nara in the late fifteenth–early sixteenth century and was probably a priest, judging from the "bō" at the end of his name. The correspondence between his name and the name of the Hannya masks has led some to postulate that he was the creator of the mask style, but it might be the other way around, or simply that he took his name from the *Hannyakyō* (Heart sutra). (MB)

NUIHAKU WITH DECORATIVE ① ROUNDELS

Edo period, nineteenth century
Silk satin weave with silk embroidery and gold leaf
56 × 58⅜ in. (142.2 × 148.4 cm)
Toyohashi Uomachi Noh Association,
Aichi Prefecture
catalogue 175, p. 209

Scattered rounds on a dark blue or black ground are a standard costume for jealous-woman roles, worn both for *Dōjōji* and for *Aoi no ue*. No stipulation sets the size and density of the rounds, or their content, but this nuihaku is typical. Smaller and larger rounds seem randomly scattered about. While some of the rounds contain flowers, waves, clouds, or are composed of leaf arrangements, others consist of dragons curled in on themselves, and still others are purely geometric in conception. The embroidery can be quite elaborate, delicately portraying texture and painterly detail. In addition to long and short, satin, line, and elaborate over-stitch, couching has been used to apply small amounts of gold thread.

Nuihaku robes with this design are almost always worn in koshimaki draping. They are first put on over the surihaku underrobe as if to totally cover it. After the front panels are adjusted so they fit snugly over the legs, the nuihaku is bound at the waist using a koshiobi. Next the top half of the garment is slipped off the shoulders and allowed to fall down over the hips. It is

then carefully arranged with explicit folds so that it falls gracefully, the sleeves hanging down at the actor's sides. The combination of surihaku top and koshimaki skirts makes an elegant two-tone suit, generally of contrasting light and dark colors. In the first half of *Dōjōji* yet another robe, a stiff karaori, is placed on top of the combination suit, but hiked up at the waist in tsubo-ori style, exposing some of the nuihaku below it. Since the tsubo-ori requires folding the karaori over on itself in a triple layer at the waist, and the koshimaki likewise involves multiple layers, the fully dressed actor has at least six layers of cloth wrapped around his waist. (MB)

SURIHAKU WITH TRIANGULAR ① SCALE PATTERN (UROKO)

Edo period, nineteenth century
Silk satin weave with gold-leaf stenciled pattern
57⅝ × 53¹⁵/₁₆ in. (146.4 × 137.0 cm)
Kyoto National Museum
catalogue 176, p. 209

The same uroko pattern, made up of rows of interlocked triangles facing alternating directions, is used on the upper undergarment in *Dōjōji* as on the kazuraobi and the koshiobi. The entire garment was first dyed red. Then a stencil cut with the triangle pattern was placed on the stretched fabric and adhesive applied through the holes. A variety of adhesives could be used, including rice paste and lacquer, the exact proportions and ingredients being carefully held secrets of the artisans. Before the adhesive dried, very finely hammered gold stored on sheets of thin paper backing was placed on the cloth. After the adhesive was thoroughly dry, the excess gold leaf could be brushed away, leaving a clean-edged pattern. This technique creates beautiful areas of solid gold, but these flake off with abrasion. Flaking occurs along fold lines and on areas of contact with outer garments, such as the shoulders and the inner sleeves. The sleeves of this surihaku are slightly longer than standard and have a gentle curve to the outer low corner.

For the first act of *Dōjōji* the surihaku is barely visible under the karaori, but in the second act it creates a flashing, strong impression as the upper half of a two-piece suit with contrasting colors. White grounds with gold or silver triangles are a common choice, but red grounds form an alternative, commonly matched with trailing red ōkuchi for variant performances. (MB)

KOSHIOBI (SASH) WITH TRIANGULAR SCALE PATTERN (UROKO)

① *Edo period, eighteenth century*
Silk satin with silk embroidery
and gold-leaf stenciled pattern
2¾ × 107⅝ in. (7.0 × 273.4 cm)
Eisei Bunko Museum, Tokyo
catalogue 177

Rows of interlocked triangles facing alternating directions form a pattern known as uroko and are used here to suggest the snake character of the shite. The same pattern appears in the hairband and the surihaku. On this koshiobi the stenciled gold-leaf triangles point down, while the embroidered ones point upward. The green, brown, and white embroidered triangles are arranged in diagonal rows, allowing the pattern to be read not only on the vertical/horizontal axis, but also along the diagonal.

In the shite's costume for *Dōjōji*, the koshiobi secures the nuihaku, which is folded over it. The waist sash is visible below the folded-down sleeves, which spread towards the sides. (MB)

177

Kumasaka

DYNAMIC; FIFTH CATEGORY

CHŌREI BESHIMI

Deme Yūkan (d. 1652)
Edo period, seventeenth century
Pigments on Japanese cypress wood (hinoki)
8 3/16 x 6 3/8 in. (20.8 x 16.2 cm)
Toyohashi Uomachi Noh Association,
Aichi Prefecture
catalogue 178, p. 214

Said to have been invented by a man called
Chōrei, this style of clenched-mouth
Beshimi mask was made expressly for the
role of Kumasaka Chōhan. As in other
Beshimi masks (cat. 88, p. 47) the lips are
firmly pressed together, with the lower jaw
jutting out from a square chin; the round
eyes glare from under sharply defined
eyebrow ridges; a black strip at the top of
the forehead indicates a hat line; and the
perimeter is rectangular. Peculiar to Chōrei
are the wide-set eyes and the straight
ridge over the bridge of the nose arching
into the eyebrows. The large scale and
the upward curl to corners of the lips are
characteristics shared with the "large"
Ōbeshimi, worn by strong humans, as
opposed to the "small" Ko-beshimi masks
(cat. 66, p. 47) with downward curling lips,
worn by demons.

The round metallic eyes of this
Beshimi mask turn inward, the left one
looking up. Onstage this imbalance
accentuates the sharp head movements
used in the dance. The presence of ears is
common on demonic masks but is not
restricted to them. The swarthy coloring
gains depth by an undercoat of red beneath
the tanned skin color. Dense overlaying of
fine brush strokes creates the thick, upward-
swerving mustache and eyebrows. Sparse
lines define a light spreading beard and
sideburns. Humor, vigor, and determination
fill the face.

The back has been hollowed with
a shallow curved knife and bears a carved
insignia of Yūkan (d. 1652), disciple of
Zekan and second in the Ōno Deme line
of carvers. (MB)

HAPPI WITH DRAGON ROUNDELS AND ABSTRACT LIGHTNING

① *Edo period, nineteenth century*
Silk satin lampas weave with gold-leaf paper
supplementary weft patterning (kinran)
47 1/4 x 78 1/8 in. (121.3 x 198.5 cm)
Toyohashi Uomachi Noh Association,
Aichi Prefecture
catalogue 179, p. 216

Kumasaka wears a lined happi to suggest
his armor. Although similar cloth can be
used to make both happi and kariginu, their
tailoring and draping differ. The happi is
draped with the diagonal front lapels
forming a broad V converging at the waist.
Below the belt the front panels flare out to
the sides and are attached to the back
panels by means of narrow cloth strips set
into the panel hems. Three typical drapings
include both sleeves on, the right sleeve
off and tucked in at the center back, and
both sleeves hiked up to the shoulders
in a style resembling *sobatsugi*. Kumasaka
can be robed with either of the later two
methods.

On this happi dragons with bulging
eyes, shaggy eyebrows, tendril whiskers,
and straight horns curl their scaly bodies
into circles. The design has been cleverly
worked out so that by reversing the pattern
to produce a mirror image of the complete
dragons on alternating panels, pairs of
facing dragons are lined up at center sleeve.
Half-dragons are woven along the sides of
the fabric and neatly matched at the
seams so four complete dragons appear
on each sleeve. Behind the dragons are
squared-off spirals, suggesting lightning,
in symmetric formation. The bold lines,
contrast of angular and circular, and
juxtaposition of gold against green make
for a striking garment suited to the vigor
of Kumasaka Chōhan. (MB)

ATSUITA WITH CLOUDS AND TRIPLE COMMA ROUNDELS (TOMOE), ARROW SCREENS, AND TRIANGULAR SCALE PATTERN (UROKO)

① *Edo period, nineteenth century*
Silk twill weave on ikat-dyed (kasuri) warp
in alternating blocks of red and green with silk
and gold-leaf paper thread supplementary weft
patterning
59 1/8 x 53 15/16 in. (150.2 x 137.0 cm)
Tokyo National Museum
catalogue 180, p. 217

Two large motifs decorate squares that
alternate red and green in a checker pattern
created by reserve-dyeing portions of the
warp threads: rows of arrow feathers lining
standing screens decorated with flower
motifs, and *tomoe* (interlocking tailed
commas) in circles floating on large trailing
clouds. An overall scale pattern of interlacing
triangles meshes the motifs into a single
design. The decorative float patterns do
not fit completely within the confines of
the checker squares, a characteristic of
mid-to-late Edo-period weaving. In addition
the added small clouds spanning the back
seam in the first two rungs form a curious
departure from the restrictions of pattern
repeat imposed by mechanics of weaving.

The motifs of arrows and screens
would be very suitable for a warrior-courtier
role. When the costume is worn for
Kumasaka, the diagonally angled screen
suggests the corridors through which
Kumasaka blindly chases Ushiwaka. The
large trailing clouds, exposed on the right
back shoulder of the dressed figure,
would complement the dragons and flaming
circles of the happi and hangire chosen
here. (MB)

HANGIRE WITH STYLIZED WAVE AND FLAMING DRUM ROUNDELS AND GEOMETRIC PATTERN

① *Edo period, nineteenth century*
Silk satin lampas weave with gold-leaf paper
supplementary weft patterning (kinran)
Front: 36 1/4 x 18 1/8 in. (92.0 x 46.0 cm);
back: 42 5/16 x 30 5/16 in. (107.5 x 77.0 cm)
Noda Shrine, Yamaguchi Prefecture
catalogue 181, p. 217

Hangire are patterned bifurcated skirts
with a broad back panel stiffened by the
insertion of straw matting between
the face cloth and lining. Cords slipped
through holes near the center of the back
panels can be pulled tight to form a large
pleat that creates the characteristic bulge
over the rear.

In this piece, giant circles made up of
waves and flaming fires are superimposed
on a lattice of thick lines forming an irregular
interlocking pattern. The large scale of the
pattern in flashy gold against dark green
suits the earthy vigor of the Kumasaka role.
Two separate warps were used to weave
the pattern, one to hold down the gold
threads and colored to complement
the metal, the other dark green to match
the silk weft threads. (MB)

KOSHIOBI (SASH) WITH TEMPLE GONG (UNPAN) CRESTS

① *Edo–Meiji period, nineteenth century*
Silk satin weave with silk embroidery
2 13/16 x 97 in. (7.1 x 246.4 cm)
Hikone Castle Museum, Shiga Prefecture
catalogue 182, p. 217

Three temple gongs in the form of crests
and lined up vertically decorate this
koshiobi chosen for Kumasaka. The gold-
color embroidered gongs stand out in strong
contrast to the black ground. Koshiobi
designs come in several types; the three-
crest type is commonly used for male roles,
particularly more vigorous ones. (MB)

CHŌHAN-ZUKIN (CLOTH HEADGEAR)

① *Edo period, eighteenth century*
Silk twill or satin lampas weave with gold-leaf
paper supplementary weft patterning (kinran)
Length: 24 5/8 in. (62.5 cm)
Hayashibara Museum of Art,
Okayama Prefecture
catalogue 183, p. 218

Zukin are cloth head-covers. Kumasaka's is particularly elaborate, with three or more layers of rounded flaps added at the base of a long rectangular strip of cloth. Sashes for tying are attached at the juncture. When a zukin is placed on the head, the base of the main strip is set at the actor's forehead. The cloth is laid over the crown of the head and held in place with the sashes tied at the back. The layered flaps fall over the ears. (MB)

Shōjō
FELICITOUS

SHŌJŌ MASK

Ōmi Kodama Mitsumasa (d. 1704)
② *Edo period, seventeenth century*
Pigment on Japanese cypress wood (hinoki)
8 1/16 x 5 3/8 in. (20.5 x 13.7 cm)
Ishikawa Prefectural Museum of Art
catalogue 184, p. 223

The sea-frolicking *shōjō* are depicted as youths, for they feast on wine, considered to be an elixir of eternal youth. The Shōjō mask with its crescent eyebrows, smiling eyes and lips, and straight hair falling like a wispy veil over the forehead resembles other masks of boy-sprites like Dōji and Jidō, except that Shōjō is bright red. The color matches the entire costume but also casts ironic humor on the wine merchant's observation, "No matter how much he drinks, his face never changes color." The carver of this mask, Ōmi Kodama Mitsumasa, was adopted into the Deme school in Tokyo, but later moved to Kyoto, where he founded the Kodama school and began to work in the style of Kawachi (d. 1645). Ōmi has been hailed as a "second Kawachi." He even followed Kawachi in placing his stamp in the temple area. In his mask of Shōjō, Ōmi has deftly caught the atmosphere of pleasurable drunkenness in the heavy eyelids and lightly parted lips that curl into rounded cheeks. (MB)

KARAORI WITH CHRYSANTHEMUMS AND WAVES

② *Edo period, eighteenth century*
Silk twill weave with silk and gold-leaf paper
supplementary weft patterning
58 11/16 x 55 1/8 in. (149.0 x 140.0 cm)
Bunka Gakuen Costume Museum, Tokyo
catalogue 185, p. 220

A red ground is a prerogative for Shōjō's costume, and in this karaori two important symbols of the play, chrysanthemums and sea waves, have been worked into the design. The chrysanthemums not only mark the season, but also evoke the phrase "chrysanthemum water," a euphemism for sake wine, referring to a story where drops of dew fall from the chrysanthemum petals, flow over mantra letters, and create an elixir of long life. The flossy bulk of the flowers contrasts with the recessed weaving of the gold thread for the waves, enhancing the sense that the flower sprigs float on the surface of the water. Dark and light patches of flowers are placed in a zigzag, giving the impression of moving down the current of a stream. The unit repeat fills the width of the cloth but is comparatively small, there being approximately five repeats over the length of the garment. These are lined up horizontally in the center section, but placed in mirror image on the left and right side (ABAB, from sleeve to sleeve), creating an impression of greater variety than actually exists. The detailing of the chrysanthemum petals, many of which are outlined in contrasting colors, uses rather short weft floats. Outlining of this sort is more typical of late-Edo pieces.

In *Shōjō* the karaori is draped over voluminous divided skirts as an overrobe. It is bound at the waist so that the upper portion lies snug over the back and chest, while the lower portion rises over the hump of the skirts in the back and flares to both sides in the front. Draping a karaori or atsuita over other garments as an outer robe is known as tsubo-ori, whether as in *Shōjō* it is over bulging divided skirts, or as in *Dōjōji* over slimmer kosode-style garments. (MB)

NUIHAKU WITH ABSTRACT WAVE PATTERN (SEIGAIHA), MANDARIN DUCKS, AND CANDOCKS

② *Edo period, seventeenth century*
Silk satin weave with silk embroidery
and gold- and silver-leaf stenciled patterns
55 1/4 x 55 1/2 in. (140.4 x 141.0 cm)
Tokyo National Museum
catalogue 186, p. 221

An irregular "sandbar" line delineates the upper and lower portions of this nuihaku, clearly designed for being worn folded down at the waist in koshimaki style. For Shōjō, however, it would be used as an undergarment, and only the interlocking wave patterns above would be visible. The idyllic water scene has a painterly, open design. This accords with trends in streetwear of the seventeenth century and contrasts with similar motifs in Momoyama garments, where the ducks are lost in a mass of foliage. As with the earlier piece, the silk floss here has no twist but is sturdy enough to support rather long stitches without fraying. Unlike the sixteenth-century pieces done primarily in the surface-only watashi-nui stitch, however, this piece employs a variety of stitches to achieve textural variation, greater realism, and a sense of three-dimensionality. The long leaves and duck feathers are executed in satin stitch (sometimes augmented by areas of overlay stitching), the bodies of the ducks in long short stitch, and general area outlining in stem stitch. The textile historian Yamanobe suggests that the comparative thickness of the lines, in both stencil patterns and embroidery, points to a date early in the seventeenth century. The contrast of patternized upper design and painterly lower half gains further emphasis by the dense wave arcs. (MB)

ŌKUCHI WITH CHRYSANTHEMUMS AND WATER

② *Edo period, eighteenth century*
Silk plain-weave lampas with silk and gold-leaf
paper supplementary weft patterning (kinran)
42 15/16 x 30 5/16 in. (109.0 x 77.0 cm)
Tokyo National Museum
catalogue 187, p. 220

Ōkuchi are one of the three main styles of leggings used in noh. Although identical in general shape with hangire, they differ in weave and construction. The cloth for ōkuchi is woven in plain weave, generally an unadorned solid color, but sometimes incorporating decoration, while that for hangire is satin weave and always incorporates a design in contrasting color, commonly gold or silver. Both garments have stiff back panels that incorporate a large pleat at the center back designed to form a large bulge extending from waist to about knee level. The pleat is formed immediately before putting on the ōkuchi, by drawing cords through holes, pulling them tight, and tying them. In order for the leggings to retain a broad, voluminous shape, the back panel has to be very stiff. For ōkuchi this is achieved by weaving in a thick, multistrand, cordlike weft and beating it tightly. For hangire, encasing a straw mat between the face and lining fabrics of the back panel creates the stiffness.

The motifs of chrysanthemums and water woven into this ōkuchi mirror the motifs of the karaori. By having a rather tall pattern unit and omitting the chrysanthemums from the upper repeat (of which only half appears), the weaver has created a sense of distance and movement, particularly in the uppermost waves. The chrysanthemums on the ōkuchi are larger than those on the karaori and lack border outlines, suggesting possibly a slightly earlier date. The bold pictorial design of these ōkuchi contrasts with the denser more generalized design of shells and waves on the ōkuchi chosen for *Tadanori* (cat. 159, p. 196). (MB)

KOSHIOBI (SASH) WITH CHRYSANTHEMUM CRESTS

② *Edo period, nineteenth century*
Silk satin weave with silk embroidery and gold leaf
95 1/2 x 2 11/16 in. (242.5 x 6.8 cm)
Noda Shrine, Yamaguchi Prefecture
catalogue 188, p. 223

The large, simple, top-view chrysanthemums with gold-leaf centers and embroidered outlines lie in a vertical row along the end panels of this waist sash. Although much of the gold has worn off, it appears as if a gold strip ran across the central section with the light-colored, central chrysanthemum, while the darker upper and lower ones were set against a red ground. As with the ōkuchi and the karaori for *Shōjō*, the chrysanthemum motif reflects the imagery of the play. (MB)

HEADPIECE

② *Edo period, nineteenth century*
Animal hair
Length: 61 1/16 in. (155.0 cm)
Tokyo National Museum
catalogue 189, p. 225

The masked actor wears something on his head to provide a context for the mask. Most common are wigs made of black human hair (*kazura* and *kurotare*) or white human hair (*jōgami*) and headpieces (*kashira*) made from masses of animal hair sewn onto a cloth, though cloth caps like Kumasaka's chōhan zukin are also used. While the wigs have long hair knotted in a strip or circle and are combed and tied into the appropriate shape on the actor's head, the headpieces are simply tied in place and allowed to cascade down the actor's back, with shorter hairs falling over the shoulders and forehead. (MB)

SHŌJŌ FAN WITH CHRYSANTHEMUMS AND WATER

② *Edo period, nineteenth century*
Ink, colors, and gold leaf on paper with lacquered bamboo ribs
Length: 13 11/16 in. (34.7 cm);
13 9/16 x 13 3/4 in. (34.5 x 35.0 cm)
Hikone Castle Museum, Shiga Prefecture
catalogue 190, p. 222

Typical of all elements of Shōjō's costume, the dominant color of this fan is red and the motifs are chrysanthemums and water. Black, wavy swirls form eddies that catch flower sprigs floating down a golden stream. The large curves radiating from spirals set left and right of the center line create the sense of a strong river current, more forceful than the lazy ripples in the nuihaku or the open waters of the karaori.

This fan would be used in a standard performance of Shōjō, but could also be used in other noh featuring characters who have drunk the elixir of eternal youth, such as Kikujidō and Makurajidō. (MB)

THE CHECKLIST ENTRIES WERE WRITTEN AS FOLLOWS:

(MB) Monica Bethe
(HG) Hollis Goodall
(TH) Tom Hare
(KS) Kawakami Shigeki
(KK) Kirihata Ken
(NI) Nagasaki Iwao
(SST) Sharon Sadako Takeda

NOTE TO THE READER

Japanese terms, with some exceptions, are italicized the first time they occur in the text. A definition is usually provided at that point. These terms are generally listed in the index as well. Words that have entered the English language from the Japanese are treated as English. All such terms, however, will not be pluralized, in keeping with Japanese usage. Translations of terms, titles, and quoted passages in the text, when not credited to a particular source, are the authors' own.

In accordance with Japanese custom, Japanese names are listed with the surname first and given name second. Prominent individuals were often referred to by their given name.

LENDERS TO THE EXHIBITION

Agency for Cultural Affairs, *Tokyo*
Bunka Gakuen Costume Museum, *Tokyo*
Eisei Bunko Museum, *Tokyo*
Fujita Museum of Art, *Osaka*
Hayashibara Museum of Art,
   Okayama Prefecture
Hikone Castle Museum, *Shiga Prefecture*
Hōzanji, *Nara Prefecture*
Indianapolis Museum of Art
Ishikawa Prefectural Museum of Art
Itsukushima Shrine, *Hiroshima Prefecture*
Kasuga Taisha, *Nara Prefecture*
Kyoto National Museum
Kobe City Museum
Los Angeles County Museum of Art
The Metropolitan Museum of Art, *New York*
Mibudera, *Kyoto*
Museum of Noh Artifacts,
   Sasayama, Hyōgo Prefecture
Nagataki Hakusan Shrine, *Gifu Prefecture*
Naratsuhiko Shrine
National Museum of Japanese History,
   Sakura, Chiba Prefecture
National Noh Theater, *Tokyo*
Neo Kasuga Shrine, *Gifu Prefecture*
Nyū Shrine, *Nara Prefecture*
Noda Shrine, *Yamaguchi Prefecture*
Nogami Memorial Institute for Noh Studies
   at Hōsei University
Nomura Art Museum, *Kyoto*
Osaka Castle Museum
Ōtsuki Seiinaki, *Osaka*
Oyama Shrine, *Ishikawa Prefecture*
Private Collections, *Kyoto and New York*
Research Archives for Japanese Music
   at Ueno Gakuen University, *Tokyo*
Rinnōji, *Tochigi Prefecture*
Seki Kasuga Shrine, *Gifu Prefecture*
Shinshiro Honmachi Noh Association,
   Aichi Prefecture
Suntory Museum of Art, *Tokyo*
Tokyo National Museum
Toyohashi Uomachi Noh Association,
   Aichi Prefecture
Tsubouchi Memorial Theatre Museum,
   Waseda University, Tokyo

CHRONOLOGY

JŌMON PERIOD   11,000–300 BC

YAYOI PERIOD   300 BC–300 AD

KOFUN PERIOD   300–552

ASUKA PERIOD   552–645

Gigaku introduced to Japan

NARA PERIOD   645–794

Bugaku and sangaku (acts that in later centuries are carried on in sarugaku) introduced from China

701 Gagaku adopted as official music of the court

751 Gigaku mask (fig. 9, p. 44), Tōdaiji, Nara

752 Bugaku and sangaku performed at the dedication ceremony of the Great Buddha at Tōdaiji, Nara

HEIAN PERIOD   794–1185

c. 1011 *Tale of Genji* written by Murasaki Shikibu

1023 Regent Fujiwara Michinaga attends *taue* performance at rice-planting festival

1042 Bugaku mask: Ōnitei (fig. 10, p. 44), Tōdaiji, Nara

1060 *Shin sarugak ku* (A record of new sarukagu) by Fujiwara Akihira mentions comic sarugaku skits similar in title to plays that appear later in the kyōgen repertory

1096 Dengaku extremely popular in Kyoto

1136 Sarugaku and dengaku performed at the first Wakamiya Festival at Kasuga Shrine, Nara

KAMAKURA PERIOD   1185–1333

Shogunal court established

Dispersion of performing arts throughout the country

1255 First record of sarugaku outdoor performance by firelight (*takigi sarugaku*), Kōfukuji, Nara

1282 Earliest record of *Shikisanban* performed by
or 1283 sarugaku actors, Wakamiya Festival at Kasuga Shrine, Nara

NANBOKUCHŌ PERIOD 1333–1392

1333 Kannami Kiyotsugu is born

MUROMACHI PERIOD   1392–1568

1349 Sarugaku and dengaku performances at Kasuga Shrine, Nara

Ashikaga Takauji attends kanjin dengaku at Shijōgawa, Kyoto; numerous casualties from the collapse of the bleachers

1352 First listing of kyōgen in a program of entertainment recorded in *Ninheiji hondō kuyō nikki* (The diary of memorial services at Ninheiji)

c. 1363 Zeami Motokiyo is born

Kannami performs *kusemai* dance for the first time in the play *Shirahige*

1368 Ming Dynasty established, diplomatic and trade relations reestablished with China

1369 Jō (Old man) mask; Nagataki Hakusan Shrine (cat. 84, p. 58)

c. 1371 Kannami establishes reputation after successful seven-day kanjin performance at Daigoji, Kyoto

1374 Kannami and Zeami perform at Imakumano Shrine, Kyoto; Shogun Yoshimitsu in attendance and becomes their patron

Nijō Yoshimoto (1320–1388), renowned literati, bestows the name of Fujiwaka to Zeami in praise of his performance

1378 Fujiwaka (Zeami) and Yoshimitsu attend the Gion Festival together, sharing the same seat

1384 Kannami performs his last noh; dies in Suruga (Shizuoka Prefecture)

Zeami becomes second head of Kanze troupe

1394 Zeami performs for Yoshimitsu in Nara; Zeami's first son, Motomasa, is born

1395 Ashikaga Yoshimochi (1386–1428) becomes fourth shogun, but does not really rule until his father's death; Yoshimochi favors the *dengaku* actor Zōami

1397 Kinkakuji (Temple of the golden pavilion) built by Ashikaga Yoshimitsu

1398 Motoshige (On'ami) is born

1399 Zeami performs for Yoshimitsu at Daigoji and also a season of *kanjin* noh

1400–1418 Zeami writes *Fūshikaden* (Teachings on style and the flower), also known as *Kadensho*, his first treatise on noh

1405 Konparu Zenchiku is born

1408 Yoshimitsu entertains the emperor at Kitayama palace with Dōami, Inuō of the Ōmi school (and possibly Zeami)

1411 Yoshimochi becomes shogun and patronizes Zōami

1412–1422 Numerous documented Zeami performances

1413 Beshimi mask by Chigusa Saemon Dayū (cat. 88, p. 47)

1419 Zeami writes *Ongyoku kuden* (Treatise on music and the use of voice)

1420 Zeami writes *Shikadō* (The true path to the flower)

1421 Zeami writes *Nikyoku santai ningyō zu* (Diagrams on song, dance, and mime)

1422 Zeami becomes a priest; begins to dictate his writings to his son Motoyoshi

1423 Zeami's *Sandō* or *Nōsakusho* (The three elements of composing a play) includes earliest mention of the plays *Hyakuman, Jinen Koji, Koi no omoni, Matsukaze, Oimatsu, Tadanori* (as *Satsuma no kami*)

Zeami dictates *Kakyō* (A mirror held to the flower) and *Go-on gyoku* (Various matters concerning the five modes of musical expression) to Motoyoshi

Yūgakushūdōfūken (Disciplines for the joy of art), and *Kyūi* (Nine levels)

Zeami made musical director (*gakuto*) of Daigoji

Zeami writes the play *Eguchi*

1424 An entry in the *Kanmongyoki* (Diary of Prince Sadafusa of Fushimi) notes that a sarugaku troupe was chastised for performing a kyōgen play about the impoverishment of nobles

1428 With *Shūgyoku tokka* (Finding gems and gaining the flower), *Rikugi* (Six genres), Zeami presents his secrets to Konparu Zenchiku

1430 Zeami's second son, Motoyoshi, compiles Zeami's memoir as *Sarugaku dangi* (Account of Zeami's reflections on the art of sarugaku), which includes earliest mention of the plays *Aoi no ue* and *Izutsu* and others

Zeami writes *Shūdōsho* (Learning the way) and *Go-on no jōjō* (Articles concerning the five sounds)

Zōami, dengaku player and possible carver of Ōmi-onna mask (cat. 170, p. 212)

1432 *Museki isshi* (A page on the remnant of a dream: in memory of his son, Motomasa), *Go-on* (The five sounds)

1432–1434 Earliest mention of the play *Taema*, in Zeami's text *Go-on*

1433 Zeami writes his last treatise, *Kyakuraika* (The return of the flower)

Motoshige is lead actor at the kanjin noh performed along the riverbank of Tadasu River, Kyoto, and becomes third Kanze Dayū

1434	Zeami exiled to Sado Island
1436	Zeami writes *Kintōsho* (Writing from the isle of gold)
1441	Yoshinori assassinated at a Sarugaku performance
c. 1443	Zeami dies
1449	Yoshimasa becomes shogun
1450	Kanjin noh forbidden by the shogun
1455	Zenchiku writes *Go-on shidai* (The order of five sounds)
1456	Zenchiku writes *Kabu zuinō ki* (The essentials in singing and dancing) that includes earliest textual reference to the play *Kantan*, *Go-on jittei* (The truth of five sounds) and *Rokurin ichiro hichū* a theoretical text on noh (Bushō bon version)
1458	Motoshige becomes a priest and takes the name On'ami
	Zenchiku writes *Enmaniza hoshiki* (The rules of Enmaniza)
1467	Ōnin Wars begin and last for a decade; cataclysmic destruction of Kyoto, artisans flee
1469	Waka onna (Young woman) mask, Rinnōji (cat. 94, p. 64)
c. 1470	Konparu Zenchiku dies
1475	Kotobide mask, Nagataki Hakusan Shrine (cat. 89, p. 47)
1477	Ōnin Wars end, but political fragmentation and civil war continue
1482–1489	Ginkakuji (Temple of the silver pavilion) built by Ashikaga Yoshimasa
c. 1490	*Te sarugaku* (amateur sarugaku) becomes popular
1512	Konparu Zenpō begins to write *Zenpō zōdan* (Conversations with Zenpō), which takes seven years to complete
1516	Kanze Kojirō Nobumitsu dies
c. 1532	Konparu Zenpō dies
1534	Earliest textual reference to *Ataka*, in the text *Utai no kokoroe no koto* (Notes in understanding singing and dancing)
1536	Ishiyama Honganji (in Ishiyama, Osaka) begins to sponsor noh performances
1553	Earliest textual reference to the play *Shōjō*, in *Zenpō zōdan*
1558	Hannya mask attributed to Hannyabō (cat. 174, p. 213)
1567	Tokugawa Ieyasu holds New Year's ritual ceremony called Utaizome (First chant of the year) at Hamamatsu Castle, which becomes the practice during the Edo period

MOMOYAMA PERIOD   1568–1615

1568	Oda Nobunaga solidifies his political authority in central Japan
1573–1592	Tenshō era: *Hachijō kadensho* (Eight volumes on flowery treatise noh) by unknown author published
1578	First collection of kyōgen plot summaries published in the *Tenshō* text
1590	City of Edo founded
1593	Toyotomi Hideyoshi, Maeda Toshiie, and Tokugawa Ieyasu perform together in the kyōgen play *Mimihiki* (Ear pulling)
1595	Hideyoshi awards mask carver Deme Zekan the red seal and proclaims him "first under heaven"
1596	Shimotsuma Shōshin (1551–1616), secretary-ambassador of Honganji temple and amateur noh actor, publishes his notes on noh performances, including *Butai-nō zu* (Sketches of noh staging), *Dōbushō* (Excerpts on children's dance), and *Shōshin nōden shō* (Book of transmission of the noh of Shōshin)
1596	Hideyoshi performs noh at Fushimi Castle
1598	Hideyoshi dies, Tokugawa Ieyasu succeeds him
1600	Ieyasu victorious in Battle of Sekigahara
1603	Ieyasu appointed first shogun of Tokugawa shogunate; celebratory three-day noh performance immediately thereafter at Nijō Castle, Kyoto
1607	Celebratory noh performance by Kanze and Konparu troupes at Edo castle is open to the public; regarded as the beginning of *machiiri* (public viewing) noh
1609	The four main troupes controlled and supported by Ieyasu

EDO PERIOD   1615–1868

Noh becomes the official ceremonial performance at government functions. The five main troupes receive government stipends and patronage from shogun and daimyo, who begin to assemble their own collections of masks and costumes

1616	Deme Zekan, mask carver of Heita (cat. 83, p. 60), Yase-otoko (cat. 86, p. 51), and Zō-onna (cat. 148, p. 191), dies
1619	Kita school is founded with shogunal approval
1637	Hon'ami Kōetsu, painter, calligrapher, and printer, dies
1642	First collection of full texts of kyōgen plays, the Ōkura school Toraakira kyōgen text (*Ōkura Toraakira bon*), appears
1645 or 1657	Iseki Kawachi, mask carver of the Chūjō mask (cat. 156, p. 197) dies
1645	First Izumi school kyōgen text, the *Kyōgen rikugi* (Six principles of kyōgen, Izumi school Tenri bon) appears
1652	Deme Yūkan, mask carver of the *Chōrei Beshimi* mask (cat. 178, p. 214), dies
1657	Great Edo Fire

1660	First of three volumes of kyōgen plays, *Kyōgenki*, not associated with any of the schools and probably collected from the observation of kyōgen performances, appears, followed by the *Zokukyōgenki* (1700) and *Kyōgenki shui* (1730)
	First book of kyōgen criticism, the *Waranbegusa* (Random notes for children) by Ōkura Toraakira appears, based on *Mukashigatari* (Old tales), the earlier work of Toraakira's father, Torahiro
1660–1700	Sagi school *Yasunori* text
1688–1704	Genroku era, first great cultural efflorescence in Tokugawa Japan
1703	Forty-seven rōnin in Akō committed seppuku after revenge, which becomes the popular theme for plays and literature
1704	Ōmi Kodama Mitsumasa, carver of the Shōjō mask (cat. 184, p. 223), dies
1792	Ōkura Torahiro text of kyōgen plays *Ōkura Torahiro bon* (Ōkura Torahiro kyōgen text)
1818–1830	Izumi school *Kumogata* (Cloud pattern) text
1848	Hōshō kanjin noh recorded in *Kanjin nō no zu*; last kanjin noh performance to be held
1855	Sagi school Kenjiro Kentsu text
1867–1868	Meiji Restoration begins

MEIJI PERIOD   1868–1912

Noh ceases to be patronized by the government, but after a period of demise is reestablished with individual backing and box-office funds

First publication of Zeami's writings

TAISHŌ PERIOD   1912–1926

SHŌWA PERIOD   1926–1989

HEISEI PERIOD   1989–present

ACKNOWLEDGMENTS

The development and organization of an international exhibition such as *Miracles and Mischief: Noh and Kyōgen Theater in Japan* would not be possible without the generous support and cooperation of the many colleagues, scholars, and lenders in both Japan and the United States, who have contributed to this project over the past five years. The initial inspiration for this exhibition came soon after the completion in 1993 of the exhibition, *When Art Became Fashion: Kosode in Edo-Period Japan*, with the desire to work again with scholars Monica Bethe and Tom Hare. Their extensive training in various aspects of noh and their enthusiastic response to my initial ideas gave me the courage to embark on what has been a long and rewarding journey.

My deepest debt of gratitude must be given to my friend and colleague Monica Bethe. Her wide-ranging expertise and deep understanding of noh have made her an invaluable collaborator. Without her encouragement, guidance, enthusiasm, and generous heart over the years, this project would not have been possible. Monica deserves much of the credit for the success of this exhibition and catalogue.

Special recognition and appreciation for co-organizing *Miracles and Mischief* must be given to the Agency for Cultural Affairs, Government of Japan, Fine Arts Division (Bunkachō) and its staff, especially Commissioner Kawai Hayao. Suzuki Norio helped launch the project and provided guidance, while Yuyama Kenichi lent his support along the way. Saitō Takamasa and his curatorial colleagues offered expert advice and worked tirelessly to secure loans from numerous collections in Japan. Noda Kiyoshi diligently coordinated the loans from Japan.

The contributing authors of this catalogue bring insightful observations of noh and kyōgen from their respective fields of specialization. They are: Monica Bethe, Professor, Ōtani University and Adjunct Professor at Japan Stanford Center, Kyoto Center for Japanese Studies; Hollis Goodall, Associate Curator of Japanese Art, Los Angeles County Museum of Art; Tom Hare, Professor of Comparative Literature, Princeton University; Kawakami Shigeki, Professor of Japanese Art and Textile History, Kwansei Gakuin University, Nishinomiya, and former

Curator of Textiles, Kyoto National Museum; Kirihata Ken, Professor of Art History at Ōtemae College, Osaka, and Curator Emeritus of Textiles, Kyoto National Museum; Carolyn A. Morley, Professor of Japanese Language and Literature and Chair of the Japanese Department at Wellesley College; Nagasaki Iwao, Professor of Art, Kyōritsu Women's University and former Curator of Textiles at the Tokyo National Museum; and Tanabe Saburōsuke, Director of Machida Municipal Museum and Professor of Art at Musashino University of Art. In addition to their duties as catalogue authors, Monica Bethe and Carolyn A. Morley brought their considerable expertise on noh masks and kyōgen, respectively, to excellent translations of essays by Professors Tanabe and Kirihata. Special thanks go to Etsuko Kuroda Douglass and Melissa M. Rinne for masterfully translating other essays that appear in this volume.

A 1996–97 Japan Foundation Professional Fellowship and a 1999 Tokyo National Museum Research Travel Grant were instrumental in helping me jump-start this project. Director Emeritus of Tōyama Memorial Museum Yamanobe Tomoyuki, textile scholar Kobayashi Keiko, Professor Maruyama Nobuhiko at Kanazawa University of Art, noh scholar Shōda Natsuko, Professor Kurosaki Akira at Kyoto Seika University, and Richard Emmert, Kita school noh instructor and professor at Musashino Women's University, all offered valuable advice in this project's formative stages. Deborah and Ian Hayden deserve special recognition for their incredible generosity.

My deep appreciation is extended to all of the lenders and for the support of many colleagues from the Japanese lending institutions who graciously allowed invaluable access to their collections. They include Dōmyō Mihoko and Ueki Toshiko, Bunka Gakuen Costume Museum; Iizaka Seiichi, Hirabayashi Akira, and Abe Junko, Eisei Bunko Museum; Okumura Naoteru and Maeda Eri, Fujita Art Museum; Nishizaki Kiyohisa, Shimamura Chiaki, and Isobe Yoshitaka, Hayashibara Museum of Art; Kita Haruchiyo, Ishikawa Prefectural Museum of Art; Shigeki Kawakami, Kyoto National Museum; Maruyama Nobuhiko, National Museum of Japanese History; Sakurai Hiroshi, National Noh Theater; Maniwa Muneo, Noda Shrine; Tani Akira and Okumura Atsuko, Nomura Art Museum; and Washizuka Hiromitsu, Nishioka Yasuhiro, Komatsu Taishū, Nagasaki Iwao, Yamamoto Tsutomu, and Kunigō Hideaki, Tokyo National Museum.

In Japan, critical information on technical issues was provided by Fujii Kenzō of the Kyoto Municipal Textile Research Institute, Fujiwara Masuo of the Fujiwara Textile Research Institute, Yamaguchi Akira of the Yamaguchi Noh Costume Research Center, and Rebecca Teele, Kongō school. On dressing for the stage, actors Kawamura Yoshihige, Kawamura Haruhisa, and Izumi Yoshio of the Kanze school, Takabayashi Kōji of the Kita school, and Shigeyama Shime of the Ōkura school all supplied insightful suggestions and confirmed costume ensemble choices. Fujimoto Keiko of the Museum of Kyoto helped in locating weaving tools and materials; the project also benefited from research suggestions from Yamakawa Aki at the Kyoto National Museum (and formerly of The Tokugawa Art Museum). Morozumi Kaoru of Sen-Oku Hakuko Kan generously allowed me to review objects in the Sumitomo collection. Ushimado Masakatsu, a master photographer of noh, provided access to his archives and use of his beautiful performance photographs for the catalogue and exhibition.

In the United States, colleagues in the following institutions were extremely supportive and encouraging: Nobuko Kajitani, Joyce Denney, Barbara Ford, J. Kenneth Moore, and the staff of the Antonio Ratti Textile Center at The Metropolitan Museum of Art; Christa C. Mayer Thurman and her staff at The Art Institute of Chicago; John Teramoto, Indianapolis Museum of Art; Felice Fischer, Philadelphia Museum of Art; Karen Brazell, Cornell University; Louise Cort, Smithsonian Institution; and Milton Sonday, formerly of Cooper-Hewitt National Design Museum. I also wish to thank Lea Sneider and Sebastian Izzard of New York and Jacqueline Baas and Stephen Walrod of Sea Ranch and Berkeley.

At the Los Angeles County Museum of Art, I am extremely grateful for the unwavering support of Dr. Andrea L. Rich, President and Director, as well as from LACMA's Board of Trustees. Former Director Graham W.J. Beal first gave the green light to this project by allowing me to accept a three-month research fellowship in Japan. The Costume Council deserves special acknowledgment for its unprecedented grant to the exhibition and for nearly fifty years of generous and devoted support of the Costume and Textiles Department. Nancy Thomas, Deputy Director of Curatorial Affairs, offered encouraging words throughout the years. Assistant Director of

Exhibition Programs Irene Martin was dedicated to this project and expertly guided it through its many phases. I am obliged to Beverley Sabo, Senior Budget Analyst, for keeping the exhibition within budget, and to Exhibition Program Coordinator Christine Lazzaretto, who ensured everything ran smoothly.

The unfailing support of my staff in the Costume and Textiles Department is gratefully recognized. Nancy Lawson Carcione, Kaye Durland Spilker, and Nicole LaBouff carefully read the catalogue manuscript several times; research assistants Rika Iezumi Hiro and Tomoko Slutsky gathered, compiled, and fact-checked the mass of information required for this project; Cynthia Cavanaugh assisted with permanent collection objects; Dale Carolyn Gluckman and Sandra L. Rosenbaum stepped in to help with the running of the department during my busiest times; Gail Stein accessed archival materials, and Danielle Sierra, Terry Satsuki Milhaupt, and Terri Niwayama all contributed to the project in its early stage of development.

Colleagues from other curatorial departments in the museum who provided expertise and advice include Robert T. Singer, Hollis Goodall, and Chris Drosse from the Japanese Art Department; J. Keith Wilson and June Li from the Chinese and Korean Art Department; and Rochelle Kessler from the South and Southeast Asian Art Department. Anne Diederick of the Research Library efficiently located resource publications.

Assistant Director of Collections Management Renee Montgomery, Registrar Ted Greenberg, Associate Registrar Portland McCormick, Assistant Registrar Jennifer Garpner, and the rest of registrar staff were critical to assembling the domestic and foreign loans. Rebecca Lachter, Laura Lambros, and Delfin Magpantay created the exhibition checklist database.

My admiration goes to Victoria Blyth-Hill, Director of Conservation, and her capable team of conservators – Catherine McLean and Susan Schmalz, textiles; John Hirx, objects; Margot Healey and Chail Norton, paper; and Marco Leona, scientist, who conducted numerous experiments, found creative solutions to environmental display issues, and prepared works of art for exhibition. Art Owens, Assistant Vice President of Operations and Facility Planning, and Bill Stahl, Manager of Gallery Services, coordinated the construction of the galleries. Manager of Art

Preparation and Installation Jeff Haskin and his staff are to be commended for their expert handling of art, assisting the art handlers from Japan, and overseeing a complicated installation. Roosevelt Simpson lit the objects to perfection. Elvin Whitesides and Megan Mellbye of the Audiovisual Department provided technical assistance and offered their video editing skills. Assistant Vice President of Protective Services Erroll Southers was sensitive to security needs.

It was a joy and pleasure to work with the talented Bernard Kester, who created an exhibition design that is not only beautiful but captures the very essence of noh. Graphic designer Amy McFarland's passion for Japan and Japanese design can be seen in her masterful solutions to important design issues. Book designer Lorraine Wild and her assistants Jessica Fleischman and Robert Ruehlman responded creatively to the challenges of a wide range and scale of objects, and produced a catalogue that is a delight to behold.

Production of the catalogue would not have been possible without the talent of the museum's Publications Department. I am indebted to Stephanie Emerson, Director of Publications, whose skillful and graceful negotiating talents have resulted in the production of a book beyond expectations. Editor Thomas Frick, with assistance from Sara Cody, undertook the challenges of the Japanese language and refining the texts of eight authors. Erika Caswell is appreciated for her assistance and calm presence. Peter Brenner, Head of Photographic Services, oversaw the quality of photographs, and Steve Oliver expertly photographed works from the permanent collection. Cheryle T. Robertson and Shaula Coyl professionally accomplished the complicated task of clearing reproduction rights for hundreds of photographs.

Jane Burrell, Chief of Art Museum Education, advised in the development of exhibition-related events, assisted by Rachel Bernstein. Associate Museum Educator Gail Maxwell took an active role of turning the catalogue manuscript into informative didactic labels for the viewing public. She also assisted Carol Fisher Sorgenfrei, Professor of Theater at UCLA, in organizing "Tradition and Fusion: The Arts of Noh and Kyōgen," a Triennial R.L. Shep Symposium on Textiles and Dress held in conjunction with the exhibition and in collaboration with the UCLA Center for Japanese Studies, directed by Dr. Fred Notehelfer.

The museum is grateful to Robb Shep for his dedication to the R.L. Shep Symposium Endowment for Costume and Textiles. Additional support provided by the Georges and Germaine Fusenot Charity Foundation.

Grateful acknowledgment is also made to the National Endowment for the Arts for a major grant. Additional thanks go to The Blakemore Foundation for support. Transportation assistance was provided by All Nippon Airways. In-kind support was provided by K-MOZART 105.1, the official classical radio station of the Los Angeles County Museum of Art, and the Radisson Wilshire Plaza Hotel. I appreciate the staff (past and present) of the museum's Development Office, including Kathy DeShaw, Tom Jacobson, Laura Hardy, Stephanie Dyas, Diana Veach, Nancy Flordelis, Anne Shisler, Winnie Jong, and Karen Benson, for their diligent professionalism. Mark Mitchell, Budget and Planning Officer, provided budgetary guidance. James Rawitsch, Associate Vice President of External Affairs, along with former Communications Director Keith McKeown and staff members Kirsten Schmidt, Mark Thie, Anne Welsbacher, and Sean Fay, oversaw *Miracles and Mischief* press and marketing.

Finally, as a third generation Japanese-American, I would like to honor the memory of my two grandmothers who each made the lonely journey across the Pacific a century ago. Their inner strength, which was inherited and nurtured in me through my loving parents, led me back to Japan and to a career in Japanese textiles. I wish to thank my family and friends, without whose constant encouragement and understanding I would not have been able to complete this project.

SHARON SADAKO TAKEDA
Senior Curator and Department Head,
Costume and Textiles
Los Angeles County Museum of Art

SELECTED BIBLIOGRAPHY

The Art Institute of Chicago. "Five Centuries of Japanese Kimono: On this Sleeve of Fondest Dreams." *Museum Studies* 18:1, 1992.

Bethe, Monica, and Karen Brazell. *Nō as Performance: An Analysis of the Kuse Scene of Yamamba.* Cornell University East Asia Papers, no. 16. Ithaca, N.Y.: China-Japan Program, Cornell University, 1978.

Bethe, Monica, and Karen Brazell. *Dance in the Nō Theater.* 3 vols. Cornell University East Asia Papers, no. 29. Ithaca, N.Y.: China-Japan Program, Cornell University, 1982.

Bethe, Monica, et al. *Noh Performance Guides: Aoinoue, Atsumori, Ema, Fujito, Matsukaze, Miidera, Tenko.* Tokyo: National Noh Theatre, 1992–97.

Bethe, Monica, and Nagasaki Iwao. *Patterns and Poetry: Nō Robes from the Lucy Truman Aldrich Collection.* Providence, R.I.: The Museum of Art, Rhode Island School of Design, 1992.

Brandon, James R., et al. *Japanese Theater in the World.* Exh. cat. New York: Japan Foundation and Japan Society, with Tsubouchi Memorial Museum, Waseda University, 1997.

Brazell, Karen, ed., and Monica Bethe, et al., trans. *Twelve Plays of the Noh and Kyōgen Theaters.* Cornell University East Asia Papers, no. 50. Ithaca, N.Y.: East Asia Program, Cornell University, 1988.

Brazell, Karen, ed., and James T. Araki, et al., trans. *Traditional Japanese Theater: An Anthology of Plays.* New York: Columbia University Press, 1998.

De Poorter, Erika. *Zeami's Talks on Sarugaku: An Annotated Translation of the Sarugaku Dangi, with an Introduction on Zeami Motokiyo.* Japonica Neerlandica, vol. 2. Amsterdam: J.C. Gieben, 1986.

Gluckman, Dale Carolyn, and Sharon Sadako Takeda. *When Art Became Fashion: Kosode in Edo Period Japan.* Exh. cat. Los Angeles: Los Angeles County Museum of Art, 1992.

Goff, Janet. *Noh Drama and the Tale of Genji: The Art of Allusion in Fifteen Classical Plays.* Princeton, N.J.: Princeton University Press, 1991.

Hare, Thomas Blenman. *Zeami's Style: The Noh Plays of Zeami Motokiyo.* Stanford: Stanford University Press, 1986.

Hare, Thomas Blenman, et al., eds. *The Distant Isle: Studies and Translations of Japanese Literature in Honor of Robert H. Brower.* Michigan Monograph Series in Japanese Studies, no. 15. Ann Arbor, Mich.: Center for Japanese Studies, 1996.

Hashimoto Ken'ichirō, and Kirihata Ken, eds. *Nō kyōgen: Zusetsu nihon no koten* (Noh and kyōgen: Illustrated books of Japanese classics), vol. 12. Tokyo: Shūeisha, 1988.

Imanaga Seiji, ed. *Geinō ishō 1: Nō* (The costumes of performing arts 1: Noh). Nihon no senshoku (The textiles of Japan), no. 7. Tokyo: Chōūkōronsha, 1983.

Kaneko Ryōun, ed. *Nō kyōgen men* (Noh and kyōgen masks). Nihon no bijutsu (The arts of Japan), no. 108. Tokyo: Shibundō, 1975.

Kanze Kiyokazu, ed., *Omote: Kanze sōke nō men* (Omote: Noh masks of the Kanze family). Tokyo: Hinoki Shoten, 2002.

Keene, Donald. *Nō and Bunraku: Two Forms of Japanese Theatre.* New York: Columbia University Press, 1966 (reprinted 1990).

Keene, Donald, ed. *Twenty Plays of the Nō Theater.* New York and London: Columbia University Press, 1970.

Kenny, Don. *The Kyōgen Book: An Anthology of Japanese Classical Comedies.* Tokyo: Japan Times, 1989.

_____. *A Kyōgen Companion.* Tokyo: National Noh Theater, 1999.

Kirihata Ken. *Kyōgen no shōzoku: Suō and kataginu* (Kyōgen costumes: Suō and kataginu). London: Thames and Hudson, 1980.

_____. *Nō shōzoku* (Noh costumes). Nihon no senshoku (Japanese textiles, vol. 8. Kyoto: Kyoto Shoin, 1993. (Bilingual)

_____. *Kyōgen no shōzoku* (Kyōgen costumes). Nihon no senshoku (Japanese textiles), vol. 9. Kyoto: Kyoto Shoin, 1993. (Bilingual)

_____. *Geinō ishō 2: Kyōgen, kabuki* (The costumes of performing arts 2: Kyōgen and kabuki). Nihon no senshoku (The textiles of Japan), no. 8. Tokyo: Chōūkōronsha, 1983.

Kitamura Tetsurō, ed. *Nō shōzoku* (Noh costumes). Nihon no bijutsu (The arts of Japan), no. 46. Tokyo: Shibundō, 1970.

_____. *Kosode nō shōzoku: Taiyō some to ori shirizu* (Tiayō textile series: Kosode and noh costume). Tokyo: Heibonsha, 1977.

Konparu Kunio. *The Noh Theater: Principles and Perspectives.* New York and Tokyo: Weatherhill/Tankōsha, 1983.

Masuda, Shōzō. "Kyōgen no shōzoku to funsō" (Kyōgen costumes and disguise). *Senshoku no bi* (Textile Arts) 14, 1981.

Matsuura Toshiumi, ed. *Mibu kyōgen ko ishō* (The old costumes of Mibu kyōgen). Kyoto: Shibunkaku, 1992.

Malm, William P. *Traditional Japanese Music and Musical Instruments,* new ed. New York and London: Kodansha International, 2000.

Masuda Shōzo, ed., and Monica Bethe, trans. *Ikei no nō shōzoku no hyakusugata* (One hundred distinctive noh costumes). Tokyo: Heibonsha, 1983.

Masuda Shōzo, ed., and Richard Emmert, trans. *Ikei no nō men no hyakusugata* (One hundred distinctive noh masks). Tokyo: Heibonsha, 1983.

Minnich, Helen Benton, in collaboration with Shojiro Nomura. *Japanese Costume and the Makers of its Elegant Tradition.* Tokyo: Charles E. Tuttle Co., 1986.

Mizoguchi Saburō, and Louise Allison Cort, trans. *Design Motifs.* Arts of Japan, vol. 1. New York and Tokyo: Weatherhill/Shibundō, 1973.

Morley, Carolyn. *Transformation, Miracles, and Mischief: The Mountain Priest Plays of Kyōgen.* Cornell East Asia Series, no. 62. Ithaca, N.Y.: East Asia Program, Cornell University, 1993.

Nagasaki Iwao. *Zaigai nihon senshoku shūsei* (Japanese textile in American collections). Tokyo: Shōgakukan, 1995. (Bilingual)

Nakamura Yasuo. *Nihon no dentō: Nō* (Traditional art of Japan: Noh). Kyoto: Tankōsha, 1967. English ed.: Don Kenny, trans. *Noh: The Classical Theater.* New York and Tokyo: Walker/Weatherhill and Tankōsha, 1971.

Nakanishi Tōru. *Noh Masks.* Color Books, no. 40. Osaka: Hoikusha, 1981.

Nippon Gakujutsu Shinkōkai. *Japanese Noh Drama: Ten Plays Selected and Translated from the Japanese.* 3 vols. Tokyo: Nippon Gakujutsu Shinkōkai, 1955–60.

Nishimura Hyōbu, ed. *Orimono* (Weaving). Nihon no bijutsu (The arts of Japan), no. 12. Tokyo: Shibundō, 1967.

Noma, Seiroku, ed. *Kosode to nō ishō* (Kosode and noh costumes). Nihon no bijutsu (The arts of Japan), no. 16. Tokyo: Heibonsha, 1965. English ed.: Armins Nikovskis, trans. *Japanese Costume and Textile Arts.* New York: Weatherhill, 1974.

Ogasawara Sae, ed. *Kinran* (Gold brocade). Nihon no bijutsu (The arts of Japan), no. 220. Tokyo: Shibundō, 1984.

Ōkōchi Sadao, and Louise Allison Cort and Monica Bethe, trans. *The Tokugawa Collection: Nō Robes and Masks.* Exh. cat. New York: Japan Society, 1977.

Omote Akira, and Katō Shūichi, eds. *Zeami, Zenchiku, nihon shisō taikei* (Complete survey of Japanese philosophy: Zeami and Zenchiku), vol. 24. Tokyo: Iwanami Shoten, 1974.

Omote Akira, ed. *Nō* (Noh). Bessattsu Taiyō Nihon no kokoro, no. 25. Tokyo: Heibonsha, 1978.

O'Neill, P.G. *Early Noh Drama: Its Background, Character and Development 1300–1450.* London and Bradford: Lund Humphries, 1958. Reprint, Westport, Conn.: Greenwood Press, 1974.

Ortolani, Benito. *The Japanese Theater: From Shamanistic Ritual to Contemporary Pluralism.* New York and Leiden, Netherlands: E.J. Brill, 1990.

Raz, Jacob. *Audience and Actors: A Study of their Interaction in the Japanese Traditional Theater.* Leiden, Netherlands: E.J. Brill, 1983.

Rimer, J. Thomas, and Yamazaki Masakazu, trans. *On the Art of the Nō Drama: The Major Treatises of Zeami.* Princeton, N.J.: Princeton University Press, 1984.

Sekine Masaru. *Ze-ami and his Theories of Noh Drama.* Gerrards Cross, England: Colin Smythe Ltd., 1985.

Shimazaki Chifumi. *The Noh: God Noh, Battle Noh, Woman Noh.* 3 vols. Tokyo: Hinoki Shoten, 1973–87.

Stinchecum, Amanda Mayer. *Kosode: 16th–19th Century Textiles from the Nomura Collection.* New York and Tokyo: Japan Society and Kodansha International, 1984.

Tanabe Saburōsuke. *Nō men* (Noh masks). Tokyo: Shōgakukan, 1981.

Teele, Rebecca, ed. "Nō Kyōgen Masks and Performance." *Mime Journal* (Claremont, Calif.: Pomona College), 1984.

Thornhill, Arthur H. *Six Circles, One Dewdrop: The Religio-Aesthetic World of Komparu Zenchiku.* Princeton, N.J.: Princeton University Press, 1993.

Tyler, Royall. *Japanese Nō Dramas.* London and New York: Penguin Books, 1992.

Ueda Makoto. *The Old Pine Tree and other Noh Plays.* Lincoln, Neb.: University of Nebraska Press, 1962.

Waley, Arthur. *The Nō Plays of Japan.* London: George Allen & Unwin, 1921. Reprints, Rutland, Vt.: C.E. Tuttle, 1976, and London: Unwin Paperbacks, 1988.

Yamaguchi Akira, et al., eds. *Nō shōzoku no sekai* (The world of noh costumes). Kyoto: Yamaguchi Noh Costume Research Center, 1989. (Bilingual)

Yamanobe Tomoyuki. *Nō shōzoku mon'yō shū* (Designs and patterns of noh costumes). Kyoto: Hinoki Shoten, 1972.

Yasuda, Kenneth. *Masterworks of the Nō Theater.* Bloomington and Indianapolis: Indiana University Press, 1989.

Zeami Motokiyo. *Kadensho.* Translated by Sakurai Chu'ichi, et al. Kyoto: Sumiya-Shinobe Publishing Institute, 1968.